MW00941609

TRUE PRETENSES

ROSE LERNER

LIVELY ST. LEMESTON, *BOOK 2*

TRUE PRETENSES
Copyright ©2015, 2017, 2020 by Susan Roth
Third edition

Cover by Kanaxa

This book is a work of fiction. The names, characters, places, and incidents are products of the writer's imagination or have been used fictitiously. Any resemblance to actual persons, living or dead, or actual events is entirely coincidental.

All rights reserved. This book or any portion thereof may not be reproduced in any form or by any electronic or mechanical means, including information storage and retrieval systems, without written permission from the author, except for the use of brief quotations in a book review.

ISBN: 978-1-5484-7555-0

RoseLerner.com

Table of Contents

For Sonia,

MY PARTNER IN CRIME.

Acknowledgments

I'd like to thank Anne Scott, my editor at Samhain, for her amazing combination of enthusiasm and attention to detail. Thank you to my agent Kevan Lyon for her support and insight, and to her assistant Clare Sanders for her help with the opening chapters.

Thank you as always to the world's greatest critique partners, the Demimondaines: Alyssa Everett, Charlotte Russell, Vonnie Hughes and especially Susanna Fraser. I couldn't do this without you. Thank you to my talented, generous friends and first readers: Kate Addison, Tiffany Ruzicki, Dina Aronzon, Greg Holt, Matti Klock, Tiffany Gerstmar and Olivia Waite. I love you guys.

Thank you to Kanaxa for my beautiful covers, and thank you to my formatter Matt Youngmark for making my books beautiful on the inside too.

I want to thank my family, especially my mother and my uncle David, who've told me so many stories about our family history (none of which are in this book), and my great-grandmother Rose, whom I'm very proud to be named for.

And finally, thank you to Sonia, for making writing this book the most fun I've ever had.

Chapter 1

Below them in the darkness, a clock chimed half past two. "Just once, I'd like to leave somewhere in daylight," Rafe grumbled under his breath as they crept down the stairs. "Wearing my boots. I'd like to take my trunk with me too."

"Shh." Their trunk and its contents were worth twenty pounds. If Ash Cohen could have brought them away safely, he would have, but they meant exactly that to him—twenty pounds. The only thing he had that he couldn't leave behind was two feet in front of him, sulking.

His brother knew perfectly well that they left places in daylight with their trunks all the time. Only certain jobs—like this one—required sneaking off in the dead of night. But Rafe was always at his worst just after a successful swindle.

Ash supposed it was natural to feel empty and frustrated when an enterprise you'd spent weeks or months on was abruptly over. Ash himself would feel giddy, if his brother didn't insist on ruining his mood. Now instead of fizzing like a celebratory mug of ale, his chest cavity filled with—butterflies was too pretty a name for them. Moths, maybe, dirty-looking gray-and-white ones, swarming about and clinging to his innards.

At least Rafe didn't let pique spoil his concentration. He stepped unerringly around the squeaking, creaking places they'd scouted in the staircase, eased open the door on hinges they'd oiled, and shoved his feet silently into his boots. Ash did the same and followed his brother out into the night.

Rafe had never been able to hold a grudge for longer than ten miles, if Ash resisted the urge to cozen him. Today, it was nine and a half (calculated using their average speed of walking and Ash's watch) before he gave Ash a sidelong, apologetic smile and said, "I could eat a whole side of beef right now."

Ash relaxed. He wished he could be less sensitive to Rafe's moods, but it had been this way for twenty-five years now and showed no signs of changing. When baby Rafe had smiled and waved chubby little arms in his direction, nine-year-old Ash had felt special, important, as if he could vanquish lions. Before Rafe, he'd been nothing, one of an army of little street thieves.

Ash smiled back and gave his brother a shove. "I've no doubt you could. Giant."

Rafe laid a large hand atop Ash's head. "Midget."

Actually, Ash was of average height, and greater than average breadth. But Rafe towered over him, and that was Ash's greatest pride and accomplishment: one look, and you knew he'd always had enough to eat.

And people did look. Heads turned when Rafe walked into a room, huge and golden. Dark, sturdy Ash looked like an ox or a draft horse, his brute strength meant to carry others' burdens. Rafe was a thoroughbred. Maybe if Ash hadn't shared so many dinners with his little brother, he'd be a giant himself, but he had no regrets.

Another five miles and they were in complete charity with

one another, and probably safe enough from pursuit to buy something to eat at a crowded inn. Rafe, more memorable, waited outside with his hat low over his face while Ash bought pasties and ale to be consumed a little way down the road.

Once the food was gone, however, Rafe's good spirits went with it. When he began worrying a worn handkerchief between his hands, Ash knew something was very wrong.

The scrap of fabric was all Ash had managed to keep when his mother died. Since he couldn't split his memories with his brother, Ash had given him the handkerchief as soon as Rafe was old enough to safeguard it from boys wanting to steal and sell it. He carried it always but almost never took it out.

"I'm sick of swindling," he said at last, with a heavy finality that Ash didn't like.

"You say that after every job. You'll be right as rain when we've found another flat. We always get on best when we're working."

"I'm sick of flats. I'm sick of a profession that hurts people. I want to be able to point to something I've done at the end of the day, something *good*."

Ash patted his pocket. "Two hundred pounds is a damn good thing, if you ask me."

Rafe frowned. "Other men give something back for money. They leave something behind them. We only take. I liked Mrs. Noakes."

"I liked her too," Ash said, stung. He liked everybody. That was why he was so good at his job—you couldn't swindle a person you couldn't get on with. "And she can afford to lose two hundred pounds."

Rafe turned his head away. "It isn't the money. Think of how she'll feel."

"Think of how we'd feel if we starved," Ash snapped. "We have to take care of ourselves—"

"—because no one will do it for us, I know." Rafe rarely raised his voice when he was angry. Most of the time, when he was trying to express an emotion other than happiness, he slowed down. It only meant he was struggling to find words, but in his deep voice, it gave every word a weight and echo, like a church bell tolling. Ash hated it. "I just want to make someone happy for a change."

You make me *happy.* The words stuck in Ash's throat. They really meant, *Don't I count?* They were weak and childish, and he knew the answer was no, anyway. He had brought Rafe up to take him for granted, to believe him strong and capable and impervious to the world's blows. He had wanted his brother to feel safe, as he himself never had. Fear, anxiety, illness, sadness—he'd protected Rafe with fierce care from them all. It seemed bitterly unfair that this was his reward.

"I don't enjoy the work anymore," Rafe said. "I'm sorry. I've tried and tried, but I find myself wishing the lies were true. That we were really shipwrecked Americans, or speculators who'd found copper on Mrs. Noakes's land, or anything other than thieves."

"You can't get—"

"—too fond of your own lies, I *know*. But haven't you ever, Ash?"

The dirty little moths settled back into his stomach and chest and clung. He had exactly one secret he'd never told Rafe. Sometimes he forgot about it for days on end, and when he remembered, it was worse than stepping out of a warm shop into a snowstorm.

"Once." The word scraped his throat like a dull razor.

Rafe waited, but didn't press him. Ash wished he would. He wished Rafe would make him tell, because by now it was obvious he'd never find the courage otherwise.

"Then you know what it's like," Rafe said finally. "I want to leave."

Everything stopped. The birds singing in the bare branches, the sun rising in the sky, Ash's heart beating in his chest—they all went silent and still. "Leave?"

Rafe held his gaze, earnest and sorrowful. It was the look he gave flats when he told them their money was gone, there'd been a ship lost at sea, a horse gone lame in the first lap, a bank failure. That was what made Rafe such a brilliant swindler: he had an honest face.

Ash wanted to put his fist in it.

"You can keep most of the money," Rafe offered. "I've thought about it. I could join the army—"

The money? Rafe thought he cared about the *money*? "You'll join the army? Even you can't be that stupid. Starve and fight and die for what? For England? What did England ever do for you? Men slice into their own legs with an ax to get *out* of the army!"

"Or I'll go to Canada. I've got to leave, Ash." He said it so slow and heavy it was like a judge pronouncing sentence. "I've done everything with you. Always. I don't know how to stop, without *stopping*. I won't be able to stick to it if you're there to talk me round. We both know it."

Resentment seared Ash's throat, sticky and hot as pitch. That was gammon. Rafe was the easygoingest man in the world right up until he dug in his heels, and then there was no moving him.

Rafe was going to leave, and Ash would be alone.

Instinctively, he bought himself time. "Well, if that's how you feel, I won't try to change your mind."

"Thank you for understanding. I didn't think you'd—you're the best of brothers." Rafe put an arm around his shoulder, his face glowing with...*relief*, Ash thought. Relief that Ash hadn't made an unpleasant scene. In spite of himself, Ash's stupid heart eased a little, that he'd made Rafe happy. "Thank you for everything. I'll—I'll miss you. I'll write you horribly misspelled letters, if you can think of a safe place to send them."

Mrs. Noakes had been a nice woman. Ash had liked her. But she'd grown up with a family, a home, and plenty of food and clothes. She'd always have those things, two hundred pounds or no.

The world had given him and Rafe nothing, and they'd proved they didn't need it. Ash looked around at the muddy little clump of trees they stood in. The morning was cold and their breath misted in the air, but they were alive and well, with food in their bellies, good coats on their backs, and good boots on their feet. This little slice of England was all he'd ever wanted. The two of them against the world, and Ash would put his money on them every time.

All Rafe wanted was to be somewhere else. Anywhere else.

Now that Rafe had said it aloud, had given it shape, it made sense in a way Ash's idyllic picture of Two Wandering Jews never had. Rafe's depression between jobs was real, and his cheerfulness during a swindle was a brief intoxication. Ash had seen it too many times—dull-eyed, hopeless men who only found a spark of life when they could forget everything but the roll of the dice, the turn of the card, the pounding of the horses' hooves. He should have recognized it in his brother.

When Rafe had been hungry, Ash had found him food. When Rafe had been cold, Ash had got him clothes. When Rafe had been sick, Ash had brought him a doctor. He'd begged, borrowed, bargained, whored, and stolen to do it—stolen every way he knew, and then made up a few new ones. He'd made it look easy, so Rafe would never feel how close they were to starving, freezing, dying of fever in a gutter somewhere and being dumped in paupers' graves.

Who would he even be, without Rafe? What right did Ash have to expect more than he'd already got?

What good did it do to be so angry, when he couldn't make Rafe want to stay anyway? It was twenty-five years too late for any sleight of hand. Rafe knew exactly what life with Ash was like, and he'd decided he didn't want it.

If Rafe wanted a new life, a respectable life, Ash would find a way to steal that for him too—one with no cannonballs or long sea journeys in it, either. And then, to keep himself from changing his mind, he'd do something he'd never done before. He'd give back something he'd stolen.

He'd tell Rafe everything.

A plan came to him, as it always did—half-formed as yet, but the first step was clear. He could do this. He could make it look easy, and be as maudlin as he liked later, when there was no one watching. "Do me one favor."

Rafe's face still glowed. "Anything."

The lump in his throat wouldn't go down. "If you must join the army, buy a commission. So you can change your mind if it doesn't suit you."

Rafe laughed incredulously. "We have two hundred pounds in the world."

"We'll do one last swindle. Two or three thousand pounds

should buy a commission, outfit you, give you something to live on."

"We've never done a swindle that big."

Despite everything, Ash grinned in anticipation. "Think we can't do it?"

Rafe eyed him narrowly, but he gave in and held out his hand to shake on it. Ash had known he would.

"We'll split up to search for flats," Ash said, and Rafe took out his guidebook without prompting. They'd done this dozens of times, planned their routes together so that they could know where to send letters when they'd found a likely prospect. Today the familiar task felt painful and new.

Ash watched his brother walk off down the road and tried not to wonder if he'd ever see him again.

Lydia Reeve sat at her desk, making a list of everything she needed to do before Christmas and ignoring the pressure behind her eyes that meant she might cry at any moment. She had prided herself all her life on being a steady sort of woman, not given to waterworks, and now, since her father's death two weeks ago, she felt as if she did little else. It was worst when she was alone, with nothing to distract her and no role as hostess, employer, or sister to fall back on.

Last year she and Lord Wheatcroft had made this list together, her father sitting on the settee just there in his old tartan banyan and cap while she took notes at her desk on alms and charitable subscriptions and Christmas boxes for the tradesmen. He'd roasted chestnuts in the fireplace for them to share.

She dared not put her head in her arms and indulge in tears even here, alone in the Little Parlor. A servant might enter at any moment, or her younger brother Jamie. There was something terrible in that moment of being discovered weeping, a sharp pang of exposure and humiliation that went all through her and became the worst loneliness in the world.

She sniffled firmly and fixed her eyes on her list. The one thing she had written so far was *new coats for the workhouse children*. She bought them every Christmas, and it looked to be a cold winter.

Perhaps she might order them early this year. Last month when she had visited the workhouse, little Mary Luff's sister was drowning in Mary's coat and Mary was pretending not to shiver.

Yes, she would order the coats now. She had only to talk to Jamie and warn him of the expense. Then perhaps she could ask him to help her with the rest of the list. He would have to begin his duties as the head of the Ministerialist party in the nearby town of Lively St. Lemeston soon enough. Why not now?

Jamie wasn't in her father's study. He'd taken the household ledger with him, however, so Lydia thought he must be around the house somewhere.

Half an hour and five fruitless inquiries of the servants later, Lydia was almost ready to cry with frustration. At last she wrapped herself in her warm cloak and went to check the hothouses.

Sure enough, she found him in his cactus shed. He jumped

when she opened the door, slicing into his finger with his knife. "Can you not knock, Lydia?" he demanded, sucking on the cut.

"Are you hurt? Let me see."

"I'm fine. But look at my poor *Cotyledon orbiculata!*" He stood at a narrow table, an unpotted succulent with flat, ruffle-edged leaves unceremoniously exposed amid a jumble of pots, dirt, and tools.

She peered at it uncertainly. "Is it very much damaged?"

Jamie huffed. "Never mind. What did you want?"

He never seemed happy to see her anymore. She didn't understand what she'd done. She didn't know why she'd left her warm parlor to find him, as if he would comfort her. "I mean to place the order for the workhouse children's Christmas coats. I wanted to warn you to expect the bill."

He frowned, prodding his plant with his bleeding finger and not looking at her. "Lydia," he said hesitatingly, "I need to...I don't..." He glanced up, his pleading expression turning abruptly into a scowl, and burst out, "You have to stop sending me all these bills!"

She drew back. "What?"

"I'm not going to be the patron of the Pink-and-White party. I don't want to."

Lydia stood speechless. He could not have said what she had heard him say. It didn't make sense. It wasn't possible.

"God, please don't cry," Jamie said desperately. "I'm not trying to hurt you, I only..."

Lydia breathed in and out. He didn't mean it. He was overset by Lord Wheatcroft's death. He was overwhelmed by his new responsibilities. She had to be strong for him. She had to make his duties in Lively St. Lemeston seem ordinary and welcoming.

Anyway, if she cried, Jamie would think she was trying to bully him.

"I know." She managed a smile. "But Jamie—"

"Don't call me that." Jamie pushed his sandy hair away from his forehead. It flopped back into his eyes. "My name is James."

"Your name is Lord Wheatcroft now," she reminded him gently. "Lord Wheatcroft has led the Tories in Lively St. Lemeston—"

"For a hundred years, I know. But, Lydia, Father spent a fortune to do it. It's two seats! The Opposition would need, what, fifty more seats at least to challenge the Tories in Parliament?"

"It isn't about the seats in Parliament. It's about Lively St. Lemeston. It's about these coats for the workhouse children. Our people rely on us."

"The home farm is fifty years behind the times." Jamie turned away to fuss at a green-and-purple plant with a strange toothy fringe. Its name was something to do with a tiger, Lydia thought. "Our people are those who work Wheatcroft land. I'm not saying Father neglected them, only it's so much money to puff ourselves up in the town when…" He glanced nervously at her.

Lydia felt as if she'd been struck. *To puff ourselves up in the town,* as if their father's years of hard work, all the good he'd done, his noble calling were nothing. As if all her own work over the last fourteen years were less than that, even. A piece of vanity.

Was that how he saw her? A pathetic old maid desperate to feel important? "But Advent is coming. Everyone will be expecting—"

"Everyone always expects something," Jamie muttered.

"What is that supposed to mean?"

His mouth set, that determined almost-pout he'd made ever since he was a baby that somehow conveyed, *I am being reasonable and you are a pack of monsters.* Despite everything, her heart turned over with affection. Why couldn't they agree?

"I don't understand why we have to pay for votes," he said. "If a man wants to sit in Parliament, let him pay his own way. And if the Tories are really the best choice, isn't that a good enough reason to vote for them, without a bribe?"

Lydia's jaw ached from holding her face still. Was he joking? "That isn't how it works," she said patiently. "*Anywhere.*"

Jamie waved aside the entire ancient edifice of British politics with an agitated hand. "Do you know how much Father spent on this election? Nearly a hundred pounds just for *ale*, Lydia."

Of course she knew how much Father spent. She knew to the penny. Lydia drew herself up, but it didn't make her feel any more in command. It still astonished her how tall her brother was; it had happened behind her back. One year he had come home at Christmas precisely her height, and at Easter he was an inch taller. After spending most of that summer at a friend's, he'd arrived back at Wheatcroft looming above her and enormously pleased about it. Lydia was no will-o'-the-wisp, but at five foot three in her stocking feet, she stood not a chance of seeming physically imposing next to her stocky brother. "Who do you think will take care of those people, if we don't?"

"Someone else will have to."

She had never noticed that people were particularly eager to take on work she couldn't. "I know you don't really feel this way. You've always wanted to continue Father's political work. You've never said a word—"

He couldn't even let her finish a sentence. "What's the point in telling you anything? You know how I feel better than I do."

"I didn't mean that. Jamie, please."

"You were both so set on me being the next patron of the Lively St. Lemeston Tories. It would have been a great row for nothing."

Her voice rose. "So you waited for him to *die*?"

Jamie looked stricken. Lydia wished she could take the awful words back.

But it was true, wasn't it? Her expectations and opinions, *her* disappointment—those didn't sway him at all.

It was so unfair. Ever since their dying mother had placed a squalling, newborn Jamie in her nine-year-old arms and said, *You must look after him for me,* Lydia had. She had doted on him, kept vigil at his sickbed, taught him to read and hired his tutors. When he went away to school, she'd written to him three times a week, every week. His holidays had measured out her years.

What had Father done, exactly, besides give him an allowance and tell him to stop crying when he hurt himself?

If only Father were here. Jamie would listen to him.

His face twisted apologetically. "I miss him too. But, Lydia, we can *both* do as we like now. You don't have to spend every minute of every day on Father's hobby, bribing tradesmen and cooing over other people's dirty babies and writing letters till your hands cramp."

Had he despised her letters too? "They aren't bribes," she said stiffly. "They're patronage."

"*Il faut cultiver son jardin,*" Jamie said. "That's what I want to do."

She frowned. One must grow one's garden?

"Haven't you read *Candide*?"

"When would I have read *Candide*, Jamie? Why on earth would I have read *Candide*?" *I've been working while you've been enjoying yourself at school.* She didn't say it.

Jamie scowled. "It's an important book. It ends with Candide realizing that the world is too large and ugly for him to mend. But he can bring order and bounty to one small patch of earth, and that's what he wants."

It was a pretty justification for turning one's back on responsibility. They were part of a class in whose hands rested the welfare and the wealth of England. Surely her brother could see that was a privilege that must be paid for? "I know you like gardening, Jamie, but—"

"It's a metaphor!"

"Well, you seem to be taking it literally." She hauled Father's careful, handsome ledger from under a pile of dirty knives and trowels and held it out accusingly.

Jamie's face flamed, and he shrank back like a little boy being shown the willow switch. "I was going to read it."

Lydia drew in a deep breath. "Oh, Jamie, I'm sorry. I know you're doing your best. Here, let me look at that cut."

He hid his hands behind his back. "My best is never good enough," he said under his breath.

He was young, that was all. Too young to know what he wanted. He'd come to his senses in a year or two (before the next election, if God was merciful), and be grateful that she'd maintained the Wheatcroft interest for him.

People in Lively St. Lemeston were counting on her. She

refused to let them down. She refused to let Jamie down.

But how was she to pay for any of it? Advent was coming, and Advent was expensive. She had no money of her own that wasn't tied up in a settlement for when she married.

Well, perhaps there was a way around that. She would send for the family lawyer and ask him about the terms of the trust. In the meantime she would warn their political agent, Mr. Gilchrist, not to make too many monetary promises.

She tucked the ledger under her arm. Her smile felt like a death rictus, but Jamie either couldn't tell or didn't care. He smiled back in relief. Her heart smote her. "Of course it's your decision, James. But…you'll take your seat next week, won't you?"

"What?"

"Parliament begins sitting next week." *You know that.*

"I…" He went a little pale. "It's too soon. Maybe next year."

"Jam—es!"

"I *can't.*"

Lydia swallowed her protests. She must make allowances for his youth and nerves. "Very well. Maybe next year. Do you mean to stay here for Christmas?"

Christmas was their family's time to be together—and, of course, to unite against the patrons of the local Orange-and-Purple Whig party, the awful Dymond family, who descended on the town for the season. Jamie had always spent his Christmases at Wheatcroft, even after he had begun going to friends' houses for the rest of his holidays.

Jamie's face contorted with remorse. "I'm going to Hal Whitworth-Perceval's. Christmas at Wheatcroft without Father…I can't. But it's to be a mixed party. You could come with me. Please do."

Lydia swallowed. She would not cry. "I don't think so. But thank you. Do me one favor, will you?"

He waited, unwilling to commit himself until he'd heard what she wanted.

"Don't tell anyone you've decided to let the Wheatcroft interest lapse in Lively St. Lemeston. Just until the New Year. Give yourself this Christmas to change your mind."

He gave her an annoyed, guilty look, and nodded.

The path back to the house took her through the Italian garden. She sat on a freezing bench for a moment to compose herself, her body so stiff with anger it should have cracked the marble. She brushed the dirt from Father's ledger, removing one glove despite the cold and licking her finger to clean the embossing.

There was no purpose to this rage. She breathed in and tried to relax. At once tears stung her eyes and panic closed her throat. She let the fury flood back so that she could breathe, and went inside to write their solicitor.

Chapter 2

Ash came into Lively St. Lemeston on the stagecoach.

He preferred walking, but a visitor who wished to escape notice in a small English town had to avoid anything with a havey-cavey appearance. Country gentlemen such as he was pretending to be did not walk long distances, and Ash hated riding, so he had bought a trunk in Brighton and filled it with a few garments, a shaving kit, and a heavy blanket to make it seem full. It had been two weeks now since he and Rafe had parted company, and he hadn't had even a whiff of a swindle big enough.

He never stayed in coaching inns. If anyone was looking for him, he'd rather see them coming from a distance. So he paid the porter to carry his trunk down the street past the market cross—a canopied stone shelter topped with a spire—to a respectable-looking pub.

He smiled up at the swinging sign painted with a cheery, haloed fellow quaffing a mug of something. It was a reminder that he was probably the only person in this town who wasn't a Christian, but he was used to that now. Riots, cries of *Christkiller*, his little brother coming home covered in bruises and pork fat—those fears were a minor itch when the shadow of the iron-and-gilt cross fell across his face.

The fine thing about the country, unlike London, was that

no one knew enough about Jews to know when they were looking at one. Give a false Christian name, and he was safe as houses.

He took a room and sent his trunk up with a generous tip to the porter. It always paid to have servants on your side. Then he sat at the bar and chatted with the publican, keeping his story vague in case he needed to change it later.

There were two gentlemen talking at a table not far from him, a middle-aged, professional-looking fellow and a young man of about twenty with a foxlike face and finicky tailoring. The young man looked and sounded upset, but over the noise in the room Ash could make out little. He wished Rafe were here; he had the gift of picking out words where Ash heard a dull roar.

He waited, drinking enough local cider to pacify the publican and not enough to seriously compromise his wits. Eventually the older man left, and the other slumped down in his seat with his head in his hands.

"What ails him?" Ash asked.

The publican shrugged. "Is all well with ye, Mr. Gilchrist?" he called.

Gilchrist stood. "All will be well, Mr. Stevens." He thrust his hands in his pockets, his cocky grin strained on his young face.

Ash felt a pang of sympathetic embarrassment. *It's not enough to smile,* he wanted to tell the boy. *You have to find a way to feel cheerful.* "Here," he called, "come and have a drink with me."

"I should be getting home to my wife," Gilchrist said without conviction.

His wife? Ash was getting old, because to his eyes the boy

looked far too young to be married. He stood and went to him, saying in a low voice, "You look like an ill omen. Sit here and I'll buy you a drink, and when you're in a more balanced state of mind, you can go home and not frighten your wife half to death. Whatever it is can't be that bad."

It took him three pints to winkle the story out of the boy, which in Ash's experience made him more than ordinarily discreet.

"I'm to lose my post," Gilchrist said. "And it's nearly Advent."

"What's your post?"

He explained that he'd worked for a candidate in the recent election and had been hired on as general political agent for the chief Tory family in the district. "You won't tell anyone this, will you?" Gilchrist reached for his pint and missed.

"I'm a stranger here. It's nothing to me."

"Baron Wheatcroft died shortly after the election." Gilchrist shifted his eyes in a way that made Ash think there was a story there too. "His son doesn't want to maintain his interest in Lively St. Lemeston at all. Wants to settle down to farming his land." He sighed. "Perhaps Mrs. Gilchrist will be pleased. She's a Whig."

"Is there any chance of the new lord changing his mind?"

Gilchrist shrugged, half cynicism and half hopelessness. "His sister wants very much to bring him round, but in the meantime she hasn't any funds to keep the interest alive. It's all tied up in trust for when she marries."

"Is she like to marry?"

"I don't understand why she isn't married already. A diamond of the first water, that lady. I was half in love with her myself until I met Mrs. Gilchrist."

Ash hid a smile. He'd noticed this newly wedded habit of referring interminably to *Mrs. So-and-so* before. From what he'd seen, that first flush of bliss lasted about as long as an apple blossom and rarely developed into anything as sweet and nourishing as an apple, but that was all the more reason to savor it.

"But I'm new to town." Gilchrist waved the publican over. "Hey, Mr. Stevens, why isn't Miss Reeve married, do you think?"

"No man with a fondness for his own breeches would marry Miss Reeve," Stevens said. "Her'd be wearing them before the week were out."

Gilchrist grinned. Now his troubles were off his chest, he was almost cheerful again. "A woman in breeches is a fine sight, I always say." He gestured in a way that clearly suggested *arse*. "If it would not be disrespectful to speak so of a gentlewoman and my employer, I'd suggest that they would suit Miss Reeve admirably."

A pretty, rich woman with a nice arse, a mind of her own, and no sweetheart, trying to get her hands on money that was tied up for her marriage. Ash could feel his plan coming clearer. This bore looking into.

Lydia sat in the window seat, hugging a cushion and staring down at the garden. The Wheatcrofts had never redone the grounds in the 'natural' style or moved their public rooms to the ground floor, being very proud of the Italian garden they already had and the magnificent view of it from above. (Lydia knew the garden was French, really, but after the Revolution they had no longer wanted the association.)

A formal garden looked particularly desolate in winter, wet green yews the only color and a stark barrenness to the angled walks and beds. Like a corpse with carefully arranged hair.

She hadn't been able to look at Father in his bier when he lay in state in the drawing room. She had knelt before him and prayed, but she hadn't been able to look. Visitors kept telling her he looked as if he were sleeping peacefully. He didn't.

Strange, how the eye could discern the difference so adeptly. Was it the lack of motion? The pallor? Or could the earthly senses somehow, distantly, perceive the presence or absence of a soul?

She had to stop being so morbid. She had to stop this. She could, if Jamie were here. But he had ridden away yesterday to stay with Hal Whitworth-Perceval and left her alone.

It began to rain outside. Only drizzling, until without warning the skies opened and torrents fell. Lydia liked the sound of it against the window, and the garden looked more lively with raindrops shaking its leaves.

She should get up and go into town. She should visit the workhouse and the hospital and the voters, and pay calls on the Tory ladies. But they would want to know her plans for the Christmas season. They'd have favors to ask of her. Worst of all, they'd want to talk of Father, and she would cry.

The road would be all over mud in an hour, she told herself. The carriage might get stuck on the way home.

She ought at least to attend to her correspondence, then. Or read this week's newspapers, waiting crisply on her desk.

Wait—was there someone out in this downpour? She rubbed a clear spot in the window with her hand, but the water was so thick on the outside the garden blurred. It was a minute before she was sure: a man was running up the drive, still nearly a quarter of a mile from the house. He had an umbrella, but in rain like this that would only protect about the top two feet of him, and it was awfully cold.

Lydia had been still so long that standing made her light-headed. She leaned against the wall for a moment, then went to the bell and pulled it.

"There is a visitor coming up the drive," she told the maid. "Build up the fire, if you please, and bring tea and brandy and something hot to eat. Would you ask Mrs. Packham to join me?" Mrs. Packham, whom Lydia called "Aunt", was in reality a distant cousin of her mother's who had chaperoned her since she left the schoolroom.

Who could be visiting her? It must be someone from Lively St. Lemeston. Had there been a political crisis? Did someone need an urgent favor? What could she sell to pay for it? Her jewels, perhaps. But she was very fond of all of them except the rubies, and those had been her mother's.

She would have liked to go downstairs and wait in the hall, but it wouldn't be ladylike, so once the man disappeared around the front of the house, she moved to a chair by the fire and listened for the sound of one of the heavy double doors opening. That was Pennifold's voice…the visitor answered too quietly for her to hear. The door to the Little Parlor opened—but it was only Aunt Packham.

However, Pennifold came soon after with the visitor's card, damp and smeared by a wet glove but still legible. Did she know a 'Mr. Ashford W. Cahill'?

"He is a stranger in these parts, madam. He had been hoping to view the portrait gallery."

Oh. He had not come to see her at all.

Lydia was surprised at the depth of her disappointment. Had she really let herself become so dreary that an unwanted caller in the middle of the afternoon was exciting?

The tea was brought in, steam rising invitingly from the pot. "We all know the portrait gallery is the coldest part of the house," she said briskly. "Probably it's the coldest part of the county. He'll catch his death if he doesn't dry off and take some tea first. Send him in."

It was improper to talk to him without an introduction, but it wasn't *that* improper, under the circumstances. The alternatives were refusing him his tour (unkind) or hiding in her own home while he was shown about by the housekeeper (too lowering to be borne).

Pennifold showed in an unassuming man with close-cropped dark hair, somewhere in his midthirties. Everything about him was broad. Broad hands, broad shoulders and chest, broad face with a broad, rather prominent nose. Indeed, his shoulders were so wide and his face so unfashionably tanned that she thought he could not quite be a gentleman despite his refined attire. But his brown eyes, deep-set under broad dark brows, were warm as he gave her a contrite smile.

Lydia opened her mouth to speak to him, enjoying the secret small thrill of doing something slightly improper—but Aunt Packham scurried out in front of her and conferred with the visitor in low tones. His voice was a pleasant tenor. She thought 'pleasant' a better word to describe him than 'hand-some', poor man, and his accent had more than a touch of Cornwall in it, but he seemed safe enough to talk to, and intent on not giving offense.

Aunt Packham turned back and whispered to Lydia, "May

I introduce a Mr. Cahill to you?"

Lydia suppressed a giggle, darting an apologetic glance at their visitor. "You may."

"Miss Reeve, may I present Mr. Cahill?" Her aunt beamed at having avoided an impropriety.

That was what Lydia needed her for, so it was pointless to be annoyed by it. She nodded at the visitor. "Mr. Cahill."

"I won't bow over your hand, Miss Reeve," he said, bowing from where he stood. "I'd only drip on you. I'm afraid my gloves are marked for death."

She looked him over. His boots had been hastily wiped downstairs, but enough mud and water remained that they would likely be ruined if they weren't cleaned soon. She doubted Mr. Cahill was the sort of man who could afford a new pair of boots whenever he liked. Besides, his feet and hands must be freezing. It was unpleasant to think of him catching a chill in her Little Parlor.

"Pennifold, please send someone to take the gentleman's gloves and boots and clean them."

"That really isn't necessary, madam," Mr. Cahill protested as the butler left the room. "I hoped to see the pictures. I shouldn't like to impose any more than that."

"Sir, the portrait gallery is chilly in winter." Lydia tried to keep her exasperation out of her voice. Why couldn't people take care of themselves? "Colder than outside, generally. It would be very foolish to go there damp."

The corners of his dark eyes crinkled in amusement, but as there was no derision in it, she found herself laughing too.

"I'm sorry," she said. "I've been the lady of the house so long I suppose I try to mother people over whom I have no authority whatsoever."

He chuckled. "I'm sorry for your loss. My mother also died when I was very young, so it's rather a comfort to be fussed over."

Lydia felt a pang of sympathy. "Please, sit." She poured a finger of brandy from the decanter and passed it to him. "How do you take your tea, sir?"

Sitting in one of the scrollwork armchairs, he tipped back his head and swallowed the brandy in a gulp. The movement of the thin strip of tanned throat above his cravat had a startling effect on her.

Beside her, Aunt Packham sniffed.

"I'm sorry." His little smile managed to be shy without being self-conscious. "I should have sipped that. I'm sure it was very fine. Only I'm colder than I thought, and I wanted the warmth. I take my tea black, thank you."

She was too experienced a hostess to grimace. At least he wasn't one of those people who put in far too much milk, like Aunt Packham. She slid the cup and saucer towards him across the table.

Luke, the footman, came in while she was adding a splash of tea to her aunt's milk. Mr. Cahill stripped off his gloves and handed them over, then yanked off his boots with Luke's help. His feet and calves were as broad and strong as the rest of him, and there was a red clock at the ankle of his stockings that wiggled as he stretched his feet towards the fire.

She looked away hurriedly. "Luke, there is a blanket on the window seat, if you would fetch it for Mr. Cahill."

The visitor spread the blanket across his knees, but it didn't help. The mind was a strange thing—put stocking-clad legs under boots and one rarely thought of them, but put them under a blanket and one could think of little else.

"This is a lovely blanket," he said. "Whose work is it?"

She blinked, looking at the blanket and seeing only his legs shifting beneath it. She had been wrapped in that blanket herself, a few minutes ago. It might yet retain enough warmth from her body for him to guess as much. "Not mine. I'm hopeless with a needle. I bought it at the Gooding Day auction last year. One of the Pink-and-White ladies made it."

His hands, cradling his teacup, were as tanned as his throat. Either he didn't often wear gloves, or that was his natural skin color. There was no polite way to ask. "Pink-and-White. That's the local Tory party, isn't it?"

"Yes. My father was their patron for many years." She straightened proudly. "The Society for Bettering the Condition of the Poor's Gooding Day auction raises money for the widows and old women of the town."

He smiled. "That's wonderful. I shouldn't like to think of a proper lady like you being one of those scoundrelly Whigs."

She smiled back, relieved. "Are you active in politics in your home district?"

"I don't spend as much time in my home district as I should," he confessed. "Wanderlust, I suppose is the word for it. I love England too much to be content with just one little piece of it. My younger brother travels with me, mostly. It's kind of him. I think lately he'd rather settle down." He turned his warm brown eyes on the fire and bit his lip—the first thing he'd done that didn't seem completely comfortable.

His lips were full, and oddly soft in his strong face.

It was rare that she found herself so physically drawn to a man. But there was no harm in it; he couldn't see her thoughts. No one could.

Lydia reflected that the percentage of her thoughts that

became somehow tangible, either by speaking or acting, must be very low. Three percent, perhaps. Was that sad? She didn't feel sad about it, only safe.

She imagined him kissing her. His lips would be soft, but she thought the skin around them would scrape. It was scarcely three o'clock, and there was already a faint dark shadow over most of the lower half of his face. His hand would fan across her lower back, holding her tight and secure.

"Well, Cornwall isn't a contested county," she said, absolving him of the sin of being away from home for the recent general election. She didn't know what to say about his brother. Every commiseration that came to mind was a complaint against Jamie, and she wouldn't voice them. "Do you mean to return home for Christmas?"

"You can hear the Cornwall, can you? Winter in England isn't the best time to travel, I suppose." He gestured at his blanket-covered legs. "But I love spending Christmas somewhere new. Every place celebrates differently. Four years ago I was in a town in Yorkshire that rings their bell once for each year since Christ's birth. One thousand eight hundred and eight peals goes on for a while."

She shook her head, smiling. "I've always spent Christmas here."

Aunt Packham sniffed. "People ought to spend Christmas at home."

Mr. Cahill looked taken aback. "I'm sorry, ma'am—"

"My aunt didn't mean you," Lydia said hastily. "My brother is visiting some friends for the Christmas season. I assure you I don't mind." She gave Aunt Packham a pointed glare for criticizing Jamie to a stranger. "He said he would miss my father too much here. Christmas was always our time together. If I weren't so stubborn, I would have gone with him."

Aunt Packham's eyes snapped. "You have responsibilities here. So does he." Setting down her teacup with a rattle, she opened her workbox and took out the lace cuffs she was tatting for Gooding Day. "Deuce take it!" Her voice shook as badly as her hands with anxious frustration. "I've knotted the thread."

Lydia was embarrassed that Aunt Packham would swear before Mr. Cahill, but then, the older generation had been born in a less genteel time. She put an arm around her aunt. "You'll fix it."

Aunt Packham pushed the work at Lydia. "You do it. My eyes aren't good enough."

Lydia winced. She was sure to make it a hundred times worse. She didn't want to fumble in front of a stranger, her fingers steady at first and then shaking like Aunt Packham's with self-consciousness and shame. Entertaining a guest made her feel like herself again, competent and serene, and she didn't want Mr. Cahill to realize it was a lie. "Aunt…"

"Let me, ma'am," said Mr. Cahill. "Have you got a needle?"

Aunt Packham eyed him with distrust, but when Lydia made no move to help her, she handed the cuff over. "Please don't let the shuttle unwind."

"I wouldn't dream of it." The white lace looked foolish and small in his hands, but his square-tipped fingers were surprisingly deft. As he slid the needle carefully into the center of the knot and coaxed it loose, frowning in concentration, Lydia found herself inexplicably blushing. She sipped her tea to give her cheeks a reason to look flushed.

Handing the tatting back, he met Aunt Packham's surprised, grateful gaze with a smile. "Aunts of my own," he said in explanation. "I'm afraid you *will* have to unwind the shuttle to pull the end through. I couldn't see a way round it."

"Thank you," Lydia said. "I'm no good with a needle or shuttle or…anything, really."

"You have excellent penmanship, dear," said her chaperone. It was less a compliment than a bewildered question. *The difficulty can't be your hands, so why…?*

"I suppose it's a matter of application. I correspond regularly, and sew as little as possible."

Mr. Cahill's eyes crinkled. "I think words are as important as stitches. Oh, we couldn't live in the English climate without clothes and blankets, but we'd die just as sure without our connection to each other."

Lydia felt warm inside and out, warmer than any blanket could have made her. "Do you really think so?"

"You have to make *something* for Gooding Day, dear," Aunt Packham pointed out before he could reply.

"I know, Aunt." Last year she had painted a smudged landscape on glass. Her father had bought it for a ludicrous sum and kissed the top of her head when she thanked him. Who would buy her contribution this year?

Someone would do it—to be polite, or gallant, or because they wanted a favor. She felt mortified and desolate at the mere thought. What if she cried at the auction before the entire town?

Mr. Cahill drank his tea in tactful silence, ignoring the tension in the air. At length his boots and gloves and coat were brought in, and Lydia, not ready to be alone again, sent for her cloak and muff.

But Aunt Packham, whose joints pained her in winter weather, flatly refused to follow them into the gallery. Lydia's maid, Wrenn, was none too eager to go either. She put on her cloak and gloves with a resigned air, muttering, "He must be a real *cognoscente* if he's willing to go in there."

"Surely it can't be as cold as all that," Mr. Cahill said.

Lydia raised her eyebrows at Wrenn. "It isn't. Well, it's colder than it is outside, probably, but it's much drier too. It isn't until the New Year that the room becomes really unbearable. The kitchen stores perishables there quite often."

Jamie had loved to play in the gallery as a child, liking the novelty of wearing his fur-lined coat indoors. He had loved to steal fruit and cheese, too. She had sat with him on the steps and told him stories about the people in the portraits, just as her mother had done with her when she was small.

She led the way through a chilly anteroom into the long, marble room. Its two levels took up two-thirds the length of the house and half its width. A grand staircase curved down at each end, and high, many-paned windows along the upper promenade looked out over the drowned garden behind the house.

The opposite wall was cluttered floor to ceiling with paintings, mostly of dead Reeves. Mr. Cahill seemed to wish to examine every one, leaning out over the balustrade to peer at the highest in a way that alarmed Lydia.

His comments left her in no doubt that not only was he fond of family portraits, but he had visited a great many of them all over the country. He at once placed the artists of several smaller works Lydia had forgotten they even had.

"Well, I don't believe he did much work in England," he said kindly, to cover her ignorance. "But I saw a pair of wedding portraits he painted at Ragley Hall once, and I never forgot them. The saddest thing I ever saw—you knew the husband was going to drive his wife to an early grave for fretting over his recklessness."

"And did he?"

He shrugged. "The housekeeper said she died of a wasting fever, but that can mean anything, can't it?"

Lydia had seen enough people give up and fade away in the course of her work to know it. "Poor lady. Do you think she loved him?"

"Who can say? That's the trouble with painting separate portraits of married people, you can't see how they are together. It's hard on a nosy fellow like me."

"Perhaps her parents made the match," she speculated. "I believe it used to be quite common to bully unfortunate girls into unions that were distasteful to them."

"Isn't it now?" he said with a cynicism that surprised her.

She sorted through her married friends in her mind. Of course they were all very good matches—except for Caro Jessop running away with a newspaperman—but no more than one or two had really been *arranged*.

"Not as it used to be," she said at last, confidently. "My father would have liked to see me married, and there were occasions when he pointed out someone who might have been suitable, but my disinclination was always reason enough for him to abandon the idea."

He looked at her curiously. Oh God, he would think her one of those harpyish females who couldn't bear to submit to a man's direction.

Aren't you?

No. She was only waiting for the *right* man. To submit to another, one had to esteem his judgment higher than one's own.

Perhaps you esteem your own judgment too highly.

"Not my disinclination to marriage," she blurted out. "My

disinclination to each specific gentleman." Oh, and now she sounded over-particular. Could Wrenn hear her? The maid, huddled in the doorway, didn't look more than usually sarcastic, so probably not.

Mr. Cahill gave her an amused, sidelong glance with no hint of condemnation in it. "I never met the woman who could tempt me, either. I don't know that I will. Not many women would care to tramp around England."

Lydia had discouraged a few suitors only because she would have had to make her home in another part of the country. Not having a home at all didn't bear thinking on. But for a brief, guilty moment, she did think of it: blowing Jamie and Aunt Packham a kiss and taking to the highway, to eat cheap tasteless food and laugh blithely at mildewed sheets and rats and stagecoaches stuck in the mud. Lydia knew she wouldn't enjoy the reality, but she thought Mr. Cahill could make the road pleasant and homey enough for another sort of woman.

"But where is Mr. Gainsborough's work?" he said after each portrait had been minutely examined. "I've only ever seen a few of his paintings, but they astonished me. That combination of life and restraint—it's quite wonderful."

Lydia hesitated. "The Gainsborough is in one of the other rooms." It would look strange if she didn't explain. But she couldn't form the words, so she led him to the library, to the unlit fireplace and the painting above it.

A combination of life and restraint: that was very apt. In the gray light from the long windows opposite, the painting looked trapped, frozen. As if its dark, muted colors were an enchantment, and if it were lifted, the subjects would come alive.

"It's you and your mother, isn't it?" Mr. Cahill asked. "I'm sorry, I didn't know."

Grief rose up from where it always lay waiting now, raking her chest with its claws. *No no no no*—but her face contorted, her mouth gaping like a wound she couldn't close. She covered her face tightly with both hands and tried desperately to stop, but it only turned the sobs into horrible wheezing sounds. Her back curved involuntarily, her body curling in on itself like a hedgehog. She wanted to apologize to Mr. Cahill, but couldn't bear to hear her own voice thick with tears.

When would this be over? How many weeks or months until she could keep her sorrow a private, containable thing like this portrait?

Wrenn came to stand quietly at her shoulder, digging through her pockets for a handkerchief.

"I'm so sorry," Mr. Cahill said. "Take mine." She reached out blindly and her hand collided with his. He'd been holding his handkerchief near her face so it would be easy for her to take it. "I'd like to ask if there's anything I can do, but of course there isn't. Here, I'll turn my back."

She was grateful that he understood that. She was grateful that he was silent after that, and that she wouldn't have to make the effort to repulse any overfamiliar comforting caresses. She had burst into tears while Charles Baverstock was visiting last week, and he'd taken the opportunity to put his arms around her and kiss her hands. And when she pushed him away, he was hurt and she had been obliged to soothe his ruffled feathers. She had felt horribly alone.

It took a long time for her tears to subside, but when she could finally wipe her eyes and open them, Mr. Cahill was still a few feet away, calmly studying the portrait as if her behavior had not put him out in the slightest.

She swallowed a few times and came to stand beside him, moving her head to politely face the portrait but unfocusing her eyes so that she didn't see it. "Thank you. If you tell me where you're staying, I can have your kerchief laundered and returned to you."

"I'm at the Drunk St. Leonard," he said. "I'm sorry I asked to see the painting. I should have known a Gainsborough would be too recent to be someone you didn't know."

"I *can* show it. It's in our library, I see it all the time. But with my father so recently gone…" Her voice trembled a little, and she shut her mouth tightly.

"Have you a portrait of him?"

She shook her head, fresh tears welling. "He was always too busy to sit for one. I'm afraid of forgetting his features."

How much did she really remember of her mother, and how much was this portrait? Had that really been the shape of Lady Wheatcroft's face? Was she remembering a painter's error instead of her mother? People said Lydia looked like her, but Lydia didn't see herself when she looked at the painting, not at all.

She didn't see herself in that laughing, carefree child, either. Sometimes she thought Mr. Gainsborough must have made it up.

"You might forget," he said. "You can't hold on to a person when they're gone. You can't even hold on to people who are alive sometimes. I don't remember my mother's face. Not really. But I tell myself—I'm still here. So much of who I am and what I do comes from her, I'm remembering her just by living. Every time I tilt my head or pick up a teacup the way she used to, that's a little bit of her still in the world."

He laughed a little, looking at the portrait with a wistfulness that made her eyes sting again. "I tell myself that, anyhow."

"Jamie doesn't want to maintain our interest in the borough," she said, knowing she shouldn't but desperate to tell *someone*. "That's what our father gave us. That's what he brought us up to do, and it's all that's left of him. My own money is tied up in trust, and Jamie—"

Drat. She was being indiscreet, and she was going to cry again. "I'm sorry, I—look at the painting as long as you like, and if you have questions about how Mr. Gainsborough worked, or—write to me and I'll tell you everything I remember, and everything I've been told, but—I'm afraid I'm in no state to entertain visitors."

"I..." He looked down. "I don't want to presume, Miss Reeve. I know we haven't been properly introduced, and I know that your crying doesn't make us friends or anything like that. Please don't think I'm presuming. But if you'd be willing, I'd love to buy you dinner in town instead of writing. I'd say it was a thank-you for your hospitality, but we both know it's yourself who'd be doing me a favor. Of course your aunt is included in the invitation, if she'd like to come."

How could she say no to that? She felt so low that even the brief sense of magnanimity it gave her to accept was gratifying.

He smiled wide when she agreed. He liked her, even though she'd been a dreary watering pot. That was gratifying too.

Chapter 3

A sh tramped back to town through the mud and rain, feeling—well, not any one thing. He was full of feeling, rather: liking and a kind of sympathetic grief for Lydia Reeve, hope that things would all come right for Rafe, exhilaration at having brought off a delicate situation with aplomb, a harsh chill from the weather, anticipation of a warm supper, pleasure at the paintings he'd seen, and a host of others.

He loved this churning in his mind at the start of a swindle, every succeeding impression sharp and clear as a bit of broken glass, the bad and the good each with a relish to them.

He had his plan now, all of it. He couldn't believe how lucky he'd been, to find this. He looked about him at the muddy parkland, fresh and smelling of rain, gleaming trees clasping the silver sky in a friendly embrace. He thought of Miss Reeve, beautiful and lonely and in need of funds from her dowry. There was something about her—that French thing that meant *I don't know what it is but I like it.*

That flood of tears had been a shock—he'd been watching her close, and he hadn't seen they were there until they were *there.* She'd seemed so warm-sun-on-calm-seas. But then, how often could you really tell what a stranger was thinking?

He'd known that the Gainsborough was likely to be of her mother. He'd thought sharing it with him might lead to some slight sense of intimacy, but the tears were an unlooked-for blessing. People were apt to like anyone who showed them tact and real understanding when they were grieving.

Rafe would have felt guilty provoking a woman to tears. But unlike his brother, Ash had been old enough to remember when his mother died. He hadn't only lost a parent—he'd lost everything he'd had that looked at all like security. Her procuress had taken her things and her money. She'd let Ash keep that one pathetic handkerchief out of a rare charitable impulse, and then she'd threatened to confiscate it every time he misbehaved. He'd been told to stop his sniveling and been pushed out into the street to steal, and on days he didn't steal enough, he didn't eat. And then she'd apprenticed him to the bodysnatchers.

Miss Reeve had grieved for her mother in peace and luxury. It was sad, and he felt for her, but a few tears wouldn't hurt her. Ash hadn't stolen anything the flat couldn't afford to lose since he and Rafe had left London and struck out on their own, thirteen years ago.

He *had* felt sorry for her, though. If she'd been a girl of his own class, he'd have put an arm around her and kissed the top of her head. Of course the Honorable Miss Reeve would have found that thoroughly unpleasant.

He wondered what her hair smelled like. It was splendid hair, peeping out from under her lace cap, thick and coppery and so shining it looked like a crisp Tudor painting. She resembled a Tudor portrait all round, with her apple cheeks and sharp chin, and her wide eyes that made brown a rich, bright color.

Well, the smell of her hair would be for Rafe to find out, one of these days. Because after all, Ash wasn't even trying to swindle her. He was trying to give her his brother. She'd be the envy of every woman in six counties.

You couldn't be obvious about matchmaking, though. People were contrary. He'd tell them both it was a marriage of convenience, that Rafe would marry her and sign over her money in exchange for a slice of it, and never again darken her door. A few weeks would be plenty of time for them to find they suited marvelously. Ash would give them a nudge if they needed it, but he doubted they would. The merits of each of them were too self-evident.

Lively St. Lemeston came into view, quaint and homey in the rain. Rafe would be set for life here, snug and warm and loved and rich. He'd forget he'd ever thought about Canada or the army.

Rafe couldn't possibly resist all this. It was perfect, the perfect honest life left lying about on a silver platter waiting to be stolen. It gave a man itchy fingers just looking at it.

Ash stood up when Miss Reeve walked in the door. She looked deliciously expensive. No hasty redying for her—he'd swear she'd ordered a whole new wardrobe in black. Figured velvet edged the bombazine bodice, and a brooch woven with silver hair ('filthy goyishe custom', his fence had always said when Ash brought in a piece like that) held the kerchief closed at her breast. There was just that faintest hint of color to her lips and cheeks that indicated a highly trained and well-paid professional had the keeping of her rouge pot.

She was the kind of art that was so valuable it wasn't even for sale, and she smiled when she saw Ash. His pulse jumped.

She hadn't brought her aunt, only the tall blonde maid with wry eyebrows. That was a good sign. Miss Reeve wasn't too bothered about keeping him at arm's length.

He bowed over her black, butter-soft glove that still smelled new. Too bad actually kissing a woman's hand had gone out in the last century—that leather would be nice against his lips. *She* would be nice against his lips.

This attraction to her was inconvenient, but it wasn't a real problem. He'd already let go of her hand and was pulling out her chair in a casual but respectful fashion. Feelings were easy to hide if you could smother the part of you that wanted to be found out.

"How are you today, Miss Reeve?" He kept his voice sincerely interested without being too sympathetic. He didn't want to make her self-conscious.

She flushed slightly under the rouge anyway. "Very well, thank you, sir. And yourself?"

"I had a splendid morning. I woke late, breakfasted on fresh bread, and was given a tour of your historic church by the sexton."

She smiled proudly. "You haven't seen it at its best until you've been to Sunday services. The acoustics are very good."

"I look forward to it." Ash was fond of attending church. It was a barefaced swindle, after all, and he enjoyed getting away with it. "What else ought I to see while I'm here?" Nothing made a person warm to you like taking her advice.

She twisted her mouth in thought. "The Assembly Rooms are impressive. They were built when I was ten, and I'm afraid they suffer from some of the excesses of style of that time— Lady Tassell, the Whig patroness, advised on the choosing of the architect—but the workmanship is beautiful…"

She talked about the town all through the soup, the fish, and the venison with removes. The river was lovely, the bridges were picturesque, the market on Wednesdays was not to be missed, there were some very old houses on Mill Street, and he should really see St. Leonard's Forest if he could manage it. She was even willing to admit that the Dymond family home several miles west of town might merit a visit. Ash listened with great interest and jotted her suggestions down in his memorandum book.

But it was when the apple tarts were served that Miss Reeve at last brought out her most treasured jewel. He could see at once in her face that she would have liked to bring it up earlier, but had had to steel herself against his anticipated lack of interest. "And…you might like to visit the workhouse, if such things interest you. At least, it's considered to be very modern and efficient. Several other towns in the district have modeled theirs on it. And the children are so sweet." Her face clouded. "I always buy them new coats this time of year. Children grow fast, you know. But this year I don't know if I can afford it." She pushed her half-eaten apple tart around her plate.

Ash felt his jaw tightening and relaxed it. After all these years, seeing food wasted still set up a frustrated, resentful feeling in his breast almost like pain. The workhouse children could probably have eaten for a whole day on what he was going to pay for that apple tart, and she didn't even have the decency to enjoy it.

"It isn't that I should hesitate to deny myself." She fixed her large eyes on his. She couldn't stand for anyone to think her hardhearted, could she? If he were going to swindle her in the ordinary way, it would be the letter-racket. Show up at her door with a tale of woe and a note from a lord somewhere saying he was a respectable person, ask for five pounds for the journey home, and she'd be eating out of his hand. "But everywhere I might trim my expenses—people rely on custom from Wheatcroft, especially at Christmastime. If I spent less, what would the grocer's wife do, or the milliner? I know! I shall cancel the dinner dress I ordered from Mrs. Miskin and offer her the custom for the coats. Only she may have ordered the black crape from London express for me, and God willing, she won't have anyone else to sell it to for some time…"

"How much will it cost to buy the children coats?"

"Oh, not above ten or fifteen pounds, I imagine. There aren't so very many of them, after all."

"I would be happy to make the donation myself, in that case." He repressed the urge to ask whether she meant to eat the rest of her tart, and if not, could he have it?

Her face glowed. "Oh, that is too good of you. Here, you must come to the workhouse with me so that the mistress can thank you. She'll be so pleased."

The invitation was a Godsend, except that Ash didn't want to go. He didn't want to see those children.

"Have you visited similar establishments in other parts of England? I'm sure she would be glad to hear your thoughts."

"I'm afraid I've avoided them." He'd toured jails and voluntary hospitals and asylums in the company of flats—it was a popular enough pastime—but he'd never outgrown his childhood terror of workhouses. "I find the notion rather distressing, to be honest with you."

In Ash's experience, when a man confessed a small weakness to a woman of about his own age, it was generally well received. Women liked to feel superior and generous as much as men, and they had fewer opportunities.

This was one of the exceptions. Miss Reeve's mouth set and her brows drew together. A moment later her expression softened, but Ash suspected it was with conscious effort. "You're right, of course," she said with melting empathy. "Institutions can be dreary. It's difficult to see children suffer. But if we wish to turn away, doesn't that make it all the more our duty to look them in the face and do what we can to help?"

Ash seldom got angry during a swindle. He didn't understand why he felt so angry now. Miss Reeve was darling. She really wanted to help, and what's more, she had little patience for squeamishness in fulfilling a responsibility. As a ruthless man himself, Ash admired that.

But he looked at her expensive mourning clothes and her perfectly made-up face and her lovely, well-fed, healthy body, and he couldn't breathe past the knot of fury in his throat.

Do what you can? he wanted to say. *I can see your sacrifices were enormous. I can see you've done absolutely* everything *you can. How dare you feel superior? How dare you lecture? How dare you sleep soundly in the knowledge of your own righteousness?*

He'd have found her easier to like if she'd simply said to herself, *It's unfair that I'm rich, but it's the way of the world, so why worry?* After all, he and Rafe had been living high too— not as high as her, but high for two kids from the East End. He'd never judge someone for taking what she could get when he did the same thing every day.

You like everybody, he reminded himself. Why was she getting under his skin? Why couldn't he keep her at a comfortable distance, unaffected by what she did or thought?

He was upset about Rafe, that was all. He was letting it tangle with everything else. He put the last bite of his own tart in his mouth, buying himself time. People liked to imagine their feelings were obvious, that their emotions were written all over their face. But generally, no one looked carefully enough to notice anything, or knew you well enough to understand what they noticed. If he didn't tell her he was angry, she'd never know.

His silence was making her nervous now. She darted little glances at him in between tiny bites of food. The world made women into swindlers, always watching and calculating, always seeking to please. It was easy enough to find the seed of tenderness that provoked and coax it to grow and unfurl.

He smiled at her, and her shoulders relaxed. Yes, here he was again, in charity with her. Poor girl. So many advantages and she didn't know how to enjoy any of them. Rafe would like her, anyway. They would get on earnestly and kindly together.

To his surprise, the idea brought Ash's anger roaring back. How smug they would be, agreeing on how selfish and careless and reprehensible he was!

No. Ash refused to be angry with his brother. Rafe didn't owe him anything. He drew up a memory of tiny Rafe, waving his chubby fists and smiling. Anger ebbed, leaving a strange, overwhelming sadness. Nonplussed by his emotions' revolt, Ash floundered.

This silence couldn't drag out much longer. To hell with it. Sorrow was close enough to penitence to fool Miss Reeve. Ash met her eyes, letting her see his grief. "You shame me. I would be honored to accompany you to the workhouse."

Her face lit up. "I didn't mean to nag." Her eyes pleaded with him not to think her a shrew.

Ash didn't know what he felt. But there was a bright scarlet thread of liking for her in it. He pulled that thread free and smiled at her, ignoring the rest of the tangle.

It took them an age to reach the workhouse. She had her footman leave calling cards at a dozen houses, and stopped at half the shops and workshops in town to chat with the folks working there. Ash didn't mind. She introduced him to all of them, and an association with Miss Reeve could only be useful when the time came to make purchases on credit.

They passed a shopfront that wafted brandy and ginger into the street, even through a closed oak door. *The Honey Moon*, the sign read. He wondered if Lively St. Lemeston was too small and quiet for a boy to safely crack a pane of the window with his penknife and make off with a jar of boiled sweets. It had been twenty years at least since he'd done any such thing, but his fingers itched anyway. That pane in the corner was low and out of sight of the till, and there were four or five jars in easy reach of it.

Miss Reeve's pattens clinked on the sidewalk ahead of him, and he ran to catch up with her and her servants. "I take it that's an Orange-and-Purple shop?"

She nodded. "It's new. We never had a confectioner in Lively St. Lemeston before. At first the novelty kept people away, but since he got a stall at the market I believe his business has improved."

"Yes, but are the sweets good?"

"Charles Baverstock told me it was fit for the gods, and Mrs. Miskin says everything is newfangled and Frenchified." She sighed. "Maybe it's a good thing Jamie didn't stay. He would be sure to see no reason not to stop there, and Mr. Pilcher the baker would be so insulted."

"My brother loves sweets too," Ash said. "When he was a

boy, he used to beg me to buy him acid drops whenever we passed a barrow." Rafe hadn't done any such thing; he had stolen the drops himself, as soon as he was tall enough to reach. He'd been a precocious little thief, and Ash had been terribly proud and shown his little brother off to his friends as a prodigy. How horrified proper Miss Reeve would be if Ash told her that!

"Will your brother be joining you in Lively St. Lemeston?" she asked. "Or—will you be leaving soon?"

"I hope he will be," Ash said. "I think you'll like him—that is, if I'm not presuming. He's about your age, and a good deal taller than I am."

She laughed and rolled her eyes. "My aunt and I should be happy to receive him."

Perfect.

"Here we are," she said, stopping before a neat white building. Her footman raised the knocker and rapped with a sound like the clanking of chains.

Ash reminded himself that this was the ultimate swindle—a street urchin striding into a workhouse like a fine gentleman, the patroness on his arm. He was Daniel in the lion's den, and it should have exhilarated him.

But he'd played this swindle before. He'd been far too lucky that last time, left a scale unbalanced behind him. This was pushing his luck, and that was something he'd learned never to do.

Well, there was a twisted satisfaction in that, too. In courting destruction as if it were a woman you couldn't resist when she'd already emptied your friends' pocketbooks and broken their hearts. Ash would have stepped off the cliff's edge a long time ago, if it weren't for Rafe.

The door was opened by a pigtailed adolescent girl. Ash followed Miss Reeve inside and let the workhouse door close behind him.

Chapter 4

I t was smaller and neater and less crowded than the London workhouses Ash remembered from his childhood. But it had the same strange smell of cleanliness without luxury or personality: brown soap, starch, human bodies, and cheap food.

It was too early for the able-bodied who couldn't feed themselves. They would come in January and February when it was coldest. Now it was the old, the mad, the simpleminded, and men and women too sick or crippled to work, all pressed up against each other in one space like odds and ends shoved out of sight in the back of a drawer—and, of course, the children, forced to care for them all.

There was a little girl of eight or nine feeding an old woman in one corner. Ash saw her notice Miss Reeve, her posture changing at once from impatient boredom into something careful and correct.

"Here you go, Mrs. Sykes," she said, her voice syrupy sweet and pitched to carry. "Nice gruel, your favorite."

Ash hid a smile.

Then another child of perhaps eighteen months toddled over and reached for the spoon. The girl snatched it away, and the child reached for it again. Ash saw the child's mouth open wide, he saw the girl's darting look of terror at Miss Reeve—

Even before the child's first wail had run out of breath, he was swooping her up. "There now," he murmured, nestling her against his coat. "Don't cry."

"She's no trouble," the girl said stridently. "She nearly never cries." Her eyes were wide with fear.

"Of course not," Ash said, pretending everything was ordinary. His heart pounded in his chest. "You seem like a very well-behaved baby, don't you?" He wrinkled his nose at the child in his arms, and she giggled.

"Her's too young for the workhouse," muttered Mrs. Sykes.

"Is not," countered the girl. "The overseers said she wasn't." She reached for the baby, her plain, square face made plainer and squarer with determination. "I can take care of her."

Ash handed the child over. "I'm sure you can. You look very responsible for your age."

"I am. I be ever so responsible, and I can take care of her." She settled her sister on her hip, even though the child was really too big for her to hold comfortably.

Miss Reeve appeared at his shoulder. "Mr. Cahill, may I present Mary Luff and her sister Joanna? How do you do, Mary?"

Mary made a clumsy curtsy, lunging a little at the end to prevent Joanna from slipping out of her grasp. "Very well, ma'am, thank you."

"Mary is a great help to Mrs. Bridger, the house-mistress, aren't you?"

"I try, ma'am."

Miss Reeve smiled. Mary watched her face intently for any possible cue as to how best to ingratiate herself. Ash's stomach turned over. He didn't want to be here. He wavered between asking to hold Joanna again so that Mary could finish feeding

Mrs. Sykes in peace, and trying to distract Miss Reeve from the children as quickly as possible. The longer those in authority noticed you, the greater the chance they would do something to muck up your life.

Miss Reeve walked away, and Ash followed. "Some of the overseers think we ought to send Joanna to a nurse in the country," she said. "They think it would be more healthful for her there."

"Surely it's better to be with her sister."

"I wish I knew." She sighed. "At a certain point you have to pray you're making the right decision."

"I don't imagine you'd have liked to lose your own brother," he said, an edge in his voice. He wasn't doing a good job of distracting her. He shouldn't have agreed to come here.

"But I could take care of Jamie. If I weren't able to, perhaps I ought to have set aside my own comfort and let him go. His own welfare must have been paramount."

"Yes, a two-year-old child, for his own welfare to be taken from his family and sent to strangers." Could she hear his voice shake? He was shaking a little all over, wasn't he? Just a fine tremor; maybe she wouldn't notice. "Would a nurse in the country have loved him and cared for him as you did—and not only while she was paid to do it, but forever? Can you be so sure it would have profited him in the end? Absolute devotion isn't so common a thing in this world that it should be held cheaper than a little clean air and fresh milk."

She looked at him with approval. As if he had taken a political stance she liked. As if it were an academic question.

He laughed self-deprecatingly. "I'm sorry. I'm rather fond

of my own brother, you know. I didn't mean to talk your ear off."

She put up a hand to her ear. It was a lovely ear. A shell-like ear, even. He had always thought that an odd phrase, but he could see it now—the creamy smoothness of the curve, the warm pink glow as it caught the light. If he leaned in, would he hear a mysterious seashore thrum from within her?

"Oh, don't apologize," she said, smiling. "My ears are very well attached, I promise you. Let me introduce you to Mrs. Bridger."

That night Ash woke from a nightmare, despairing and soaked in sweat. *Your blanket is too thick and the windows too snug,* he told himself. *It's not a portent. You've had that dream like clockwork since you were a child.*

It was a simple enough dream. The place varied, and his own age in it, but the core of it was that he couldn't find Rafe. He was looking and looking and could not find Rafe.

Usually when he woke, Rafe was there. It was easy to know Rafe was there because he snored, a fact Ash was secretly grateful for no matter how he teased.

But it *was* a portent this time. Rafe would be gone soon enough, gone forever. Ash wondered how long he himself would last after that, and what purpose he'd find to drag him through his days. Maybe he'd die in a workhouse like the one he'd seen today, charming the staff into granting him small and useless privileges.

He threw back the covers. Chill air rushed in, welcome and unpleasant. He ought to wait a few days longer to be sure of Miss Reeve. He lit the lamp and wrote to Rafe anyway, and told him to come.

Even if Rafe were in Arundel and received the letter at once, he would have to journey to London and take the stagecoach from there to lend credence to coming from Cornwall. He could not possibly come sooner than Wednesday, and the coach never arrived in Lively St. Lemeston before one and often not until three.

Yet on Tuesday Ash found himself in the Lost Bell coaching inn at half-past ten. There he sat, reading the *Lively St. Lemeston Intelligencer* and buying drinks for the local population, until the stagecoach rattled in at a quarter past two and disgorged a number of disgruntled passengers, none of whom were Rafe.

On Wednesday he toured the powder mill and put off arriving at the Lost Bell until noon. He shared a dinner table with a large family breaking their journey to Brighton, then removed to the coffeehouse across the street, where he sat by the window pretending to cherish an infatuation with the owner's daughter Imogen, a pretty black woman with dark eyes and a Sussex burr.

Fortunately she enjoyed the attention, willing to be bought a mug of chocolate and carry most of the conversation besides, in between tending her pots and beans. For a couple of hours he was absorbed easily enough in her brother's apprenticeship at the Honey Moon, the difficulties inherent in the importation of coffee, her father's trying insistence on double-checking her figures, and gossip about Miss Reeve's great rivals, the Dymond family.

"He's devoted as can be to Mrs. Sparks, Mrs. Dymond now of course. I never much thought of marrying, but to see how he looks at her—"

The coach rolled into the yard across the way with a great squelching and splashing.

"Oh, are you waiting for somebody on the stage?"

He turned back to Imogen with an effort. "Yes—my brother. I don't know if he'll arrive today. We're usually inseparable, and I haven't seen him in a few weeks."

"Isn't that sweet? Do you spy him?"

Ash knew Rafe was there even before he ducked out of the low coach door, last of everyone. He knew because all the passengers looked happy and in charity with one another. Ash could get along with anyone, but Rafe had an instinctive knack for bringing people together and raising their spirits.

He pointed. "That's him. My brother Rafe."

She took Rafe in appreciatively. "You don't look much alike."

He laughed. "No, he got all the looks in the family."

She grinned at him. "I don't imagine you do too bad yourself."

Ash pretended not to see the invitation in her words. "Thank you for your kindness in keeping me company, Miss Makepeace." He stood, smiling, and offered her a shilling tip.

"Oh, you needn't." Her tone said she'd take it if he pressed, but wouldn't mind if he took it back either. The coffeehouse must do well for itself.

He pressed it into her hand, almost wishing he could offer her more than a flirtation, and see if she liked to accept it. But he never took more than someone could afford to lose, and a girl who had decided she could afford casual tumbles would know he ought to have a foreskin. It wasn't a good risk.

He didn't mind, except when he was feeling particularly lonesome. There was no reason he should feel lonesome now. Rafe was here.

He hurried outside, and in spite of everything, when Rafe broke into a smile at the sight of him, Ash was happy. Rafe gave him a great bear hug that lifted him an inch or two off the ground and set him down. His eyes searched Ash's face. "How are you?"

A small, mean impulse made Ash smile unconcernedly back and say, "Never better. You?"

Rafe looked disappointed, hurt, even a little angry. It wasn't fair. It wasn't fair for his brother to want to leave *and* to want Ash to want him to stay.

Then Rafe's smile broke out again. "I'm very well. Where are we staying?"

The safest place to talk privately was in the open, so once Rafe's luggage had been dropped at the Drunk St. Leonard, Ash took his brother on a walk to Wheatcroft.

"…It isn't even a swindle," he finished his explanations. "Or rather, she's in on it with us, if she agrees. All you have to do is marry her and see that the settlement is arranged to her satisfaction, and she'll give us a slice of that lovely fortune."

Rafe frowned. "But she'll be *married* to me. I'll be married to *her*."

"She doesn't want a husband. You'll buy your commission and you never have to see her again. If you like, you can even send her a condolence letter from the War Office in a few years."

"But if she marries again, she'll be a bigamist—"

"Who's ever to know? Just keep away from Sussex and don't use the name Ralph Cahill again." He knew perfectly well that the best way to reassure was to listen patiently to Rafe's concerns, agree with all of them, and resolve each to Rafe's satisfaction. It was easy to do with a flat, but nearly impossible with his brother.

Why should he have to swindle Rafe? Why on earth was his brother fretting over bigamy, of all things? If there was ever a crime that harmed no one…and it would all be moot once Rafe and Miss Reeve made a love match of it. But of course he couldn't say *that*.

"I won't," Rafe said. "I'm going to use my own name after this. Our name."

Ash blinked. "You'll use Rafe Cohen? To buy your commission?"

Rafe looked at his feet, grimacing. "I haven't decided on the army for certain. I know I'd have to profess Anglicanism. But it's only a formality. You…would you mind?"

"Of course not," Ash said, startled. "I wouldn't mind if you changed your name, either. You'll have a lot of petty prejudices to contend with, else."

Rafe shook his head. "I want to be who I am, Ash. Can't you understand that?"

Ash was stung. "This *is* who I am. I'm a swindler. So are you. You'd still be you with a different name."

"I don't want to be a swindler anymore. I told you that. I just want to be Rafe Cohen."

"Do you now?" Ash smiled his mildest smile. "And will

you tell your fine new officer friends that Rafe Cohen was a housebreaker? That Rafe Cohen's mother was a whore? You can set up shop as an honest man all you like, but you'll have to lie to do it."

Rafe's face darkened. "You're the one who wants me to be an officer."

Drek, Ash thought. Drek drek drek. This was what happened when he lost his temper. If he wasn't careful Rafe would run off and enlist before he even met Miss Reeve. He wouldn't have to convert to serve in the rank and file. "Yes," he said promptly. "Yes, I do, and I'm sorry. I lied with all that 'never better' claptrap. I'm on edge. You know Rafe Cohen is my favorite person in the world; anybody would want to be him."

Rafe slung an arm around his shoulders. "Thank you, Ash." His voice was thick. "I don't—I'm not proud of what we do, not anymore, but I'm proud to be your brother. We were dealt a bad hand. I don't blame you for how you brought me up."

It was a harder blow than blame would have been. To be magnanimously forgiven for his hard-won, improbable accomplishments—he thought suddenly of the two little girls in the workhouse, and Miss Reeve's question. Would Rafe have been better off if Ash had given him up? Would he have been happier apprenticed to some low trade, plodding through his simple, hungry, honest life?

They came round the bend and saw Wheatcroft. The house sprawled—or rather, reclined elegantly, looking enormous even with a good five minutes' walk between them and it. Ash let the view sink in. Lights beckoned in the windows, and a faint homey noise drifted towards them.

He and Rafe hadn't been 'dealt a bad hand'. They had never

been in the game. Now Ash was going to give his brother an interest in that house and all it stood for, and better than that, Rafe wouldn't seem a jot out of place. That was nothing to feel guilty about.

The house didn't need any embellishment to make it seem tempting—and if it did, Miss Reeve ought to do the trick. But for good measure Ash turned up his coat collar and rubbed at his arms—*it's cold out here, and warm and dry in there.* "Why don't you meet her?" he said. "You can decide then."

Rafe shrugged. "Why not? Here, take my muffler." He dropped it around Ash's neck without waiting for a reply. "You never dress warmly enough."

Ash sighed.

Lydia was in the Little Parlor window seat again, alternately staring at the garden and at the ever-growing pile of unanswered correspondence on her writing table.

She had responsibilities. She had stayed at Wheatcroft while Jamie went off to a house party, specifically so that she might discharge them. And yet she couldn't open those letters. Some of them carried condolences. Some were from people who hadn't heard the news yet, and would ask after her father's health.

Tears swam in her eyes, merely at the thought.

Read a magazine. Plan your contribution to the Gooding Day auction. Do something. Do anything but sit here feeling sorry for yourself. Her father would be ashamed of her.

A tear spilled over and dripped down her cheek. Ugh! She hated the slippery feel of it. She hated how dry and sore the skin under her eyes felt when she wiped it away.

Two figures appeared on the drive. The shorter of the two looked like Mr. Cahill, which was a silly schoolgirl fancy as they were much too far off to tell.

But when they drew nearer, it *was* Mr. Cahill. So she hadn't been looking for him, or hoping to see him, or thinking about him at all. She had only recognized him, because her eyesight was good. Who was that with him? His brother, perhaps.

She felt a glimmer of satisfaction at having her guess confirmed when their cards were brought in to her. "Please ask my aunt to join me, and bring some tea," she told Pennifold. "Once Mrs. Packham is here, you may show them up."

She examined her face very carefully in the mirror. Would they be able to tell that she had been crying? She thought not, in this light. But ever since that first day when Mr. Cahill had seen her cry, when he met her eyes she felt as if he could see everything, as if he knew her. As if all the ghosts of thoughts not acted on were tangible and solid to him.

She was in mourning. Crying was expected. Why should she feel this embarrassment, this vulnerability?

Aunt Packham bustled in, and Lydia put on a smile for her. "Oh, you poor thing," her aunt said. "When the visitors are gone we'll put a warm compress on your eyes, with an infusion of rose petals. It will be just the thing."

Lydia felt panicked out of all proportion, as if the whole world were looking at her. She *had* to wipe the strain from her face.

Well, and she could. She had been a political hostess since she was seventeen. Taking a deep breath, she shut her eyes and tried to find something glad that didn't have her father in it. But even the roar of the crowd when the Tories won both seats in the recent election was tainted. She had been overjoyed; so had her father, and he'd had too much champagne and galloped home in the dark and now he was dead.

She thought of tea. Tea, and jam on toast. She breathed in deep, imagining she was smelling rich black pekoe tea. She imagined the crunch of the toast and tart sweet raspberry jam.

Luke carried in the tea tray. The smell wafted from the pot, adding to Lydia's calm. She smiled at the footman and thanked him, feeling almost herself.

"I don't know how you do that, dear," Aunt Packham said, comfortably admiring. "A born hostess. Your father always said you could smile when the world was ending."

Lydia's fragile serenity wobbled. She took the lid off the teapot and leaned over it, breathing in the bittersweet, luxurious scent.

The door opened. She replaced the lid without hurrying, so as not to look as if she had been caught doing something strange, and stood with a smile. She felt genuinely well on the surface. Underneath…she could ignore that. "I do love the smell of fresh-brewed tea. How do you do, Mr. Cahill?"

The corners of his eyes crinkled warmly. "Very well, thank you. Miss Reeve, Mrs. Packham, may I present my brother, Mr. Ralph Cahill?"

She held out her hand. "A pleasure to meet you, Mr. Ralph."

Mr. Ralph stepped forward, into the light. Lydia drew in a breath. He was—she couldn't find a word. She was speechless.

He's good looking, she told herself firmly. *That's all. Plenty of men are good looking.*

But Mr. Ralph was something out of the common way. He was well above six feet, his shoulders like something cast in bronze. His hair, tied in a short, old-fashioned queue, was molten gold in the firelight. His features were chiseled, his movements graceful, and best of all, his smile lit up the room. Solid, bright, a hint of wickedness with nothing of disrespect.

"It can't be half as nice as meeting you, Miss Reeve," he said. His voice was special too, a deep, confident, comforting rumble.

He wasn't what she'd expected from unassuming Mr. Cahill's brother. She fought a blush and sat as he bowed over Aunt Packham's hand with equal grace. "Please, sit. Would you like some tea?"

They clustered round the fire, Mr. Ralph taking the seat by her while Mr. Cahill took a chair by her aunt. "Tea would be splendid," Mr. Ralph rumbled, smiling again. His simple good humor was infectious. As she poured tea and listened to his earnest compliments on her biscuits, her earlier depression melted away like frost on a window when the fire was lit.

"How long have you been in town?" she asked.

"I came in on today's stage. My brother said you were the thing best worth seeing in the neighborhood."

"I promise to show him the church and the workhouse another day." Mr. Cahill looked up at his brother, obvious affection in every line of his plain face, and she felt a great pang of liking for him. A pang of envy too; his little brother, who wanted to settle down, had come to be with him at Christmastime.

Jamie wanted you to go with him, she reminded herself. "Mr. Cahill is very kind," she said, and meant it. His deep brown eyes met hers and he smiled. Just a tiny quirk of the lips, but her face felt hotter than it had at first sight of Mr. Ralph's cast-in-bronze glory.

She was lonely, that was the problem, lonely and susceptible to being paid attention to.

"Have you any plans tomorrow morning?" Mr. Ralph asked. "I had hoped that if I borrowed a horse from the inn, you might accompany me on a ride about the countryside. I know it's cold, but it looks to be beautiful country."

Her heart swelled with pride. "It is, and I'd be happy to loan you a horse myself. It's too cold to go far, but if you dress warmly, in a couple of hours we could see part of St. Leonard's Forest. Well, a lot of it is heath now, but…" Her gaze went to the writing table. "I really should spend the morning working at my correspondence. I'm sadly behind."

Mr. Cahill gave her a sympathetic smile. "Surely under the circumstances no one will blame you. Take care of yourself, this once. Enjoy yourself."

She nodded without conviction, wishing she *could* be so carefree, and not the sort of person for whom an unanswered letter gnawed away at the back of her mind. Nobody liked a stick-in-the-mud…but they liked all the things sticks-in-the-mud did for them, didn't they? They liked not having to worry because someone else, someone who couldn't sleep when she had left a duty unperformed, would make sure that nothing too terrible happened.

I'll do it tonight, she promised herself. *I'll do it tonight and cry and put warm compresses on my eyes, and tomorrow morning I'll feel better and go on the ride and be jolly company, and no one will have to know but Wrenn.*

Mr. Ralph frowned. "Are you expecting bad news, Miss Reeve?"

She tried to laugh. "No, it's only the condolence letters for my father. I don't—I ought to want to read them. People have taken the trouble to be kind, but I—"

Mr. Ralph's eyes widened. "Oh, of course! I ought to have begun by telling you how sorry I am for your loss." He looked awkward, and angry with himself.

"Thank you." She held her hands very still in her lap, trying to sound gracious and at ease.

He put his hand over hers for a moment, meeting her eyes. Aunt Packham frowned, but his hand was warm, and the gesture didn't feel forward. It felt sincere and natural, comforting her as his words did not.

"They've written because they want to make you feel better," Mr. Cahill said. "If reading the letters won't make you feel better, there's no purpose to it."

Lydia knew he was right. She also knew people would feel slighted if she didn't answer their letters.

"I could read them for you," Mr. Ralph offered.

She blinked.

"I could, and help you answer them."

Aunt Packham made a disapproving sound. So did Mr. Cahill.

"It's too much to ask," Lydia said, breathless.

He gave her that wide, infectious smile. "You didn't ask."

Aunt Packham made another disapproving sound, somewhat louder. To be sure, it wasn't proper to let a gentleman read one's private letters. But half of her correspondents kept secretaries, anyway. She supposed she ought to ask Aunt Packham to read the letters for her, if she wanted them read. But Aunt Packham would cry and insist on reading all the bits about what a wonderful man Father was, and *no*.

"It would be very kind of you," she said. "But surely you and your brother would rather be enjoying yourselves…?"

Mr. Ralph shook his head, and Mr. Cahill looked between them in satisfaction as if—

As if he were matchmaking. She hoped it was only her own conceit; the idea made her more uncomfortable than it should have. "Then I would be very grateful. Really, I can't thank you enough."

"All I ask in return are several dozen more of these macaroons," Mr. Ralph said. They all laughed, and Lydia tried to forget that look on Mr. Cahill's face.

That evening, after they had gone—had Mr. Ralph bowed over her hand a little longer than he ought, and how did he make a country-squire queue seem dashing?—Lydia sat at her desk, sorting out the letters that really might be private from those she could show him. There were only a few, mostly from women near her own age who, as well as political correspondents, had become friends and confidantes.

She broke the seals and skimmed them to see if there were any urgent requests or news. At least, she began by skimming them. Grief was strangely like a toothache—one couldn't help poking at it.

She didn't *want* to feel better, not really. She was afraid of it. This grief was the last connection she had to her father, and when it was gone…he would be too, completely.

It was nice, anyhow, to read the letters. Painful, but nice. Her father was gone, but people were still thinking of her. People still loved her. Mrs. Innes had sent a book of mourning poems that helped her when her older sister died. Jane Gillingham tried to cheer her with a series of cartoons depicting her failures at foxhunting during the Devonshire county election.

Lydia put the private letters in a drawer to be answered later, bathed her eyes in rosewater, and went to bed. For the first time in a fortnight, she was rather looking forward to the morning.

Chapter 5

It did not take Lydia long to realize that Mr. Ralph would never make a great secretary. He obviously found the written word a struggle, and was self-conscious about it. He sat squinting and reading each sentence over in his mind before he would venture to read it out loud in his deep, confident voice.

To be fair, some of Lydia's correspondents had abominable handwriting. But even Emily Rathbone, who had won a penmanship prize at school and was still proud of it over a decade later, gave him difficulties.

He also had very little grasp of what was political and what was not; she skimmed the first letter after he had excerpted it for her, just to be sure, and found that a newly vacant living in Lady Maugham's brother's gift had gone unmentioned because Mr. Ralph "thought that was gossip about her relations".

Once she had written her urgent request that Alderman Wood's nephew, recently ordained, be considered for the post, she asked Mr. Ralph to summarize thoroughly instead. It was not efficient, but she only teared up once, when Mr. Ralph said softly, "She says your father was very proud of you."

The things people asked for at a distance—letters of recommendation, advice, information, putting in a kind word with one of her other correspondents—she could mostly supply. But requests were piling up from Lively St. Lemeston too, and those—for pensions and annuities and warm clothes for the children and apprenticeships and loans to get through the winter—she couldn't. She hadn't said so to anyone, though. She had said she would see what she could do.

Could she ask one of her friends for a loan? It was for the Ministerialist party, after all…but she shrank from it.

In the pauses while Mr. Ralph wrestled with the written word and she wrestled with her conscience, Lydia watched Mr. Cahill talk to Aunt Packham across the room. Aunt Packham did most of the talking, actually, her soft, plaintive tone carrying clearly if her words did not. Mr. Cahill listened with every appearance of interest and enjoyment.

It was rarer than she liked to think that one of her visitors paid so much attention to her aunt. It was to his credit, whether he was only being kind or whether, unlike most men, he was willing to see the value in a poor middle-aged woman's conversation.

Or perhaps—she remembered that matchmaking gleam in his eye. Was he keeping the chaperone occupied for his brother's sake?

Don't puff yourself up, she scolded, and tried not to like him more on that account, that he would efface himself in favor of his handsome brother without a trace of resentment. She wondered what he would think if he knew she would rather he had read her letters for her. Of course, he hadn't offered.

He laughed at something her aunt said, a gold back tooth catching the light.

Lydia wrenched her gaze away. "I can't thank you enough, sir, really," she told Mr. Ralph.

"Evidently not." He gave a warm rumble of a chuckle.

Everything about him and his brother was warm, she thought. What a pleasant family they made!

She didn't even know what the stab of longing that pierced her was for. She missed Jamie, of course, but Jamie had been at school most of his life; she had got used to missing Jamie. Besides, Jamie didn't make her feel warm or safe. He was her little brother—her darling, nervous, funny, brilliant, stubborn little brother—and it was her job to take care of him, not the other way round.

You took care of your father too, said a stray disloyal thought, which she quashed.

It was a lovely feeling, though, to be taken care of, to be surrounded by friendliness and solicitude. She might wish Mr. Ralph had let her cut her own pen—she liked a narrower nib—but she drank the courtesy gratefully in nonetheless. She didn't understand why the dozens of condolence calls she had received had made her long to be alone, and the Cahills had appeared from nowhere yet she already felt so comfortable with them.

"That's the last of them," said Mr. Ralph. "Would you still like to go for that ride?"

"Certainly. Do you—do you think your brother would like to come?" Her face heated at her fumble, and the note of self-consciousness in her voice. She was usually better than that at making an invitation sound casual.

He laughed. "No. Horses make him nervous."

Lydia had, somehow, assumed this golden creature would sit on a horse centaur-like, as though he and the beast shared one thought, one breath. Instead, Mr. Ralph asked for a gentle mount and sat on it like the proverbial sack of potatoes. But unlike with reading, he laughed at this deficiency without embarrassment. The muscles in his thighs certainly showed to great effect.

St. Leonard's Forest was too far to go with an indifferent rider, so she contented herself with a tour of the estate. Although her toes and fingers ached for hot water and a fire, and Mr. Ralph called cheerily, "I'm learning why Sussex mud is famous," she had become so sluggish indoors that it was a relief to feel the wind on her face, however biting. But she kept to a canter—in courtesy to Mr. Ralph, and not at all because her father's accident had given her a fear of even a mild gallop.

Trailed by a groom, they viewed the gardens, the greenhouse, the trout stream, the topiary, the antique statuary, and the shuttered Dower House.

"Does no one live here?" he asked.

"I wanted my father to let someone live in it—it would have been a splendid favor to do someone. We're the Ministerialist patrons here, you know. But he was saving it for Jamie and me, when one of us married, or when Jamie's wife became Wheatcroft's mistress and I needed a home of my own."

That might be a good many years, since Jamie was only twenty-one and had said over and over again that he didn't want to marry despite her most forceful representations about the Wheatcroft legacy, the need for an heir for the estate, and the value of a screen in case anyone guessed that he preferred men.

She looked at the snug house studded with small windows—casements and dormers and a little round window like a Cyclops's eye peering from above the arched doorway. The yellow stone walls and reddish clay tile roof made it look warm even in winter. Perhaps Jamie would be willing to let it. It was too bad for such a charming dwelling to stand empty, even if part of her had liked it every time her father said, *That house is for my children and that's more important than any favor.*

"Do you think you'll like living in it?" Mr. Ralph asked.

She'd miss being Wheatcroft's hostess. She would miss her home. "I don't know. But if I don't, it won't be the house's fault."

"You don't mind that it's so close to where you grew up?"

The question took her aback. "I love my home. I thought—your brother said you wanted to settle down yourself."

Mr. Ralph frowned. "Did he now?"

Had she said something wrong? "Don't you like Cornwall?"

After a moment, his face cleared. "Cornwall is splendid," he said, in that way he had as if he wanted nothing more than to share his happiness with her. "The sea there is only kissing cousins to the sea in Brighton. It's wild and lovely and wants to tear you to pieces."

She shivered and raised her eyebrows at him, half-teasing and half-appalled. "That doesn't sound very lovely to me."

He laughed. "I like a challenge." He was very handsome when he said it. He was so tall, and his hair shone even in the gray, misty late-November light. He glowed with health and vitality; he looked as if he belonged somewhere that was trying to tear him to pieces.

She wondered if he had been so hale and hearty as a child. One couldn't tell, of course. Sometimes sickly children grew up as strong as anyone. Jamie was rarely ill these days—but when he was, he still took everything much harder than his friends. When he'd been younger…she remembered his small-pox inoculation, and the mumps and the measles and scarlet fever (three times), the influenza and the whooping cough and pneumonia, a hundred nights she'd thought Death was going to reach out and gather him up in her arms.

She shivered again. Had Mr. Cahill had an easier time of it? Or had he kept vigil too?

She wondered what Mr. Cahill and Aunt Packham were talking about—but that was rude. She was here with Mr. Ralph, and he had been very kind to her.

"Are you cold, Miss Reeve?" he asked her with swift concern.

"Only my hands."

She realized too late that it had been the wrong thing to say when he reined in his horse and slid off. "Come here," he said.

She dismounted, because it would have been rude to refuse, and because he was unlikely to really do what she was imagining. But no—he drew his gloves off and held out his hands for hers.

Well, she *was* cold. She took off her gloves, conscious of the groom's eyes behind her, and let him take her hands and rub warmth into them. His hands were as good as heated bricks. She felt breathless, blushing when he met her eyes.

"It was kind of you to come and be with your brother at Christmas."

His eyes searched her face. "Not particularly," he said at last, cheerfully. "I don't much care where I am for Christmas."

"Do you like seeing new customs and ways of celebrating, like your brother?"

He nodded. "But I like the spring holidays better, May Day and the beginning of mackerel season. Holidays that happen outdoors when everything feels new." He flicked a glance at the soggy, bare landscape.

Lydia felt a surge of protectiveness. She loved Wheatcroft at every time of the year. She had always loved the naked branches curling and catching at the sky, the wet sheen on every stone, the gleaming green of the yew trees, and how everything felt secretive and full of possibility. Looking around, she saw that again, and not her own sadness. It was an intense relief.

"I like winter," she said. "I like…you can feel the world waiting, and not minding the wait. People say things die in winter, but it isn't true, mostly. They just gather their strength." That had been a strange thing to say, she realized. She wished she hadn't said it.

"Anyway, everything *does* feel new at Christmas," she said hastily. "What's more hopeful than the birth of a child?" She would have gone rambling on about the season of charity and giving, but he stopped her, his hands tightening on hers.

"Do you hope to have children?" He watched her closely, as if her answer mattered.

"I don't think so." She knew it was almost always the wrong answer for a woman to give, and was glad of it for once. She didn't want him to get ideas. Smiling to soften it, she said, "I already brought up my brother. It was lovely, but I think once was enough. I'd like to be an aunt, though."

His hands didn't relax. "Was it difficult? When you were so young too?"

Oh dear, she had said exactly the wrong thing. "Everything worth doing is difficult. I wouldn't exchange it for anything."

He looked relieved and let her go. She felt a pang, because what she had said was true, but it was a lie, too. She would have answered the same question from Mr. Cahill differently.

"Did Ash really tell you I wanted to settle down?"

"Perhaps I misunderstood him," she said hastily, hoping she hadn't hit on a sore point of some kind. *Ash.* The nickname suited him.

Mr. Ralph smiled at her attempt to shield his brother. "Perhaps. Ash—" He sighed. "It's hard to explain things to him sometimes." He gazed out over the wet garden as if he wasn't seeing it at all. Even in the gray light, his eyes were bright, piercing blue. "We've been together all our lives. I owe him everything. But he can be—he wants me to be happy. I'm grateful for that. I am. But no one can be happy all the time."

He wanted to leave Mr. Cahill because his brother wanted him to be *happy*? Was it such a burden, to have someone care for one's happiness?

Mr. Ralph glanced down and read her incomprehension on her face. "He has a strong personality. Growing up in his shadow has been…I love him, but I need…" He sighed again, searching for words.

She gazed up, up, up at his face. "Not in his *shadow,* surely." Unassuming Mr. Cahill, a strong personality? That was either the voice of deep affection, or Mr. Ralph himself could not have very much ballast.

But she was drawn to Mr. Cahill, wasn't she, without knowing why? Maybe he did have a strong personality.

Mr. Ralph's mouth tightened. "You're right, I'm tall," he said flatly. He shook his head, giving up his explanation as a bad job. "I'm thinking of taking up a commission."

Mr. Cahill hadn't mentioned that. Perhaps he disliked the idea. "Which regiment?"

"I haven't decided."

"Oh, but you must look into it first." For Mr. Cahill's sake she prompted Mr. Ralph in the direction of the safest regiments, lingering particularly on the 1st Dragoon Guards, still on home service. "If you need any help getting your letter of recommendation, you must let me know. I correspond with General Beresford's sister-in-law."

He didn't answer right away. "May we talk privately for a moment?"

She was taken aback, but it was far too early in their acquaintance for him to make any overtures of love to her. He must want to tell her something about his financial circumstances. It would be awkward, but she was curious, and she could already feel the instinct to help uncurling inside of her and reaching out, like a hungry baby squid. She was a busybody, and that was that. "Of course. Tom, can you fall back a little while we walk? But keep us in sight, please."

"I want to deal plainly with you," Mr. Ralph said when Tom was at a safe distance. "You're a woman of character, and I—I think we can help each other." His blue eyes glinted seriously. Now that he had given up on describing his own emotions, he seemed again a man to be reckoned with.

She turned away from him to feed her mare a piece of apple, so as to seem a little distant. She had an uneasy feeling that this would be a proposal that was unladylike merely to hear. "What do you mean?"

He looked at his boots, mouth twisting. "I can't afford that commission. Ash told me you're having money troubles too."

Mr. Cahill had shared her confidences with his little brother.

Well, of course he had. He'd known her a few days, and he'd known Mr. Ralph nearly all his life. That was nothing to condemn him for.

"Yes," she said cautiously.

"If you married me," he said soberly, meeting her eyes, "I'd sign over your dowry to you. All but the few thousand pounds I'd need to set me up in the army. You'd have your money, and no husband to get in the way." His gaze slid warmly over her. "I wouldn't ask you for anything you didn't offer first. I swear." She flushed hotly. *I'd take it if you offered, though,* was the clear message.

It was shocking. A *mariage de convenance* was one thing, but to come right out and say it, to her face—as she thought the words, she knew them for the worst sort of hypocrisy, as if cloaking the thing in polite courtship and flattery and negotiations between fathers and lawyers and men of business made it any different.

This still felt naked and brazen.

"You can trust me," he said, trying to take her hand.

She took it back politely and smiled at him, her heart pounding. "I believe you. But it's a very big decision." She ought to say no. If he ever told anyone she'd even considered a bargain like this—with a stranger, no less—her reputation would be ruined. But she needed that money. "I have to think on it."

He nodded, accepting it without demur. "When should I come back?"

She tried to think. It wasn't easy, with him looming like a Greek god and *I wouldn't ask you for anything you didn't offer first* in her ears. "I'm going to the workhouse in town tomorrow. Meet me there at one o'clock. I can't promise to have an answer, but I'll have thought about it."

"Very well. Have you any questions for me?"

She shook her head. "Let's go back to the house."

Tom came forward to help her onto her horse. Mr. Ralph

made a move as if to do it himself, then looked at the mud on her boots and hem and stood aside, laughing. She really did like him when he laughed.

She wondered what she would have said, if his brother had made her the same offer.

Ash tried to be patient. He tried not to let his annoyance show. "Do you not like her?" he asked his brother. "Admittedly, she's a bit of a mouse."

She wasn't, but if you wanted Rafe to like someone, criticizing her helped. Rafe liked to protect people.

"What has that to do with anything?" Rafe demanded, not trying to hide his own annoyance at all.

"Rafe, if you'd wanted her to say yes, she would have. You sprang the offer on her out of nowhere after a discussion of your commission, of all things. You didn't trouble to remind her of how badly she needs this. You didn't try to persuade her. You barely *flirted* with her. You couldn't even agree with her about the wonder of Christmas. So I think asking if you don't like her is a fair—"

Rafe flopped heavily back onto their bed. "I'm sick of Christmas."

Ash breathed in and out and looked at Rafe, at the furrows in his honest brow, at one big hand outstretched on the bed, at the clumsy straggling tie of his queue. Rafe was impossible and stubborn but Ash loved him. He wasn't angry. There was a knot in his chest but—it was as if his heart grew smaller while the rest of him expanded away from it, almost aching with affection. "Why?"

Rafe sat up, frowning. He'd always had those thick eyebrows; his face had grown into them now, but as a child it had made him look like a tiny disgruntled rabbi when he frowned. "Aren't you tired of celebrating other people's holidays? Don't you ever want a holiday of our own? A family tradition of our own?"

"No," Ash said honestly. He loved celebrating other people's holidays. Moments were as satisfying to steal as money, and besides, sharing things with strangers made him feel as if the whole world was really one family.

Ever since they'd left London and struck out on their own, he'd tried to make sure Rafe had a happy home—someone's happy home—to spend holidays in, and when he couldn't, he'd made sure they had enough for a room to themselves. He'd loved those Christmases and Easters too, he and Rafe lying on their bed talking all day, sharing cold goose and mince pies, or hot cross buns and a bowl of richly dyed eggs. Just the two of them, still and warm while the world bustled on around them. He'd never realized Rafe minded.

We could start a tradition if you wanted was on the tip of his tongue, before he remembered that Rafe was leaving.

"You said this was a deal, not a swindle," Rafe said. "So I dealt honestly with her."

"Honest men swindle too. Everybody swindles, only they don't call it that. What's so wonderful about honesty, anyway? What's so wonderful about honest folk? Honest folk never helped us when we were starving, unless we swindled them into it."

Rafe wanted to be an honest man, now. He wanted to feel as if he deserved what he had. But no one deserved anything. Ash thought of Lydia Reeve in her fine house, thinking it was hers by right. He didn't envy her that terrible blindness. He didn't understand why Rafe—

But that wasn't really true, was it? Ash did understand. That was what he did, why he was so good at his profession: he always understood, and he always accepted.

I don't understand myself, he thought. Why, with Rafe, the one person he loved more than anything in the world, did understanding not lead to acceptance?

He'd have to force it to.

Rafe watched him, quiet and assessing, and Ash wanted him to be happy so intensely it was like something crawling out of his stomach and up his throat. Which was disgusting, so he swallowed it and smiled at his brother.

"Do you lie to me?" Rafe asked.

Only once. But that wasn't even the truth. He didn't answer.

"I thought brothers didn't lie to each other." Rafe didn't sound angry, or surprised, only sad.

The moths were at it in Ash's chest. He'd repeated that maxim to Rafe a thousand times—and tried to live by it, mostly. But he had really said it because he didn't want Rafe to lie to *him.* No secret a child was asked to keep from his family was an innocent one, and he'd meant for Rafe to know that he should always come to Ash with everything.

"I don't lie to you. I've—" But he couldn't make his tongue form the word *never.*

"I want to know. I want to know what you've lied about. Even if it isn't anything important. I can't bear it that you treat me like a flat."

Ash's heart stopped. "Like a flat—Rafe, I've *never* thought of you as a flat!"

Rafe simply looked at him, and it seemed to Ash that there

was too much sadness in his eyes for only twenty-six years of life.

He had failed as a brother. If he could repair it somehow, would Rafe stay? What could he say that would make Rafe stay?

But he couldn't—he couldn't swindle Rafe, and he couldn't ask Rafe to stay, and he couldn't hope. He couldn't stand to hope. "Can we not do this now? I'll tell you everything before you go. Let's not spoil these last days."

"You always do this. You always insist on pretending that everything is fine."

"Everything *is* fine."

"Ash…" It struck Ash that *Rafe* was trying to be patient now, that he was breathing in and out and trying to sound as if he weren't angry, and that it wasn't working at all. "I know you're angry with me—"

"I'm not angry with you," Ash said gently. "I want you to be happy. If you're doing what will make you happy, then we share a common goal. Why should I be angry?"

"So I'm selfish for not staying and cheating old women?"

We've only cheated a few old women. Even Ash knew that wouldn't sound good spoken aloud. "That isn't what I said." Somehow, now that Rafe was losing his composure, Ash found it easy to keep his voice steady. "What's so bad about being selfish, anyway? Everybody's selfish. I selfishly want you to stay, you selfishly want to go, Miss Reeve selfishly wants her little brother to come home and sit on the throne she's been at such pains to carve for him. Selfishness is as natural as breathing. Unlike you, I don't blame people for how they're made. Next you'll be talking about original sin like a goy."

Rafe pulled the handkerchief out of his pocket and

crumpled it in his hand. "You aren't selfish, not really." He didn't look at Ash. "You have such a big heart—if you could open it a little farther. The sacrifices you've made for me—"

Ash tried to imagine opening his heart farther than he already did. All he could think was how much it would hurt, to have people with their boots and pointy little heels and squirming toes walking on the soft wet linings of his insides.

"There's no such thing as a sacrifice," he said. "Only swaps. I suppose I've made some swaps for you. I think they were all good ones, for what I got in exchange."

You have no idea how selfish I've been.

Rafe worried his handkerchief. Embroidered in one corner was a Hebrew *L* that had once been red and was now a faded mulberry color. Ash knew the letter was there, but he couldn't bring himself to look at it.

He couldn't remember his mother Leah's face, except that he'd thought she was pretty. Gainsborough probably wouldn't have agreed. He would have seen a greasy Jew.

What would she say, if she knew what he'd done? Would he have been better, if she'd brought him up? Or—would he have been worse? She'd found him his first job, after all.

Well, she was dead, and what she didn't know couldn't hurt her.

There was a long silence, and then Rafe sighed. "You'll tell me everything before I go?"

Before I go. Ash shut his heart tight to keep the words from hurting too badly. "I promise."

Rafe began reluctantly to describe the Wheatcroft dower house, a house big enough for half a dozen families just lying fallow. Soon enough the conversation moved on, comfortably and with much laughter, as if everything was fine.

Later, Ash lay in bed, the pressure of unsaid words building in his throat. He didn't even know what they were, what they would become if he let them out. He couldn't predict a single one.

Chapter 6

"Jack Sparks is agreeable to taking on Christopher Tobill as an apprentice, if we can pay the fee," Mrs. Bridger said when they were closeted together in the master's office. Mr. Bridger was out helping move a recent workhouse inmate's furniture.

Lydia's heart sank. "How much?" Mr. Sparks was the only printer in Lively St. Lemeston. He was also a devoted Whig, which meant that all Tory pamphlets and handbills and the monthly Tory journal had to be printed elsewhere at Wheatcroft expense. *Oh, and it's almost time for the December edition!* Perhaps the printer in Lewes would extend her credit.

Her head did not quite ache, but there was a pressure at her temples as it debated with itself whether to begin. Printing apprenticeships weren't cheap.

"Seventy-five pounds, ma'am. I believe he's making alterations to his home to accommodate his new wife and her wheelchair, and the cash would be most welcome. Some of it can come from William Turner's will, and Mrs. Dromgoole has pledged something as well, but that still leaves fifty pounds."

Only a few weeks ago, Lydia could have promised the money on the spot. Then perhaps in time there would be a Tory printer in Lively St. Lemeston—nothing was certain, of course, but it was a great favor to do a poor child. That would be a triumph. "Will he take five pounds a week?" It was a sixth of her own income, but she could do it.

Mrs. Bridger shook her head, looking surprised at Lydia's haggling. "He'd like to have the matter settled by Christmas. I beg your pardon, I hadn't ought to have presumed. I'll go to Martha Honeysett, and ask if the Society for Bettering the Condition of the Poor can help. And Lady Tassell will be in town next week. I can—"

"*No.*" Lydia ought to tell the house-mistress how matters lay. But she shrank from it. When Jamie changed his mind and wanted to be these people's patron again, how little confidence they would have in him! "Please don't. My brother is from home, but I'll write him and see what can be done."

"That would be wonderful." Mrs. Bridger straightened the ledgers on the desk, hesitating. "I'm sorry to press you, ma'am, but the sooner the better. Mr. Sparks can take an apprentice anywheres, while we won't find another printer so easy."

They wouldn't find another printer at all, and they both knew it. Christopher Tobill was clever and likable, but he would need months of lessons, if not years, before he could read and write as well as the children Sparks *could* have sold the apprenticeship to. "Of course. I'll write directly I get home."

Mrs. Bridger now arranged her husband's pen and pen-knife at perfect right angles. "There's something else, ma'am."

"Yes?"

"We've had an offer to employ Mary Luff. Deborah Tice saw one of the baskets she made here and was quite impressed."

Lydia's heart pounded. She did not want to make this decision. "And Joanna?"

"Of course Miss Tice can't add an infant to her household.

I know you didn't want to see them separated, ma'am, but Miss Tice says Mary might have the makings of a milliner."

It was another place they were lucky to be offered. But Lydia knew Mary wouldn't want to go.

Nobody who wanted to take Mary would take Joanna. Must Mary grow up in the workhouse then, feeding old women gruel, and know no trade at all when she was older?

Mrs. Bridger asked Lydia's advice on these matters because Lydia was a reliable source of income. If that changed, she and her husband would make these decisions themselves, or leave them to the overseers.

Lord Wheatcroft had been an overseer, and Lydia was well acquainted with those who remained. For the most part they were kindly, generous men and pleasant dinner guests, but their visits to the workhouse were perfunctory at best. They would never think that the feelings of an inmate should guide them in any way.

Lydia imagined the wreck of a conversation that would ensue if she tried to convince Jamie to be an overseer.

The maid of all work poked her head into the little office. "Pardon me, Miss Reeve, Mr. Cahill and Mr. Ralph Cahill are here to see you. What shall I tell them?"

Mr. Cahill would understand how much this decision mattered. She wanted to hear his opinion. She wanted to share this responsibility. "Do you mind if I ask them in?"

Mrs. Bridger smiled at her, deferential as always. "Of course not, ma'am."

Her skin tingled a little when Mr. Ralph walked in and gave her one of his conspiratorial smiles—mostly from embarrassment. Mr. Cahill's cheerful nod set her positively buzzing. She thought that was mostly not embarrassment.

His coat was ill-tailored, rumpling over his brawny upper arms and tenting behind his neck. It would have made him appear hunched had it not been for his bearing—nothing like his brother's confidence, but a simpler comfort, as if he gave his body the same friendly, undemanding acceptance he seemed to give everything else.

She didn't understand how or when she had gone so quickly from *more pleasant than handsome* to *I notice the way his coat wrinkles.*

When greetings and introductions were over, she said, "Mr. Cahill…Mary Luff's been offered a position."

He stiffened. "What about Joanna?" He remembered their names.

"Joanna would have to be boarded out. But it's a good place," she said pleadingly. "She might be a milliner someday, if things go well. I don't know what place she'll find that will allow her to bring an infant with her. What do you think we should do?"

"This is the little girl with the sister?" Mr. Ralph asked.

Mr. Cahill's eyes flickered to his brother. He nodded.

"Maybe Mary deserves a chance to live her own life," Mr. Ralph said. "Maybe—maybe a nine-year-old girl shouldn't have to be a mother."

Mr. Cahill's tanned face went very still. Lydia felt a pang of vicarious humiliation. She wouldn't have liked it much either if the brother she'd struggled to make a happy home for and cherished from birth gave her a measuring look and said she'd have been better off without him. Before strangers, no less.

But Mr. Cahill smiled the next moment and turned to her. "Maybe so. Miss Reeve knows the child best. What is your opinion, ma'am?"

She twisted her hands together. "I don't know. Mary adores Joanna. But she hates it here."

"Why don't we ask her?" Mr. Ralph said.

Lydia drew back. "Oh, she's too young! What if she abandons her sister, and later regrets it? No one should have to make that choice."

"Ralph is right." Mr. Cahill gave his brother a look that was a little sad and very proud. He shook his head. "If you'd told me at nine that when I was grown I'd be like all the other adults and think I knew best about everything…" He turned his deep-set brown eyes on her. "Mary's got two things in the world. Her sister, and this choice."

Lydia was never afraid to meet anyone's eye. She knew they couldn't see a thing she didn't want them to. But for a single vertiginous moment, she had to remind herself that her eyes were little balls of flesh and jelly, not a shop window to her soul with all her secret thoughts prettily displayed for his perusing.

It would be stupid to marry his brother, when he himself made her feel like this.

"I agree with Miss Reeve," said Mrs. Bridger. "And we can't let it get about that paupers may simply choose to stay here if they don't like the situations we find for them. What will the overseers say?"

"I suggest we don't tell anyone," Lydia said ruefully. "If it gets out, I'll talk to them."

Lydia didn't think Mrs. Bridger was convinced, but she clearly didn't feel strongly enough to start a genuine disagreement with three gentlefolk. She shrugged and rang for the maid, instructing her to bring the girl in. "Ask her to leave Joanna with one of the other children, please."

Mary curtsied as she entered, her eyes going from face to

face, trying to guess why she was here. Everyone waited defer-
entially for Lydia to speak.

Lydia's heart bled. "Mary, I want to ask you something."

"Yes, ma'am?"

"We—we have an offer of a place for you. Miss Tice, the
milliner, saw the basket you made and would like you to come
and work for her."

"At first it will be weaving straw," Mrs. Bridger added, "but
she tells me if you show promise, there'll be a chance for you
to learn the whole trade."

"Thank you, ma'am." Mary's square little face was still.
"What about Joanna?"

"Joanna couldn't go with you," Lydia said. "That is the
question I have for you—do you want to go live with Miss
Tice, or stay here with Joanna?"

Mary hesitated. "I'll stay, ma'am. Thank you."

Somehow the bleeding in Lydia's heart didn't stop. "You
don't have to answer so quickly. You must consider what's best
for you and what's best for Joanna, and not only now, but for
the rest of your lives. It isn't likely that you will find a place that
will allow you to take your sister, and then when you're older,
you will have no trade and be less able to help her. But perhaps
being with a sister you love, who loves you, is more important
than that. It's a big choice for a little girl, but we thought it was
too big for us to make it for you."

Mary was silent for nearly a minute, thinking, her small
shoulders tense. "What would happen to Joanna if I left her,
ma'am?"

"She'll go to a nurse in the country until she is older, and
then come back here until a place can be found for her."

"Could I still see her?"

"Yes, but perhaps not very often. You will be working most of your time," Lydia said. "If our usual nurse can take her, she'll only be a few miles off, but that's a long walk for a little girl."

"What do you think I should do, ma'am?"

Lydia looked around the room for help, but there wasn't any. Mr. Cahill was watching her, and Mr. Ralph was watching Mary. Mrs. Bridger merely looked patient.

"I don't know," Lydia said haltingly. "I think there are good and bad aspects to both choices. Love and duty may guide you equally in either direction. All you can do—all any of us can ever do in this life—is your best. I think that you are a brave, good girl, and—and no matter how you choose, I'm very proud of you. So are your parents in Heaven."

Mr. Ralph stepped forward abruptly, and knelt down so he was looking the little girl right in the eye. "Good afternoon, Mary. My name is Ralph Cahill. Of course you don't know me, and have no reason to value my opinion, but I want to tell you that when you're turning this over in your mind, it's all right to think about what's best for you, as well as what's best for your sister."

Mary glanced doubtfully at Lydia. Lydia hesitated. Of course one must think of others first; of course one's duty to one's family outweighed all else. Lydia herself had always acted on that principle. But Mary had been here three months, and she was thinner and paler than she had been, and more discontented about the shoulders.

Lydia nodded. "Mr. Ralph is right, Mary. If you ruin your health or your happiness it will profit no one, really."

Mr. Cahill, who had been silent and still through this whole scene, turned his face away and pressed his knuckles to his mouth. Lydia, her gaze caught by the movement, saw that he was hiding a smile at her hedge, brown eyes crinkling. Even at this terrible moment, she felt a flash of desire.

She turned back to Mary. "You may have until tomorrow to decide, if you like."

Mrs. Bridger nodded. "But if you wish to take up the position with Miss Tice, you must start the day after. Christmas is one of her busiest seasons."

Mary's eyes widened. "You mean—you mean I won't be with Joanna for Christmas?"

Now, finally, Mr. Cahill spoke. "The shop will be closed for Christmas, I imagine. If you want to go to Miss Tice, and you trust me enough to travel with, I'll take you to visit Joanna on Christmas Day."

Mary gave him a narrow scrutiny, though whether gauging his sincerity or his trustworthiness Lydia couldn't tell. "Do you promise?"

"On my mother's grave."

Mary took several deep breaths, chest swelling. Then she said in a deflating rush, "I want to go and earn my own money."

Lydia swallowed hard.

"There's a clever girl," said Mrs. Bridger, looking relieved. "Now come along with me, and we can talk about what you'll need in your new life."

Mary looked around the room, not sure who to talk to. "If Joanna cries, she likes to be picked up and sung to. 'Ye Sons of Albion' will quiet her every time. She likes to feed herself, and she hates raisins and dogs—the little ones, big ones are all right—and people shouting—"

Lydia stood very still and tried not to cry as Mary was led away by Mrs. Bridger, still giving detailed, slightly desperate-sounding instructions. She remembered Jamie at Joanna's age, how suspicious he was of strangers, his inexplicable fear of wardrobes, the way he put the end of her braid in his mouth.

"It isn't fair," she said. "It isn't fair that some people have everything and some people have nothing."

"It's God's plan. Isn't that what the Tories believe?" There was an edge in Mr. Cahill's voice. Lydia looked at him in surprise; he had seemed so calm. Now he was stony-faced, eyes fixed on the door.

"*Ash.*" Mr. Ralph gave her a sympathetic glance. "When *I* say something like that, Ash always says, 'Yes, and the world should be shook out and made over like an old dress, but it probably won't happen today.'"

Mr. Cahill smiled, a polite, meaningless curve of his mouth. "I'll be outside. Miss Reeve." Bowing in her direction, he strode jerkily out and shut the door softly behind him.

Mr. Ralph sighed, looking troubled. "He doesn't usually take things so much to heart. I—I'm sorry, I think I should go after him."

Lydia wanted to go after him too. She wanted to tell him that she didn't think this was God's plan at all. There had always been rich and poor so God must have a reason for it—she didn't know what it was but there must be one—but she knew He couldn't want anyone to be *this* poor. No one needed to be, if the rich would do their duty.

She wanted him not to be angry with her. She wanted to stop feeling as if what had happened to Mary was her fault somehow.

What right did he have to make her feel this way? He was a gentleman, just as she was a gentlewoman. He gallivanted around England, living to please no one but himself, while she worked every day, and—

What difference did Lydia's hurt feelings make, when Mary had had to give up her sister?

Mr. Ralph smiled at her, squeezed her shoulder, and left her there. She tried not to cry.

Rafe didn't say anything when he came out the front door, just bumped Ash's shoulder with his own—well, with his upper arm, given the difference in their heights—and stood at his elbow, silent and hulking, as if misery could be physically intimidated. Maybe it could, because Ash felt better at once. "Did she give you an answer?"

"I didn't wait," Rafe said. "You were upset."

"And I would still have been upset in five minutes after you'd talked to Miss Reeve."

"It isn't like you to let something get to you this way."

"I know. I'm sorry."

"Don't be," Rafe said, almost shyly. "It's—it's nice. You always brush things off so easily, and I—can't."

"There's nothing nice about the way I feel," Ash said sharply. This was why he was careful to open his heart so far and no farther, because England was full of Mary Luffs, and there was only so much Ash to go around.

He needed that pane of glass between him and the world. Why couldn't he manage it this week? Was it because Rafe was leaving? Or was Miss Reeve's damned earnestness getting to him?

When he didn't keep his heart under control, he made mistakes. He'd worked so hard to make Miss Reeve like him, and now he'd put everything in jeopardy. His brother's future depended on this. What good did this rending pain do anybody?

Rafe looked away. "I didn't mean…I'm sorry."

Ash couldn't be angry. If he could behave like Mary and give Miss Reeve a list of foods Rafe did and didn't like, he would.

You're thirty-four years old. Stop behaving like a child. But he felt like a child, adrift in a large world whose rules were both arbitrary and stacked against him.

"Mary'll be all right," Rafe said.

"Everybody is until they're dead," Ash agreed lightly. He looked around for somewhere to sit and wait for Miss Reeve. In these small towns, people didn't want you to sit on their stairs.

She came out before he'd finished his assessment, marching right up to them with a smile and saying to Ash, "Mr. Cahill, might I talk to you privately?"

Ash blinked. But it wasn't that unusual for a flat to trust most the brother she'd met first, to want a little reassurance before agreeing to a deal. It was a good sign, really. "You don't mind, do you, Rafe?"

Rafe shook his head, and Ash followed Miss Reeve down the street a little ways before she gestured him into a narrow space between two houses—neither of which, he saw, had windows on the facing wall. She was a woman who noticed things.

She looked at him, that chin of hers tilted up. Her eyes were red. "Do you know of the proposal your brother has made to me, Mr. Cahill?"

"I do."

"Do you approve?"

Ash shrugged ruefully. "I suppose I always thought he'd

marry for love, but he needs the money and I don't have it."
He smiled at her. "He likes you, though. He could do worse.
Maybe in time—"

She shook her head. Ash's heart sank. "I like your brother
too. But…" She squared her shoulders, her chin going up even
higher. He could see her pulse hammering just under the black
ribbon of her bonnet. "I like you better. If you've any inclination, I'd rather take the same offer from you."

Ash's heart stopped, or maybe his ears. He couldn't hear a
sound from the street. "What?" *What* was common. He should
have said *I beg your pardon*. He should have said something
cleverer than either.

"I know it's very forward of me." Her voice trembled but
her gaze didn't falter. She had bottom. "But we're past the
proprieties, and marrying a man for convenience's sake while
nursing a *tendre* for his brother is something out of a tired
French farce."

"A *tendre*?" Trust her to use a word he didn't know. But her
meaning was all too clear. "For me? But—Rafe is—"

The corner of her full mouth curved up softly. Tenderly,
even. Maybe that was what *tendre* meant, tenderness. "Mr.
Ralph is very handsome. But *chacun à son goût*, as they say."

He looked at her blankly.

"Tastes differ?"

The enormity, the implausibility of this reversal—had he
done something, said something—

Of course he had. He liked her. She'd attracted him from
the first moment, and somehow he'd let her see it.

Could he find another life for Rafe this good again? Would
Rafe be willing to wait while he tried? He'd been practicing his
whole life for this swindle, this moment, to give Rafe this. He

couldn't—wouldn't—fail like some amateur, like a *flat*. But he couldn't speak.

"We have a—a connection, do we not?" she tried again, her words almost echoing in the silence. Those big brown eyes wobbled back and forth a little over his face, where she apparently saw something she wanted to marry.

I have a connection with twenty people a day, he wanted to shout at her. *What does a connection matter?*

She stepped forward. She didn't want him to see how nervous she was, but it showed in her silent staccato breaths. The fine hairs on the fur trim of her pelisse trembled as her breasts went up and down.

She stood there for a second, waiting for him to say something, and then she sighed and undid that black velvet ribbon under her chin.

He should leave. If she was ready to take the deal from him, then once he'd turned her down she'd probably take it from Rafe.

But she'd only do that if he could get out of this without embarrassing her. He had to turn her up so sweet she wouldn't mind seeing him again. He would be her brother-in-law, and she didn't know that soon he'd be out of the picture for good.

She took off her bonnet.

He tried to not want her. If he could just find a part of himself that didn't want her, he'd know what to say and how to make it sound natural.

He couldn't even find a part of himself that could *breathe*.

He stepped back, but that put him squarely against the wall. She wasn't short, exactly, but even in her pattens she had to put a hand on the wall for balance and strain up to kiss him.

He shut his eyes, hoping he'd want her less if he couldn't

see her. "Miss Reeve, please—" It was supposed to sound unmoved, maybe even gently amused. It didn't. He put out a hand to hold her off, but it was too late. His hand went right past her.

Her mouth was on his.

He could feel her heat against his cold cheeks. She wanted him, she'd chosen him, and now he knew that her hair smelled like jasmine. Her lips were warm and a little chapped, and her breath puffing into his mouth was a small intimate thing. It had been so long, so long since anyone touched him and it had been a bad week and he couldn't breathe.

You chose her for Rafe. She was Rafe's, she was going to be Rafe's *wife*—

He pushed her away, gently. He wondered if she could hear his heart pounding. Her brown eyes were coffee-dark with passion. "I do like you." He sounded almost normal—unless he was jug-bitten with lust and could no longer judge what he sounded like. "You're good company and you're beautiful, and I'm a lonely man. But I'm a friendly man too; you mustn't think it means more than it does. I could say the same about a dozen women I've met this month. Rafe—it means something, when Rafe likes a person. He'll be good to you."

It was the truth, but she didn't look convinced, simply uncertain and assessing, as if he were a flat she was swindling and she was deciding how far to push him. She nodded. "Talk it over with your brother. See what he says." She bit her lip. "If you really aren't interested, and he is, I'll consider his suit. I—I very much want that money."

Ash knew gently bred women weren't any less coarse than anyone else. Somehow, he was still startled at how straightforwardly she bargained, at how little pretense of maidenly modesty she made. He liked that she didn't pretend.

He liked her far too much.

He'd thought he had at least another fortnight with his brother while the banns were read. He'd hoped for even longer. He'd meant to keep his promise to Mary, and take her to see her sister for Christmas.

Rafe would have to do it for him. Ash wasn't going to ruin this. It was time to say goodbye.

"Rafe, I've got to talk to you," Ash said, thinking that he'd rather never talk again than say this.

Rafe followed him out of town to where the fields stretched empty on either side and the muddy road was deserted. He said nothing when Ash kept walking, either.

When they stopped, Ash would have to say it. This was the last time he and Rafe would ever walk down a road side by side, matching their strides together with the ease of long practice.

Eventually, his feet slowed. Rafe stopped when he did and waited, a faint line between his brow the only sign of his nerves.

Ash had to put this exactly right. The moths in his ribcage had spread up his throat into his skull and were now squeezing into his fingers and toes. "Miss Reeve has said that she would prefer to marry me."

Rafe blinked, then shrugged, spreading his hands wide and laughing a little. "I've no objection."

"I know." Ash couldn't help smiling at him. "But I don't think I can do it. You saw me today. I'm out of twig. I could bring off being her future brother-in-law, but weeks of courtship—I won't manage it. She's said if I'm not interested, she'll likely accept your offer. I think we should stick to the original plan."

Rafe frowned. "As you like."

"She'll be embarrassed to be around me now, I think. This is the biggest deal we've ever done and it's in the palm of your hand. I don't want to risk souring it." He took a deep breath. "We should part company now."

Rafe gaped at him.

"You take the money. Buy yourself a new life."

Rafe flushed, his brows drawing sharply together. He never responded well to surprises from Ash. "Now?" he demanded. "You told me—"

"There's something I have to tell you before I go." Ash talked over Rafe because he couldn't hear him anyway. The words went in his ears and got lost in the flutter of moths. Would he even be able to say it? He'd opened his mouth to bring it up hundreds of times over the years.

Surely Rafe would be happier not knowing. It was cruelty to tell him like this, to tell him and then leave him to try to understand on his own. Ash could make up another lie, something shocking but forgivable. *My father was hanged for murder,* maybe.

How could Ash bear telling Rafe and leaving him? What would be left to connect him to his brother then?

He tried to take another deep breath, but his lungs wouldn't expand. "I'm sorry, and I love you, and you will always be my brother."

"I know that—"

"That isn't what I have to tell you, though. That's just a true thing." He'd planned this so many times. He'd tried to think how to make Rafe understand, how to twist the facts around so they didn't look so bad. He'd given it up for a bad job. "We don't have the same mother. We don't have the same father either. I stole you."

Chapter 7

Rafe froze, his mouth open and about to speak. Then he laughed, as if Ash were lying, as if Ash were playing some cruel practical joke. "Ash, I know you're angry, but—"

"It's the truth. I told you I'd got too fond of my own lie once. That lie was 'we're brothers.'"

"But—but how—" Rafe's flush deepened into crimson incomprehension. The expression was so familiar. All of Rafe's expressions were familiar. Ash had brought him up from a baby.

He'd had no right, and he'd always known it. "I've told you about working for Izzy Jacobs the bodysnatcher and his gang."

Rafe nodded.

"That was after my mother died."

"No. No, it was before—"

"She died when I was five." Ash had said *when I was eight* so many thousands of times that the truth seemed as unfamiliar and new as a lie. Rafe stared as if Ash's face were undergoing a similar transformation, as if without changing at all he had become unrecognizable.

Ash's tongue felt numb and swollen, but it kept on shaping words. "I told you sometimes we took bodies from the workhouse. Well, once, one of those women had a child. You. You were about a year old. I liked you and I took you."

"My name—" Rafe's deep voice scraped painfully in his throat. "My name isn't Rafe Cohen?"

"It is if you want it to be. I wasn't born Asher Cohen either, but it's my name now."

For some reason that made Rafe look angrier than anything else. "Your name isn't Asher Cohen?"

"I changed our names when I left Izzy's gang. He would have looked for me. It's nothing but a name, what difference does it make?"

"So my name isn't Rafe Cohen," Rafe said slowly and angrily. "And I'm not Jewish." His voice cracked on the last word.

Rafe was the one person Ash had never wanted to steal from. He'd taken everything anyway.

"Your name is Rafe Cohen and you're Jewish," he said, as if he could make Rafe understand that if he spoke with enough conviction. It had always worked before, or Rafe had been willing to pretend it did. "You weren't born those things, but you are now, same as you're my brother—"

Rafe shook his head in terrible, heavy denial. Ash was only this moment realizing that a part of him had hoped Rafe wouldn't think it was so bad.

"What is my name?" Rafe demanded. "Who am I?"

"I don't remember."

"You don't remember, or you won't tell me?"

"I don't remember. It was a quarter century ago, and I was nine years old. It was something—a common Gentile name, John or James or—I think it started with a J." He hadn't tried to remember. He'd wanted to cover his tracks.

"My—my mother's name?"

"No."

"What happened to her?"

Ash bit down hard on his lip, silently begging Rafe not to ask that, not to make him say it, not to care.

But Rafe cared about everything. "*Tell me!*" he roared, face red and fists clenched and tears in his eyes. This was why Ash had brought them out here, so Rafe could lose his temper.

"I left her with Izzy." There was nothing else he could have done. That didn't seem like much of an excuse.

Rafe made a choked, despairing sound.

"She was dead," Ash said. "He couldn't hurt her. Nobody could hurt her."

Rafe pulled Ash's mother's handkerchief from his pocket and stared at it. His mouth contorted with revulsion. "So you gave me this, when you knew my mother was in pieces on some medical student's table."

"You asked me for it."

Rafe shook from head to toe. It was a curiously blank movement, as if he were trying to find something that would be angry enough and couldn't, as if nothing could encompass the magnitude of this moment. "Why didn't you tell me?"

"I meant to. I meant to tell you when you were old enough to keep a secret—no one would have let me keep you if they knew. Then I meant to tell you when you turned thirteen, then when we left London, when you were twenty-one, and—I couldn't."

"You were afraid I would leave."

Ash nodded.

"Now I know how a flat feels."

"*No,*" Ash said. "No, I never—"

"I knew it didn't make sense. I knew we didn't look alike, that I wasn't circumcised—but you told me my father was a goy, you told me our mother died in childbirth and no one bothered to arrange for a mohel, and I believed you even though it made no sense because I *trusted* you. When you never trusted me."

It wasn't like that, Ash wanted to say. But it was exactly like that.

"We've done this to people all over England."

"We don't take more than they can afford to lose," Ash said desperately.

"You don't *know* what anyone can afford to lose!" Rafe was shouting again, a thick, growling, whining sound that Ash had always hated because it meant that he'd let things get out of hand. "Maybe faith and self-respect were things they needed, things they couldn't live without!"

"We couldn't live without food."

"I would have stayed with you," Rafe said. "I'd stay with you forever if we could have been honest, if we could be *honest*—"

"I am not honest," Ash said flatly. "It's not in me. I don't want to be honest, any more than I want to be a Christian, or a gentleman. I'm not ashamed of who I am."

"Is honesty in the blood, then? I thought you said blood didn't matter. I thought you said we were brothers."

"For—" *For Christ's sake,* he almost said, but Rafe hated him to use Christian oaths. "I didn't *say* that. You're from the East End too. You're the second-best swindler I've ever met."

"Blood has nothing to do with it." He looked at the handkerchief, and Ash could see that he still wanted it, that it still meant something to him. "People choose. You can pretend all you like that this was fate, or luck coming back around, or whatever makes you happy. But you chose this. You made this happen all by yourself." His face closed, and he held the handkerchief out with a deliberate motion.

Ash knew that nothing would change Rafe's mind now. He took the handkerchief and slipped it into his own pocket. It felt right, as if he'd never given it away. He didn't like that it felt right.

Rafe rubbed angrily at his eyes. "We're not doing this to Miss Reeve. I'm telling her the truth. She deserves that. Then I'm leaving. Don't go back to our room until after six o'clock. I'll be gone by then."

Ash made one last convulsive effort. "Rafe, please—"

He was glad, in a way, that Rafe ignored him. That *please* had been unfair. If Rafe wanted to go, he should go. And he did. He turned and walked away down the road. Ash watched him. This might be the last time he would ever see his brother, and he didn't want to miss any of it.

About a quarter of a mile away, Rafe crouched down, a dark spot on the pale road. He put his elbows on his knees and his fists against his forehead and knelt there.

Ash's skin crawled with the knowledge that there was absolutely nothing he could do to make Rafe feel any better. There never would be again.

The moths died inside him, one by one. Dead moths were more disgusting than live ones; they carpeted his stomach with their faint, tickling weight.

Ash's knees buckled and he gagged. He did his best not to waste the luncheon he'd paid for, but up it came, leaving him empty. Bile and cooked pears lingered on his tongue.

When he stood, Rafe had passed out of sight.

Lydia took dinner with Reggie Gilchrist at the Drunk St. Leonard. He spent most of the time talking about how expensive it was to set up a new household. He might as well have been shouting, *Don't sack me!*

Lydia had helped Jamie copy out *Poor Richard's Almanack* once, and she still remembered the axiom, *If you would keep your secret from an enemy, tell it not to a friend.* It had struck a chord with her, because she had lived by it all her life. Mr. Gilchrist was making her nervous, reminding her that too many people knew the truth. The town's faith in the Reeves hung by a thread. She shouldn't have told Mr. Cahill, either, though that had worked out to her advantage in the end. She hoped.

She leaned in and interrupted Mr. Gilchrist's amusing story, delivered with anxious eyes on her face, about the offensive Whiggish habits of his mother-in-law. "Have you told anyone?"

Mr. Gilchrist blanched. He hid his face behind his mug and choked on a mouthful of ale.

"Who?" she hissed.

"I was drunk," he said pleadingly. "I had just found out, I thought I was going to lose my place—"

"You still may," she snapped, despite knowing she couldn't dismiss a man with a new bride. Especially when said bride was a daughter of one of the most prominent Whiggish families in the town, who would seize any opportunity to blacken Lydia's name.

"He was a stranger." Mr. Gilchrist looked miserable. "He said he was passing through. I've actually—I've been wanting to warn you that he may be a fortune hunter. Only I didn't—"

"Only you didn't want to tell me that you had betrayed my

confidence." Actually, it would have been impertinent in him to give her that kind of advice in any circumstance, but she was in no mood to be fair-minded. "Wait a moment—who do you mean?"

"Mr. Cahill. I told Mr. Cahill."

So this is what feeling faint is like. There was a tingling in her neck and everything looked bright and shaky, as if the distance between objects had skewed. But after a few moments, her head stopped swimming. Her hand, when she reached for her teacup, was perfectly steady. She wasn't really faint then, merely indulging in melodrama.

How bad was it? Mr. Cahill must have had his eye on her for his brother from the beginning, but that wasn't a crime. People did want their brothers to marry rich wives. Mr. Gilchrist had put a solution to her problem in her way. She ought to be thanking him.

She felt awful, though: humiliated and sick.

Mr. Ralph appeared in the doorway of the dining room, a huge dark shape limned in silver-gilt winter light. It was only when he stepped forward and the door swung shut behind him that she could see his face. He had been crying, and he was coming towards her.

Could he be upset she had preferred his brother? She had no reason to think his heart particularly engaged, but men didn't like to be rejected. It made them angry and vindictive. Whatever the cause, it was in her interest to prevent a scene. "Sir, you look ill!"

She stood, calling to the barman, "Would you show us to a private parlor and bring up some tea and brandy for Mr. Cahill? No, no, it's quite all right, Mr. Cahill, Mr. Gilchrist and I have finished our dinner."

Mr. Gilchrist gave Mr. Ralph an apprehensive look, but he straightened up and said, "Would you like me to accompany you, Miss Reeve?"

Lydia was touched. Mr. Ralph could not be *literally* twice his size, but it struck the eye that way. "No, but thank you."

"I shall wait here in case you need me." He gave Mr. Ralph a minatory glare that went, Lydia thought, quite unnoticed by him.

When the door of the private parlor shut behind them, Lydia stayed by it. Mr. Ralph looked around the room suspiciously. "Anyone could overhear us here."

The same thought had occurred to Lydia, but there was no help for it. "If you have something to say to me, sir, here will have to do. I had rather speak with you in earshot of other people just now."

His bloodshot, blank eyes focused sharply for a moment on her face, then slid away. It came to her uncomfortably that he was not as straightforward as he seemed. But he gave in, taking a chair with an exhausted thump. Even seated, he filled the room. "Come here."

"I had rather not."

"I don't want to be overheard."

Was it a threat of blackmail? Reluctantly, she drew near him.

"My brother and I…" He whispered so softly she had to lean in still farther, turning her eyes away so as not to see the individual beginnings of a blond beard glinting on his cheek. He swallowed, a jerky blur in the corner of her eye. "We're swindlers. We grew up in a thieves' kitchen. We aren't gentlemen, we aren't Cornish, we aren't even Christians."

"Not—not Christians?" she whispered back foolishly, as

if *that* were the most shocking thing he'd said. Could it really be true? But why was he so upset? Surely not because she had preferred his brother.

"My name is Ralph Cohen. Short for Raphael." He made an unhappy choking sound and put a hand to his pocket as if to take something out—and then let the hand fall empty in his lap.

Her feelings had not yet caught up with her. She felt numb, as she had after her father died: *Surely I should be upset? What's wrong with me?* "Mr.—Mr. Raphael, why are you telling me this?"

"I'm finished with swindling. I thought you should know the truth." There was something eerie about such a big man speaking so quietly.

I think lately my brother would rather settle down, Mr. Cahill had said—no, he was Mr. Cohen. Mr. *Cohen*? He was a *Jew*? But he was so clean, and when she kissed him he'd smelled—well, of course Jews didn't really have an unnaturally foul stink, but she hadn't expected one to smell so *good*, like pears and wool and clean skin. "Where is your brother?"

He turned, his red-rimmed, pale eyes staring directly into hers from too close. "It's always better to know the truth, isn't it? Even if the truth is unbearable?" He bowed his head, fists clenched in his lap. "He's not my brother."

At first she thought she had misheard him, so garbled were the words, with almost no breath in them.

"Not—not by birth. He lied to me. He stole me. And I would have—I would have forgiven him if he'd *told* me."

"*Stole* you? Stole you from where?" She had never given much thought or credence to the rumors that Jews stole Christian children, but it must be true. Yet she was sure Mr.

Cohen loved his bro—he loved this man, and—to steal a child like that, out of covetousness of its golden hair and strong limbs, and raise it as one's own—it was unnatural—diabolical. Mr. Cohen didn't seem—

Her head spun. "Can you return to your family? Did they take other children? Can we find them? A—a Parliamentary inquiry—"

He blinked at her. "Pardon? I don't—what 'they'?"

"Mr. Cohen must have been a child." Relief flooded her. Yes, of course, that was it. He had been a child. He wasn't responsible. "There must have been men who told him what to do—"

He frowned in blank confusion, and then horror dawned on his face. "You've made up a story already, haven't you? A story that fits what you already believe. What did we ever tell you about ourselves? That we have aunts? That we're from Cornwall? We barely had to lie; you did the work for us. I don't know why I thought telling the truth would work differently. You don't know anything about me or my brother. Stories like yours aren't real. They're an excuse to murder Jews in the street and feel good about it. What would we want your children for, when we can barely feed our own? If that filthy slander gets out in the town, they'll hang Ash to a lamppost."

Lydia could not move, stuck in the moment like a drop of water freezing on a windowpane. Had she really been so gullible? What *had* Mr. Cohen told her? She cast her mind back. The only thing she remembered with any certainty was that he had lost the memory of his mother's face, and that he loved his brother. That had seemed like enough.

Mr. Raphael pulled out his watch. "I told him I'd be gone by six."

He took her wrist in his hand. "I don't want to hurt you. I don't want to hurt anyone anymore. That's why I'm leaving, and why I've told you this. But he is still my brother and I will still protect him. You keep our secret, and I won't tell anyone you said you'd marry whichever of us we thought best to get at your money."

Her blood was freezing now, crackling along the length of her arms. She nodded. Incredibly, she thought, *How will I get the money now?*

Then she realized that Mr. Cohen was wandering around God knew where in God knew what state of mind. She had kissed him. She had kissed a child-stealer, a thief, a Jew. She had offered herself to him.

She squeezed her eyes shut, remembering. The moment had felt almost holy. His breath had stuttered. She had been so sure he was as overwhelmed as she was. Had he been despising her?

"Does he know you meant to tell me this?"

He nodded. Mr. Cohen must think her money entirely out of his grasp—which it was, of course. He might go to the Dymonds. Their matriarch Lady Tassell would love to hear about this.

Father would be so ashamed if he knew. Jamie—what would *Jamie* say? "Where is he?"

"I don't know. I asked him not to come back until six. He may not come back at all. He never cared much about his things."

Mr. Cohen might disappear into the night and take her indiscretion with him? No. She had to speak to him. She had to know what he would do.

"Where did you last see him?"

He frowned at her. "Why?"

"I have to speak to him." Her throat hurt from whispering. "I have to know whether he'll tell anyone that I…"

"He won't. Not if you don't do something to make him."

"You will pardon me if I don't take your word for it." She was suddenly furious with the man in front of her. *If he's so honorable, why are you leaving him?* She wasn't stupid enough to say it out loud.

"Somebody ought to see that he's all right," she said placatingly. "Don't you think?"

He nodded reluctantly. "On the road towards Nuthurst, near the stand of aspens. Be—be kind to him."

"I will." This would be the last time she ever saw Mr. Cohen, if her luck was good. Better to send him off well-disposed towards her.

"Thank you. I'm sorry." He crushed her hands painfully in his. Lydia didn't like the reminder of how strong he was. She gave him a sympathetic touch on the shoulder and went out, glad to be escaping.

Chapter 8

It was nearly dark. The shadows of the aspen trees stretched out of sight. Even poking her head out the coach window into the chill wind, Lydia could make out little beyond that something was stopped in the road ahead, a cart perhaps. She heard Mr. Cohen's voice before she saw him.

"No, no, thank you!" he was saying in a loud, cheery voice. "I'd like to walk back. I've only stopped for a moment to rest." He sounded as if nothing whatsoever was wrong.

He was precisely where his brother had said he would be. That meant he had been in one spot for at least an hour in this biting cold. For a moment, exasperation that other people could not manage to properly care for themselves swamped everything else.

"Pull up alongside," she told the coachman. It was Madge Cattermole's cart, no doubt on her way back from the market in Steyning. Lydia leaned out the window. "You are a good Samaritan, Mrs. Cattermole. Mr. Cahill has had rather a shock. His brother sent me to fetch him."

She could not see his face, but she saw how he swung towards her at the words, flinching back.

"Mr. Ralph has gone on ahead to see your aunt. He didn't think you would be recovered enough to travel." She turned back to the farmer's wife. "Their great-aunt has come down with the influenza and is very ill."

Mrs. Cattermole shook her head sadly. "It takes the old ones and children the worst."

"Everything does," he said.

There was an edge in his voice, but fortunately the woman did not seem to remark it. "Ben't that the truth?" she said. "Well, my Lucy is expecting me. You'll take him back to town, won't you, ma'am?"

"I certainly will, thank you. Did you do well in Steyning?"

Mrs. Cattermole smiled. "Bettermost winter broccoli in the county. Good health to you and your family, sir. Evening, Miss Reeve." She touched her whip to her forehead and drove off down the road.

Lydia opened the carriage door.

"If it's the same to you," he said, sounding perfectly normal and cheery again, "I'd rather walk. I think the air and the exercise will do me good." He started off in the direction of Lively St. Lemeston.

By now the last sliver of sun had slipped below the horizon, leaving the road in darkness outside the faint circle of light provided by the coach lamp. But Lydia had seen him shiver. She eyed the road reluctantly, then climbed out into the faint, chilly drizzle.

The round iron rings of her pattens sank into the ground with a squelch. She followed him and promptly stepped into a puddle much deeper than it appeared.

Living in Sussex, Lydia spent a great deal of time almost falling over in the mud. Wet feet were also familiar. But she had never learned to enjoy either sensation. "You are damp and chilled and you have had a severe shock. Kindly get in the carriage."

"I'm hardy as an ox." His breath misted on the air in shuddering white bursts. "My brother needn't have sent you."

"Your brother didn't send me."

He flinched again. She stripped off her glove and reached out to feel his cheek, expecting him to flinch away from that too.

He didn't. He stopped to look at her—the same look that had been driving her wild, the one that said he saw more than she meant him to. Now she knew it must be an acquired professional skill, which made it less frightening. It somehow did not make it any less enjoyable.

His cheek was cold and clammy. In the darkness, his eyes were black. "And our aunt?"

She jammed her chilled fingers back into her glove, conscious that they were in full view of the coachman. "Please get in the carriage, sir. It will not help your aunt for you to catch your death."

His eyes narrowed. "Perhaps I ought not to go back to town at all. What did my brother tell you?"

At least he retained *some* instinct for self-preservation. She leaned in, muttering, "Mr. Cohen, if I meant to set the constable on you I would have done so, instead of ruining my shoes in this manner."

He blinked at her. "You can't like me *that* much," he said at last, as if racking his brains for an explanation of her behavior and finding none. His shivering was growing worse.

Strange, how Mr. Raphael's distress had repelled and frightened her, and his did not, when he was so much guiltier. Even knowing everything, she wanted instinctively to share her warmth with him. Had he used some trick to make her feel this way? Could she trust her instincts, or were they swindling her too?

"There is no unhappy creature that I would leave to die in the road," she said. "Please. I brought hot beef broth in a flask, and hot bricks."

He began again to walk. "I can't be back before six. Rafe asked me—" His mouth crumpled a little, and he turned his face away.

Lydia was a stubborn, fretful patient herself. When she had had an inflammation of the lungs at fifteen, she had refused to eat. Aunt Packham had convinced her with one simple sentence: *You're scaring your brother.*

"Think how your brother will feel if he hears you've made yourself seriously ill," she called after him, knowing it was cruel. "He'll blame himself."

He stopped. For several long moments he stood there, head bowed, unmoving except for his uncontrollable shivering. Then, without a word, he turned and walked past her to the carriage, mouth set.

She breathed a sigh of relief and allowed him to hand her in. "Here," she said, passing him the rugs she had kept wrapped round the hot bricks.

It was so dark out, and the road had been so muddy. She hesitated—and then, opening the panel, asked the coachman to drive slowly. She knew he must have noticed her new caution since her father's accident, even if he was too tactful to say so. It embarrassed her, made her feel exposed, like being caught crying.

Did Mr. Cohen know how her father had died? Had Mr. Gilchrist told him that too? Could he guess that dark, muddy roads had never troubled her before? *He has other things on his mind,* she reminded herself.

Setting his wet hat and gloves on the seat beside him,

he swathed himself in soft wool and leaned back against the squabs, the shadows under his eyes stark in the lantern light. Silently she offered him the flask.

He wrapped his olive-skinned fingers around the warm leather and drank. There was no relief or pleasure in his face, only methodical efficiency as he went about staving off the chill that would distress his brother. When the flask was empty, he pulled off his boots and set his feet on a hot brick.

After his row with his brother, he had stood in the cold and wet for an hour, not moving.

She passed him a packet of sandwiches, and a second flask filled with hot tea. He shook his head. "I'll only cast them up again." He gave her that look—piercing was too harsh a word. It did not invade; it noticed, taking in everything she gave. "Are you all right? This must have been a shock to you."

She could not reconcile this with what Mr. Raphael had told her. It was all so outlandish that she couldn't feel the enormity of it. Her conversation with Mr. Gilchrist had upset her more.

Learning that he was a professional swindler should have made her shame a hundred times worse. Instead, it took the sting out of it. The whole affair was disgusting, and she was unwise to have trusted him, but she had been one of many victims. She wouldn't stand out in his mind as more foolish than other women.

What a strange, vain thing the mind was.

"Do you mean to blackmail me?" she asked.

He smiled at her. "Not if you don't mean to prosecute." There was something boyish in the way he said it, as if he had broken something at play and was trying to sweet-talk the housekeeper.

Only he'd been orphaned very young, and never had a housekeeper. She didn't like to think whom he must have had to sweet-talk, growing up alone in a rookery. Then, as if life weren't difficult enough, he had taken on a baby that didn't even belong to him.

Yes, she still liked him. But she was mad, to be considering what she was considering.

"Tell me what happened." She took off her damp bonnet to let her cap dry.

"Didn't my brother?"

"I don't mean the quarrel. Tell me what happened, when you—adopted him. The coachman can't hear us. I know it."

The corner of his mouth curled a fraction. "Do you now?"

"I used to like to ride on the box as a little girl. I could never hear what my parents were saying inside."

"Adopted." He made an amused sound. "That sounds so legal." He said *legal* the way Lydia's friends said *Whiggish*, a little disdainful and a little bemused. "There is absolutely nothing legal in this story."

"I've been the patroness of Lively St. Lemeston since I was seventeen," she said, as much for her own benefit as his. "I'm not easily shocked." She clung to that. She thought this story would be bad. Lively St. Lemeston wasn't London.

He gave her a sorry look as if he was thinking the same thing, but he said, "My mother died when I was five," in a storytelling sort of voice. In Lydia's experience very few people who had had a bad upset could really resist talking about it, when pressed. It ate at them until they did.

"Do you remember how I picked your aunt's knot out, when we met? At five, I had already been employed for a year picking the embroidery out of stolen handkerchiefs. After my mother died, the woman who kept the house she worked in didn't think that income alone was worth the expense of keeping me."

His mother had been a whore, then. He didn't seem to find that notable enough to comment on.

"She sent me out to steal with a gang of boys a little older than I was. I was good at it, but not so good she didn't hope to make more a couple of years later by apprenticing me to a gang of bodysnatchers." Most people, by this point in a story, would go on as if by compulsion. He stopped, and asked gently, "Do you know what that means?"

It annoyed her that he was behaving as if he were being kind to her when the shoe was quite on the other foot. "Men who steal corpses for dissection," she said sharply. Then she realized what that meant. He had stolen corpses.

As a child, she reminded herself, *as a child,* but she drew back in her seat nevertheless. She thought of her father, recently buried. There was still an armed watch over his grave at night to keep away men like this.

He saw her thrill of spiritual horror and smiled. "Yes, it *was* rather disgusting," he said so matter-of-factly that her throat closed. A child among such horrors—how could he help but grow inured to them? "I wasn't a squeamish boy, though, and I was too young to be much help in digging. I mostly fetched and carried and held the dark lantern and kept a lookout for guards. Besides, even in London there isn't work for more than a few big gangs, and we weren't one of them. We only robbed graves when the opportunity came our way, and the rest of the time I went on learning to steal. It wasn't a bad life, but I was lonely."

Not a bad life? It sounded like a nightmare.

Her disbelief must have shown on her face. "It was hard," he said. "But poor children work. I'd rather steal than scramble up chimneys or work in the mines, or be up from dawn to dusk scratching in a field. But all *that* seems ordinary to you, I imagine, because the law permits it—that a child should get up at dawn and thread machines until it's too dark to see, and then go home to a place that isn't even warm and fall asleep hungry."

"Not at all," she said. "I and my friends have been pushing for a Royal Commission for years to investigate the conditions in factories. The Act of 1802 has no teeth and I'm assured that it is ignored with impunity…"

She trailed off, sensing that the next part of her speech would not be well received, about how factory owners had not been brought up to be masters and had no sense of their sacred responsibilities to those under them.

He gave her a look that was startlingly fond. "You're like Rafe. You want to make over the world all by yourself. It is what it is, and that's not a tragedy. Rich folk go on as if not being born one of them is the saddest thing in the world. As if we must go about weeping and wailing and wishing we could change places. Well, Miss Reeve, I like your house, and I like your fine tea, but I wouldn't like to be you." She bristled, and he laughed. "It's nothing against you. I'd just rather be me. I'd always rather be me. Would you really give up your own life to get something you thought was better?"

Lydia couldn't think of anything better than her own life. But she took his meaning loud and clear. *Don't pity me.* She knew people hated to be pitied; usually she hid it better than this. But a child, in the resurrection trade—never mind. She smiled back. "No, I wouldn't."

His eyes lit with warmth, and that little grasping baby squid of pity turned to something leafy-green that twined around her heart and reached out tendrils towards him.

"Rafe would." He smiled at her for a moment, a spasmodic curve of the lips, as if that would keep her from seeing how he felt. Lydia remembered that smile on her own face, speaking to her father's friends across his coffin. "He'd rather anything than what I gave him."

She quashed the impulse to reassure. Contradicting rarely helped the way one hoped it would. "How did you meet?"

"One of our tricks was to keep an ear out in the work-houses. If a pauper dies with no family, the expense of burial is the parish's. The parish would rather save their money, so a respectable-looking person who presents himself as a relative can generally claim the body without much trouble. I was the only one in Izzy's gang who spoke English without a foreign accent." He spread his hands. "And I'm persuasive."

She snorted, ignoring him to unwrap a sandwich.

He grinned at her, then looked at his hands. "I shouldn't be able to laugh. Not so soon."

She glanced up in surprise from removing her gloves. She had thought him more tolerant of human frailty. "What would you say," she asked, "if I said that to you?"

He watched her, considering. Some people, in a conversation this personal, avoided their companion's eyes, while some watched for the other's reaction. He was one of the latter.

So was she, as it happened; she didn't like the idea of people seeing her in an unguarded, private moment. But that wasn't a bond between them. There was no bond between them. She took another bite of sandwich to hide her self-consciousness.

"I would say the heart can't feel any one thing for too long," he said. "Nature made us that way a-purpose, to keep us sane. I would say not to worry, grief will be back soon enough."

She took a satisfied swallow of tea. "Well, there you go."

"Would you find that convincing, if I said it to you?"

"I think I would."

"I suppose the difference is that *I* should believe it, if I were saying it to you. But I've been tolerant of myself too long. I don't like to dwell on things. People torture themselves, you know—they put themselves through a regular Spanish Inquisition, and nobody asked them to do it. Nobody enjoys it but themselves."

He took a sandwich and began to peel off the paper. Lydia felt a thrill of triumph. "I told myself it didn't matter, because we were brothers just the same and what difference did it make?"

He ate in great mouthfuls. She tried to imagine him a small, dirty, hungry child. The image was—*darling*, she thought, and was ashamed of it.

"One day, when I was nine years old, we heard about a woman dying in St. Mary's workhouse. No family at all, except a baby. We waited for days while she died, afraid someone would get in ahead of us, but in the event I was the first to present myself. I said she was my mother's cousin. The man was suspicious, I could see it. 'Bring over my little cousin,' I said. 'He'll know me. You'll see.' My nerves were eating me up on the inside. If the truth came out, I didn't know whether they'd send me to prison or keep me there. I didn't know which was more terrifying."

She recalled with painful embarrassment her own speech to him on the subject of workhouse children.

"Well, he brought out Rafe. He wasn't crying, but the next

best thing to it, that sort of whining sniffling noise that means they're thinking about a real scream." His voice was terribly fond. She remembered that noise. She could almost feel Jamie's warm heavy weight in her arms, thinking of it. "I went up to him bold as brass. 'You're all right now, coz,' I said. 'I've got you. Remember me?' And I picked him up."

"What did he do?"

Mr. Cohen smiled, shifting in his seat. For a second his tears caught the light from the lantern, his brown eyes blazing gold. "He had the thickest eyebrows I'd ever seen on a baby, and he gave me a frowning look like a little beardless rabbi, as if he knew I was trying to put one over on him. Then he giggled and grabbed my hair and babbled some baby talk. I was faint with relief. He sat in my lap all the way home."

His smile twisted. "He'd no notion his mother was in the back of the cart. He started to wail and scream fit to wake the dead when they unloaded her—only the dead can't be woken, can they? Not if that heartbroken screaming couldn't do it. 'What did you bring the child here for?' Izzy asked me. 'He's louder than a church-bell. Go and drop him somewhere.'"

Lydia gasped.

"It happens every day," he said simply. "But it didn't happen to Rafe. I went out to drop him, and I never went back."

"But—but where did you *go*? You were a child!"

He smiled. "Clever boys of eight or nine are in great demand in London. They make the very best thieves—so small, they can get in anywhere. I went to another Jewish gang in another part of the East End, made up a new name, spun them a tale about the workhouse trying to take my brother away. At first I worried all the time that Izzy would come after me, but London is a big place and I probably greatly overestimated my importance to him. After a few years I had grown so much I doubt Izzy would have recognized me."

"But your brother—he's blond, surely that would have given you away."

He laughed. "Blond Jews are more plentiful than you imagine. We've lived among Europeans for centuries, after all. I said his father was a Gentile. No one questioned it. He didn't question it either." He ate a morose bite of sandwich. "He was so upset, to find out he wasn't born Jewish. He's more Jewish than I am. He won't eat pork, if you can believe it."

"Do you?"

He waved his ham sandwich at her.

She cringed. She hadn't thought of that when she'd ordered them. "Sorry."

"You don't have to apologize. I love ham. But Rafe—he took a bad beating once. Ten years old and he'd rather die than eat pork when some boys tried to make him. I said God would want him to be safe, and he said—he said *I* wasn't God, and it wasn't about God anyway. He never touched pork again."

He squeezed his eyes shut for a moment. "He told me that I thought he had honest blood. What's blood got to do with any of it? Swindling doesn't sit right with him because I grew up lying, and he didn't. I brought him up to expect what was inside him to matter to someone. I suppose I brought him up to leave me."

"Don't *you* want someone to care about what's inside you?"

He made a face as if he'd bit into a lemon. "Never in life. When no one's looking at you, you can do as you like."

Lydia privately agreed. "And what do you like to do?"

"Damned if I know." He exhaled, sounding exhausted. "Everything I've done since that day, I did for him. I don't know how people go on, who haven't anyone. I'm like a watch—I need winding. I'd have stood in the road all night if you hadn't fetched me."

Lydia remembered how empty she had felt at seventeen when Jamie left for Eton. How the days had stretched out like an unrolling ball of yarn, infinite and thin. The only thing she had wanted to do was write to him, and she'd sat at her desk unable to think of anything interesting to say. That was when she'd taken up politics.

She thought Mr. Cohen would laugh at her if she said, *There are always plenty of people who need to be taken care of.* So she didn't say it. She knew it herself, and she was going to take care of them. Whatever it took.

They had been watching each other so long it was like the reverse of saying a word out loud until it lost its meaning. Each feature of his face seemed full of significance. "If it was only ever a swindle, why was it so important to you that it be Rafe who married me?"

He leaned forward, elbows balanced on his knees, and spread his hands wide. Even now, telling her things he must never have told anyone else, his brother gone, tear-tracks on his cheeks, he seemed physically comfortable in a way that startled her.

Your father always said you could smile when the world was ending, dear, Aunt Packham had said, and Lydia had felt self-conscious and wrong. *He* would understand.

"It was never only a swindle for me." He gave her an apologetic smile with a hint of self-mockery in it. "He said he might go in the army, or emigrate. I thought if I could find him a better prospect...I thought in a few weeks you'd be sure to fall in love with each other."

His mouth compressed, a sudden hard edge. "It would have worked if I hadn't mucked it up by letting you see I was attracted to you myself. He might do anything, now. He could *enlist*."

The idea of someone enlisting as a common soldier whom Lydia had entertained as a guest, whom she had considered an equal, appalled her. She could not think of a single comforting thing to say; the *Lively St. Lemeston Intelligencer* had been publishing a series on the terrible conditions among the enlisted men in the Peninsula.

Of course it was nonsensical to assume that, without her attraction to Mr. Cohen, she would unfailingly have fallen in love with Mr. Raphael. But there was no use in saying so. He would only want to argue about his brother's merits.

"It *is* possible to get enlisted men out, with the proper influence," she said at last. "If you ever need that sort of help for Mr. Raphael, you must come to me."

The movement of the coach changed. They had gone over the bridge and were driving on clinkers now. That meant they were in town. She didn't have much time.

There was an edge of cynicism in his fond smile. "You can't resist someone who needs help, can you?"

She blushed, more because of the smile than the words. "I would prefer to say that I see no reason to withhold help I can easily give. But in your case my motives are quite selfish. I still need my money, so I still need a husband."

His eyes narrowed. "You can't mean me."

She meant to think of tea—but she thought of their kiss. Calm filled her. "I do."

"You can't like me that much."

"Liking is beside the point," she said, although it wasn't.

Her liking for him, foolish as it was, was what made this feel safe. Or not safe—obviously it wasn't safe—but something she could do. She had kissed those lips. They'd been soft and warm. She had thought she would recognize the sound of his breathing anywhere. How could she be afraid of him, after that?

"I am a Jew," he reminded her. "I am a bodysnatcher." She flinched at the word, and he smiled, so gently it made her shiver. "My mother was a whore, and my father could have been anybody. I'm a swindler and a thief. You can't seriously mean to marry me."

A thought struck her. "But—how did you mean for Mr. Raphael to do it? The banns must be read in your home parish, and you haven't one!"

He waved a hand. "There's a pastor in Cornwall who's made a profession of having lost all his records in a fire about twenty years ago. He's our home parish now. I have a banker there too, who provides me with letters of reference upon request."

Lydia knew she shouldn't be so shocked. She had seen plenty of graft in the Church of England. It was a repulsive bias to find small crimes worse than large ones.

"Look at you," he teased. "You're thinking of turning him in to his bishop right now. You can't enter into a false marriage."

She could smell his wet coat, just as she had when she kissed him. She inclined towards him a little, breathing in. "It wouldn't be false. Once the vows are read and the register signed, it will be a real marriage. Your history only makes it easier for me. You will know how to look upon it as a simple transaction. You won't expect anything from me."

He shook his head in disbelief. "You shouldn't decide this now. Grief clouds the judgment; that's how undertakers make their money. You're making yourself a target for blackmail."

For a moment she felt cold. He could come to her at any time and threaten to expose her, for the rest of her life, and she would have to pay him. In politics, blackmail was the ultimate terror. She had worked hard all her life never to do anything that would justify it.

But it hadn't been for its own sake. She had done it so that she might protect her family's interests, and be in a position to help Lively St. Lemeston. There was little use to her spotless reputation if the Wheatcroft interest were let to lapse.

It was unlikely anyone but her, Mr. Cohen, and his brother would ever know what she had done. Mr. Raphael had used blackmail only as a threat for self-protection. She didn't *think* Mr. Cohen would try it unless he was in some terrible need, in which case she would certainly help him regardless.

After all, in exposing her, he must expose himself. She thought, with calculation and a sneaking sense of shame, of Mr. Raphael saying, *If that filthy slander gets out in the town, they'll hang Ash to a lamppost.* But she wouldn't need to threaten him with that. He had been a bodysnatcher. That alone was a public revelation a man couldn't hope to survive.

She chose to run the risk. She knew her father would have hated the idea, alive, but perhaps in Heaven he wouldn't blame her. "If you don't wish to make the bargain, say so. But I find all these scruples unconvincing, when you planned for me to marry your brother in earnest, whose background is equally scandalous."

He leaned forward, eyes kind. "You don't owe these people this. Don't sell yourself so cheaply. You're worth more. I thought you would be happy with my brother."

Tears pricked unexpectedly at her eyes, that he would say that. She blinked them away. "I'm glad you think you know how to set a just price on me," she said dryly. "But I don't consider that I am selling my *self* at all. I am choosing to do what I must to get what I want. I don't want a real husband, who'll ask me to arrange my life to suit him. Even if I contracted a marriage of convenience with a gentleman of my acquaintance— and I cannot think of any who would suit—who's to say he might not later desire more? Expect more? And it would be very awkward to refuse him. I think I can trust you to be practical. Do you agree?"

He leaned back against the squabs, legs spread. His brown eyes glittered as he considered her. There was admiration in his face, and what she thought—*hoped*—was desire.

For a moment she entertained a silly fancy that he would say, *I don't feel very practical right now.* He'd pat the seat beside him, saying, *Come here*, and she would, because where was the harm? It was no worse than anything else she meant to do. Then he'd kiss her, desperately but with a touch of wonder.

But he only blinked, the desperation and wonder in his eyes vanishing so completely she wondered if she had imagined them. There was nothing there but sadness, now. "You can trust me to be practical," he said. "Very well."

Chapter 9

Miss Reeve showed no sign of relief at Ash's acquiescence. He had never before thought how near trained aristocratic reserve could be to swindling. When she leaned forward to continue bargaining, the flickering lamplight shone full on her composed face. She was calmer than he was, and he didn't like it.

"I would need you to stay here a half-year afterwards," she stipulated. "There must be no hint of scandal. It must seem to be an ordinary marriage, and then we can come up with some excuse why you're obliged to go away."

Six months here with her, pretending to be married? He ought to leap at the chance. Three thousand pounds for half a year's work was more than he had ever made in his life.

But…it felt like disloyalty to Rafe to take what was to have been his the moment he left the scene. How would it sound to Rafe, if he heard of it? It would seem as if Ash didn't miss him.

"Half a year is a long time to expect me to pass as a gentleman. The longest I've ever managed was a month or two."

"You were then found out?"

"No," he allowed. "Then the swindle was done. But I've had some close shaves."

A smile split her face, startling him. "Not recently."

He blinked, confused, and then rubbed his fingers over his

rough cheek with a grin.

She swallowed visibly, her eyes tracking the movement.

He was flooded with heat, of a sudden. It felt wonderful, after how cold he had been. After how cold his heart still felt.

But Ash's inability to resist temptation was what had ruined Rafe's chance at this. So he resisted, this once. "I shaved just this morning," he said as if he hadn't noticed her reaction. "Close as you please. My hair grows fast. I've to have this cut every couple of weeks as well." He put a hand instinctively to his close-cropped head, and tried not to think about how her hand would feel there.

"Yes, if you wish to keep it so short."

"If I don't, it curls and makes me look the Jew." He'd had a mop of curls when he left London at twenty-one. He still remembered them falling silently to the floor in some barber-shop in Brighton. He had grinned to show Rafe he didn't mind.

The grin had been real later, when he'd barely recognized himself in the mirror. Ash had known his limits; he hadn't been sure he could make it outside London. But in that moment he'd realized he was going to get away with it. He was getting Rafe out, and no one could find them, and there was no telling what that stranger in the mirror might be able to do.

Then she said—her face reflected nothing but kind concern as she did it—"Your brother might come back."

That hurt like a thousand spikes being driven into his body. He hadn't allowed himself to consider that.

"If you leave, he won't be able to find you."

Rafe wouldn't come back. Ash knew that. But Rafe might want to know that Ash was all right. If there was to be a crash, if he was going to stop like a watch someone forgot to wind, it couldn't be for another year or two, until he was sure Rafe wasn't watching any longer. This would keep him going while it lasted.

She would keep him going.

"Ruthless," he said, his misery fading to a dull background throb as he focused on plans and strategy. "That's good. You'll need that."

She looked surprised. She was used to gentlefolk, who valued a smooth flow of conversation above everything, or else people who wanted something from her. She didn't expect anyone to openly question her motives. That made her forget that they could still do it silently. It made her feel safer than she should. She would need training for this deception. But she had it in her.

"Does that mean you'll do it?" she asked after a pause.

"Yes."

She smiled. "Thank you."

He hoped she would still want to thank him in six months.

Rapping on the partition, she directed the coachman to the vicarage. "I want us to be married in time to prepare for Christmas if possible. I'd prefer the banns to be read for the first time this Sunday. If the vicar writes to Cornwall at once, we can get the letter on this evening's mail coach."

"Why trouble with banns?" he asked, surprised. "You can afford a license. We needn't rush, and you'll do better with your brother if you wait and ask his permission."

She drew herself up. "I am a Reeve of Wheatcroft. We belong to Lively St. Lemeston. Our banns are read in St. Leonard's Church and we are married there." She deflated a little. "I suppose you're right that I should ask Jamie's permission, but I don't think I could make *that* convincing."

Well, it was she who stood to lose, and her risk to run.

"We'll need to discuss terms more carefully. And I think you might need a few acting lessons. If I come to your house tomorrow, might we speak privately?"

She raised her fine eyebrows at him. "We're engaged to one another. Naturally we may dispense with a chaperone now and then."

She had asked him for no assurances of any kind. She had trusted his yes, when he said he would stay for six months after he had his money in hand. Now she was trusting him with her reputation. He meant to play fair with her, but she had no way of knowing that. There was a streak of recklessness in her indeed.

He wanted her. He couldn't resist anymore.

He leaned forward, bringing their faces closer together. "I don't want to make unjust assumptions. You've said you can trust me not to expect anything, and that's true. I promise our bargain shall go forward however you answer. In the six months we live together, do you intend us to…" He searched for a polite way to say it. "To have carnal knowledge of each other?"

He knew it sounded ridiculous, but it was unambiguous, and if she meant there to be nothing of the kind, he needed to know *now*.

She didn't laugh. Her brown eyes searched his face as if she expected to find something. She made him feel as if maybe she could, when he knew there was nothing on his face he didn't want there.

"I don't consider that part of the bargain," she said at last, leaning back against the cushions. Without the light directly on her face, he couldn't tell if she was blushing, but her voice was a little too nonchalant. To an unmarried gentlewoman, this must be unimaginable boldness. "I hope we will neither of us feel entitled to expect it. But I don't see that there would be any harm in it, if we found at some point that we both wished it. We will, after all, be married."

He felt, actually, a little relieved that there was to be no set understanding. A thing like that developed best naturally, sure as a wild rose was prettier than a cultivated one. Besides, he'd got used to celibacy. He'd fumble and look unsure, and that had come to mean danger to him. It wasn't as if he could practice on his own before a performance was required, like billiards or tying a cravat.

Yet he said, "And now? If I should want, by way of example, to kiss you—I don't want to make you uncomfortable. I want to clearly establish the rules."

She bit her lip. "So long as you accept a refusal gracefully, I won't mind if you ask. I think I may trust you to…"

"Be a gentleman?" he suggested, amused.

"It's not a good word, is it? I haven't found that gentlemen take a refusal better than anyone else. Let us say that I believe you will not offer me disrespect or cruelty or—or force. Will you believe the same of me?"

She wouldn't have asked a gentleman that, he thought with a touch of sourness. But it wasn't her fault she was richer than him, or that she could probably turn this town into a howling mob with a snap of her fingers if the fancy took her. Plenty of women in her position would have assumed they'd bought whatever they liked. He wouldn't even have minded. He wanted her, and besides, what was sex compared to the six months of marriage he'd already promised her? It was pleasant, really, to be asked.

She had a lawyerly mind behind that Tudor-portrait face.

She understood everything should be laid out separately and clearly, with no room for misunderstanding. He wondered what she'd be like in his arms. Like a wildfire? Methodical? He hoped for both at once. "I trust you," he told her.

"Thank you." She licked her full lower lip. "Do you—*do* you wish to kiss me?"

"I do, yes." Saying it without urgency, so as not to frighten her, was more difficult than it should have been. He was half-hard already.

Her lips parted and her eyes unfocused. Then she moved to sit beside him, sliding his hat out of the way with a jerky movement. "I—yes. Let's."

Chapter 10

Ash twisted round in his seat to kiss her. She tasted like tea and roses and human warmth, but it wasn't enough. He hauled her into his lap and yes, that was it, that was what he wanted, to have her curled against him. Now it felt real.

Her hip pressed against his cock, and the chill under his skin faded. His hands felt hot again as he gripped her waist.

He held her snug against him and kissed her while he explored, tracing the bones of her stays up her side and following the edge of the corset with his fingers to where it cupped her breasts. He dragged his thumb hard along the busk, down her front to her belly.

She broke off the kiss to brush her cheek against his, making a tiny satisfied sound in the back of her throat, so light and sweet his heart contracted.

He knew, distantly, that he was unhappy. He focused on this instead, on her hunger and how he could satisfy it. He knew they must be almost to the vicarage but if he just had time to give her this, if he could just feel her shudder in his arms, if he could just accomplish this one small thing—he cupped her cunt through her skirts.

She went absolutely rigid, and he thought that if she pulled away he might not be able to hold in his tears.

There was a long moment, and then she spread her legs

and pushed up into his hand. He made a sound that was barely human and pressed his mouth to her throat, rubbing his hand against her.

Even through all that expensive cloth, he could feel the yielding of her soft flesh, and the bone beneath. She urged him on with her hips and made not a sound except for her desperate breaths. Her skin was soft and sweet and hot, and she quivered against his mouth, straining. Every movement she made rubbed his cock. With his whole soul he willed her to spend, if he could, if she could, *please.*

She put a hand up to his head. She must have noticed that his ear was cold, because she pressed her warm palm flat around it. There was a sharp pain in his chest—

The carriage jolted to a stop. They both froze, and then she whisked herself back to her own seat. Ash felt as if he were made of lead.

"Oh, damn," she said quietly. Her mouth trembled and curved up, and then she laughed, straightening her clothing and putting on her bonnet. "You have rose lip salve on your mouth. Hopefully only on your mouth, it's too dark in here to be sure."

He laughed back, but underneath he felt terribly exposed and didn't know why. He pulled out his handkerchief and rubbed at his mouth. Looking down, he saw he had taken out his mother's handkerchief by mistake. He had forgotten he had it. It was supposed to be in Rafe's pocket. He couldn't do this.

Yes. He could.

He tucked the handkerchief away, buttoned his greatcoat over his erection, and inhaled and exhaled slowly. He could smell her in the close air. That was good; it distracted him. "We have to look happy," he told her. "It isn't enough to smile. You have to *be* happy."

Six months of her. He could manage to feel happy about that.

She blinked, and the door to the carriage opened. He leapt out and swung her down. She stumbled, crushing his toe with her patten, but she tilted up her chin and beamed at the coachman, a blinding victorious grin. The servant's smudged lantern turned her skin a dark gold and made the red in her hair seem a trick of the light.

"Congratulate me, Gideon. I'm getting married!"

Lydia was painfully aware that despite a good start, her performance last night at the vicarage would not have won accolades upon the stage.

In the face of the vicar's stares and dismay, she'd grown nervous and a little panicked, and been unable to do anything but assert that she was long since of age, that there was no impediment, and that that must be the end of it. She had felt sick and guilty at deceiving him; he had baptized her, for Heaven's sake!

She would have to do better now. "I have something to tell you, Aunt."

Aunt Packham raised her eyes from her tatting. "What is it, dear?"

"Mr. Cahill has asked me to marry him."

Aunt Packham blinked. "Which one?"

Lydia calmed the tense fluttering in her chest. To her surprise, when it was gone she was able to laugh. "Mr. Ralph is a little young for me, surely!" Although really, she'd believed Mr. Cahill's lie that she and Mr. Ralph were of an age. It was only that she hadn't been able to stop thinking of him as a little brother.

Aunt Packham looked amused. "At my age, it's hard to understand all that fuss about a few years. The elder Mr. Cahill, then. I *thought* he liked you."

Lydia smiled, thinking how annoyed Mr. Cahill—he had instructed her to continue to think of him under that name— would be by that.

"What did you tell him?"

"I told him yes."

Aunt Packham's needlework fell forgotten into her lap. "You did? Oh, my dear!" She stood, opening her arms for a hug, and stepped on her needlework. She fumbled, trying to pick it up and unable to see through the tears misting her eyes. "I wish you all the joy in the world, darling."

Straightening, she gave Lydia the hug, a kiss on the forehead, and a kind of soft back-rub that meant she was overflowing with emotion and that Lydia had always disliked on account of being ticklish. "When do you mean to be married?"

"Before Christmas." Lydia kept still for the back-rub with an effort. "The banns are to be read for the first time on Sunday morning."

"Oh! That's a little soon, surely?"

"I don't want to wait. I want—" She blushed, realizing that anything she said would sound as if she were eager for the marriage bed. "That is to say—it would be nice to spend Christmas in my own establishment."

Aunt Packham's eyebrows went up. "Well, if you're

sure—oh, my dear, you're going to be so happy." She gave Lydia another hug, beaming.

Lydia was ashamed of her own emotion as she hugged her aunt back; it rose in her throat quite as if this moment were real.

"Oh, if only your father could be here!" Aunt Packham said. "I had almost given up hope that you would find someone, but he never did. He wanted so much to see you settled and happy."

Lydia began to cry, and, incredibly, her longing for her father to be at her wedding felt real too. She had to remind herself that she wouldn't be getting married at all, if her father were here. This whole desperate undertaking was only necessary because he was gone.

She was seized by fear that the anticipation fizzing like champagne in her stomach at knowing she'd see Mr. Cahill soon was the same as being glad her father was dead.

She tried to think what Mr. Cahill would say to that. He'd have *something*, even if she didn't know what, and somehow that comforted her enough that she was able to stop the tears with a horrible sniffling sound.

Blowing her nose, she said, "I know Jamie will want you to stay on as his hostess."

Aunt Packham's smile wobbled. "You children are too good to me."

Lydia thought how galling it must be for Aunt Packham to have to defer to a woman half her age, simply because Lydia was rich and she was poor. She'd thought of it before, of course; the misfortune of poor relations was hardly a new idea. But for the first time it didn't seem a sad necessity, as unavoidable as the weather, but an active injustice. She remembered Mr.

Cahill's flash of resentment in the workhouse: *Isn't it God's plan?*

"Not as good as you deserve," she said at last, quite truthfully, and submitted to another back-rub. "I—I must write to Jamie."

"He will be so happy for you. Oh, you look so happy, my dear! I don't know how I missed the signs, it's clear on your face that you're in love."

Aunt Packham was always claiming to be able to read things in Lydia's face that were not there at all. *I can tell your headache is better* when it was worse, *I can see you're hungry* when Lydia had just eaten, *Poor girl, you look wretched* when an unpleasantly insinuating neighbor finally went off to London to practice law. Lydia was deeply thankful for such a forgiving audience. She had no idea what to tell Jamie, who was more perceptive and who had to sign the settlement.

Dearest James, she wrote, and waited for inspiration. She had been waiting a quarter of an hour when, with relief, she heard hoofbeats on the drive, and was given Mr. Gilchrist's calling card.

"May I ask how you do?" the young man asked once he was settled in a chair with a cup of tea in his hand. "I heard Mr. Ralph Cahill has left town."

He said it with a significant air and a piercing look of sympathy, as if he imagined she had sent Mr. Ralph about his business and was now nursing a broken heart. She was touched by his concern and amused by how far he was from the truth.

The two things combined to make a very convincing smile. "I am better than I have been, thank you, Mr. Gilchrist. I am—I have news, if you have no pressing business." Aunt

Packham quivered in her chair with excitement, but kept her eyes on her tatting.

Mr. Gilchrist's eyes brightened, and he leaned forward in his chair like a little bloodhound, which his strong resemblance to a fox made especially comical. "None at all."

"I hope I can trust you not to gossip," she said severely.

His face clouded. "I've learnt my lesson. I assure you, my lapse was entirely out of character. I have kept worse secrets better."

Really, he was only very young. At his age she hadn't always remembered to guard her tongue, either, and in this instance, his slip had helped her enormously. But irrepressible Mr. Gilchrist needed occasional repressing, so she waited a few moments to give his regret time to sink in. "I am to be married."

There was a long silence. "I wish you joy, of course, but—to whom?"

"The elder Mr. Cahill."

"A charming young man," Aunt Packham said. "I am very fond of him already." Lydia was seized with a wave of affection for her aunt.

Mr. Gilchrist stared. "But…after what I have told you…"

It would be tricky to carry this off. "I spoke to Mr. Cahill about what you told me. You were right; he brought his brother up from Cornwall as a result, in the hopes we should suit. But you cannot blame him for his pragmatism. I—ordinarily I wouldn't confide in you so far. It's none of your affair. But since you already know so much, I will tell you that he's agreed to take only the smallest percentage of my money, to set his brother up in the army. The rest will be entirely mine. There is no question of fortune-hunting, and I hope very much you will not embarrass me or my future husband by implying otherwise in the town."

Aunt Packham had listened to this speech with a deepening frown. "Certainly not! If you spoke to your own wife more than five times before marrying her, Mr. Gilchrist, it is more than I'm aware of."

Mr. Gilchrist flushed bright red. "People in glass houses, eh?" he said with a laugh that didn't come off. "This wretched tongue of mine. I'd give it a tongue-lashing if I could do so without its cooperation."

Lydia could see from his expression that he had thought of something coarse to say on the subject of tongue-lashings, but after several firm setdowns early in their acquaintance, he knew better than to say it in her hearing.

Having wrestled with his demons and won, he told her with evident sincerity, "I hope you will be very happy, Miss Reeve. No one could deserve it more."

"Thank you. If Mr. Cahill makes me half as happy as I hear you're making Mrs. Gilchrist, I shall consider myself lucky." Mrs. Gilchrist, though one of the prettiest girls in town, had always had rather an anxious air about her. Lydia had caught sight of her the other day, and while the anxiety lingered, it was suffused by a gentle, beaming glow.

He grinned, equilibrium recovered. "I could give him pointers, if you like." There was a slight pause, which she suspected he'd have liked to fill with a wink. "Do you mean to remove to Cornwall after your marriage?"

Lydia smiled, flattered by his ill-concealed dismay at the prospect. "Mr. Cahill has led a wandering sort of life and has no objection to settling here. Other than removing to the Dower House, I imagine I shall go on very much as I have."

Mr. Gilchrist lit up with relief. "I am very glad to hear that, madam. It is a pleasure working with you, and not only because of your extraordinary personal beauty."

Lydia laughed, trying not to think about how soon his salary would come due. "Thank you, Mr. Gilchrist. On that note, let us work."

They spent the next half-hour discussing the recent parish vestry meeting, the petition being got up by the local Whigs asking their MPs to sponsor a Police Act for the borough, Lady Tassell's imminent arrival in the district, and half a dozen requests for favors and small loans.

It was all so familiar that Lydia could almost imagine that her father was away in London for the opening of the new Parliament, and that his account of the day's work might be expected in tomorrow's mail.

"There is one more thing." Mr. Gilchrist hesitated. "It's about the new Mrs. John Sparks."

"Ah," Lydia said, taunting him a little, "your sister-in-law's new sister-in-law!"

Mr. Gilchrist looked embarrassed, and she wished her words back. It was no easy thing for a young Ministerialist agent to be related, by however many marriages, to a man so reviled by his party.

"You haven't yet called upon her in her new home," he mumbled.

"I had not planned to."

The new Mrs. Sparks had been Caro Jessop, daughter of the borough's longstanding Ministerialist MP. A few weeks ago, in the midst of a hotly contested election, she had left all her friends to elope with Jack Sparks, possibly the most obnoxious Whig in Lively St. Lemeston—and that was saying something.

Calling upon her in the printing office from whence issued the scurrilous *Lively St. Lemeston Intelligencer* was not a tempting prospect. Lord Wheatcroft, not six hours before his death, had actually forbidden it.

Mr. Gilchrist cleared his throat. "The other Pink-and-White ladies won't go if you don't. Several of them have confided in me that they'd like to see her, but they don't want to offend you."

Lydia hadn't thought of that. "Perhaps I might leave my card."

"You and Mrs. Sparks used to be very good friends," Mr. Gilchrist said delicately. "That will look like a snub." They both knew that that was because it would be one.

"She didn't come to call when my father died," Lydia said quietly. "We could not have been such good friends as all that." They'd been friends for so long. Lydia had helped and guided Caro when Caro was a brand-new hostess. For Caro to send a kind note, on such an occasion… Of course it was difficult for Caro to get about, but she might have made the effort.

"Her husband would have had to come with her." Mr. Gilchrist looked even more embarrassed by this evidence of his knowledge of the inner workings of the Sparks family, but he soldiered on. "She doesn't have a man any longer to help her with her wheelchair. They would have had to rent or borrow a carriage, as Sparks doesn't keep one. It would have been a deal of expense and trouble if you hadn't received them."

Lydia wasn't sure she *would* have received them. Receive Jack Sparks, when dozens of times she'd had to talk her father out of a libel suit over some unforgivable insult in his family's horrid rag? When she could remember her mother doing the same? She had picked up Lord Wheatcroft's obituary in the

Intelligencer with dread, knowing from long experience that it was bound to be full of small digs and insults—

But she had found it respectful, kind and thorough. She knew Caro must have written it.

Caro had always been so proud. She would hate to be publicly turned away, from a home where she'd been such a welcome guest.

It occurred to Lydia abruptly that if Caro could influence the contents of the *Intelligencer*, it would profit the Pink-and-Whites to keep up her old loyalties. And she had no desire to stand in the way of any of Caro's other friends who might wish to see her. There was no good argument *not* to go, except her own reluctance.

"Of course I will go. This very afternoon. I hadn't realized the Pink-and-White ladies were waiting for me. Thank you for making me aware of it."

Mr. Gilchrist broke into a relieved smile. "Thank you, Miss Reeve." He visibly screwed up his courage once more. "Miss Reeve—I have no desire to press you, but my wife is so concerned—do you think the new Lord Wheatcroft will stick to his guns? Ought I to be inquiring after a new situation?"

His *wife* was so concerned, indeed. Poor Mr. Gilchrist was young and inexperienced; he would be a brilliant political agent one day, but he had no great connections and had made a highly imprudent match. In the period after an election, there would be dozens of more seasoned men looking for work.

"When I am married, I will pay your next year's salary out of my own pocket," she promised. "By next Christmas I'm sure Jamie's little freak will have passed."

Mr. Gilchrist thanked her fulsomely and took his leave

soon after, still spouting extravagant compliments as the door closed behind him.

Lydia began several drafts of her letter to Jamie and hated all of them. Finally, after wasting two perfectly good sheets of paper, she scrawled *Why are you doing this to me?* across one ruined page. Then she fed both sheets to the fire so that Aunt Packham and the servants couldn't read them, and climbed into the embrasure of the window.

Strange, how a week ago she had gazed out at this garden and thought only how desolate it was, and how dead. Now she remembered what she had told Mr. Ralph: that she'd always liked how things looked in winter. She remembered taking Jamie into the garden in January, all bundled up, to learn to identify trees without their leaves.

It was merely a coincidence that from the window, she could also see part of the drive.

"Aren't you cold, dear? Come and sit by the fire."

"I'm not cold," Lydia lied.

Aunt Packham laughed. "But you're watching for your young man! How silly of me. Is there any sign of him?"

"Not yet," Lydia admitted. But it was only a few minutes more before he appeared. In his heavy greatcoat, a little too large for him, his solid frame looked like an enormous brick with ankles and an umbrella.

"Oh, you've spotted him!"

Lydia realized a smile had spread across her own face. She stood, embarrassed. "Aunt, if you wouldn't be offended—if after some little time you might make an excuse to leave the room... We are betrothed, after all, so there can be no impropriety in it."

Aunt Packham smiled knowingly. "Of course, dear."

Lydia hadn't been thinking of it, but now the memory of last night in the carriage swept over her. She flushed hot as a banked coal exposed to air. In an instant she was desperate for the completion she'd been denied then.

She'd found it on her own later, alone in her bed. She didn't think she could have slept otherwise, but she regretted it now. How could she be near him again without thinking of it?

He walked up the drive with a cheery, confident stride. There was no trace of the man who had wept last night. He knew he could be seen from the house, she realized.

Or could his emotion of the night before have been a show, and this was the truth? How would he have looked, if she could have seen him before he came around the curve in the drive?

She felt sure the suspicion was absurd—but after all, yesterday morning she had been sure he was a gentleman of integrity.

She ought to care more that he wasn't. Instead she was tempted to rush downstairs and meet him at the door. No one would marvel at it. It would even help their charade, but she couldn't bring herself to do it. She was too old to behave like a lovestruck girl.

It seemed to take him an eternity to climb the drive, and then it was far too long before he was shown into the Little Parlor, his boots hastily cleaned and his hat and greatcoat no doubt drying in the hall.

Everything froze for a sharp glittering moment as their eyes met. She thought it would be he who moved, he who broke the silence—but he simply stood there, his body relaxing a little from the bluff good humor she had watched come up the drive. His shoulders slumped almost gratefully.

"How do you do?" she asked, the words sticking in her dry throat.

His grave mouth didn't even curve; the corners twitched, faintly. "Better, for seeing you."

If it was false, his talent was beyond anything. She ought to care whether it was false instead of marveling at his skill.

"This is so romantic!" exclaimed Aunt Packham. "My dear boy, you must allow me to wish you joy."

He allowed it at unpardonable length, and inquired after her collars for the auction with wholehearted interest. He would do splendidly with voters. Lydia couldn't wait to show him off in Lively St. Lemeston.

It was twenty minutes before Aunt Packham remembered her promise, saying with a sly twinkle, "Oh, but I have just recalled, I must speak with the housekeeper. You won't think me rude if I leave the two of you alone, will you?"

Mr. Cahill twinkled slyly back. "We shall never forgive you for depriving us of your company." Her aunt laughed, and whisked herself and her workbox out the door.

Chapter 11

Mr. Cahill sighed and sprawled a little on the sofa, eyes drooping. She gave him a few minutes of silence before asking quietly, "How do you do? Really?"

He smiled at her. "Better for seeing you. Really." He smiled wider at her uncertain frown. "I'm sorry. It's going to drive you mad, isn't it, not knowing what I mean and what I don't? Listen—I mean most of it, and that's God's own truth. It wouldn't be convincing if I didn't. It isn't the *whole* truth, that's all. I do feel better for seeing you. I also feel like someone's turned over my chest with some of those farming implements you country folk are so fond of. And…I like you. You know that. But I like everyone. Maybe not as much, but I'd have felt better for seeing anyone. I'm always worst when I'm alone. I stayed up late last night in the common room with a party of travelers, and when I woke early this morning, I went down the street to the coffeehouse and talked with the proprietor's daughter."

She didn't know how to react to that. "I hope you told her you were engaged," she said tartly, and then found herself grinning. "And Imogen Makepeace is a Whig. If you must have coffee go to the Cocoa Seedling, on Forest Road."

He grinned back. "Miss Makepeace says they serve coffee-colored water at the Seedling."

"I like weak coffee."

He laughed. "So do I. Don't ever drink a cup of the Makepeaces' coffee on an empty stomach. I've calmed down a bit now, but I thought I might shake to pieces on my way here."

She raised her eyebrows. "You haven't eaten?"

He gave her one of his slow smiles. "I was in a hurry to see you."

Even if it was only part of the truth, it made her happy. She rang for a hot meal.

"I didn't tell Miss Makepeace I was engaged," he said when the servant had left the room. "I wanted to give you a last chance to change your mind."

"I haven't changed my mind. I wondered, though—how many depredations have you committed under the name Ash Cahill? Are you likely to be discovered?"

"As luck would have it, none. We change names a few times a year. As we meant our next swindle to be a big one, we picked new ones, had new cards printed, all of that."

"Isn't it difficult, to learn to answer to a name that isn't yours?"

He shook his head. "The trick is finding one you'll recognize even if you aren't paying attention. I've been through dozens, all of them sounding enough like mine or Rafe's to make my head turn. Mr. Ashford, Cash Mohan, Mr. Rafferty, Ashley Caine…"

The hot meal arrived, toast and butter and bacon. It disturbed her now to see him eat pork. It reminded her how little he respected anything, if he could so easily ignore one of the most ingrained strictures of his people. "Do you really mean to go to church tomorrow?"

"They're reading our banns," he said in some surprise.

"And I love Stir-up Sunday."

The Collect for the last Sunday in November began, *Stir up, we beseech thee, O Lord, the wills of thy faithful people...* After church, the streets would echo with children singing,

Stir up, we beseech thee,
The pudding in the pot,
And when we get home,
We'll eat it all hot.

The Monday following, the grocer's windows would be filled with raisins and almonds, and the whole town would smell like ginger and cinnamon and nutmeg.

"Oh—I know the country folk round here think it's ill luck for a man to hear his own banns called," he said. "Is that it?"

She shook her head, embarrassed to explain.

His expression changed. "Ah. I'm not used to talking to someone who knows me for a Jew." He was silent, eating and watching her.

She was starting to understand that those pauses in his speech were a form of calculation, though whether he was gauging her response or trying to marshal his own she couldn't yet guess. She fixed him with a friendly, open look and waited.

"I've been to church in dozens of parishes all across England," he said at last. "I've been to mass and Quaker meetings too. I like it. It's all the same in the end, a ritual to make us feel closer to each other, to lift us up a little."

"Do you believe in God?" It was a rude question. Piety was a private matter, between oneself and the Almighty. But she wanted him to say yes. She wanted to know he believed in *something*.

His eyes stayed steadily on hers, but his sensitive mouth jerked a few times, uncertainly. "I can't today," he said at last, softly. "I can't—I'm alone now. Completely. I can't not mind feeling like a curiosity. I can't explain myself to you with any grace. I don't blame you for thinking me as strange to you as if I lived in the Antipodes, or for wanting to know more. I hope you won't take offense. I just can't today."

"I'm not offended." She hid her mortification. "It's I who ought to apologize, for prying." A dozen thoughts went through her mind. Ordinarily, it wouldn't have occurred to her to share them. But now the unsettling idea came to her that she could.

She tried to choose a thought that wouldn't be too dangerous. She could tell him that she had always imagined God as rather like her father: affectionate, ever-present, but distant somehow. His commands were to be obeyed rather out of love and duty than out of a conviction of their rightness, and on occasion creatively interpreted for the good of all.

She could tell him how alone she felt, that usually she didn't mind it, but this month she did.

She couldn't say that out loud. Or could she? He felt alone too. She wanted to tie them together, so he would keep their bargain. So he would like her.

She could think of nothing to tell him that wouldn't more deeply underscore how different their lives had been. "I know we have few points in common, as far as our experiences go. But I believe we can learn to understand each other." His expression didn't change. That wasn't enough. She added, "Quite well."

He laughed, his gold tooth winking at her.

"I didn't mean *that*." Strange, how she had almost forgotten.

Now desire was back, not sure and predictable like the tide but all at once like a hurricane. She hoped her cheeks weren't flushing. Her womanly parts tingled and ached; so did her breasts and, inexplicably, her ears and fingers. She had never been so conscious of her own body before.

"I know you didn't," he said. "Thank you. I think we can too. Shall I give you a little acting lesson, before our debut tomorrow?"

Even the innocent act of speaking, lips and tongue forming sounds, now seemed suggestive. The words *Shall I give you* were quite obscene. "Certainly," she said.

"I think you're very accustomed to acting in one sense. You're very good at hiding your emotions, at seeming friendly and even-keeled. Would you agree?"

She smiled involuntarily. "Yes, I would."

His gaze sharpened. "What are you thinking of now?"

She was imagining him taking her hard on the sofa, and he had not an inkling of it. She gave him an innocent look. "I'm sorry if I appeared abstracted. I was only giving your words my full consideration."

He smiled. "That's a good one. Hiding things is just one part to acting, though. The other is showing things. You've mastered looking cheerful, concerned, that sort of thing. Mild, friendly emotions. But if this is going to work, you're going to have to pretend a lot more than that. You're going to have to make everyone in this town, including your brother, believe that you love me so madly you can't wait to be married to me."

The jangling of her nerves only heightened her aroused state. She nodded, taking a few deep breaths to relax the muscles in her throat and stomach.

"The easiest way to do it is to imagine that you do love

me," he said. "At least, that's what I've always done. I find a little part of myself that feels the thing I want, and bring it out and feed it. You like me, so it shouldn't be too hard."

She shrank inwardly, that she had told him that, before she knew what he was.

But knowing hadn't made her like him any less. She'd let him pleasure her last night, and she would allow it again.

She'd always known she had in her the seeds of rebellion and wantonness. She'd thought she could simply choose never to let them grow. Evidently she'd been wrong.

"The biggest obstacle to a good lie is your own hesitation," he said. "There's a part of us that wants people to know the truth, to see us for who we are. But if you can stop wanting to get caught…you're the sole witness to your own thoughts, and so you can perjure yourself without fear of contradiction."

Though she had never thought of it in those terms before, his words felt uncomfortably familiar. She'd never meant to be a liar—only a good daughter, sister, hostess, patroness.

"What would you think of someone else who did what you're doing?" he asked. "An heiress who married a gentleman of limited means on a week's acquaintance?"

"I would think her a very great fool," she said promptly.

He nodded. "I imagine you don't want everyone to think you a fool. That will stand in your way. And then—" He cleared his throat. "Have you ever been in love?"

"Twice or thrice," she admitted.

"How did you behave?"

She flushed. "I hid it very carefully. I didn't want anyone to guess."

"Not even the objects of your affection?"

"Especially not them."

"Why not?"

She wasn't sure she could explain the panic that had seized her at the idea that someone might see the truth in her face, in her laugh, in the way she angled her body. "I didn't want to be pitied or mocked. I wasn't pining, or even particularly miserable, and I hated the idea that someone might think I was."

He nodded, considering her. "You have to let go of that too. Folks expect people in love to behave in a particular way. Maybe if you were really in love with me, you wouldn't show it. But you can't afford to play it that way now." He paused. "I suspect it might embarrass you if *I* thought you really were falling for me."

She hated the very idea. Even nodding in agreement made her squirm a little.

"I promise not to think it. No matter what you say, no matter what you do, no matter how besotted you may appear to be—even if you sink into the role so thoroughly you begin to question your *own* feelings—I've swindled before. I'll know certain-sure it's part of the lie. All right?"

She nodded again, bizarrely reassured.

He frowned. "Maybe it isn't a good idea for us to go to bed together. When you're exposing parts of yourself to view like this, it's important to keep something back, to help you feel safe. You're new to swindling. You probably need to hold more back than I do."

Frustration burned hot in Lydia's chest. It was a familiar feeling, one she almost never allowed free rein, as it had no purpose. She wanted to ask him how many women he had pretended to love—not because she was jealous, but because she thought it would hurt him.

That wouldn't get her what she wanted, though. He was

lonely. He wanted to feel as if they were two of a kind. She smiled demurely at him. "I'm a quick study."

He gave a crookedly surprised smile, his eyes crinkling admiringly. "You've got nerve and a cool hand, I'll give you that. Just be careful. Take care of yourself, because no one else will do it for you. No matter how good my intentions might be, you can't count on me to look out for you when all my self-interest goes the other way."

His meaning didn't immediately strike her, and then it did—he wanted to take her to bed too. "Does it?" she asked, to be sure.

He laughed a little. "You have no idea how arousing I find the idea of you pretending to be besotted with me."

The sensation of power was what she had always liked best about flirting. Now an even headier sensation joined it: the expectation of fulfillment.

Lydia left her armchair and came to stand beside Mr. Cahill. He sat at one end of a bulging, inlaid, and be-scrolled Baroque sofa, which had gone hopelessly out of style in the fifty years since its manufacture. "When I updated this room a few years ago, I tried to modernize this sofa by recovering it."

She kicked off her slippers. It was impossible to tell if he was looking at her feet, or at the pale green and white stripes on the silk upholstery. "It wasn't a great success, but the sofa is so comfortable we couldn't bear to part with it."

In particular, it was at least eighteen inches deeper than an elegant modern one would be. When she sat beside him and leaned her head on his shoulder, she could pull up her legs and feet after her with perfect comfort. He had been outside recently enough that the fabric was not quite warm against her cheek.

He went very still. "It's a fine sofa."

His bare hand rested on his thigh in the center of her field of vision. She laid her smaller, paler hand atop it; his fingers tensed, shifting beneath hers in tiny jerks. She slid her fingers between his and held his hand, her nails resting against the wool of his pantaloons. Ignoring his taut muscles, she breathed in.

She liked the way he smelled. Was that a vulgar affront to all the men and women who had striven to form a polite, rational England out of the bawdy past?

No, she decided. Manners mattered. They enabled people to live comfortably together with all these animal urges safely hidden.

She lifted his hand in hers and kissed his fingers one by one. He drew in a long, audible breath through his nose, his shoulder rising and falling against her temple. Abruptly she was filled, not with lust, but with affection. Tears pricked at her eyes, and there was an achingly sweet pressure against the inside of her ribs.

She was trying to act besotted, so that was right. Tentatively she let the emotion grow, groping her way along the curve of her instincts. He knew it didn't mean anything.

She turned his hand over and kissed his palm, then his wrist. Sitting up, she pressed his hand to her heart and met his eyes. "Do you feel that?"

The moment trembled in the air between them like a wire strung taut, and even so the corner of his mouth twitched. She doubted he could feel a thing through all her clothes. She tamped down her own smile.

He nodded solemnly.

"It's yours," she said.

His lips parted. His chest heaved, and there was such hunger in his face—his eyes were bright, as if with tears or fever—

He whooped with laughter, the exhilarated sound smashing the moment into buoyant, giddy shards. "You *are* a quick study. There, wasn't that as good as the real thing?"

"Better. Less messy."

She couldn't stop smiling. He was right, she had made herself feel a lot of mild, friendly things, but she had never summoned up something so intense within herself.

She had known lying was safe, and satisfying. She had never realized it could be *fun*.

His hand was still on her chest. He pushed her down on the sofa and bent over her, kissing her and still laughing, giggling almost. She kissed him back, feeling drunk.

"I don't mind a little mess," he said, making it wicked with his tone.

She flushed bright red, suddenly conscious of the slick wetness between her legs.

"*That* embarrasses you?" He shook his head. "I'll never understand gentlewomen."

She turned it over in her mind. "It's more like fear than embarrassment. Fear that you won't think I'm a lady anymore."

He propped himself up above her on his forearm, clearly delighted. It occurred to her that he must have picked up everything he knew about being gentry through observation. He had never been able to ask anyone directly before. "Ladies have bodies like other women," he said.

"Yes…" She couldn't think how to explain it. "It's as if…as if one is trying to avoid reminding men that one *is* like other women. Men don't always treat women very well."

His mouth twisted. "No." He sat up. "I'm sorry, I shouldn't

have done that in your parlor, even if we *are* out of line of sight of the keyhole. I forgot how much you have to lose."

She felt bereft, and sad. Sad about the world's unfairness, and sad for him too, because he didn't have anything to lose. She wanted to pull him back down and feel that giddy warmth again.

She sat up too. "You're probably right."

"I had an idea last night. Something that would make it make sense, how fast we're getting married and then me dis-appearing a while later."

"Yes?"

"We could say I'm ill. Nothing contagious, but definitely fatal." He grinned at her. "We don't know how long I have left, so every day is precious."

It was a brilliant idea. Lydia's entire body went rigid in protest. "No."

"Surely you aren't superstitious," he teased. "So common."

"Have you done that before? Pretended to be dying?"

"Once." His mouth did something lopsided and compli-cated. "Rafe didn't object. He could work himself up to tears about it. It was heartbreaking. I had a couple of handkerchiefs spotted with blood. We could have made a fortune raising money to send me to Italy. But Rafe was never as good as me at stopping a feeling when he didn't need it anymore. A few days in he started crying at night too. So we stopped."

"You could have done it the other way round," she sug-gested, to see what he said. "Had Rafe pretend to be dying."

"Bite your tongue!" he said, half sharp and half laughing at himself. "I never said *I* wasn't superstitious. Poor folk learn to respect the evil eye, keeping body and soul together day to day."

As always, a wave of fellow feeling hit her at how much he loved his brother. She searched for a reason to object to his plan that wasn't *The idea of your dying upsets me.* She didn't want him to think she was too soft for this.

"I don't want to be back in mourning, just when I'm out of it," she said at last. "I don't want to have to pretend to grieve. It sounds difficult and painful."

There was a pause, and then he shrugged and smiled. "Then you'll have to act extra infatuated."

He went on with her lesson: tell as few lies as possible, keep them vague and simple, be prepared to change them if necessary. Lydia listened in fascinated horror to rule after rule for dishonesty and betrayal, clearly distilled from long and varied experience—aware all the while that there was more fascination than horror.

"…Let the other person create the story in their own mind. They'll do it better than you could, because they know what kind of story they like best."

She remembered Mr. Ralph saying, *We barely had to lie; you did the work for us.* There was a lovely alchemy to it, really. She had done it herself, in a smaller way, when paying charitable visits or talking to a guest.

She had never thought of it as cheating anyone of anything.

"What is it?" he asked.

She could smile and say *Nothing.* Lydia hesitated. "I was reflecting that I do something similar in my own work. I learned it hostessing. I used to let my father's guests do all the talking, when I first started at seventeen. I thought that was what they wanted. But I discovered they all thought me very dull, even a little proud. So I began giving them a few charming speeches, carefully doled out."

He smiled. "Oh, they did want to do all the talking. They just also wanted to believe that a brilliant, beautiful woman liked the sound of their voices as much as they did."

It was a cynical thought. "I suppose so," she said, feeling protective of those well-meaning, self-important men and their fragile pride, "but there's no harm in wanting to be liked. I didn't mind listening."

His smile broadened. "A girl after my own heart."

She froze.

He saw it, and his smile faltered. "Don't let it trouble you. A blacksmith and a burglar both pick locks, but that's no shame to the blacksmith."

Then, perversely, she wanted to avow the connection that had so unsettled her. Instead she said, "I don't know what to write to Jamie. I've tried and tried, and…I'm going to hate lying to him."

"You could tell him the truth."

She tried to imagine telling Jamie the truth, that she was marrying a Jew swindler to get her money. He would be horrified. He would think she was pathetic and obsessed, that she was throwing everything away for nothing. "He would believe it was his duty to stop me. For my own good. He said—he called Lively St. Lemeston Father's hobby. He said we spent a fortune to puff ourselves up in the town."

She felt so embarrassed, saying the words—afraid that Mr. Cahill would agree, that it was true, that she was a frustrated spinster drunk on her own consequence.

Mr. Cahill frowned a little. "All right, we won't tell him."

"It's not a hobby," she insisted. "We didn't do it for our own pleasure. I don't—"

He looked surprised. "What's wrong with liking your

work? Isn't that the point of being gentlefolk, that you can choose a profession that pleases you?"

That made her feel guiltier than all the novels of Hannah More. She had never had to work whether she liked it or not, only to eat.

She'd been told all her life that women were inclined to base their conduct on the gratification of shifting impulses at the expense of principle, that if she enjoyed her work she was self-indulgent, that it was unchristian to be proud of what she had accomplished. She hated hearing it, and hated even more how it got into her bones so she believed it herself.

There was something freeing in realizing that the question, which had been so large to her, did not even make sense to Mr. Cahill. It mattered to a great many people whether her pursuit of philanthropy was proper, Godly, and self-effacing. That didn't mean it had to matter to her, so long as she made the right show.

"I'm going to give that letter another try," she said. "Do you mind waiting and coming to town with me? I have to visit a friend. She—well, thereby hangs a tale, but she recently married the man who publishes the newspaper."

"The *Intelligencer*? It's a good paper." He laughed at her grimace. "Even if it is Whig. I don't mind at all. A newspaperman is a gossip with a speaking trumpet. If we can convince him, we're halfway there."

She hadn't considered that aspect of things. It made her even more anxious about the proposed visit. Could she really fool Caro?

If she could fool Jamie, she could fool anyone. She went to her writing desk, and instead of trying to imagine what she would write if she were in love, she tried to feel it. She tried to *be* in love and writing to Jamie.

My dear James, she wrote, and suddenly she had a hundred things to say. Her pen swept across the page with an authoritative scritching sound. She looked up halfway down the page to see Mr. Cahill watching her, pleased as a tutor with a clever pupil.

"You were right," she said, pleased enough herself to wish to gratify him. "Once I stopped feeling as if I deserved to get caught, it was easy."

He beamed.

"You…" She hesitated. "Can I ring for anything for you? I know from experience that it takes me at least an hour to write a good-sized letter."

"It's only been five minutes."

"Yes, but I'll agonize over every word when it's done, and copy it over at least once. I do that with all my letters. I know it's probably not necessary, but—" She checked herself. "I write good letters, and this is how," she said firmly. "It's easy to be misunderstood when one isn't there to explain."

He nodded. "I don't much care for the written word, myself. It's like touching marble when you expect flesh."

She was taken aback until she thought. "You haven't had occasion to receive many letters, have you?"

He shook his head.

"I love letters," she said. "They *are* different from conversation. But they aren't like books or magazines, or something that isn't addressed to you. I find myself quickly losing interest in those too, unless I plan to make use of the information in them. Letters are more like—more like a clothed embrace."

His eyes gleamed. "With a charm of its own. I see."

"Yes, and there are practical obstacles to incessant nudity."

She bent her head demurely over her letter. "One doesn't always live in the same place as one's friends."

Chapter 12

"Mmm," Ash agreed. "And it would be cold."

Her hair shone a dull bronze in the gray winter light, and her skin looked like ice cream; inside that still head were a million whirring thoughts, and he wanted to know all of them. At the moment, her thoughts about nudity interested him in particular.

Being with her was like a Frost Fair on the Thames, life and noise and a welcoming, solid sheen over filthy, freezing water. He really had thought he would shake to pieces on the walk here. He'd known he wasn't dying, but it had felt that way, like how people described seasickness. Now the earth revolved steadily under his feet.

He walked around behind her chair. She turned her head sharply to look at him and put a hand over her papers.

"Don't worry, I won't read your letter." He ran a finger along her shoulder, through her clothes. If a letter was like that, it was a fine thing indeed. She shivered and didn't pull away, so he traced her shoulder blades and the collar of her dress. He ran his finger lower, aiming at her nipple.

"Not when I'm writing to my brother!" She set down her pen, though, and let him nuzzle the nape of her neck. Turning her face towards him, she kissed him for slow minutes, just long enough that it didn't sting when she pushed him away.

"Now let me finish my letter."

She was swindling him, letting him think it was a struggle to resist him when he was pretty sure she could resist anything. He smiled at her sneaky, upright back, and her hair piled up and covered with lace like icing over a fancy dessert. "Can I have a look around the room?"

He was a little surprised when she nodded, but he didn't ask twice. Permission to snoop in a house like this was too good to be true, a little slice of paradise on earth. She even let him look through her desk drawers, smell her sealing wax and test the edge of her penknife and feel the weight of her writing paper.

She smiled at him while he did it, even, and when he could pull himself away from her to look around the room at the pictures and knickknacks and doilies and carved cabinets, she patiently paused in her writing to answer his questions about who had bought them, and who had made them, and how old they were.

She gave him a few narrow-eyed looks, but she was too polite to ask if he was planning to steal anything. As it happened, he wasn't, but he was incurably nosy and liked touching other people's things and seeing how they lived.

This was different than anything he'd ever done. He was burrowing right into someone else's life and pulling it shut behind him, and she seemed to want him to. It was too much luck, but Ash didn't mean to look a gift horse in the mouth, even if everything he touched, he wanted to tell Rafe about. *Sometimes they burn cherry-wood for the smell,* and *Her grandfather's snuffbox isn't gilt, it's gold,* and *They buy new curtains every ten years, can you believe it?*

He could picture the appalled wonder on Rafe's face, and

the pain of it was so sharp that he almost wanted to stop and sit by the sweet-smelling fire. But then he'd have nothing to do *but* think about Rafe. He was examining the workmanship on the wrought-iron poker when she finally stood.

He came to give her his arm out of the room, and she handed him a folded, sealed paper. "Read it later and see what you think about letters."

He was absurdly touched that she'd thought of it. Kissing the note reverently, he put it in his left breast pocket. Her brown eyes shone with amusement.

He was going to have her. For six months he'd have her—morning, noon and night if he could make her want it badly enough. Six months was a long time, so there was no point thinking about after that. He'd have to find somebody else, that was all.

Sitting opposite her in the carriage into town reminded Ash of last night. He wanted to pull her into his lap and make her laugh and moan—but this visit would be their first test. Miss Reeve was new at swindling, and this woman was her friend and had something real to compare the false to.

So he asked about Caro Sparks. It was juicy gossip—illicit meetings between a poor Whig and a rich Tory, at the circulating library of all places, the suitor turned away by a stern father, a daring elopement, and Caro gone from living in clover to slaving dawn to dusk over a newspaper that, though she didn't come right out and say it, Miss Reeve clearly regarded as a mouthpiece of Satan.

"Do I need to hate this paper too?" he asked. "How friendly do you want me to be to this Sparks fellow?"

She made a face just at the mention of his name. "You should be friendly. Then I won't have to be."

"What about Caro Sparks? How intimate is your friendship?"

Her brow furrowed as she tried to decide what to say. "*I* would have said we were the best of friends."

"And she wouldn't?"

Miss Reeve shrugged. "I suppose I don't know what she would say about much of anything anymore."

"Just because she fell in love with a Whig?"

Her eyes flashed. Politics seemed to be the one thing that really made her angry. He'd seen this in other small towns: rival parties like street gangs, fighting tooth and nail over an inch of territory and demanding absolute loyalty. He didn't understand why wanting to belong always had to go hand-in-hand with other people not belonging, and hating them for it.

"She abandoned her friends in the middle of an election," Miss Reeve said stiffly. "She was to have been hostess at a whole round of events that week." She hesitated, evidently not wanting to seem petty, but Ash could guess to whom the work had fallen in her absence. "She left us for *Jack Sparks*, who'd like to make out we're all either stupid or evil, who puts ideas in honest folks' heads to make them discontented with their lots, who wants to turn tradition on its head and have committees of his own friends snooping into every corner of this town's life. The things he said about my father…"

Ash privately thought that most politicians were neither stupid nor evil. They were good at serving their own interests, that was all. They ran the country for themselves and their friends and made sure it stayed that way. He didn't voice this opinion. To Miss Reeve, it was a question of loyalty. He could go along.

When they reached the door of the printing office, Miss Reeve hesitated.

"We don't have to go in if you don't like," Ash said.

She dismissed this with an abortive motion of her hand. "It isn't that. It's only—ordinarily I would have to ask if she's receiving visitors, and send in your card to make sure she wished to be introduced to you."

"She doesn't have a butler anymore."

"I know that. It seems rude, that's all." But she gestured at him to open the door, and preceded him into the shop. It amused Ash, how it confounded the gentry not to know which of their mazelike sets of manners to apply to somebody.

Jack Sparks's shop was a tidy little place, or as tidy as a printing office could be. The shelves were full of the odds and ends that seemed to accumulate in printing offices everywhere in the calm certainty that advertising was free—everything from patent medicines to mathematical instruments, and an inexplicable crate of lemons with a beautifully lettered sign reading *1/2d ea.* Then there were the racks of books and pamphlets, magazines and forms and prints.

Ash knew a moment's regret that he was too respectable today to ask to see the lewd pictures; it always reassured him to see how much of it was the same across England. He'd wager a half-crown this place had the same tired engraving of nuns flogging a priest that he'd seen in dozens of other towns and villages.

Behind the counter were the press, the drying racks, and several long tables, all as close to the windows as possible. The room was crisscrossed by strings from which dangled drying broadsides. A man and a boy worked the press while a thin young woman bundled in shawls sat at one of the tables going over stacks of correspondence.

The woman looked up with a wary expression, and the

man, a barrel-chested, fair-haired fellow, came to stand behind her chair. He glowered at them so fiercely, and crossed his powerful arms so emphatically, that Ash began to consider the possibility this visit would end with a pummeling. According to Miss Reeve, Sparks had recently beaten an earl's son bloody merely for withdrawing his candidacy for Parliament at a politically inopportune time. Once Ash could have easily whipped the printer, but he'd softened up since leaving London, and Ashford W. Cahill didn't fight dirty.

Miss Reeve edged a protective shoulder in front of him. He should have expected it—she was a woman who took care of everybody—but he hadn't, somehow. It made him feel a little raw.

The young woman laughed. "Heel, Jack. How do you do, Lydia?"

"Very well, Caro, thank you. And you?"

"Splendid, thanks," said Mrs. Sparks with a touch of defiance. "I believe you know my husband?"

Miss Reeve gave a strained smile. "Mr. Sparks."

He gave an even more strained nod. "An honor, Miss Reeve."

Miss Reeve, evidently deciding that violence was not in the immediate offing, moved to the side. "Mrs. Sparks, I hope you will allow me to introduce Mr. Cahill? I have—I have recently agreed to marry him."

Mrs. Sparks gaped delightedly. "Mr. Cahill, it is a pleasure," she said with aplomb. "Pray excuse my not being able to rise to greet you. Do sit down, both of you."

Miss Reeve seemed startled by this sudden warmth, but Ash had long remarked that most people were charmed by the merest hint of a betrothal. He felt it himself; it made the world seem a handsome place after all, where two people could find each other.

"Please don't apologize. It's an honor to meet you." Ash found the hinge in the counter and lifted the flap so Miss Reeve could pass into the back of the shop.

She had warned him in the carriage that Mrs. Sparks used a wheelchair, and that he was on no account to stare or ask prying questions. He couldn't help glancing over her chair when they got closer, though. It was a good one, with great big wheels that would have graced a farm cart. Ash suppressed a pang of bitterness at the memory of his childhood friend Mo, who'd pulled himself about on a board with four filthy, tiny wheels that would barely go over the uneven London pavement. Mo wouldn't have wanted a chair that needed someone else to push it, anyway.

Mr. Sparks put his hand on a chair as if to pull it out for himself and looked questioningly at his wife.

"You don't mind if Jack works, do you?" she asked. "He has several jobs to finish before dark." The printer was moving away even before Miss Reeve's gracious "Of course."

"But before I wish you joy"—Mrs. Sparks looked at Miss Reeve apprehensively—"I must offer you again my deepest sympathies for your grief."

Miss Reeve's unconcerned smile was as good as a slap in the face. If you liked someone who offered you condolences, you showed them a little bit of your sadness. "Thank you. I was very glad to get your letter."

There wasn't a trace of emphasis on *letter*, but Mrs. Sparks flushed. "I wanted to come. I—Lydia, I wanted to. I'm sorry."

Miss Reeve hadn't mentioned that. She hadn't wanted to admit she was angry on her own behalf.

Mrs. Sparks had presumably had her reasons, but in a fight between friends, a third party picked sides based on loyalties, not facts. Ash was on Miss Reeve's side. He laid a hand over the fist she'd clenched in her lap where Mrs. Sparks couldn't see.

She glanced at him and straightened her shoulders. "Is that all you're sorry for?" she asked, completely surprising him.

Mrs. Sparks looked surprised too. "If you mean you had to take over hostess duties for me, ask my father for an apology," she said after a moment. "I wouldn't have had to run away, if he hadn't shut me up in the house."

Ash thought that was pretty convincing, but Miss Reeve didn't say anything.

Mrs. Sparks tilted up her pointy chin. "I'm not going to apologize for loving Jack."

"Caro," Miss Reeve said with faint incredulity, "I once saw him and his sister-in-law spit on the sidewalk outside your house."

The printer, across the room, flushed beet red, but Mrs. Sparks laughed. "You take things too seriously, Lydia."

Now there was a sentence that never got a good reaction. Miss Reeve's face set. "Perhaps you take them too lightly."

Mrs. Sparks's mouth twisted. "You *would* say that. I worked like a dog for the Pink-and-Whites, and it was never enough for you."

Miss Reeve frowned. "What do you mean? I think you've been a skilled hostess and a very effective campaigner. If I ever said anything to make you think differently—"

Mrs. Sparks snorted. "Yes, a hostess and a campaigner, that's all I was to you. You were my closest friend in this town, Lydia, and you never confided in me about a thing! You never thought I was good enough to *really* be your friend, did you?

Not genteel enough, not serious enough, not a devout enough Tory, I don't know. I tried so hard, but you saved it all for those letters you were always writing. You obviously don't want to be here. Did my father ask you to come?"

She threw up her hands. "I suppose the other Pink-and-White hen-hearts can't be far behind now that you've deigned to give them permission. Wonderful, I've been missing those afternoon-long conversations about the vicar's health and the weather! Can you blame me for wanting someone to see me as something more than a magic purse that is always full of dinner parties no matter how many it gives?"

Ash wished he could blame Mrs. Sparks for the look on Lydia's face. He wished he could be angry with her. But it wasn't anyone's fault.

There was only one thing she was wrong about. *You never thought I was good enough to really be your friend.* Ash was sure Miss Reeve had thought they were friends.

If he didn't seem offended on her behalf it would be suspicious. "Miss Reeve? Would you like to go?" He pushed his chair back.

She shook her head. "I'm sorry you felt that way," she said slowly. "I am—I have—there was nothing in those letters that you didn't know. My friendship might not have been to your taste, but it was sincere."

Conflicting emotions chased each other across Mrs. Sparks's narrow face. "*Did* my father ask you to come here today?"

Miss Reeve met her eyes. "Mr. Gilchrist did."

Mrs. Sparks's laugh was half a moan. "Mr. *Gilchrist*? That lascivious little weasel had more weight with you than I did?"

"He made some good arguments." The words could have meant anything but Miss Reeve made them sound like, *He made me see what an ass I was being,* or maybe even, *I wanted to see you.*

"Besides," she said, and then she smiled a real, happy smile, and dropped her eyes to the table, "I suppose—even if there were some reason Mr. Cahill was a bad match for me, someone my family and friends could not approve—I think I should find it impossible to give him up."

Out of his welter of contradictory reactions, Ash picked out admiration and dwelled on that, in case Mrs. Sparks glanced at him. Miss Reeve had found stray fibers of truth—that he was beneath her, and that she had chosen to marry him anyway—and spun it into a fine lie that was precisely what her friend wanted to hear.

Mrs. Sparks's face softened entirely, and she beamed. "I never thought I'd hear *you* say that. I'm so happy for you, Lydia! Marriage is wonderful, you'll see."

Lydia beamed self-consciously back.

It amazed Ash how, seeing someone you'd known all your life behave completely against character, the simplest explanation was still *She's in love,* and not *She must be lying.*

"I'm sorry I made a scene," Mrs. Sparks said. "I wanted us to be friends pretty badly. I suppose I took things for slights that weren't."

"Oh, please don't apologize," Miss Reeve said. "It wasn't much of a scene, and it's always better to know the truth, I think."

Mrs. Sparks grinned. "Generous to a fault, as always." That made Ash a little angry. Miss Reeve wasn't a magic purse either. "Mr. Cahill—I hope you know what a lucky man you are."

He looked at Miss Reeve's bashfully bowed profile and the creamy skin on the nape of her neck. "No. I don't think it's possible to wrap the mind around this much luck."

Mrs. Sparks made one of those delighted, cooing sorts of noises that women made at babies and kittens and other things too darling for words.

Miss Reeve's glance at him had a touch of skepticism in it. Was that real or part of the act? Ash had never agreed with Miss Reeve's platitude—it was more *useful* to know the truth, but he loved this thrill of doubt better. It kept things full of possibilities.

"Mr. Cahill has a silver tongue." Ash's chest hurt at the fond sarcasm in her voice. "Don't let him twist you around his finger."

"Oh, I'm sure he'll save his fingers for you." Mrs. Sparks's smile was beatifically innocent.

Miss Reeve rolled her eyes. "That was worthy of Mr. Gilchrist."

Mrs. Sparks snickered.

"That's my cue," Ash said. "I'll leave you ladies to talk, if you don't think Mr. Sparks will mind showing me his press. I've never seen a cast-iron one at close quarters before."

Mrs. Sparks gave the contraption a glance of fond pride, clearly already looking on it as her own. "Jack loves that press. He'll be happy to show it off."

So Ash learned all about the workings of a Stanhope press and was even allowed to pull the lever and see how easy it went compared to a wooden one, while Miss Reeve and Mrs. Sparks sat with their heads bent together whispering happily. When Miss Reeve finally rose, his reluctance at being pried from the machine was quite genuine.

"How are you?" he asked quietly when they were once more on the street.

"I think it went well, don't you? Caro agreed to take Sparks's apprentice from the workhouse, and wait until we're married for the fee."

"Oh, yes, I think they were thoroughly convinced." He tried to decide if she would like him more if he let it go tactfully, or if he tactfully pressed the point. "You shouldn't take what she said to heart. Different folk look at friendship differently."

She sighed. "I knew she thought I was dull and stiff-rumped. But I didn't mind her shortcomings. I thought she forgave mine."

"You're like me." It was a thing he said often. People liked to hear it, and he liked to say it. It shouldn't feel significant now.

He'd always had Rafe before, he realized. To remind him what was real, to keep the pane of glass between Ash and everyone who wasn't his brother. They didn't know it was there, but he did. He needed it.

He didn't like how important she felt to him. He didn't like the idea that maybe he'd fasten on to the first thing he saw, like a barnacle. Rafe wasn't just convenience. He wasn't replaceable.

"Like you in what way?" She was looking at him with concern.

He thought about how much he liked the little furrow in her brow, and that smoothed out his face. "I'm a friendly man. I like most people. If I choose to spend enough time with someone, I'll feel an affection for him, consider him my friend. So my loyalty—it's to my brother first, always. Then it goes by seniority, and my best judgment. Rafe, though, he's choosy—he dislikes plenty of people. So he judges friendship by something else, some kind of intimacy, a feeling inside himself. He wants to fit with someone like a dovetail joint."

He interlocked his fingers to show her and tried not to think about the gaps inside him now Rafe was gone, like torn gums where teeth had been pulled. He remembered teaching Rafe to clean his teeth, so he'd never have to go to the dentist. He remembered having his own gold crown put in, so Rafe would have something to fall back on if he died.

She didn't say anything, only glanced up at him and knew about Rafe. Knew about everything. Her hand tightened on his arm, and he remembered her kissing his fingers, suddenly.

"People who look at things that way think they have a right to you," he said, surprised at his own intensity. "Your friend wants the two of you to treat each other's minds the way I treated your desk drawers this morning. You don't owe anybody that."

Chapter 13

A sh couldn't see Miss Reeve's face past the brim of her hat. "I knew she wanted me to tell her things," she said at last, a little sadly. "Women always do. She wanted to hear about who I thought was handsome, my quarrels with my father, that I found political philosophy as dull as she did on occasion. I had no real reason to think she'd repeat any of it. But I couldn't bring myself to risk it."

"Most people repeat things."

"Most people don't have the discretion God gave a chattering magpie." She gave him an assessing look. "You talk about things—personal things—all the time. How—how do you do that? Is it because you have no reputation in a community to protect?"

"It helps, knowing I can disappear if things go south," he said slowly. "But I had a reputation to protect when I was a kid. That's how it started out. I had Rafe. I needed everyone to like me, so they'd let me keep him. So they'd help me out when I needed it. I needed every advantage I could get, and confidence and courage are everything in a gang. I learned sleight of hand, the way a sharper shakes his sleeve to show he's got no cards hidden in it. Show enough to make it look like you've shown everything, and people will think the fear and sadness you're hiding don't exist. That's a common enough trick for little boys. Gentlemen probably learn it too, if what I hear about those public schools of yours is even half true."

Something on her face made him think she knew it was all true. Poor Jamie.

"The other part—do you want me to tell you the other part? As far as I can see, respectable married people like to pretend they've never even had eyes for anyone else."

She froze for a minute, then laughed, a tense little laugh. "I ought to pretend to be insulted, that you'd speak of such things to me."

"I don't want to insult you," he said quietly. He wasn't ashamed of his past, but if she didn't want to look at it, that was all right.

"Tell me," she said, finally.

"It's not uncommon for boys like me to keep mistresses."

She turned to stare at him. "But—how old were you?"

"Ten. I was ten when I kept my first girl."

It had been ordinary. When he stopped being somewhere it was ordinary, he stopped telling people. He didn't like this feeling. He didn't like the horror on her face. He didn't like wondering if something terrible had happened to him and he was too much of a flat to realize it.

He tried to imagine how she'd look if she knew that when he was older, he'd done a little streetwalking. Only a week or two a year, when they got too deep in debt. He tried to imagine telling her that the worst thing he could say about it was that he liked stealing better. She'd never understand.

"Everyone did it," he said. "And I needed someone to watch Rafe when I was working. I needed someone who liked me enough she'd look after Rafe even if I went to jail. So I got them to love me. I confided in them. I put false bottoms on the drawers in my mind and let them think they had the run of me. It worked out well for me, but there's no reason you should do it, just so as not to hurt Mrs. Sparks's feelings."

There was a long pause. Then she said, "Did you love them?"

He didn't know if she wanted him to say yes, so she could pretend he was an upstanding man, or no, so she wouldn't have to be jealous. He thought about Speranza, who had wanted him to read her anything he could get his hands on, Ruchl who loved oranges, Dvoire who always pushed his head between her legs, redheaded Faige who could talk for hours about what a shithole Poland was.

"Of course," he said honestly. "How could I not love someone I knew that well? People are beautiful, most all of them. I don't know why some folks can't see it."

She chewed that over. "Did you ever go to jail?"

His pulse raced at the memory. "Only twice. For a little bit each time. It scared Rafe something awful, though."

Lydia had never thought much of the mania for visiting prisons. It was a prime example of Whiggish sentimentality, feeling virtuous for gawking uselessly at another's misfortune. In her opinion, the money the Opposition wished to use to make prisons more hospitable would be better spent on schools in the districts that mainly fed them.

But a friend had dragged her to Newgate once. She remembered the stench and the clamor, and the horror of—dear God. She swallowed. The horror of seeing children in among the hardened criminals.

Oh, they're every bit as hardened as the men, her friend had said. *No, don't give them money, Lydia, it will only be taken from them, or they'll spend it on gin.*

Mr. Cahill must have been terrified. But he'd told her not to pity him. He'd said that his *brother* was scared.

So she thought of his brother, a small child left alone in a brutal, violent world. Jamie had disliked it quite enough when Lydia went away to visit family. "It's frightening for children, when constants in their lives are no longer constant," she said, and her voice barely shook.

He nodded. "Have you heard anything of Mary and Joanna?"

She shook her head. "We can visit Mary this afternoon. It's too early to go and see Joanna. They always cry the first few days they're with the nurse, and it doesn't mean much about how she'll do when she's settled." When she had first started working with the parish, she had had to learn that lesson many times over before she could stop herself from going.

"When Jamie first went to Eton…" she began.

It had been on her mind since he said *public school*, and now it wouldn't stay inside. "Well, all little boys of his rank go to school. If he hadn't gone, he'd be left out of everything now. All his friends are boys he met at school."

She turned her head, not liking that she couldn't see him around the brim of her bonnet as they walked. He was listening, open to whatever she might say. She had never had anyone to talk to, before, who didn't have a stake in the value of public schools.

"He was eight, and he didn't want to go. He cried and cried. Papa said that was why he *had* to go, he couldn't grow up tied to his sister's apron strings. And then—he wrote to me three times a day, begging me to let him come home. He wrote that the other boys were cruel to him, that—terrible things. Papa said it was nothing to worry about, that it was difficult at first but in a few years, Jamie would barely remember it. Papa said he couldn't come home."

She felt squirmingly disloyal—when Lord Wheatcroft was not even alive to defend himself. "But I didn't want to tell Jamie I wanted to bring him home and Papa refused, it seemed—oh, disobedient, or maybe I was only embarrassed that I had so little influence with Papa, or I wanted—I wanted to seem like a grown-up, as if Papa and I were really his parents together, speaking with one voice. Maybe I *was* being a sentimental woman for wanting to give in, I don't know. I wrote back and told Jamie he must be brave and strong…and his letters did begin to sound more cheerful after the first term. He did well, he made friends…I don't know if he even remembers those letters."

She didn't know what she wanted Mr. Cahill to say. *That's life, and it isn't a tragedy?*

Or perhaps she wanted someone to admit that it *was* a tragedy, that ordinary life—the things everyone told you were just how it was supposed to be—that it was all right to feel this overwhelming sadness about them.

He didn't say anything for a long time. "We did our best. But maybe we could have done better."

That was what she'd wanted, after all: *we.*

Oh God, if she kept on like this, she'd be crying about her father within five minutes. She turned her head towards Mr. Cahill again. He looked about as cheerful as she felt, and even more than she wanted to feel better herself she wanted to make him feel better.

He was beautiful when he was sad, though. When he wasn't smiling, she could see how full and lovely his lips were, and his brown eyes looked larger. The brim of his hat was unfashionably wide and the crown too short, but she liked that—it made him look like a country man. She would never guess he was a Londoner from looking at him.

She would never guess anything about him from looking. He was like an unremarkable brown-paper-wrapped parcel she'd been waiting for anxiously—holding it in her hands was all the more exciting because no one else knew what was inside.

He tugged her to the left, and she realized she'd almost walked straight into a hole in the sidewalk that had been there for a good five years. He gave her a sidelong crinkle-eyed smile; he couldn't help but know she was staring at him.

They were coming to the Market Cross, with its long line of irate cart drivers going in single file around the wide stone canopy. A drop of rain fell, and another.

"We'd better take cover," she said, and pulled him between two stopped carts into the shelter of the old timbered roof. At dinnertime the cross would be full of people with pies and sandwiches, but right now they were alone.

"Jamie used to love this place when he was an infant," she said. "He'd hide behind the columns. He'd giggle all the time he was hiding, and then be surprised when I found him."

"Mmm." Mr. Cahill maneuvered her so her calves pressed against one of the stone seats that ringed the canopy's pillars. He leaned in to kiss her.

"You know that pillar only blocks us from view from one angle."

"I do know," he murmured. "All to the better." He didn't

really kiss her, not the way he had earlier. It was a quick soft press of closed mouths, for the benefit of anyone who might be watching.

And knowing that people *were* watching, that she and Mr. Cahill were performing together, gave a weight and electric charge to everything she did—when she tilted her head up to meet him, arched her back slightly, made a small humming sound. A clean burst of happiness swept everything else aside. When he pulled back, she smiled, *tsk*ed, and hit him on the arm with her muff, saying to anyone looking on, *I'm a good girl, but I'm not angry.*

He leaned in one more time, and oh God, the brief brush of his lips, she wanted his hands too, his body, all of him. He was already pulling back when she pushed him gently away with a breathy laugh and a not-very-indignant, "Mr. Cahill!"

"Yes?" he said innocently, looking as electrified as she felt.

She held that moment close through the long afternoon. Visiting was, for now, another reminder of grief: she would never relay the news she got to her father.

But its rewards remained, and to the satisfaction of efficiency, usefulness, and community was added the *frisson* of doing it all while firmly yet indulgently preventing Mr. Cahill from removing her gloves, playing with her hair, whispering in her ear, stealing her pencil or notebook, or otherwise demonstrating his admiration for her person and desire for her attention.

Of course it was all a show, but he was clearly enjoying the game, and she could feel the smug happiness on her own face as she smiled apologetically at person after person and confessed, *Mr. Summers will read the banns tomorrow.*

Mr. Cahill paid attention, too. Once, while Lydia listened patiently to a list of sick Mrs. Goacher's symptoms and promised to ask the grocer to extend her credit, he chimed in with, "Which grocer is that?...How much can you afford to pay him down?...Even sixpence will sweeten him...I'll be back in a bit, ladies."

Twenty minutes later, he was back with the news that the grocer had extended Mrs. Goacher's credit for another month.

By the end of the afternoon he had wheedled three grocers, two butchers, a tallow-chandler, and a baker. She tried not to beam with pride at the beneficiaries of his efforts—and then she remembered that she was supposed to be madly in love, and beamed away.

They visited Miss Tice, the milliner. Mary Luff was wan and fidgety and asked anxiously after her sister, but Miss Tice had nothing but praise for her progress.

"Thank you," Lydia said at the end of the day.

He shrugged. "I'm a master at sweet-talking tradesmen."

So was she. It was exceptionally lovely nevertheless, having something done for her that she could have done herself.

But then, she was paying him three thousand pounds to be the perfect husband for six months, so it was really no different than if Mr. Gilchrist had helped her.

She invited him for dinner and they stopped at the Drunk St. Leonard so he could change his clothes. To her astonishment, in under twenty minutes he was back in the carriage in breeches, pumps, a gray waistcoat, and a dark coat, his fresh cravat in a knot whose plain serviceability would have embarrassed Jamie and his friends.

"That was fast."

"Really?" His eyes glinted with curiosity. "Was it too fast? How long do men of your set usually take?"

"Well, I—I don't know for sure," she said with the peculiar uncertainty that came from being asked to quantify something one had never given a moment's thought to. "Father generally took half an hour. Jamie…Jamie always goes up to his room forty-five minutes before the dinner bell, and then we wait fifteen minutes for him. The cooks have started planning dinner accordingly, when he's at home."

"What do they *do* with all that time?" Mr. Cahill asked, fascinated. "Take one set off, shave, put another set on, and off you go. Or do they just have so many clothes it takes that long to choose?"

She rolled her eyes. "Oh, you know how young men are. Jamie can spend half an hour in front of the mirror worrying over his hair." It was incomprehensible, when he was such a handsome boy.

"Rafe is vain of his hair too. He…" He trailed off.

Lydia's heart lurched in sympathy—but she was suddenly distracted by something he had said. "You shaved?"

Now she could see that the stubble whose progress she had watched throughout the day was gone. She wanted to touch his clean, smooth skin. She wanted it very badly.

He grinned and tilted his head from side to side, exposing the smooth underside of his chin and a sliver of throat above collar and cravat. Oh, why not?

"May I?" She tugged at the fingers of her glove to loosen it.

He frowned in puzzlement at her hand. Then his generous mouth curled up at one corner, slyly. "I promise it's an even shave, but you can check if you don't believe me."

She raised a brow severely. "We'll see about that." She ran
her hand firmly down one cheek, over his mouth and up the
other, sweeping her thumb under his chin. "Hmm. I'll need to
take a closer look."

She slid forward in her seat and tilted his chin up, leaning
in to press a kiss to his jaw. She slid her mouth along it. Her
lips, more sensitive than her fingertips, could feel the texture
of his skin, a patch by his ear where he hadn't shaved as closely.
He smelled like Eau de Cologne and soap.

She felt him swallow. "You can shave me yourself one of
these days if you like."

She was plunged headlong into desperate lust. "Really? I—
but what if I cut you?"

"Then I'll have to go about with sticking plaster on my
face, and people will think me clumsy. I imagine the experience would be worth it, don't you?"

She turned his face towards her and kissed him, abruptly
overwhelmed with gratitude. He held very still and let her; it
reminded her of that first kiss, and this morning when she'd
leaned her head on his shoulder. When she pulled back, he
drew in a breath with a small, protesting sound, but he didn't
move.

"Sometimes you go still," she said. "When I touch you, or
when I ask you something." She didn't know how to phrase
her question. *Does it mean you want me to stop? Does it mean
you're afraid I'll stop?*

He did it again, watched her for a moment perfectly still,
like a hare that sees the hunter. She half expected him to
bound out of the carriage, but instead he leaned back against
the squabs, relaxed and confident, and laughed. "It means I
haven't bedded anyone above twice or thrice in the last thirteen

years, and I'm nervous. I don't want to look green." He didn't look nervous, or green.

She remembered that that didn't mean anything with him, but her moment of skepticism had lasted long enough for her to realize that didn't explain when he did it in conversation. "Did you just lie to me?"

He gave her a rueful smile. "It's God's own truth. One of the hazards of pretending to be a Gentile—there's one part of me that can't pass muster."

He'd already told her he lied with the truth. If the truth was distracting, as this one was, she was sure that was all to the good.

Well, if he didn't want to talk about it, she didn't need to know, so long as she knew one thing. "Does it mean you want me to stop? We agreed that refusal would not affect our agreement. You don't have to win me over." She thought of those girls he'd lived with in London, how he'd made them love him.

She'd worked at being easy to love too. She'd made her father love her, and her brother—or at least it had felt that way. She'd made this town like her. It seemed sad, somehow; she wondered whether other people were loved naturally, without trying, even when they were difficult and useless. Whether she could have been, too.

"Sweetheart, if we were going at my pace I'd have my tongue between your legs right now."

She could feel her eyes turn to saucers. His tongue? Between her *legs*? Did people do that?

He ran his tongue along his top lip, filthily.

So—he didn't want to talk about it, and he was annoyed that she'd asked. She felt a brief flare of anger herself, tempted to lift her skirts and say, *Well, have at it then.*

The flare wasn't just anger. His tongue—she imagined it— only she couldn't imagine it. She didn't have the slightest idea what it would feel like, only knew she wanted it. Even the jolt of her secret places against the carriage seat when they went over a hole in the road made her ache.

She was tired of this. She was tired of aching, of hot frustration, of desperate desire. She wanted to be *satisfied*.

She wished she could turn the tables, leave *him* aching and unsatisfied. She wanted to say coolly, *May I?*, calmly unbutton his trousers, and pull out his—his male part? She was dissatisfied with the word too, but still shrank from using coarser ones. Never mind. She imagined toying with it until he made desperate sounds—and then the carriage would pull up in front of her house and they would have to stop. That would serve him right.

She wanted to do it, and she probably could, but she refused to turn the attraction between them into a weapon, the way he had done. It was petty, and not a precedent she liked to set. So she gave him one more kiss, to show she wasn't punishing him, and leaned back against her seat.

Chapter 14

"I'm sorry," Mr. Cahill said after a moment. "I shouldn't have spoken so crudely."

"You can speak as crudely as you like, if you do it because you want to and not because you're annoyed with me."

He gave a surprised laugh. "That's fair." They watched each other for a minute or two, and then he said, "I did mean it, though."

Lydia's intimate muscles contracted instinctively. "Have you…have you done that often?"

He grinned. "Not recently, but yes. I can't wait to see if you smell as flowery down there as you do everywhere else."

She bit her lip. "Probably not."

"Good." He made the word a suggestion all its own. "Not that I don't love how flowery you smell. It's a little strange, but I like strange. Lavender for your clothes, roses for your lips, orange blossom for your skin, jasmine for your hair. I learned those smells stealing perfume bottles, as a boy."

She'd learned those smells in the garden and the hothouse, and in the housekeeper's room making sachets for wardrobes and drawers. She tried to imagine not seeing flowers every day. "We have a rose garden. Some of them should be blooming by the time your six months are up."

She wished immediately she hadn't mentioned that he was

leaving, even if it was true, and foolish to want for a moment to forget it. But she was glad she wouldn't have to let him go until summertime, when it would be warm and sunny and she would miss her father a little less. Jamie would be home in the summer.

"Of course you do. Do you have a greenhouse with orange trees too?"

"Yes."

His eyes took on a faraway look. "Won't you miss all that, when you move to the Dower House?"

"I imagine most people miss their home when they leave it. But as for oranges and lemons, Jamie will let our cook take what she needs."

He smiled. "Our cook. I've never had a cook before."

She smiled back, thinking how much fun it would be to play the role of besotted bride, eager to make the perfect home for her new husband. "You must tell me all your favorite foods."

He hesitated. "Duck," he said finally. "Roast chicken, pheasant...er. Fowls generally, as you see. Anything with cooked fruit or raisins. Potatoes and cabbage. Tipsy cake. I don't like rosemary."

"You don't?"

"It's a very English herb. I never had it growing up. I thought it sounded lovely in the song, but when I had it—well, it was a nasty surprise. I don't like too much cinnamon, either, which I did have growing up."

"Do you like mutton?"

"It's all right."

She smiled. "Father loved it. I put it on the menu three times a week, and I hate the stuff. I even hate the way it smells."

"Did you ever tell him that?" He sounded like he already

knew the answer, though.

She shook her head, and he smiled at her, a crooked smile that said *I know you* and *We're the same*, and for a moment she imagined what it would be like to leave everything, to walk off with him in the clothes on her back and go across England lying and stealing.

She'd imagined it before, she realized, that first day in the portrait gallery before she even knew lying and stealing would be involved. It was a lovely, impractical daydream, like giving Lady Tassell a real piece of her mind.

Why had she never felt this way about a man of her own class? Did she only like him because he was dangerous? Or was it as he said, and she knew so little about him that she was making up a story that would inevitably please her?

Was there something common in her blood? She'd assumed other ladies hid the same urges she did, that they were all playing the game, but maybe…maybe there was something wrong with her, and when she was old she'd be one of those dreadful dowagers who slavered over the grooms and the village blacksmith.

"Do you only desire me because I'm rich?" she asked, and knew herself for a coward. "No, I'm sorry. Don't answer that, please."

He sucked part of his lower lip into his mouth, considering his answer. "It's hard, isn't it? The human heart is like a big mess of embroidery silks, and the more you pull, the more they tangle. The thing is, the threads have only got one end, if that. You can't sort them all out into colors. You just have to pick the ones you want and hold on to them as best you can. I'd have desired you if you were poor. But I wouldn't have acted on it, because I wouldn't have had anything to gain." He watched her, to see if she'd be angry or hurt.

She didn't know how she felt. "Have you—have you made up to a lot of rich women before?"

"Some."

Which could mean anything. He looked rueful, probably because he knew it would appeal to her. Well, he didn't owe her the truth. Did she even want it? She wanted her money, and she wanted a little fun. She had no right to ask for more, when she had nothing more to give him. She'd told him that one little thing about Jamie, for everything he'd told her.

"There is a thrill to it," he said. "Like holding antique porcelain in someone else's house, that I could never afford to own. But I'm sorry if I made you feel like a China dish. I'll try not to."

It thrilled her too, that he was forbidden. So long as she didn't make him feel like a slavered-over groom, perhaps that was all right—and if it was something wrong in her, something twisted, then it was wrong in him too. "Do you know the proverb, 'Stolen waters are sweet, and bread eaten in secret is pleasant'?"

He nodded. "But isn't that said by a woman who knoweth nothing to a man who wanteth understanding?"

"Yes," she admitted. "But it always—it always felt true to me."

"That's because it is."

If he wanted a China-dish thrill, she could give him one. She spent the rest of the ride telling him about the time her grandfather was treating the voters and ran out of port, so he opened up a cask of his best claret—and the voters went over to the Tassells in retribution for his being so cheeseparing as to fob them off with sour port.

He was still laughing when the carriage pulled up in front of the house.

Lydia looked at her watch. Still an hour and a half to dinner. "If you'll excuse me," she said, ignoring a qualm at sending him to wait alone in a room full of expensive knickknacks, some of which could fit into his pocket, and went upstairs.

Dot Wrenn, her maid, was waiting for her, quiet and watchful.

Lydia wanted to ask Wrenn to make her look pretty and rich. But in the end she was too self-conscious. "I'm sorry, Wrenn. I would have told you last night that I was getting married, only I hadn't told my aunt yet, and I should have told you this morning, only I wanted to consult with Mr. Cahill about something first."

It was a lie. She had put it off because she had known this would be a tricky conversation. Wrenn was lazy in a very particular way that meant she prized efficiency above all else. She was very, very good at her job, because she liked things to be done properly and because it allowed her the greatest possible time and indulgence for herself. Lydia wanted her for a housekeeper, but the additional responsibility would be a stumbling block.

Wrenn smiled, still watchful. "I wish you joy, madam."

"Thank you. I'm afraid our income will not support a lady's maid in my new household." She let that sink in while Wrenn unbuttoned her walking dress and helped her out of it—long enough for Wrenn to think about all the work involved in finding a new position, but not long enough for it to seem deliberate. "I would be honored if you'd consent to be my housekeeper. I know the Dower House will be a much smaller establishment, with less scope for your talents. If you'd rather look for a new position as a lady's maid, of course I'll give you an excellent character. It has meant so much to me to be able to rely on you all these years."

"Thank you, madam." Wrenn helped her into her evening gown. Lydia couldn't get a good view of her face in the mirror. "It's very good of you to ask me."

"Naturally you must think it over. But I do need to know soon. The housekeeper will engage the rest of the staff, and it really wouldn't be fair to give Mrs. Jenner less than a fortnight's notice of whom she is to lose, particularly in the kitchen."

Wrenn's hands stilled in the act of pulling pins out of Lydia's hair. "You'd want me to choose the other servants, madam?"

This was the great lure Lydia had been counting on. "I know everyone who works at Wheatcroft. I wouldn't object to any of them, and you know better than I do who'd be suited to such a situation. We'll need a cook, of course, and four or five others."

Wrenn took her time combing out the morning's rolls and twists. "Perhaps we might do something special with your hair, madam? For your gentleman?" She pulled out the velvet box containing Lydia's gold combs.

Wrenn wanted to butter her up, then. Was that a good sign? "Please do. No new curls, though. I don't want to keep him waiting too long."

Wrenn slept in Lydia's dressing room, and she had been sneaking out nearly every night for the last six months. Lydia did not *know*, but was morally certain, that she had made a match of it with her bosom friend Abigail Gower, the second undercook. The prospect of presiding over a small, hand-picked household with Gower might be tempting enough to offset the added work, but if Lydia hinted too broadly, it would make Wrenn nervous. So she waited, and watched her hair rise slowly but surely into a masterpiece. Mr. Cahill would like it.

"I think Jeanie and Jenny would like a smaller establishment," Wrenn said at last.

Lydia grinned at her. "You don't think having housemaids named Jeanie and Jenny will be too confusing?"

"We're clever women," Wrenn said dryly, her amused eyes meeting Lydia's in the mirror. "We can rise to the challenge."

They discussed grooms and gardeners for a minute or two, and then Wrenn said, as if it was an afterthought, "For the kitchen, what do you think of Abby Gower? You've complimented her pastry, I believe, madam."

Lydia pretended to consider. "She's only the second undercook. Would Polly Turvill think it a slight not to be asked first?"

"Turvill wouldn't work anywhere smaller than here. If she has five minutes to stand still, she's unhappy." Her tone said this was a mystery to her.

"In that case, anyone who can turn a pastry like that is welcome in my establishment. Does all this mean you'll come?"

Wrenn hesitated.

"I'll raise your salary ten pounds per annum."

Wrenn chewed her lower lip, then smiled. "Fifteen."

"Done. If Cook can spare her, perhaps you and Abby might go to the Dower House a week early, to put it all to rights." She turned her head from side to side, examining the careless tumble of combs and pearls and thick shining loops and pretending not to notice Wrenn's weighing glance.

Perhaps she should just say, *I know, and I'm happy for you.* She didn't know how to do that, though. She knew tactful silence, and how to disguise generosity as no trouble at all. "It looks splendid, Wrenn, thank you. Will you still condescend

to help with my hair when you're my housekeeper?"

"Of course, madam. It's a pleasure to dress you. I hope I don't seem ungrateful. I couldn't ask for a better mistress."

Their eyes met in the mirror, and Lydia thought that whatever of politic falsehood there was in this moment, there was some truth too. She worked hard to be a good mistress. Why shouldn't she accept a deserved compliment? She thanked Wrenn, and after a few emotion-choked moments, added a casual afterthought of her own.

"Fetch my cloak, would you, Wrenn? Mr. Cahill wants to see the greenhouse, and I think we have time before dinner."

Left to himself, Ash would have sat by the fire until dinner, but he had no objection to a tour of the greenhouse instead. Mentally saying farewell to the shilling he would have to pay the inn's boy to clean his flimsy evening pumps—he supposed gentlemen wore them a-purpose to show off that they could afford to be driven about—he followed Miss Reeve and her clinking pattens out the door and down a gravel path.

The greenhouse was a long, tall, narrow building of the same stone as the house, with tall, arched sash-windows and even taller arched double doors that nearly brushed the roof. Miss Reeve passed them by, unlocking a small door in the sidewall. "Quickly. We mustn't let in the cold air." She shut the door behind them and slipped her pattens off.

In the dim light, the smell hit Ash first: earth and green things. But not green like the English forest—this was an exotic greenness, rich and delicate and foreign. The lantern's light glinted strangely off the glossy orange trees that marched up and down the stone floor in wooden tubs, flashes of green and gold where fruit of various ripeness hung together.

Around the edges of the room, small-leaved shrubs and delicate vines grew out of pots and up the whitewashed wall, and there—Ash stared. A short line of shiny trees were in flower. Flowering in December!

He went to look more closely. The flowers were white, round, many-petaled, and peculiarly regular in shape. They looked phosphorescent in the darkness. He put his nose to one—a very faint, slightly sharp smell, like honeysuckle without the honey.

"Those are our camellias," said Miss Reeve with proprietary pride. Really, there was nothing money couldn't buy. Ash turned to thank her, to apologize for having wanted to stay by the fire, and realized she hadn't brought him here to show him the greenhouse at all. She watched him with banked hunger, biding her time.

For a brief moment he resisted, wanting to explore, and then he thought about kissing her in the warm, fragrant darkness, surrounded by orange trees, and it was the most luxurious thought he'd ever had. It was exactly how he'd imagined a nobleman's life, as a lust-addled adolescent.

Then he remembered Rafe. The dead moths in his ribcage fluttered and twitched. He had meant this life for Rafe.

Or had he planned to take it all along?

He couldn't forget how this town and this house had given him itchy fingers. This giddy, glorious emotion properly belonged to Rafe, and Ash had stolen it. Thief that he was, he hadn't been able to help himself.

Where was Rafe? How much money did he have left? Was he warm?

Ash knew his brother was a grown man, who could find work and feed himself. But he'd promised himself Rafe would never want for *anything*, had sworn it over and over. He'd wanted Rafe to have this plenty, this excess of everything—and not on a six-month loan, but forever.

Her beautiful forehead creased. "Are you well?"

Ash knew better than to tell a woman that he'd planned to give her to his brother as a gift. He had her now, and he might as well enjoy her. He let go of the tightness in his face and chest. For a moment he couldn't understand why that didn't feel like enough, and then he remembered to inhale.

"I love your hair," he said. "It looks like a braided loaf." Coming closer to her, he ran a finger along a strand of pearls that danced through the smooth loops, wondering if they were real and how they would feel between his teeth. He was tempted to bury his nose and mouth in her hair and find out. The jasmine scent must come from this greenhouse.

"Thank you," she said. "I think. May I kiss you?"

There it was again, the simple pleasure of being asked for permission. "Yes." With the word, everything in him rushed out to meet her.

She wrapped her gloved fingers firmly around the back of his neck, lifted up on her toes, and gave him an open-mouthed, undemanding kiss that he felt everywhere, as if she'd got hold of all those silken thread-ends poking out of his heart and given them a gentle tug. She herded him firmly until his back hit the wall.

The wall was hot—not like a stovetop, but like a flat rock on a late summer morning, or pan-warmed sheets. "Mmm," he moaned, surprised, and she smiled smugly against his mouth.

He kissed her smile, feeling drugged and lazy, until she stepped away. "May I?"

Might she what? He blinked and saw that her ungloved hand was extended towards the front of his trousers in clear inquiry. He gave her a dazzled smile, unable to believe his luck. "I'd take it as a kindness."

Her mouth curled up. He watched her fingers on his buttons, and then she pushed aside his flannel drawers and pulled out his cock. He felt a moment's self-consciousness. Male equipment never looked more foolish than when peering out of evening dress. Besides, when not called upon to act, his own had always rather resembled him, short and squat and a little rumpled.

But she curled her fingers round it and gave a firm, experimental tug, and his head knocked against the wall. "Unh."

"It's growing," she said, startled.

He laughed. "It does that."

"I thought they just…stiffened."

"It depends on the man. Mine grows."

Frowning at it, she tugged again. He made a strangled sound. She met his eyes and smiled, as if pleasantly reminded that the strange thing in her hand was attached to him. Running her thumb in a circle over the head, she gave another few tugs.

Unable to believe how good it felt, he watched and reveled in the simple luxury of this moment, of not having to do anything to get what he wanted.

"Is this right?" she asked, dubious.

"When I do it myself, I go a bit faster and harder. But I'm in no hurry."

Her mouth curved. "We do need to be back in time for dinner." And she squeezed tighter and sped up.

She liked making him feel good, he thought. She was used to taking care of people. Ash usually said to women like that, *Tonight, let me take care of you.* It was extremely effective.

But this was so nice, and it would tie her to him anyway with the warm glow of successful generosity. So he let heat seep into his bones and made small, contented noises, and it was all so dreamlike that he almost expected to wake up before he spent.

His pleasure peaked all at once. Miss Reeve jumped when seed spurted onto her hand, and he realized he should have warned her. But all he could say was, "Please." The word staggered drunk and laughing off his tongue. This felt unlikely, mythological, a sensation too intense to ever duplicate, like biting into a hot rich pie when you hadn't eaten in days. He trembled and gasped and wanted it never, ever to be over.

When it was, he handed her his handkerchief—not Rafe's, but a plain white one—and slumped to the ground. He felt exhausted, wrung out. He wanted to stretch out on the warm flagstones with her and gaze at the ceiling as if it were the night sky.

When she gave the handkerchief back, Ash wiped himself clean with it and set it aside to dry. "Thank you." Buttoning his trousers, he sat there, feeling heavy and weightless at the same time. "Thank you very much," he added after a minute or two.

She laughed and settled down beside him. "You're welcome."

It was that, her calm patience, which finally prodded him into action. "Did you like that?" he asked her.

She shot him a sidelong glance. "Yes."

A last warm ripple of pleasure spread through him. He tried to wipe the smile off his face and gave it up as a bad job.

Tugging her into his lap, he palmed her breasts. "Feeling all tingly and sensitive?" She squirmed, legs falling open, and he slid a hand down and cupped her there too. "How much time do we have before dinner?"

"Show me your watch," she said breathlessly. He did. "Ten minutes." There was frustration in her voice.

"Don't worry. It won't take me that long."

Chapter 15

Ash's head spun a little when he stood, but he fetched her fur-lined cloak and laid it out on the stone. "Lie down."

She obeyed. He put his hands on her silk-stockinged ankles above gossamer slippers and slid her skirts up the dizzying curves of her legs, resisting the temptation to unhook her brightly embroidered garters.

"I thought no one would see them," she said. "I know I shouldn't be wearing colors, but buying new ones seemed such a waste."

"I like them." He had never thought before about how intimate it was, to know what someone's underthings looked like. They'd be sitting at dinner, respectable as you please, and he'd know these were there. He crooked a finger around the ivory satin before abandoning them for the bare skin above her stockings.

Curving his hands under her thighs, he drew them apart. Her skirts pooled. When she pulled them out of the way, there was her cunt, laid bare to him.

He felt like a virgin, a fumbling boy overwhelmed by the very idea that women had bodies. In the dim light her pale skin and darker hair looked like milk and honey, like the Promised Land. Kneeling, he reverently kissed her inner thighs, the left and then the right.

She lay very still, but she wasn't calm or patient now. He could feel the tension radiating from her. Mostly lust, of course, but he remembered her saying, *It's more like fear that you won't think I'm a lady anymore,* and thought that there must be some of that mixed in.

He hated the idea of fear threaded through this moment. But promising he'd never use this against her would only make her realize he was thinking of all the ways he could.

"Thank you," he said at last, smoothing his thumbs along the creases of her thighs. "I'll treasure this memory forever."

She didn't answer, so he bent his head and licked up her until he found the right spot. When he sucked it gently into his mouth, she drew in a deep, heaving breath, her hips tilting up and her thighs pushing into his hands.

He raised his head to tell her it had been a while, and she could give him instructions if she liked.

"Please do that again," she said in a taut voice.

He obliged her. She tasted incredible and smelled better, nothing like flowers at all. He loved the way she surrounded him, how she moved slow and urgent as planets revolving. Her skin was like nothing else, not satin or silk or cream, just human flesh, hot and wonderful in his hands. He loved the way her curls poked at his nose, loved her short, desperate breaths, loved *her*.

He teased her slit with his finger. She was so wet he slipped in almost without meaning to. She froze, clamping around him.

"Sorry," he said, wiggling his finger. "May I?"

There was a long, hopeful moment. "Yes."

"Good. I want to feel it when you spend."

He could feel her give up whatever control she'd still been

holding on to, her legs thumping to the ground, her head hitting her cloak with a muffled thud—had she been watching him? He could feel her pushing towards him, welcoming him, giving him what he wanted—generous even with her own pleasure. "Please," she said, "I—*please*."

He frigged her slowly and insistently, putting his mouth right where she needed it and working her until she fell apart, her muscles rippling around his finger with the force of a shipwreck.

"Oh," she said. "Oh, thank God. I needed that."

He didn't understand why his stomach started forcing its way up his throat at her words. He didn't understand the sudden piercing stab of loneliness. But there it was, a physical sadness so immense it felt as if a door inside him had opened onto the chilly, airless expanse of space. Maybe he'd used up his store of happiness in one intense burst, and this was all that was left.

"Does my hair look all right?"

He nodded. Her hair looked perfect, as if nothing had happened at all.

Ash wiped his mouth and fingers on the clean half of his soiled handkerchief and put it in his pocket. Standing, he offered her a hand up. Her eyes searched his face, but for once, he couldn't manage to meet them.

"Are *you* all right?" she asked.

This was what he did. He took a deep breath full of oranges and jasmine and rich earth and thought about how he was about to have dinner with her, how he was going to be served good wine and waited on by footmen and—

Just now, the idea of being waited on made him feel cold too. Liveried servants had seemed impossibly well-off to him once, when he'd watched them coming in and out of a fine house he was planning to rob. What right did he have to their deference? What right did anyone have to the deference of another human being? Why did people fight so hard to create distance between themselves, when all anyone wanted was closeness?

For so long, when he wanted to smile, he'd used a memory of his little brother. Rafe had always been a sunny orb of happiness behind his ribs.

Drek. If he wasn't careful, he'd cry.

"I'm fine." It wasn't even a tremor, barely a hum, but his voice gave him away. He could see it in her face. "It's a reaction, that's all. An imbalance of humors. I enjoyed that far too much, and I'm crashing back to earth with a vengeance."

There was silence. He wished he hadn't said anything. He should have brazened it out. He should have managed.

"Very well," she said. "We'll wait before going back to the house. Do you want me to stay, or would you like a moment alone?"

He gulped in a breath, his chest feeling less tight at her simple, matter-of-fact acceptance. "We'll be late for dinner."

Miss Reeve smiled. "I've learned today that nothing is a surer symptom of love than uncharacteristic rudeness."

Her staff would be watching them at dinner. They knew her, and they probably also knew the servants of every other major family in the district. He had to be in high form at dinner. "I'll take a quick turn in the air. Wait for me here. I won't be above five minutes."

He put on his overcoat and stepped outside. Then he stood there—not even like a statue, but like stone before the statue, a shapeless lump of rock without a story…being a rock sounded terribly quiet and soothing…

He shook his head and forced himself to walk, to breathe in the chilly air, to wake up and get his heart pumping again. He pulled out the tangled mass of threads in his chest and looked at it.

It wasn't much of a surprise. He knew why he felt this way. He hadn't liked the way she'd said *I needed that.* He hadn't liked to be reminded that for her this was a physical urge, an itch to be scratched. She hadn't even said *Thank you.* She had said, *Thank God,* as if Ash hadn't been there at all.

He'd known from the start that he'd be in love with her before their time was up. He'd known it would break his heart to leave her. He hadn't thought much of it; his heart had been broken before, and mended.

But something new occurred to him now. If he played his cards right, maybe he could have this to come back to.

Of course he couldn't *stay*—he was a whoreson thief and she was the next best thing to a princess. He was a wanderer and she was planted in this town like an oak tree. The idea of wearing starched collars and being waited on and mouthing respectable Tory sentiments for the rest of his life was preposterous. It tickled and choked like smothering in down.

But there was no reason he couldn't visit her a few times a year, if he confined his swindling to the middling sort of people and avoided the surrounding counties.

Now that he had a goal, he felt better. He didn't think it would be hard to make her fall in love with him. She had a heart wider than the Thames. But she wouldn't change their bargain just because she wanted to. No, he'd have to convince her he was a good decision. That would be a challenge, because he was a terrible decision.

But he thought he could do it. He'd be the perfect husband

for six months. Rafe, genius that he was, had taken the right tack at once when he'd offered to help with her correspondence. Ash would be useful. He'd be unexceptionable. He would make himself popular in the town and adored by the servants. He'd win over her little brother. He'd make sure the Tories came out ahead in their charity auction.

Hope and plans blocked up the doorway to that bleak empty wasteland. Ash's body felt solid again, his clothes snug around him, the air cold on his skin, the ground crunching beneath the soles of his shoes. He went back to the greenhouse suffused with mild embarrassment at having made a cake of himself.

When he opened the door, she was sitting curled up with her cheek against the heated wall. She started to her feet, and he realized she was feeling more uncertain than she'd let on.

"I'm sorry," he said before she could speak. "This should have been special for you, and I spoiled it."

He meant it, but she shook her head so vigorously he felt as if he'd manipulated her into contradicting him. "You don't owe me anything. I don't need you to pretend."

"I pretend. That's what I do." He shouldn't have said that. It wouldn't help. He smiled at her. "It scares me a little, when I find I can't."

She shook her head again. "You don't have to win me over by confiding in me," she said earnestly. "I've been thinking, and—you can tell me whatever you like. You can tell me the truth or you can lie, I don't care—but tell me things because you *want* to. Please." She twisted her gloved hands together, and added, "Unless the truth could have a material impact on our plan, of course."

Ash didn't know what to say to that. He didn't know what

he felt, and he didn't have time to sort it out. He wished he hadn't told her so much about himself.

Only—she'd said she didn't mind if he lied to her. No one had ever said that to him before.

"And you didn't spoil anything," she said. "Even if we don't repeat the experience, I'm very glad to have had it."

Even if—*what*? Ash's composure wavered. "Have you decided you'd rather not repeat it?"

She shook her head, blushing. "I thought maybe—you—"

He gave her his very best smile. "On the contrary."

It was only her relief now that told him she'd been disappointed before. "Oh. Good."

He leaned in to kiss her. "It took me by surprise, that's all." She clutched at the lapels of his coat, and when he pulled back, she actually laid her cheek against his shoulder and leaned on him. He put an arm around her and kissed one of those shining copper loops. "Next time I'll be prepared."

She made an amused sound.

"You're right. That's ludicrous. No one could be prepared for how beautiful you are."

She laughed outright. He squeezed her. She shifted a little, almost squirming, and he was suddenly very conscious of how close she was, of what they had done, of everything they hadn't done yet. It had been all of a quarter of an hour, and he wanted her again. He slid his hand lower to cup her buttocks and pull her hard against him.

She made a sound that was half squeak and half moan and drew away. "We have to go to dinner." She stretched her neck and tried to peer down at her bodice to make sure it was straight. Adjusting it a little, she bit her lip hard as if the shifting of her stays against her breasts felt all too good.

"We *just* did that," she said, exasperated. "How can I already want to do it again? What an ill-regulated appetite."

Ash felt giddy. Maybe he hadn't spoiled it after all. She still wanted him, she was still willing to lean on him. And, she was adorable. "Indeed," he agreed solemnly. "What can the Almighty have been thinking of? Makes him seem rather a Peeping Tom, doesn't it?"

She gave a shocked laugh. "Mr. Cahill! I am sure He was thinking only of the propagation of the race."

Right. There was that. Now probably wasn't the time to bring up children, and how he didn't want them, and anyway he hated the idea of having one he wouldn't be there to raise. He couldn't say that to her, when it was so obvious she would give a child a far better life than he ever could. Only—she'd told Rafe she didn't want children, either, hadn't she?

He winked at her and went to the door. She put on her pattens and out they went, shutting the plants up snug and warm in their house.

"About the propagation of the race," he said. "We—I—"

"I don't want children," she said flatly, and stumbled over the gravel because she was watching for his reaction.

"Neither do I."

She sighed with relief. "Good."

"How do you plan to prevent it?"

"There's a woman in the town who grows pennyroyal. I'll go on Monday."

Good old pennyroyal tea. He thought his mother must have used it, because the sharp, minty smell always brought him a sense of happiness and a still image of a reed-bottomed chair he thought had been in their room, a red shawl draped to hide its cracked back. He wondered if she had been sorry she'd let him be born. He didn't think so.

"Mr. Cahill—"

"You can call me Ash, if you like."

"I rather like calling you Mr. Cahill. It feels terribly proper and domestic. A fortnight from now, you can call me Mrs. Cahill."

It was a strange and wonderful thought that had entirely failed to occur to him. He was to become one of those new husbands, referring unnecessarily and often to *Mrs. So-and-so* and *my wife*. It seemed a miracle, that she and him could be marked as belonging to each other, just like that. "Mr. and Mrs. Cahill. I like it. Will you miss being Miss Reeve?"

"Maybe a little. But Jamie isn't Mr. Reeve anymore, either. He's Wheatcroft. So I don't know that it makes much difference."

It struck Ash that Rafe would be using a new name now. A name Ash didn't know, a name he might not even recognize if he saw it in a newspaper. He felt a little sick.

"Does it bother you that it isn't your real name?" she asked.

"No. Does it bother you?"

She gave him a sidelong smile. "I like it."

She was the most darling woman in the world, and his luck was beyond anything. All he had to do was not ruin it.

Too bad ruining things was his second-best skill, after swindling.

Lydia thought Mr. Cahill still seemed sad at dinner. He had enjoyed that story about Grandfather's claret, so she brought out more tales from the riotous elections of the last century.

The more extravagant and financially irresponsible, the more his eyes shone.

"I don't know the last time I saw you so gay," said Aunt Packham, wondering, and Lydia felt self-conscious and guilty. Lord Wheatcroft had been ashamed of these stories. He had worked hard to do away with the drunkenness and revelry that had made devoted government men, to whom the people entrusted their well-being and their country's fate, look like a pack of greedy, wasteful children.

Of course, *she* wasn't giving all fifty voters a whole pineapple. She was merely talking about it.

But she *had* given away her virtue. Her father would have been sick over that, if he knew. She should feel different—cheapened, damaged, as if something precious had been cracked and spilled like an egg.

She did feel different. She felt better, as if she'd been *given* something precious—and nothing she had to be so careful of as an egg. This new knowledge was a strong, living thing that leapt from between her hands, dancing in the air above her head and showering her with gold and silver sparks every time she looked at Mr. Cahill.

If the thought intruded, every so often, that their tryst had not had the same effect upon *him*—well, he had said his melancholy was a reaction, and no reflection on her. If Jamie had broken with her yesterday, she couldn't be happy either.

Mr. Cahill had been patient with her grief, had made her feel that she could show it without troubling him. She would do the same for him. She'd do her best to cheer him, without demanding he be cheered.

He had apologized for spoiling things, but Lydia refused to let them be spoiled. She couldn't remember the last time she had felt so happy either, and she held on to the feeling as hard as she could.

If Mr. Cahill noticed that not one of her stories was about herself, he didn't say anything.

Ash had never heard a reaction like this to the reading of banns. The entire church, hundreds of people, erupted in a buzz of gossip. The backs of the pews were high enough that, sitting, he couldn't see anyone in them. But the poorer folk leaned out of the gallery, staring and pointing down at them.

He was already a little on edge from being in a church with Miss Reeve. Even though no one else would know how to interpret it, the way she kept looking at him to make sure he knew his cues felt like a giant signboard reading *JEW, THIS WAY*.

I know how to behave in an Anglican church, he wanted to tell her. *I made us go every day for the first three months we were on our own, to learn. Rafe hated it.*

So when that buzz of talk erupted, aimed right at him, fear and adrenaline blazed across his chest like fire licking up cheap paper. It was exhilarating, and he beamed up at the gallery and kissed Miss Reeve's hand.

She beamed too, looking absolutely thrilled at the prospect of being his wife, thrilled that he had kissed her hand, thrilled that she was important to this parish.

Some people wouldn't be able to afford mince-pie spices, come Monday. Ash could never forget that. But sitting beside Miss Reeve, who had spent her morning planning out exactly who she needed to speak to at church as part of her endless campaign to manage the supply and flow of mince pie and the associated pleasures and necessities of life in Lively St. Lemeston—he had always thought charity a small drop of warmth in a very large bucket of cold water. He still did, but today he thought also, *It's better than nothing*.

Children from all over the church raced out the doors the moment services concluded, bursting into the Stir-up Sunday rhyme. Ash loved how holidays grew, so slowly and inexorably that now pudding seemed like a sacred element of the human condition and forgiveness of sin smelled like ginger and nutmeg.

One child, however, pushed her way through the congratulatory crowd outside to stand solemnly at Ash's elbow. Mary Luff bobbed a careful curtsy, offering Miss Reeve a sprig of evergreen.

There had been exactly one juniper among the bare trees on the path to the church, so she must have run and broken it off just now, or else held it in her hand all morning, waiting. "I wish you joy, ma'am, sir."

Ash wanted to compliment her on her shoe-licking—and caution her to be a little less obvious, but that would come with practice. "Thank you, Mary. What a lovely gesture." He hid his smile.

Miss Reeve did not. "This is the very first bridal gift I've received," she said. "I'll treasure it."

Mary glowed triumphantly.

"How are you doing with Miss Tice?" Miss Reeve asked. The question was unlikely to be answered honestly, should the answer be *very badly* or *Miss Tice mistreats me*, but it didn't hurt to ask.

"Very well, ma'am. I asked Miss Tice if I could make a

hat out of scraps for the Gooding Day auction, and she said I could. I want to be counted with the Pink-and-White ladies, if I may, ma'am."

Miss Reeve looked ready to burst with pride. Ash was bursting with pride himself. The kid had a future.

Having thus prepared the ground, Mary asked, "Have you seen Joanna yet, ma'am?"

It had only been half a day since she had last asked, but Miss Reeve's face fell guiltily. "We're going to visit her tomorrow. Babies always miss their families very much the first few days. By now we can see if she's really settling in. We'll come by directly after we've seen her and let you know. How's that?"

Mary bobbed a disappointed curtsy and tried to make a grateful face. "Thank you, ma'am. That would be lovely. And I'll see her myself on my Thursday afternoon." In her thick Sussex burr, the precise grammar sounded almost comical. Ash knew what that was like, to have to fight your own mouth.

He was turning into a flat, because he said, "Miss Reeve, may I speak to you a moment?" She wore a bonnet, so he had to lean in close, their cheeks almost touching. "May we send your carriage to take her? It will be half her afternoon walking there and back, and her coat and shoes look none too new."

She bit her lip. "It can't be every week," she murmured. "It won't do anyone any good to make a pet of her."

"I know." He glanced down at Mary, who had guessed they were talking about her and was standing on tiptoe trying to hear. Ash remembered the first time he had gone to prison, how he hadn't been able to sleep for missing Rafe's squirming and kicking in the bed with him. He looked Miss Reeve in the eye. "Please."

Her face softened. "Is your coat keeping you warm, Mary?"

The little girl thought before answering. "Warm enough," she hedged. "But it's got some holes."

Good answer. That way she couldn't be told it wasn't safe to go, but she left the door open for a little charity.

"I will send a cart to take you then," Miss Reeve said. "Just until Christmas, when you and the other children get your new coats."

The girl's face lit up. "Really?"

Miss Reeve nodded.

Mary stood speechless, overcome by the unexpected success of her toadying. Then she remembered herself and began a barrage of thanks and kissing of Miss Reeve's hand that was curtailed only with difficulty.

You couldn't make the world over like an old dress. But maybe you could patch it around the edges. The world was full of Mary Luffs, true. But he'd helped this one, a little, and that was better than nothing.

"What a calculating little girl," Miss Reeve said with some amusement when she was out of earshot.

"Mmm. She must remind you of yourself at that age."

Miss Reeve gave him a shocked, severe look. "I should hope not," she said primly. "*I* did not overact."

He laughed loudly enough that people close by turned to look, so he leaned in to speak in her ear again and give them something to look at. "Everybody overacts when they're learning. But kids are strange enough anyway that people don't realize what it means." Eight-year-old Rafe had overacted with an intense, pleading-eyed earnestness that Ash had enjoyed no end.

There were less than a hundred feet between them and the Market Square, and they had to stop and introduce Ash and be congratulated and inquire after someone's health a couple of dozen times at least. He wished people would stop talking about Miss Reeve's father: *Lord Wheatcroft would have been so proud,* and *Did you know Lord Wheatcroft, Mr. Cahill?* and *Your father will be missed.* Couldn't they see she hated it?

Well, very likely they couldn't. Ash put his hand over hers, but she stiffened and pulled away, evidently not liking that *he* could see it. So he went back to pretending obliviousness.

The next person to stop them was a queenly little woman of middle age with graying blond curls at her ears. Miss Reeve had already pointed her out as Lady Tassell, the chief Whig patroness. She'd been sitting alone in the pew opposite, her husband and eldest son being in London for the opening of Parliament, and her two younger sons, according to Lydia, ignoring her and in South America respectively since the November election.

The countess held out her arms with imperious motherliness. "Oh, Miss Reeve! How are you? I have been thinking so much of your father these last days that I can't imagine how hard it must still be for *you.*"

Ash could feel the tension in Miss Reeve's arm, but she smiled, disengaged herself from Ash, and gave Lady Tassell a gracious embrace. "He has done so much for this town, I imagine we will all be reminded of him pretty often for years to come. I miss him very much, but I'm better than I was, thank you."

"And how is your brother? My husband writes that he's been too broken up to attend the opening of Parliament. He was always such a sensitive boy. I do hope his nerves don't give way."

There was a pause. Ash had to admire the countess's temerity, but he thought that was a low blow even for politics.

"Jamie will be all right," Miss Reeve said. "He needs time, that's all. Only imagine how devastated your own sons would be to lose you."

Ash kept his jaw from dropping, but he couldn't quite contain his smile. She was a cool hand, all right.

Lady Tassell's face reflected the blow, spasming a little. Her eyes darted to the side before returning resolutely to Lydia with a sickly smile.

Ash followed the direction of her gaze and saw the back of the second son's blond head. The young man stood a little farther down the path in conversation with the Sparkses, one arm around a plump woman in an ancient bonnet who must be his new wife. Ash didn't think it was a coincidence that his back was to them.

People said family was forever and blood was thicker than water, but Ash had seen families come apart like dry pie crust more times than he could count. Everyone had. They just didn't want to believe it, because they didn't want to think it could happen to them.

Miss Reeve looked as if she was already sorry for her words and would have liked to take them back. But it wasn't the kind of thing you *could* take back; trying would only bring the awful thing you'd hinted at squarely into the light.

"Quite so," said Lady Tassell. "Will you introduce your young man, so that I may wish you joy?" And they all continued their conversation as if nothing were wrong at all.

They spent most of Monday morning at the nurse's, fussing over babies. Beth Pye, the nurse, was a responsible, hardworking young woman, but despite her best efforts Lydia had always found the place a little dreary. Its shabby cribs and cradles, dusty corners and dirty windows, and unadulterated smells of children were so different from the spotless, lovingly appointed nursery where Lydia had grown up.

But Mr. Cahill seemed to see nothing wrong at all. He descended on the children with delight, glowing every time he coaxed a smile or gurgling laugh. In an hour he had discerned every child's character and preferences and learned to cater to them. It was a talent that should not, perhaps, have charmed Lydia quite so much.

All in all Lydia—fond enough of babies herself that their small faces could distract her even from Mr. Cahill—could not remember when she had spent a more pleasant morning.

Mary seemed both relieved and disappointed to hear that Joanna was doing well. Lydia, very glad she'd agreed to send the cart on Thursday, hoped Joanna would be suitably over-joyed to see her sister.

She tried to put it out of her mind during their after-noon of visiting Pink-and-White ladies in preparation for the Gooding Day auction. Mr. Cahill was endlessly, improbably willing to be interested, asking every lady in detail what she hoped to buy, why she wanted the Pink-and-Whites to win, and what she was contributing. He admired each unfinished project with unassailable sincerity.

"Do you really care about all that?" she asked as they came out of Mrs. Howlett's house, whom he had drawn out for nearly half an hour on every piece of worn linen in her home and how much replacements would brighten the place.

Lydia had been listening to Mrs. Howlett's ramblings for the better part of fifteen years and had consequently grown fond of them, but Mr. Cahill's presence made her oddly self-conscious. It was hard to believe that a stranger, and a man, could really have enjoyed the conversation.

He laughed. "I've been priming them to spend as much as possible, didn't you realize? Encouraging them not to wander off and leave their needlework half-done, too. But I don't find it tedious. Mundane details make me happy."

The revelation that he had not just been making conversation, but actually working at winning the auction for the Pink-and-Whites, left Lydia a little breathless.

"Mrs. Gilchrist is a Pink-and-White, isn't she?" he asked, still scheming. "He works for you, but her sister is the shabbily dressed one married to Lady Tassell's son, isn't she?"

"She's been Orange-and-Purple all her life. Do you think we can convince her to change?" Almost every woman they'd talked to was planning, despite party loyalty, to bid on either Mrs. Gilchrist or Mrs. Dymond's quilt, two of the centerpieces of the auction for the last few years.

The finicky geometric complexity of Mrs. Gilchrist's patchwork always made Lydia feel as if she'd drunk too much coffee, while Mrs. Dymond's sloppy, droll scenes from popular novels made her cringe. But people raved that art was in those girls' blood and bid ferociously on both, and it was all very annoying.

Mr. Cahill grinned at her, a martial light in his eye. "I know we can."

It was only with the greatest willpower that Lydia did not seize him by the lapels and kiss him then and there.

She didn't have to wait long, however. The evening was rainy, so she closed the carriage shutters and launched herself at him with an enthusiasm that would have embarrassed her if he hadn't seemed so pleased by it. The parcels of pudding ingredients gave the carriage a spicy, fairy-tale atmosphere which the smell of damp straw from the floor could not extinguish.

Before last night Lydia had thought a few convulsions would satisfy her hunger, but they'd only stoked it. Now she found she didn't want to rush. She wanted time to go over Mr. Cahill slowly, for hours, without interruption. She wanted to take his clothes off—she couldn't get at nearly enough of him. More than anything, she wanted to see his square-built chest and shoulders.

Later she would think of a way to get that. For now she gave up and kissed him with slow, friendly kisses that led nowhere. He fidgeted when he kissed—he had traced the bones of her corset, that first time. Now he slid his finger inside her collar, ran his thumb over her buttons, *bump bump bump,* unfastened and refastened the frogging on her pelisse, explored the shape of her up-swept hair.

Each touch seemed to say how much he liked her. It felt proprietary, as if they were married already and in and out of each other's pockets, and she read him the paper every morning while he lay on the sofa with his head in her lap.

Arriving at Wheatcroft was like waking gently from a nice dream. "Two weeks," he murmured as he tied her bonnet strings.

But the lingering warmth didn't even survive the walk from the carriage to the front door. This desire was a double-edged sword. It would cause talk among the servants if she was always trying to be alone with him. Yes, it would make people believe she was in love with him, but it would do little to support the idea that he was in love with her. People would say he had seduced her for her money, and make jokes about gullible, frustrated old maids.

Even his extraordinary kindness to the townsfolk would seem suspect. They would say it was too good to be true.

They wouldn't be wrong about any of it, which was a creepy-crawly thought.

Wrenn was brushing Lydia's hair when they heard the unmistakable sound of hoofbeats on wet gravel. A rider, at this hour? Had something happened in town?

She went to the window. It was dark and the figure was still too far away to make out. "You'd better do a simple coil. Whoever it is, they're in a hurry." She was back at the window as soon as her hair was in place. The rider was close enough that—

"Jamie."

Chapter 16

"Wrenn looked over her shoulder. "Are you sure, madam? I can barely make out anything."

Lydia could barely make out anything either, but she was sure. Impatient happiness filled her like a balloon, even if he *was* riding too fast—and then she thought, *He's come because of my letter, and Mr. Cahill is upstairs alone.*

"Hurry," she said. "As quick as you can, please."

So Wrenn rushed her into fresh petticoats and an evening dress, and Lydia put her slippers half-on and ran out into the corridor without any jewelry or perfume.

She met Jenny coming to tell her of Jamie's arrival. "Mr. Pennifold put him in the saloon with Mr. Cahill, ma'am." Lydia thanked her and almost turned her ankle on the stairs in her haste.

The door to the saloon was ajar. She heard Mr. Cahill say with his faint Cornish lilt, "I hope you had a pleasant journey."

"Pleasant enough," Jamie said, shortly enough to be rude.

Jamie was shy, but his manners were good. If he was being openly rude, he was very angry. Suddenly Lydia wanted to linger here eavesdropping, as if this weren't her own life but a play for which she had no responsibility. She stopped to pull on the backs of her slippers.

"You don't like me much, do you, my lord?" Mr. Cahill

said. That ruefulness of his could charm anybody. "Well, I don't blame you. I wouldn't like a man who made such a whirlwind courtship of my sister either. But—"

"Have you got a sister?" Jamie did not sound charmed.

"I haven't, as a matter of fact."

"Mm. I didn't know that. I don't know a single thing about you, do I? Not one, and until I do, you aren't getting a penny of Lydia's money."

Lydia's heart sank like a rock. She had not wanted to consider this possibility. She had very carefully not considered it. Jamie was trying to protect her, but—it was so very inconvenient. It was *her* money. Why couldn't she have it?

"Jamie!" Aunt Packham said weakly.

"I suppose that's fair," Mr. Cahill said cheerfully. "What do you want to know?"

She was filled with wonder at his sangfroid—wonder and protectiveness. Why should his ability to take lumps make her want to shield him from them?

Any moment now Pennifold would come to announce dinner and find her listening. She pushed open the door and went in. For a moment, her dread vanished and she was simply happy to see Jamie. Angry or not, he gave her a great hug that lifted her off her feet.

"It's too cold and wet to ride from town," she said, knowing it would set his back up and unable to stop herself. "You'll"— she couldn't say *fall*—"catch a chill."

His face set into an expression of fidgety resentment that always made her nerves jangle. "Don't fuss, Lydia."

I wouldn't have to, if you would all take care of yourselves. But she'd said that to him thousands of times, and it had never made any impression. She smiled stiffly. "I'm sorry. I'll try not to. Has Aunt Packham already introduced Mr. Cahill to you?"

"I did, dear." Aunt Packham fluttered a little—evidently not wanting to be blamed for the room's chilly atmosphere, as if anyone could blame her for anything when she never *did* anything.

Oh, no. That had been a nasty thought. How had her mood soured so rapidly? She tried to find her adoration of Jamie poking out of her tangle of feelings, as Mr. Cahill had instructed her, but her chest was one great knot. She could only think that everything would be ruined—that her life was slipping away—when there was no reason to be so afraid.

She wanted Jamie to like Mr. Cahill, she realized. She wanted it with startling desperation.

Mr. Cahill came and stood beside her—not touching her or speaking to her or doing anything that required a response, only silently offering anything she might need. Lydia almost burst into tears at how splendid a feeling it was to have some-one focused on her and not the other way round. Someone paying attention to her not because he wanted anything, but because he thought she might want something from him and wished to be on the spot to provide it.

Of course that was his profession, but she didn't care; she nestled against him, and he put an arm around her and kissed the top of her head. She wished miserably that she could have this for real.

"I hope you'll like each other," Lydia said to Jamie, and let the almost-crying show in her voice.

Jamie looked poleaxed. "Lydia, can I—can I speak to you a moment? Mr. Cahill, Aunt Packham, if you will excuse us?"

When they were two rooms away, he hissed, "What *is* this?" Lydia hoped the servants couldn't hear.

She tried not to think or plan. She had to *be* in love with Mr. Cahill and eager to marry him. "I don't know what you mean," she snapped.

"This charade. We both know you're doing this to get at your money. Or maybe to blackmail *me* into agreeing to follow in Father's footsteps, in exchange for a longer engagement."

She found herself giving him a teasingly speculative look. "Would that work?"

"*No,*" he growled.

"Then give me credit for more strategy."

"*Lydia.*" He took several steps towards her. "Please tell me the truth. The timing is too coincidental to be accident. You find yourself in need of money, and a husband appears?"

It was folly to feel stung by the truth, and yet she did. "Is it so impossible to imagine I might have fallen in love?" she asked quietly. "Do you think me so cold?"

He threw his hands in the air. "Those martyred eyes might have everyone else wrapped around your finger, but I've been watching you do that for twenty-one years and it isn't going to work on me."

That stung a hundred times worse. "I beg your pardon? I have *never* tried to martyred-eye anyone into anything!"

Jamie rolled his eyes. "Every time you disagreed with Father about anything, out they'd come—the sad, stoic face and 'Very well, Father' and he'd crumple like cheap paper."

"If you mean how I got him to extend your school holidays, believe me, I tried begging and it didn't work."

It had never been an act—not *mostly* an act. She didn't think it had been. The decision had been her father's to make, so she had gone along with it. *Everything* had been her father's decision, always.

So she hadn't been able to hide her disappointment, as a girl barely out of the schoolroom! Had she been supposed to act *happy* about sending Jamie away early because Lord Wheatcroft chose to imagine the boy longed to reunite with his friends? Jamie had dreaded going back to school those first few years.

Then she had begun to feel as if he couldn't wait to leave, as if he only came home to be polite. She'd put effort into acting happy, after that.

Jamie's lower lip crept forward. "Lydia, you have always been very good to me. You've always been very good to *everyone*. I won't let you throw yourself away like this because you feel some kind of obligation to Father's legacy. Let it go. You can do as you like, now. You deserve that."

"This *is* as I like." It would do no good to tell him how much it hurt her to see him let their father's legacy go so easily. It would be unkind. "And Jamie, I—" She tried to think of something she could say to her little brother about Mr. Cahill that would not make them both blush. "Mr. Cahill—"

"I can't decide if he's a fortune hunter, or your unfortunate dupe."

Lydia was diverted by this idea of herself as a ruthless Delilah duping poor besotted Mr. Cahill into marriage. "Please don't be rude to him," she said, more calmly than she'd managed yet.

Words piled up in her throat: *I've never even been tempted before, and now I can't wait to be married,* and *If you offered right now to take charge of the Pink-and-Whites if I gave him up, I'd have to talk myself into accepting,* and *You're right, I do want something just for me, and it's him.*

If she were really, uncomplicatedly making a love match,

she would be too self-conscious, too English to say any of those things. She was too self-conscious now. "Please, Jamie. He's had a difficult life and I want—I want him to be happy here."

"I've asked you to call me James." Jamie gave her a narrow-eyed look. "I won't be rude. But I'm not signing any settlements."

"He doesn't even want my money. He only wants a few thousand pounds to set his brother up respectably. He's absolutely refused anything more than that."

"What more does he need? He'll be living off you."

Lydia's fist clenched. "If I don't mind that, why should anybody else? Ugh, I can't abide odious remarks about men with less money than their wives, as if it were some grotesque overturning of the natural order of things. Why shouldn't a woman have money? Why shouldn't a man like her anyway?"

Jamie blinked. "I didn't mean anything like that. Plenty of men have liked you, Lydia. Which is why I find it so suspect that you've waited until now to succumb, when it's so very convenient."

She took a deep breath. "Do you mean to make me ask your permission to spend my own money for the rest of my life? You can't. Jamie—James—I'm a grown woman."

She'd bought him his first pair of trousers when he was breeched, for God's sake. She'd supplemented his pocket money his entire childhood. If she were to read over the letters she'd saved from Eton, hardly a one ended without cajoling her to send him money on top of what he got from Papa, for things he *needed*, positively couldn't live without, marbles and parakeets and a new species of cactus for his collection. "James, *please*."

He looked as uncomfortable as she felt. "It isn't your money, Lydia. It's Mama's money. It's for your children some day. I can't give it to you free and clear when I know charity-mongers will wheedle you out of the principal by next Christmas."

Lydia's jaw dropped. "You can't really think I'm that bad a manager! I've been running this household since I was out of the schoolroom." She couldn't bring herself to touch that scornful *charity-mongers*.

He gave her a sheepish smile. "I wouldn't have to fuss if you'd take care of yourself," he said, repeating her own words back to her. It was sweet of him, really.

Later, she might feel grateful. "I *am* taking care of myself. I love the work I do. Why can't you believe that? You'd love it too, if you'd give it a chance."

He looked at her and didn't say anything. What was he thinking? She squirmed inwardly at the idea that he saw something about her that she couldn't guess at.

"I wish you'd be honest with me," he said at last, sadly.

Lydia tried to imagine telling him that Mr. Cahill was really Mr. Cohen, and that he'd grown up thieving in the East End. Even in fantasy, she couldn't find the words. God only knew what Jamie would do with that information.

God only knew if he could ever hold her in esteem again. He would think she had lost all respect for himself, that his sister was trading herself for money in the meanest commercial fashion. He wouldn't understand that it didn't *feel* that way.

Even if it did, she thought suddenly. *Even if I didn't like Mr. Cahill so very much, and I had offered him a plain business proposition of a home and some cash and free use of my body*

*in exchange for thirty thousand pounds, why shouldn't I, if I
thought it worth my while?*

God would not approve. Her parents would not approve.
But why should this one thing be so sacred, when money
bought everything else? She could see no reason except that
God had said it, and that gentlemen liked ladies to be the
repository of their daydreams of innocence and virtue.

She could never say that to Jamie, or to any of her friends.
But it wouldn't shock Mr. Cahill. He had doubtless considered
the matter himself and had some opinion on it. Did that mean
he had corrupted her?

Jamie would think so.

I wish I could be honest with you too, she thought, and
smiled at him. "I am being honest with you. I know I never
showed much interest in matrimony, but…I hadn't met Mr.
Cahill then."

Jamie's frown didn't dissipate. "It isn't…it isn't that you
think this isn't your home any longer, now that Father's dead,
is it? You know I don't plan to marry." He said it awkwardly
and a little defiantly. "I'd be glad, more than glad, to have you
here forever."

"Oh, Jamie." She hurled herself at him, and he folded his
arms around her. He was unbearably young. How could he
talk about forever? How could he know how he would feel in
five years?

Lydia felt better about everything, suddenly. Who cared if
the townsfolk knew he had given up politics? No one would
hold that against him, if he chose to pick up the reins five years
from now. They would understand that he had been a grieving
boy. By the time he was forty no one would remember anything about it at all. So long as she maintained the interest in

the meantime, this inheritance would still be his.

"I would be glad to live here with you forever too," she said. "But I'll be right down the drive. It will be almost as if I hadn't left." When Mr. Cahill went away, perhaps she could even be Jamie's hostess. She rubbed at the stubborn crease between Jamie's brows. "You'll give yourself wrinkles. Everything is all right, truly. You'll see."

"I hope so," Jamie said, sounding unalterably unconvinced.

"Please get to know him. You'll like him."

He sighed. "At least postpone the wedding."

It would only upset Jamie to point out that she had spent enough time alone with Mr. Cahill now that her reputation would be in tatters if she didn't marry him. "I'm sorry, Jamie, but no."

"Why not?" he demanded. "But wait, I know. It's because you can't wait to get your hands on your money."

She hesitated.

"You can't deny it, can you?"

She raised her eyebrows. "I thought it would embarrass you if I admitted it was because I couldn't wait to get my hands on Mr. Cahill."

"Lydia!"

"Well, it's the truth. Don't ask questions you don't want to hear the answers to."

With a squeamish, defeated look, he offered her his arm to go back to the others.

In the saloon, Aunt Packham was blooming under Mr. Cahill's attention. When they were called in to dinner, he offered Aunt Packham his arm and let Lydia go with Jamie. He was full of small kindnesses, and if they were calculated, she didn't think that made them less kind.

For a moment Lydia was furious with Jamie—with anyone who would say she ought to give this up, who would look down on Mr. Cahill if they knew the truth.

It would have been a stretch to say Jamie was polite. He had no knack for skating pleasantly on the surface of a conversation, and he could find nothing cordial to say to either of them. Mr. Cahill, with the tact she was beginning to find actually arousing, refrained from filling the silence, deferring to Lydia.

But her own conversational gifts deserted her painfully and embarrassingly. If she spoke of her work, Jamie would think she talked of nothing else. Gossip seemed frivolous, informing him which servants she meant to take to the Dower House would be dull, she had read no books since she saw him. Her brother replied in obstinate monosyllables to all her questions and to the few ventured by Mr. Cahill—good questions, referencing things about Jamie she had forgotten mentioning to him.

She couldn't bear that Mr. Cahill was witnessing this. *Usually Jamie and I can talk for hours,* she wanted to protest.

"I love your greenhouse," Mr. Cahill said after a particularly long pause.

Lydia flushed scarlet.

Mr. Cahill did not look at her. "What do you think of the new fad for glass roofs? When I was at Barnsley Park, I saw a greenhouse designed by Mr. Nash that is almost *all* glass, except for the stone columns and the latticework."

"When you were at Barnsley Park?" Jamie's skeptical tone dared Mr. Cahill to presume any acquaintance with the proprietors of such a fine place. Lydia blushed again, this time for Jamie's manners.

Mr. Cahill laughed—not even as if he were unaware of the insult, but as if he thought it rather witty. That half-inch of throat above his collar would be the death of Lydia yet. "I wasn't a guest. We visited the house to see the paintings, and the greenhouse is just behind, so we peered in. I chatted with one of the gardeners a bit, and he told me for truly tropical plants, a glass roof can't be beat."

"Some collectors swear by them," Jamie said shortly, clearly intending to leave it at that. But half a minute later, he burst out, "The difficulty is keeping out drafts," and then, "and keeping the more delicate plants out of direct sunlight," and by the time he said, "Of course, most greenhouse glass has a greenish tinge to it, to protect the plants," the Reeve passion for accuracy and complete information had taken over. Jamie embarked on an explanation of fish-scale glazing, cast-iron, and the difficulty of housing citrus and succulents in the same house.

He was louder and more halting than usual, which meant he was nervous, and his suspicious looks said, *I know you aren't really interested, you're just conniving.* But he talked, and Mr. Cahill patently *was* interested. By the end of the evening Jamie had extended an extremely grudging invitation to re-pot an ailing orange tree the following morning.

"Do you mean it?" Mr. Cahill leaned so far forward in his chair that Lydia—whom gardening made sore and muddy and not much else—suspected him of sarcasm herself.

Jamie frowned.

Mr. Cahill sat back. "I'm sorry—I collect other people's enthusiasms. Someone who really loves a subject can make anything fascinating."

"I found the same with the dons at Oxford." Jamie paused. "Where were you at school, sir?"

Chapter 17

Lydia tensed, then wished she hadn't. Mr. Cahill showed no sign that this was dangerous ground.

"Not Oxford," he said ruefully. "I never had the staying power to prosper at school. I think my brother would have done well at Edinburgh, if I could have afforded to send him."

Lydia wondered if that were true, or if Mr. Cahill had somehow guessed at an old grievance, which was about to be aired. The University of Edinburgh didn't mind so much about the classics, emphasizing the practical sciences instead.

On cue, Jamie said, "I would have liked to attend Edinburgh. They teach botany and agriculture there. But all the Reeves go to Oxford."

Lydia didn't want to go over this bitter ground again. University in Scotland held few advantages for a Ministerialist political heir, and that had been that. "Jamie, will you stay for the wedding, or will you be going back to the Whitworth-Percevals?"

Jamie frowned at Mr. Cahill. "I'll stay."

For the first time in her life, she was not wholly happy to hear Jamie say that. She didn't like the feeling.

It had been a long evening, Ash thought as he walked back into Lively St. Lemeston. A long evening of swindling on his own, for when it came to dealing with her brother, Miss Reeve didn't have the faintest idea what to do.

He understood that: brothers were difficult. Ash would have to handle it, that was all.

The invitation to re-pot a tree was a Godsend, because Lydia wouldn't be there. It had taken far too much of Ash's energy tonight to be glad for her that her brother had come to see her, and not envious.

Ash couldn't remember ever being so envious of anyone.

But he was lucky, really. He'd lost Rafe, yes; but while he'd had him, Rafe had been the best brother possible, worlds better than anyone else's. Jamie was a nice boy, and Ash liked him, but he would be no fun at all to tramp across England with and worse than useless in a swindle. He couldn't even pretend to be polite for five minutes at a time.

When the ladies left them alone after dinner, the young man had fidgeted silently, misery all over his chubby, good-looking English face. When Ash said, *I must admit I've never much cared for port or cigars,* Jamie had shot up out of his chair in relief. How could he share the cast of Miss Reeve's features and her porcelain-doll coloring and entirely lack her finesse?

Shy people could be swindled, but it took longer, and pressing them was never shrewd practice. Maybe Ash should suggest postponing the wedding again.

He didn't want to. He couldn't sleep in the solitary silence of empty streets and thick interior walls. He'd been catching a few hours' rest in the early morning, when carts started moving in the road below. He wished he liked to read, so he'd have something to do all night, instead of wasting a candle playing patience with a deck of cards he and Rafe had used for piquet, or lying awake looking for faces in the knots on the ceiling and wondering whether he should have told Rafe the truth sooner, or never told him at all.

For all Ash knew, he and Miss Reeve would have separate rooms even when they were married. How many rooms did the Dower House have? How rich did you have to be, exactly, before you didn't share a bed with your wife? Miss Reeve had probably never shared a bed in her life. What if she hated it?

He put his hand up to his breast, feeling the reassuring crinkle of paper in his inner coat pocket. He hadn't yet opened the letter she had written him.

It was a simple trick, but an effective one. He'd used it as a child, keeping a boiled sweet in his pocket and telling himself he'd eat it when he was *really* hungry. As long as he had the willpower not to eat that licorice drop, he knew the pangs he was feeling must be bearable, and so he could bear them. Besides, it had given him a treat to look forward to.

So he took out the letter, looked at it, and put it back in his pocket, thinking, *I'm only a little lonely. If I were* really *lonely, I'd open it.* He occupied the rest of the walk home in wondering what was in it. Poetry? A lock of hair? He'd like to have a lock of her hair, tied with a bit of ribbon. Sky-blue velvet would look nice against that satiny copper.

There was nothing wrong with swindling yourself a little, in a friendly way. He wondered sometimes if flats ever knew they were being swindled, and went along with it because it was better than no one paying them any attention at all.

"So you're from Cornwall," Jamie said as they carefully washed the roots of the orange tree, suspended in mid-air by a pulley.

Ash nodded. "Have you ever been? It's beautiful country, and so wild it's easy to believe pixies are hovering just out of sight."

"I haven't," Jamie said.

"Do the local folk believe in fairies hereabouts?"

"Where in Cornwall are you from?"

"I was baptized in Blight's Penryth," he said. "But my parents died when I was young, and after that my brother and I went from aunt to aunt."

"And what have you been doing since you were old enough to leave your aunts behind?"

The gardener studiously kept his eyes on the tree, his discomfort obvious. Jamie was as single-minded as his sister, and much less concerned with manners.

"Wandering about, mostly, the two of us. I like seeing new places."

"You've never spent much time in any one place?"

"A few weeks," Ash said. "Not much more than that."

"So if I wanted to inquire as to your character, there's absolutely no one I could ask?"

"May I speak to you for a moment?" Ash pulled Jamie into a corner. "We've got to come to some kind of truce, you and I, or we'll make Miss Reeve the subject of vulgar gossip."

Where Ash grew up, no one had cared about gossip. Everyone knew everything about everybody. But he'd quickly learned that it was a magic word to almost everyone else.

Sure enough, Jamie immediately looked uncertain of his ground. "Time enough for a truce when I'm satisfied you haven't got anything to hide," he muttered.

"Such as?" Ash said in exasperation. "What on earth do you think I'm hiding?"

Jamie glared and didn't answer, reassuring Ash that his suspicions were nonspecific. "You've never stayed anywhere more than a few weeks, and now you want to spend the rest of your life in one place and I'm not supposed to find anything about that peculiar?"

"Your sister is an extraordinary and beautiful woman."

"I know that. It doesn't answer my question."

He was right, it was peculiar. Of course Ash had no intention of staying in one place for the rest of his life. But when he took a moment to think, his answer was easy. "Home has never been a place to me. When I was young it was my mother, and later it was my brother. The places I've gone, they've all been home because he was there. Miss Reeve is my home now. Whither she goes, I'll go, and her people will be my people." He gave Jamie a half-smile. "If they'll have me."

"I don't expect she'll object to traveling now and again if I get itchy feet. I'd like to show her Cornwall."

As he said it, it became true. She'd look like a sea creature in the Cornish mist. If he took her hair down, the wind would catch it like a banner, and then they'd sit in the shelter of a twisted tree and he'd comb the tangles out and kiss her. She'd love the seals.

Jamie snorted. "Lydia gets anxious more than twenty miles from home. She doesn't even like going to London for the Season."

Ash didn't voice his opinion that she'd like traveling with him better than she'd liked traveling with her father and brother, or that she might enjoy a real holiday better than a Parliamentary session. "Then I'll go off on my own every so often. We'll sort it out." He looked Jamie in the eye. "I promise I'll make her happy."

"And you think she'll make you happy?"

He smiled. "She makes me happy already."

There was silence. Out of the corner of his eye, Ash could see the gardener with his back to them, fussing over the tree. Jamie seemed to be considering his options.

In Ash's experience, flats like Jamie didn't soften gradually. They kept up the appearance of mistrust long after they'd already given in in their minds, because they felt in some obscure way that letting you know they were thinking about trusting you would make them look foolish if you weren't trustworthy. Then when they'd entirely, *entirely* made up their minds, they gave way in a flood of apologies and smiles and relief, and you had them. He could be patient.

Suddenly he heard Rafe say, *You don't know what anyone can afford to lose. Maybe faith and self-respect were things they needed, things they couldn't live without.*

He didn't want to hurt Miss Reeve's brother. He didn't want to push him further apart from her. He'd seen at dinner last night how Miss Reeve had sat silent and guilty, the consciousness of her own deceit precluding easy conversation. He might be envious, but he was glad for her too, that she still had what he'd lost. He wanted her to keep it.

But she'd already flatly refused to tell Jamie the truth. Ash's loyalty was to her, and she wanted to lie.

"A truce, then," Jamie said reluctantly. "In front of the servants."

"Thank you." Given the quality of Jamie's performance up to now, Ash didn't expect much from the truce, but if it prevented the most pointed remarks, it was worth it.

Jamie shifted uneasily. "We'd better get back to that tree. The roots must be put in water as soon as possible."

Lydia sat alone in the Little Parlor, reading her correspondents' accounts of the Prince Regent's speech on opening the new Parliament. It was difficult to think of him with respect as *the Prince Regent*; her father had still called him *Florizel* with gentle satire.

There was no letter from her father in the pile. There would never be a letter from her father again.

She wished Mr. Cahill were here, flitting about the room and asking nosy questions. That would help with the vacant place in her heart. Most people only made it echo, the way talking in an empty church made you notice how high the ceiling was. With Mr. Cahill, the emptiness felt comfortable somehow, as natural as a bare-branched winter morning.

She'd asked him not to expect more from their marriage than a simple bargain, but she was becoming terribly afraid *she* would expect more. One empty space in her heart she could handle. Two…she didn't want two.

She didn't need Mr. Cahill here, anyway, not when there was so much work to occupy her. She turned back to her neglected letters. There would be a motion put forward for Catholic emancipation after the Christmas recess. It was a question on which even Ministerialists were permitted by the government to differ, but sentiment among the Lively St.

Lemeston Pink-and-Whites was strong against it.

The subject had arisen at a voters' dinner during the recent election. With a sinking feeling, she remembered that someone had said, *Who's next? The Jews?*

At the time, Lydia had agreed.

Mr. Cahill had been born in London. He spoke English. Was his first loyalty really to an overarching Jewish nation with ties to Bonapartist Europe, or some such fancy of the pamphleteers? The idea—previously remote but plausible—was now patently asinine. If he did not feel a part of England, it was because England pointedly excluded him.

The last Jacobite rebellion had been in '45. Perhaps it was time to reconcile. Surely great men could find better uses for their talents and their money than keeping Papists out of public office.

Oh, but Mr. Jessop and Mr. Dromgoole would both vote against it. Even if the motion never reached the Lords, it would look very bad if Jamie didn't bother to attend. And if Catholics became voters, in Lively St. Lemeston they would all be Orange-and-Purples, and the Wheatcroft interest in the borough would slide still further.

High politics always left her feeling ill with uncertainty. A vicar in Crawley had died, so she calmed her nerves in writing another letter of recommendation for the alderman's son. When Mrs. Jenner rapped at the door to tell her it was time to stir the pudding, she was enough herself again to start up with anticipation. "Have you sent to the greenhouse?"

"I've sent to everyone, Miss Reeve. They're all here."

"Of course."

Every member of the household stirred the pudding, down to the lowliest stable boy. She and Mrs. Jenner smiled at each other, for a moment not servant and mistress but only two people united by years of memories. Lydia loved Christmas.

Christmas hit her in the face when she went through the kitchen door: brandy and suet and spices and lemons and a dozen other smells, emanating from the great cast-iron pot on a table in the center of the room. A long wooden spoon lay across it, wreathed in steam.

The room was warm, the only *really* warm room in the house, and crammed with people. They should have been chattering excitedly—and they were, but they were doing it very quietly and darting glances at Jamie.

Poor Jamie. Lord Wheatcroft had been the first to stir the Wheatcroft Christmas pudding for going on forty years, and he had done it with convivial charm and boyish enthusiasm. Jamie stared silently at the spoon as if it might bite him.

He glanced up at Lydia, and for a second a really awful look crossed his face, as if she might bite him too. Was Jamie afraid of her? *Why?* She wanted more than anything to be a comfort to him. She didn't know what to do or say. Anything she did would be wrong.

Her eyes went to Mr. Cahill, chatting with one of the gamekeepers. He put his hands in his pockets and smiled at her. "Your father always used to do this, eh?" he said to Jamie. "You must miss him."

It must be hard for Mr. Cahill to see her and Jamie together, when he had lost his brother. What was his kindness costing him?

Jamie nodded, then gave a short burst of self-deprecating

laughter. "I wish I could be more like him," he said, trying for confident ruefulness and missing.

"No doubt *he* wasn't much like himself at twenty-one," Mr. Cahill said easily. "I imagine lording starts out stiff as brand-new boots, and comes to fit you over time."

Jamie looked startled.

"I met a Russian woman once who said in her country they have a proverb," Mr. Cahill continued. "It translates to 'the first pancake is always lumpy'. I'm sure, Mrs. Marsh, that you'll agree with the truth of that."

The cook laughed. "Oh, aye. The griddle's never at the right heat, and the oil is too much or too little. I don't mind much as I always eat that one myself." She gave Jamie a sympathetic look. "My lord—the first time it fell to your father to begin the stirring, he dropped the spoon on the floor."

Lydia had never heard that story. Why had her father never told her?

"Aye," said Andy Weller, "and remember when his lordship sliced his leg open, cutting the first sheaf of wheat?"

There was a chorus of mingled clucks and laughter, and then all the older members of the staff were sharing stories of Lord Wheatcroft's youthful ineptitude. Lydia had never heard any of them.

She thought of her own firsts. Plenty of them were Jamie's firsts—Jamie's first fight, Jamie's first lesson, Jamie's first heartbreak. She hadn't performed particularly well through any of them.

But she'd learned early that if she didn't call attention to her own failures, often no one else noticed. Now she couldn't open her mouth and say, *The first time I saw you run a high fever, I cried and frightened you into a frenzy.* Shame clogged her throat, a host of small shames she'd locked away and lost the key to.

Now that he wasn't the center of attention and she wouldn't embarrass him in front of the servants, she went to Jamie and took his hand, with a grateful smile at Mr. Cahill.

"I don't wish you were more like anyone," she whispered in her brother's ear. "I wouldn't change a hair on your head."

"As a brother, maybe," he said. "As Lord Wheatcroft…"

She didn't know what to say to that. Jamie hated to clash with anyone, and he rarely put much stock in his own opinions, unless it was about plants. She *had* worried that he lacked the firmness to be master of an estate, leader of a political interest.

Surely he would grow into command, as Mr. Cahill said. But *It will be different when you're older* never pleased anyone.

"My first dinner party was a disaster," she blurted out, and flushed hot.

Jamie stared at her. "It was?"

She remembered writing to him about that evening. She had tried to make it sound like a great success. Her face had flamed all through the letter. She couldn't tell this story.

She looked at Mr. Cahill. Eager warmth lit his eyes, as if he were already filled with fond amusement at her endearing younger self. The heat in her body suddenly meant something very different from embarrassment.

"I put on rouge," she said. "I wanted to look older. Father laughed and told me I looked like a strumpet and to go and wash it off."

The corner of Mr. Cahill's mouth turned up, but even years later, she couldn't find it funny. And yet—what was so terrible about it? Why did humiliation crawl over her skin at the memory? Surely every girl had heard that at one time or another.

"I don't remember that, ma'am," Mrs. Jenner said, surprised. She had been cook then. "We all thought you behaved like a little queen through everything. I so wanted to do you credit, and then I forgot how walnuts make Mr. Baverstock's tongue swell and put them in the cake." She shook her head. "You were that good about it."

"It was an honest mistake." She didn't say she had blamed herself for *that* too. "Then I spilled pickled beets all down my dress. I ought to have gone and changed at once, but I was so mortified I couldn't think. All I wanted was to smooth it over and say it was nothing."

She had tried to laugh ruefully; it had been as painful a sound as Jamie's, she was sure. The comparison made her uncomfortable in a way she didn't really understand. "Father told me not to be ridiculous and to run and change my gown. I felt like a fool, and the new dress was a completely different color and much less fine. All night, guests kept on asking me why I had changed it and I had to explain."

The story seemed suddenly anticlimactic. Oh, there was more, but it was all that sort of thing—tiny awkwardnesses etched into her mind with strong acid. She told Jamie how she had invited two men engaged in a lawsuit against each other, how she had made an innocent remark that struck her neighbor at dinner as uncommonly dirty, how the ladies had quarreled over precedence going in to dinner, and the more she told him, the less significance it had.

"You never told me any of that," Jamie said.

"I was embarrassed."

Mr. Cahill leaned in and kissed her cheek. Even through the brandy and spices in the air, she could smell his skin. How had his scent become so familiar so quickly? Suddenly she was thinking of the first time they had shared in the greenhouse, and all the first times that still awaited them.

"Shall we?" Jamie picked up the spoon. "Happy Advent! Peace on earth and goodwill towards men, and don't forget to make a wish, everyone."

He stirred a few times, shut his eyes, and wished.

Lydia wondered what he had asked for. She always wanted to know other people's wishes. All these people living so close to her, and the nearest wish of their hearts was as great a mystery as if they were on the far side of the world.

But that meant they couldn't see her wish either. She took the spoon from Jamie and leaned over the pot, breathing in brandied steam. It made her feel a little drunk. She smiled at Mr. Cahill and wished for a really spectacular wedding night.

Chapter 18

L ydia always tried to go into town on Market Day. The Whig newspaper came out the night before and everyone had something to say about it by Wednesday noon. It was a wonderful opportunity to see Pink-and-Whites who lived outside of town, and Lydia looked forward all week to salmagundi on a fresh roll from one of the food stalls. Even the drive to town was an enjoyable weekly ritual, with Mrs. Jenner and the still-room maid in the carriage, planning the week's meals.

It was drizzling in Lively St. Lemeston today, and the market less busy on that account. Lydia and her umbrella had no difficulty going from errand to errand. She turned away from promising to find an apprenticeship for Mrs. Bickerstaff's third son and almost walked into Phoebe Dymond.

Funny, that girl had been through three family names, and all of them among the most unpleasantly prominent Whig names in town. This last was unquestionably the worst.

"How do you do, Mrs. Dymond?" Lydia said politely, and waited for the woman to step aside.

"Well. And you, Miss Reeve?" Mrs. Dymond glared a little as she said it, and showed no sign of moving.

"Very well, thank you." She glanced across the square, about to pretend to see someone waving to her.

"May I speak to you a moment?"

Lydia's eyebrows went up, but there was no way to refuse, and anyway, she was curious. Furling her umbrella, she let Mrs. Dymond draw her into an empty doorway a little apart from the crowd.

Once there, the young woman seemed at a loss for words. "This is going to sound awfully rude," she said at last. "It's going to *be* awfully rude, and I don't know why I ought to stick my neck out for you, but you're friends with Caroline and you came to visit her." Lydia didn't know how Mrs. Dymond, when she was uncomfortable, contrived to look as if she were peering out from under her own eyebrows. "She was very happy about it, so thank you."

Lydia smiled. "I was glad to do it. Mrs. Sparks is my friend. Now if that was all you wished to say—"

Mrs. Dymond shook her head, loose curls jostling. She always looked as if she'd put up her hair in the dark. "You probably heard that me and Will Sparks didn't get along so well when we were married. Ma'am."

Actually, I heard you and Will Sparks not get along so well, on a number of occasions, Lydia thought. The Sparkses having a row in the street had once been a familiar sight in Lively St. Lemeston.

She affected a distant frown. "Now that you mention it, I suppose I do remember hearing something like that once."

Mrs. Dymond's mouth twitched, as if she thought that was funny but was too nervous to actually smile. "I married him right after my father died. I mean right after, as soon as you. I thought I loved him. Oh, I did love him, but—I—"

She drew in a deep breath. "He was a good man and I loved him, but I didn't do him any favors marrying him. He made me forget and I thought it was on account of a sympathy between us, but you know—on his side, he couldn't have understood quite what he meant to me. I thought he was comforting me, but really it was half not being alone that made the difference, not—not *him*. On his side, he was just walking out with me. I don't—I don't want you to make the same mistake. I know it's awful and lonely, but it'll get better, I promise, and staying at home can't be so bad, can it? Your brother seems nice."

Unlike your mother, Lydia thought, but there was no sting to it. She was suddenly, terribly afraid that Mrs. Dymond was right. What had Mr. Cahill said? *Grief clouds the judgment; that's how undertakers make their money.*

Her own judgment could not be trusted, other people knew better, she was making a terrible mistake—after a girlhood spent making adult decisions, those fears wrapped around her like a comfortable cloak.

She had told herself Mr. Cahill could be trusted. That he wouldn't cheat her, that he wouldn't blackmail her, that he wouldn't demand things from her she didn't want to give. What evidence did she have for any of it? Just a feeling, a grief-addled feeling.

If he was lying, he could hurt not only her but also Jamie. He could take money from Wheatcroft. She felt sure in her heart that the idea was absurd—but all of his victims must have been sure.

Then she caught sight of him, bareheaded, leaning much too far out an upper window of the Drunk St. Leonard and waving to her. He was a hundred yards away and he'd picked her out of the crowd.

She lit up with happiness. It would be unladylike to wave back, but she raised a hand slightly to show she'd seen him. He kissed his hand to her and disappeared back inside.

"Thank you," she said to Mrs. Dymond. "I appreciate your candor, and your kindness. I hope you will not think too badly of me if I don't take your very wise advice."

Mrs. Dymond shrugged resignedly. "I didn't really think you would, ma'am."

The woman's manners were appalling. Just to point that out, Lydia said graciously, "Please, allow me to wish you and Mr. Dymond every joy."

For the first time, Mrs. Dymond smiled. "Thank you, ma'am…I wish you the same," she added, somehow making it clear that she did wish it, only thought it unlikely.

Wednesday morning Ash slept like a stone. The streets were flooded with carts and people going to market, jostling and shoving and cursing each other. When he finally woke at eleven o'clock, a little groggy, he wanted to see Miss Reeve. He could sense the black cloud of melancholy hovering somewhere near the ceiling above his head, but it hadn't descended yet.

He shaved and dressed hastily, trying to keep ahead of it, and when he spotted Miss Reeve out the window, he seized his hat and hurried downstairs. Stepping out the door of the Drunk St. Leonard, he found himself in the midst of a country market day.

He froze.

Rafe loved market days. When they first left London, the brothers had used to specialize in working small swindles at country markets and disappearing into the crowd. They still did when they needed a few pounds in a hurry, but they went after richer flats. Now Rafe liked to scatter largesse by losing a shilling or two to the thimble-riggers and the pin-and-girdle men. Sometimes, if the brothers were particularly flush in the pockets, Rafe would even let the Jewish peddler who seemed to crop up at every market sell him a cheap watch for more than it was worth.

I liked hearing his accent, he'd say if Ash teased him about it. *We can always sell it again ourselves later.*

So Ash would say, *You overacted your surprise when the pea was under the wrong thimble,* and Rafe would laugh, and Ash *wanted his brother back.* Maybe if he left town now, he could still find him.

Ash had built his life on the principle that when a man disappeared into the highways and byways of England, there was no good way of tracking him. It wasn't fair that even a simple, comforting truth like that could turn on him.

It was December, and rainy; there wasn't really enough of a crowd to attract petty swindlers. But when Ash rounded the Market Cross, hoping to spot Miss Reeve, he came face to face with a Jewish peddler, who said, "Ribbons and lace, good sir, watches and buttons," and thrust the box that hung around his neck into Ash's chest.

Ash avoided other Jews unless he was in a particularly reckless mood. Eventually one of them would give him away— maybe by word or sign, maybe merely by sharing a physiognomy. When he'd had Rafe, this eternally optimistic hawker's cry with its thick accent—Dutch, he thought—would have been pleasant enough, but hardly magnetic. Now it sounded painfully like home.

Rafe had wanted to keep on speaking Yiddish when they were alone. Ash had flatly refused. It was dangerous, a bad habit to get into, an unnecessary risk. He didn't know if the overwhelming temptation to speak Yiddish to this peddler was homesickness or atonement.

How the fellow would stare! Ash was getting old, because the peddler—in his early twenties and with a week's growth of beard—looked like a child to him, too young and too scrawny to safely walk the highways in winter. Rain misted in his blond curls. Ash wondered where he'd sleep tonight, and if he'd sold enough on this slow chilly day to buy dinner *and* a bed.

Of course he must be tougher than he seemed, and his coat and shoes looked free of holes, at least. Ash should let him go about his business. He should stop standing here waiting for someone to notice the family resemblance. But the strong lines of the young man's face—after so many years of English folk, to talk to someone who looked like the people Ash had grown up with!

Maybe I should go back to London. But he hadn't wanted to be in London when he *was* in London. It was a peculiar trick of the human mind to want something simply because you'd shut yourself off from it.

"I'd like a blue ribbon," he said. "Blue like the sky."

The man probably didn't speak enough English to understand anything but "ribbon", but he tapped his finger on the bottom left drawer of his box. Inside were ribbons of every hue and texture.

Ash selected one of pale-blue velvet sewn with tiny glass beads. "How much?"

The young man eyed him consideringly and held up two fingers. "Two shillings."

It was highway robbery. The peddler himself looked a little disgusted when Ash paid it. But recognizing a flat when he saw one, he said, "Very fine lady's watch," and indicated a watch that Ash knew from experience would probably stop ticking the first time it was dropped. He almost bought it because Rafe would have, but he looked over the jewelry instead.

It was mostly pinchbeck and paste. Ash thought it friendlier and gayer than the real thing, but Miss Reeve would be mortified if her necklace stained her skin with green. He picked out a string of malachite beads that tied with black satin ribbon, and ignored the string of coral beneath it, twin to the one he'd given Rafe as a baby to ward off illness. Paying about ten times the necklace's worth, he slipped it into his pocket.

Two people walked by with a copy of the new *Intelligencer*. Mr. Dymond had another article in it about the horrors of enlisted life, apparently. "Those poor lads, stung so bad by mosquitoes they couldn't open their eyes!"

Rafe wouldn't really have joined the army. He was too smart for that.

It's his life, Ash told himself. *His to enjoy, and his to throw away if he likes to.* Every bone in his body resisted the idea.

There Miss Reeve was, on the other side of the square. Relief lanced through him like pain, only backwards.

The deep, even black of her coat stood out against everyone else's drabs and colors. He couldn't see her hair, which was a shame—could only see, in fact, the slight curve of her cheek and chin below the black brim of her hat. That one line was as confident and splendid as the charcoal sketch of an old master.

Running wasn't respectable, but Ash walked towards her so fast he had to hold his hat on with one hand. When she turned her face towards him, he was already grinning at her and didn't know when he'd started.

"How did you get your eyes that color?" he asked her.

"Perhaps you can sell the secret at the Gooding Day auction and make a fortune."

She laughed and grimaced at the same time. "Don't remind me. I still haven't started anything for the auction."

She looked a little on edge. Maybe a present would cheer her up. Ash pulled his purchases out of his pocket, dangling the beads before her. "For you."

She made a moue. "I don't know if it's proper to accept jewelry before we're married," she said slyly, reminding him a-purpose of the things they'd done without being married. Those hands in their black leather gloves, demurely holding the strings of her reticule, had been on his cock.

"It's traditional among your set to give one's bride-to-be a family heirloom or two, isn't it?"

She laughed. "You bought that half a minute ago from the Jew peddler. I saw you."

He didn't say anything, but she glanced from him to the peddler, and maybe there was something on his face or maybe she was just clever, but he saw her realize that this was the closest thing to a family heirloom he'd ever have—that silly as it was, he almost meant it.

She took the necklace with a half-smile and ran it between her fingers. "How did you know green was my favorite color?" she said in that voice she had for flirting, as though she didn't mean a word of it but was willing to play the game if it meant they could get to the good part later. It was the most seductive thing Ash had ever heard.

"Is it really?"

"No. Lavender is. But I'm very fond of wearing green."

"I thought you must be. Redheads always wear green."

"I'm not a redhead," she said, surprised and evidently

stung. Her lower lip pouted a little, stubbornly. He'd noticed her brother did the same thing.

Ash knew abstractly that red hair wasn't elegant. It always surprised him when people really believed it. He supposed it was too Jewish, or too Irish, or something, and that its beauty meant nothing in the face of that. He took a moment to make sure his voice wouldn't sound flat when he teased, "You'd better take your bonnet off so we can decide for sure."

"I know what color my hair is. It's auburn."

Ash felt sad at all the stupid things people had to worry about. "So that I won't make the same mistake again, maybe you could give me a lock of it?" He held up his blue ribbon, feeling a little shy.

She gave him a pleased, startled smile. "You want a lock of my hair?"

He laid his hand over his heart. "I'll carry it here."

The smile spread. "Give me the ribbon. Wrenn will help me cut it for you."

He handed over the ribbon. "Can I cut it myself?"

"Only Wrenn and I are allowed near my hair with scissors." She put the ribbon in her bag and tied the malachite around her neck, tucking it beneath her pelisse so she wouldn't break mourning. Ash felt a deep sense of satisfaction as she took his arm.

But now that they were silent, that edgy look settled on her face again. "Is something wrong?" he asked.

She started, looking almost guilty. "It's nothing."

I'm fine was the lie people most wanted to get caught in. "I see," he said with clear skepticism. "Nothing." It was all right if she didn't want to tell him, but maybe she only wanted a little encouragement.

She glanced at him. "Mrs. Dymond said I shouldn't get married so soon after my father died. She said it was clouding my judgment."

Ash's heart sank. *If she threw me over, that would be all right,* he told himself. *I'll go to Brighton and fleece tourists and marry a mermaid.* He believed it for the second it took to say in a neutral voice, a voice that would let her do whatever she wanted, "I told you the same thing."

"She was nineteen when her father died, though. I'm thirty. I know my own mind." She was trying to convince herself, not Ash. She wasn't sure.

Ash didn't trust his voice, so he put his arm around her and hoped she'd interpret his silence as wordless understanding.

"Do you mind if I don't invite you for dinner tonight?" she said after a little bit. "I don't want Jamie to feel left out."

Coming out of her room the next morning, still feeling unsettled, Lydia's eyes fell on the silver tray that held the outgoing post. Had she remembered to put her congratulations on the birth of Lady Saunders's grandchild with the pile, or was it still sitting on her desk?

She flipped through the stack—and saw a letter addressed in Jamie's neat hand to *The Viscount Prowse, the Priory, near Kellisgwynhogh, Cornwall.*

Chapter 19

Lydia's stomach turned to ice. Why was Jamie writing to Cornwall? What should she do about it?

She was tempted to steal the letter and burn it, but if Jamie found out later it had never arrived, he would know. Worse, he might notice it gone from the salver before the post was taken into town.

Jamie came through the front door fresh from a morning ride, looking flushed and relaxed. Lydia's chest seized with worry. He had inherited their father's love of going very fast. Was he riding safely?

"Good morning," he said. "Lord, riding past those empty barns makes me wild! We'll keep twice as many cows next winter, and feed them on turnips. I know Father was old-fashioned, but planting fallow fields with clover and turnips is barely an innovation anymore."

Then he caught sight of the letters in her hand, and the slack went out of him like a rope pulled taut. "Are you looking for something?"

He *was* investigating Mr. Cahill, then. She could confront him and start an argument, or she could pretend she hadn't seen the letter. She dropped the post back in the salver with a tranquil smile. "I was making sure my note to Lady Saunders is here. Did I tell you her daughter was brought to bed of a healthy boy?"

Jamie's relief was obvious, which meant her lie was not. How could they be so close, so connected, and yet so distant from each other?

"Will you help me go over the guest list for my wedding breakfasts today?" she asked to distract him entirely. She was having one breakfast in town and one at Wheatcroft, for the convenience of guests without carriages. "I'm terrified of leaving someone off."

"Guest lists are an unadulterated horror," he commiserated, making no promises. "Are you inviting Caroline Jessop—Caroline Sparks, I mean? I like her."

Lydia sighed. "Yes. I hope Jack Sparks doesn't start a brawl."

"Might liven things up, anyway."

She frowned at him. "My wedding breakfasts are going to be delightful!"

"Not if Mr. Pilcher bakes the wedding cake."

"Mr. Pilcher baked the cake for your christening, young man."

"Yes, but I didn't have to eat *that* one."

Lydia laughed. "Mr. Pilcher's cakes aren't *bad*. Only…lackluster." She enjoyed them. They had the unmatched flavor of childhood.

Jamie's face turned serious. "You deserve better than lackluster, Lydia. In everything. Don't marry Mr. Cahill."

"Mr. Cahill isn't lackluster." She sounded absolutely smitten even to her own ears. She hoped Jamie would take the breathlessness in her voice for wide-eyed adoration, not the sure and certain carnal knowledge it was.

He scrunched up his face. "Do you think he rumples his jacket like that in advance, or does it happen naturally when he puts it on?"

"I like how rumpled he is," she said, flushing. "I think it—er—" She didn't know why she liked it. Was it because it drew attention to the shape of his body? Because there was a boyish sweetness about it? Because it looked as if she could tumble him into bed right then and there and he wouldn't mind a bit?

Jamie frowned at her. "You really do love him, don't you?"

"Yes!"

"This isn't about the money for you."

Her heart pounded. This was her chance. She should ask him not to send the letter. Maybe, while she was at it, she could ask him all the questions she never had the courage to: *Why don't you ever bring your friends home?* and *How have I failed you?* and *Do you love someone?*

"It was never about the money." It sounded true because it *was*. It was about her brother, about Lively St. Lemeston, about protecting what she loved.

If she did nothing and that letter ended by exposing Mr. Cahill—if anything ever exposed Mr. Cahill—that would be the ruin of it all. The end of her influence and her respectability. The end of her life as it had been. She had been thinking of it ever since her conversation with Mrs. Dymond yesterday.

But right now she honestly didn't care enough to change her course, and even more fiercely than she wanted Mr. Cahill, she wanted to hold on to not caring. She wanted there to be, at last, something in her life more important than what other people thought, something no one but herself could measure the worth of.

Jamie shook his head. "His story won't hold water. You must see that."

"What's so suspicious about being from Cornwall?" It didn't sound convincing because she knew exactly how right

Jamie was. She paused and thought about her lessons.

There was nothing wrong with Mr. Cahill. She didn't want him slighted. There. *That* was true.

"It isn't fair of you to judge him only because he didn't go to university." This time the ring of truth was in her voice. "I know him. I know he isn't going to hurt me. And I hate watching you treat him as if he doesn't belong here."

Jamie's face set. "I'm sorry, Lydia. But you sound like every willfully deceived woman since Eve. Father isn't here anymore to look after us. If I don't stop you, no one will."

"Yes," Lydia said furiously, "and then I would do as I like. How terrible that would be!"

It was an awful, awful thing to say. To have Father back, she would have given anything, bartered anything—*except Jamie*, she added, afraid to commit herself too far even in her own mind. No freedom was worth the price she'd paid. But freedom was sweet all the same. Her face burned with anger hastily papered over shame.

She wanted to ask Jamie if he felt it too. Lord Wheatcroft had never known that Jamie liked men; the two of them had kept the secret from him carefully. Lydia had even pretended once or twice that Jamie had confided in her about girls, not knowing if she was doing the right thing but knowing that Jamie was terrified Father would find out.

Father would never find out now.

"I only want you to be happy," Jamie said.

"I *am* happy! I was happy before you started a quarrel." Her eyes welled with tears. "I miss him."

"He was a good father."

Lydia thought that that was almost entirely true, but also just a tiny bit a lie she and Jamie would always tell together, and then she cried all over his riding coat, not caring about the smell. Jamie sniffled a little himself and was very embarrassed about it, and then they laughed over the impossibility of sharing a handkerchief.

Lydia wished she knew whether she ought to do something about that letter.

"You did absolutely right," Ash said, glad it was the truth. "It's all part of my trade. The odds are low he'll find anything. I wasn't using this name in Cornwall, and when the answer comes back, he'll feel justified in letting it go. Waiting is never easy, but the risk is worth it to ease his mind."

Miss Reeve toyed with a jasmine leaf from the vine that grew along the greenhouse wall, looking unconvinced.

"If he can find something out," Ash said gently, "better now than when we're married."

"I wish we were already married." Her voice was tight. She must be really worried.

"If you want to tell him the truth, I'm game." If she did, the marriage would be quietly called off. Ash felt that the generosity of his offer was only slightly marred by his conviction that she wouldn't take it.

"It doesn't concern him," Miss Reeve said in the small, defiant voice of one who knew herself in the wrong.

She loved her brother so much. Ash picked through the tangle of screaming red *let it go*s in his heart to find a thread that wanted nothing but her happiness. "It's not his choice who you marry," he said. "But it concerns him that the person who loves him most in the world is lying to his face. If you want to be close, maybe you have to be honest."

"Honesty isn't necessary for closeness. Look at us. We're close…aren't we?" Of course she was unsure. For all she knew, this was a game he'd played with flats across England.

It wasn't. Before her, there had been exactly one person in his life whose interests he'd consider putting above his own.

He'd offer a third time, the magic number, and if she still resisted, he'd done his duty and he could have her with a clear conscience. "Secrets are my profession. I know them inside and out. What separates me from someone I'm lying to isn't the false information. It's that I know I'm lying. It's a pane of glass—they can't see it, but I don't forget that it's there. My"—*my brother,* he started to say, and then the wound was too raw and he couldn't.

"When I have a drink with a man in a pub, and he doesn't know I'm Jewish…what's the difference between a Jew and a Gentile, really? It makes no difference, but I believe it would to him, so I don't mention it, and we can go on drinking together." It wasn't only practicality. But somehow, he was ashamed to explain how it would hurt, to see himself turn from a fellow soul to a dirty Jew. The pane of glass kept the distance between him and his own sadness too. "But when it's someone you love, that fear, or shame, or mistrust, or whatever isn't letting you tell the secret…" He couldn't finish the sentence.

I would have stayed with you if we could have been honest, Rafe had said. There wasn't an honest bone in Ash's body, there were panes of glass in his heart, but maybe if he'd been braver, if he'd smashed the glass for his brother and let the blood flow, maybe…

"It makes a difference in *you,*" he said finally.

She chewed on her lip. "There are a lot of things I haven't told you."

He'd noticed. She barely talked about herself at all. He smiled. "There are a lot of things I haven't told you too."

"Does that mean we can't be close?"

They might have shared a skin, that's how close he felt to her. He leaned down, his mouth a hairsbreadth from hers, sharing her breath. Her eyelashes brushed his cheek as she kissed him. He couldn't feel her heart beating, but even if it wasn't keeping time with his, it might as well have been.

Let it go, he told himself. *She's ready to bet. You don't tell a flat the game is rigged.*

He didn't want to think of her as a flat, though. "We agreed," he said quietly, leaning back against the hot wall for comfort and breathing in the smell of rich green things. "You told me it was all right to lie, that I could say what I wanted to you. Did Jamie offer you the same deal?"

She made that Reeve half-pout. "It isn't fair. It isn't fair that he has control over my money."

To Ash it looked as though no one really rich controlled his own money. It was trustees and allowances and entails and settlements and jointures and life interests as far as the eye could see, as if a pile of money or an expanse of dirt were a beloved grandmother whose life had to be stretched out at all costs. Miss Reeve wasn't allowed to have her money because she might spend it, instead of keeping it locked up to make sure her children were rich people too. Nothing about any of it was fair.

"You're right," he said. "I'm not saying you should tell him, or that you owe it to him, or anything like that. I'm saying… think about all of this. The town, your brother, the money."

Me. "Decide what you want. Then go after it, whatever that is, and I'll back you."

Ash knew what she wanted. She wanted her brother. He traced his fingers over the embroidery at her gown's high waist, wanting to touch her one last time if this was the end of it.

Her eyes glimmered with tears. "No one's ever said that to me before. Not my father. Not Jamie." She blinked; now her lashes were wet. "Jamie will never understand. I brought him up not to understand. What we wanted has never mattered. It's always been our duty. I understand, I do. We've been blessed and that means we have responsibilities. I want to do my duty by Lively St. Lemeston, as my father taught me. I will do it. But I want to choose, too. I want my money, and I want…" Her glittering eyelashes swept down over her cheekbones.

"You can have me," Ash said, gambling that was what she'd meant to say. He felt a little sick. This was what he did: he made people feel safe and accepted and then he hurt them. But there were no false pretenses this time. She knew the risks. Why should he feel guilty?

He traced a line of expensive black silk thread, nearly invisible against black bombazine. "But your money…if he doesn't sign it over before the wedding, what do you want to do?"

She pressed both her hands on top of one of his, holding it flat under her breast. "No one's ever said they would back me even if they didn't agree with me. Of all the good opinions in the world—and I've cared about all of them, Mr. Cahill, I doubt there's a person in England I haven't tried to please— Jamie's is the one I cherish the most. But I'm ready to care about my own opinion."

She was magnificent. She was a queen, a goddess.

Admiration and relief made him restless. He wanted to lift her up and swing her around, or pull her down into his lap on the floor, or go on his knees and press his cheek into the softness of her belly. He wished the shutters weren't open behind them.

With an effort he stayed still, only stroking his thumb lightly down the busk of her stays. "And what do *you* think?"

"I think if Jamie doesn't sign the money over before the wedding, he'll sign it over afterwards. He can't hold out for six months. I think we're getting married in eleven days, and that boys don't need to know everything about their big sisters."

When she squared her shoulders like that, it took super-human willpower not to bury his face between the perfect globes of her corseted breasts. "I was hoping you'd say that." He grinned at her, expecting her to smile back.

Instead worry clouded her face again. "It's dangerous for you, though, isn't it? If I don't tell him, and he finds something out?"

She was impossibly sweet. He had been running exactly this risk for years, of his own free will, and now she was ready to make it her responsibility. "Even if you did tell him, there are plenty of other folk who live here. It's not likely anyone will find anything out, but it isn't impossible. Fear of discovery is part of the game." She'd be living with it for the rest of her life, if he could talk her into it. She could do it. She liked walking the cliff-edge. She just needed to be reminded of that.

"You can't control everything," he said. "You can't control hardly anything. Let it go and enjoy the ride."

Their gazes held, and he could see her do it. It was the most arousing thing he'd ever seen, the way she relaxed and straight-ened like an acrobat about to walk the tightrope. Eleven days was an eternity.

"Oh," she said, "I forgot. I have something for you." She handed him a sealed packet. "Open it later."

Ash broke the seal as soon as he was out of sight of the house, careful not to spill the contents in the mud. The note was folded around an intricately braided circle of hair, threaded through and tied in a neat bow with the blue ribbon he'd given her.

Ash kissed it with a flourish, even though there was no one to see. Slipping it into his left inside breast pocket with her as-yet-unread letter, he read the note.

Mr. C— You were right. My hair is red. I didn't mean to be cruel, but I think perhaps I was. I'm sorry. Please accept this as a token of my undying esteem and regard. Yours aff.ly, Lydia Reeve.

Drek. He was definitely in love with her now.

He stood in the road, strangely panicked. She'd figured out what was bothering him, and she'd apologized. He was too close to her.

He realized, all at once, that he'd never put up any glass between him and her, and it was too late to fix it. Again and again, she'd asked him questions, and he'd told her the truth, because he wanted to. He'd told her things he'd hid from everyone, even Rafe.

Was he simply lonely? Was it only that she already knew part of it, so what did he have to lose from telling her everything?

No. It was her. It was the way she said, *tell me things because you* want *to*. She didn't push, and she didn't grab, and he felt safe for the first time in his life. As if he could let her rummage through all his secret drawers, and she'd be careful to put everything back where she found it.

His heart was wide open, and he didn't know how to shut it. He'd have to make damn sure he didn't lose her, now.

To Lydia's surprise, the days until her wedding passed quickly if not painlessly. On Sunday the banns were read again, and on Monday Dot Wrenn and Abby Gower (who would be Mrs. Wrenn and Mrs. Gower henceforward despite never having married, which Wrenn clearly found a little silly and which Abby enjoyed enormously as proof of her new status) removed to the Dower House to put it in order.

On Monday, too, Lydia bought pennyroyal, and hid it where she hoped Wrenn wouldn't look.

After that her mornings were occupied with visitors and her correspondence, her afternoons with arranging furniture in her new home, planning the menus for her first week of married life, and more than once tying on an apron and scarf and helping to beat carpets or stuff mattresses with fresh straw.

Mr. Cahill followed her about as much as possible, and when he couldn't, he occupied himself helping in the stables and the garden. In the evening, they walked back to the manor house for supper with Jamie in tired, accomplished silence. Lydia's bonnet swung unceremoniously from her fingers.

She glanced sideways at Mr. Cahill. Small, carefully doled-out transgressions like not wearing her bonnet had contented her once. No longer.

He grinned and plucked a bit of straw out of her cap. There was no point—she was covered in the stuff—but she smiled at him anyway. "I hear you learned to make holly wreaths today."

"Not good ones."

"Practice makes perfect."

He put his hands in his pockets and gazed contentedly up at the sky. "Nothing is ever perfect. That's part of the beauty of the world."

Why should those words provoke such a rush of affection? The world's beauty sprang into sharp focus, of a sudden—a gleaming black patch on a drying branch, the sky's light, bright gray, the contrast between Mr. Cahill's dark hair and eyes and his warm olive skin, the energetic line of his hunched shoulders in his greatcoat, its collar askew.

"Jamie wants to know if you rumple your clothes on purpose, or if it just happens when you put them on."

"That's a trade secret." He gave her a sidelong, laughing glance. "And the secret is that my clothes were usually made for someone else."

She wanted to kiss him. She wanted to drag him behind a topiary sphere and have her way with him. Yet she somehow felt that neither of those things would be enough.

After a moment, she recognized the feeling: she wanted to throw her arms around him and say *I love you.*

He had warned her she might begin to question her own feelings. He had promised her he would know, no matter what, that it was all a lie. She tried to tell herself this was amateurish confusion, that she didn't love him, that she would feel this way about anyone with whom she'd done the things she'd done with Mr. Cahill.

But I wouldn't have done those things with anyone else.

He leaned towards her, breathing in deeply. "I love the smell of clean straw," he said. "We'll be sleeping in that bed in a few days."

She eyed him. It was clear he hadn't been sleeping well. In moments of quiet his eyes went glassy, and once or twice she'd seen him almost irritable, especially when supper was delayed by Jamie's dawdling. "I have some letters to write. Why don't you take a nap on the sofa while I do that?"

He was disarmed by her concern, as he always was. The look on his face said that basic human consideration was some sort of remarkable gift of hers.

Her heart felt as if it were actually bloating unhealthily in her chest.

It isn't anything special in me, she wanted to say. *It's only that you've let me know you well enough to guess at what you aren't telling me.*

But…he'd chosen to do that. With her.

Could she really let him go in six months, only because a real marriage between them was unthinkable? She rolled the idea around her tongue, silently: *the daughter of a baron, pillar of her community, marries a Jewish street thief.*

Yes, it was preposterous. Sometimes men of high rank married actresses, and she could think of one dowager who had married her groom. Even that was rank folly to be mocked and condemned by all one's friends, and all their friends and their friends' friends besides. *This* was worse than anything she had ever heard.

But when she set that aside and looked at Mr. Cahill, it didn't *feel* preposterous. It felt like exactly what God intended marriage to be.

She had plenty of time to decide. She would see how she felt in six months. Or was that only plenty of time to get in deeper? What were the odds that after six months of sharing his bed and his hearth, she would love him less than she did now?

But that was preposterous too. The odds were excellent. One saw it all the time. People married, they shared a home, they became hopelessly disenchanted and despised one another. She had nothing to worry about.

She repeated that to herself as she watched him sleep on the sofa, limbs sprawling, the lines on his face smoothed away and his mouth hanging faintly open. This adoration, this desire to sit and watch him, the ease with which she produced a letter filled with effusions about her upcoming marriage and her splendid husband-to-be—it was all nothing to worry about.

I thought you were supposed to be a good liar, she told herself.

Chapter 20

A sh couldn't quite believe that he was standing before the vicar in a parish church at nine o'clock on a Tuesday morning, getting married. Miss Reeve was beside him on her brother's arm, looking nervous and wearing a dress that was all the same colors as a pansy. If he glanced over his shoulder, he'd see her family and friends watching him with expectant smiles, handkerchiefs at the ready. He felt like an actor who'd wandered into the wrong play.

Growing up, Ash had hardly known anyone who was married. The people he moved among now set so much store by it, but Ash had never stopped thinking of it as one more excuse for the law to stick its nose where it didn't belong, into what should be sacred between two people. It made it illegal to leave, a prosecutable offense to love someone else. What was solemn or beautiful about that?

He was already bound to Miss Reeve, vicar or no vicar. Her tiniest motion called up an answer in him, the way on a good day wind among the wildflowers could make his heart flutter as if it had petals. If this official blessing meant she would live with him, then it was worth it to stand here and try to look awed.

"Are you all right?" she asked him, stiff-lipped. Her fingers gripped one another tightly.

He leaned in and brushed a kiss on her cheek. "I've never seen you in colors before. It's a bit overwhelming."

She didn't laugh, but she made a little huffing sound and her shoulders relaxed. Jamie glared at him across the top of her head. Ash hoped he wouldn't do anything to embarrass Miss Reeve.

The ceremony did nothing to decrease his sense of unreality. Anglican weddings were so strange and staid; there was no sense of joy in them at all. Ah yes, here came the bit about marriage signifying the mystical union between Christ and his Church, a metaphor Ash had always found bizarre and a little perverse. But the English thought the Song of Solomon was about Christ and his Church too—or politely pretended to, anyway. Ash and Rafe had laughed silently about that in churches across England.

"…And therefore it is not by any to be enterprised, nor taken in hand unadvisedly, lightly, or wantonly, to satisfy men's carnal lusts and appetites, like brute beasts that have no understanding; but reverently, discreetly, advisedly, soberly, and in the fear of God…"

Miss Reeve breathed deeply and evenly, gazing straight ahead—too deep and even and straight. Ash could guess the effort it cost her not to flinch at those words. Childhood fears and beliefs never really left you. But she was carrying it off beautifully.

She didn't flinch when the vicar asked for impediments, either. Jamie gnawed on his lip and glanced over his shoulder at the empty pews. He didn't have anything, clearly—only wished he did, or that a woman would suddenly rush in at the back of the church crying, *Stop! This man is already married—to me!*

But when asked who gave this woman to be married, he said in a voice whose tension could easily be interpreted as shyness, "I do," and let her go.

Then there was a blur of repeating after the vicar, and trying not to snicker at the idea that any of the Hebrew patriarchs had marriages one should try to emulate.

Ash kept his eyes on Miss Reeve through the interminable remainder of the ceremony, shutting out the clergyman's voice so as not to look sarcastic or remember all the places he and Rafe had once looked sarcastically at one another.

He wished Rafe were here, only—he had meant to stand back there with the teary relatives while Rafe married Miss Reeve.

Rafe, he thought, could have taken these vows in earnest. Ash shouldn't be happy that he was here instead. He shouldn't be happy at all.

But he had to be happy, because everyone was watching them. So he kept his eyes on Miss Reeve—Mrs. Cahill now, he remembered, and his smile felt as if it would split his face. She was beaming too—she *glowed*, quite as a bride should, and darted little glances at him. Ash didn't know how he was going to make it through *two* wedding breakfasts before getting her into bed.

Lydia's jaw ached from smiling. The Lively St. Lemeston Assembly Rooms were full to bursting with food and people, and she and Mr. Cahill had spoken to most of them.

Lydia had never known anyone who liked crowds as much as she did before. Aunt Packham was weeping quietly in the corner, where Jamie kept her company, not exactly glowering but not smiling either. Her erstwhile best friend Caro sat by the wall, taking notes on everything for the *Intelligencer* and giggling behind her hand with her new sister-in-law.

Caro had always wanted Lydia to giggle in a corner with her at parties, when Lydia was *working*. Caro had wanted to be friends, she realized now, and had thought that was what friends did. Lydia was glad Caro had found people who understood what she wanted and wanted the same thing.

Lydia, on the other hand, had barely spoken to Mr. Cahill directly in an hour, and yet she could feel the thread between them humming. She knew very well that he was thinking mostly of their wedding night, just as she was, and yet he smiled and shook hands and remembered details about guests' children, half of which she hadn't told him. She quickly realized that he must be talking to people all the daylight hours he wasn't with her.

Miss Tice, Mary Luff's new employer, walked in. Lydia had been campaigning to make a friend of her, in hopes that a desire to please her might win good treatment for Mary, where showing favor to the girl herself might lead to resentment and secret cruelty from the milliner and other girls alike. She thought it was working; Miss Tice's congratulations sounded heartfelt enough.

"We're all that happy for you, Mrs. Cahill," she said. "All of us. We did so hope you'd find a gentleman worthy of you."

"Oh, I don't pretend to be worthy," Mr. Cahill said, and Lydia thanked her, full of sloshy warm embarrassment and the pleasure of being called *Mrs. Cahill*.

Miss Tice smiled the particular sentimental smile of a guest at a wedding breakfast and gave Lydia a small box. "I hope you like these."

Inside nestled delicate sprays of winterberries, so carefully made they looked almost real. "They're *beautiful*." Oh, it was nice to wear colors again. It was a kind rule, that brides left off mourning. Wearing black had been a good thing those first weeks, announcing her grief to the world so that she wasn't obliged to. But it had begun to *make* her sad too, every glove and hat and scrap of fabric arrayed against her slipping for even a moment and forgetting what she had lost.

"They'll look splendid on my white winter bonnet. You don't think a low crown is hopelessly outdated, do you?" After a pleasant discussion of fashions in hats, in London and the country, Lydia turned to Mr. Cahill so he could compliment the gift too.

"Your most cunning work I've seen yet, ma'am," he said. "Though I must admit, my favorite is still the love-lies-bleeding."

Miss Tice smiled. "I saved a few berries for the auction, never you fear."

So Mr. Cahill had been visiting Miss Tice too. Not only Miss Tice—as the breakfast wore on, woman after woman whom Lydia had brought him to meet now told him in detail about her auction contribution, referencing conversations Lydia hadn't witnessed: *I've decided on a yellow border instead of the purple* and *I thought I could offer to sew the buyer's initials on it after* and *I realized a half-crown was precisely the right size to use as a pattern.*

With every exchange, every new proof of his skill, his dedication and his generosity, Lydia's arousal grew until she was desperate with it. She and Mr. Cahill had been creating static electricity between them all through this party, and now she was fully charged. When the Gilchrists arrived, she could not even manage to care about Mrs. Gilchrist's quilt, though she had resolved to speak to her on the subject at the first opportunity.

"I'm so glad we saw you!" she told the agent and his wife. "We're about to remove to Wheatcroft." She exclaimed over the fussy embroidered cuffs Mrs. Gilchrist had made her, and then gathered up Jamie and Aunt Packham and whisked them all out the door, leaving the Pink-and-Whites to enjoy themselves and eat the rest of the food.

The drive was interminable, the conversation for once dominated by Jamie and Aunt Packham. Lydia's whole mind was occupied with her thigh pressed against Mr. Cahill's, his arm brushing hers when the carriage swayed. She didn't dare turn her head to look at him.

"Are you all right, Lydia?" Jamie asked at length. He looked half desperately worried and half I-told-you-so, as if he imagined she felt the first stirrings of regret.

Lydia had no idea what to say.

Aunt Packham laughed. "It's natural for a woman to feel anxious on her wedding day, Jamie. She'll be blooming tomorrow, never fear."

Jamie flushed bright red. "Lydia?" He shot her a defiant, loyal glance.

Her heart skipped a beat. She'd done that for him when he was small. He'd been a quiet boy. Nursemaids, tutors, doctors, other boys, Lord Wheatcroft, and Aunt Packham had all rushed to speak for him, to tell Lydia how he felt, how his day had been, what he wanted, whether his head ached, or where that bruise had come from.

And she had always said, *Jamie?* so he'd know that if he wanted to contradict, to tell her the truth, she would listen and she would care.

He never had. Eventually she'd stopped, afraid she was making him feel conspicuous. But he must have marked and appreciated it after all, because now he was trying to do the same thing for her. She wished she had something to say besides, "I think Aunt Packham is right."

Mr. Cahill's quiver of suppressed laughter might have been imperceptible to someone not pressed against his side.

Jamie sighed and looked out the window.

As the carriage rolled up the Wheatcroft drive, Jamie said, "Mr. Cahill, may I speak with you a moment in the Little Parlor?"

"Of course," Ash said, with a small show of surprised confusion. His brain whirred with trying to guess what Jamie wanted, but that wouldn't help him. Only a relaxed state of readiness could do that. So he uncluttered his mind and imagined that Jamie was his new brother-in-law who could only want to speak to him about something quite harmless.

Mrs. Cahill's gaze went between the two of them. Ash gave her a reassuring smile.

"Perhaps I should come with you," she said.

Jamie shook his head. "I have a gift for you that I don't want you to see yet."

Mrs. Cahill—no. He would call her that aloud, and enjoy it immensely, but he couldn't possibly think of her that way in the privacy of his own mind. *Lydia* looked surprised and annoyed for the space of a moment before an expression of fond gratitude spread over her face. "You got me a gift?"

Jamie grinned. "I know you hate surprises, but I think

you'll like this one."

Ash didn't understand how it was possible to dislike surprises, especially surprise gifts. But he also didn't understand why you would give someone a surprise gift when you knew she disliked it.

"If it's from you, I know I will." Lydia ruffled his hair. "Be nice to my husband."

Jamie pulled him into the parlor. The gift was immediately obvious: the huge, bulging sofa Lydia had reupholstered with stripes was missing. Jamie looked embarrassed. "She loves that sofa," he muttered.

Ash thought she loved that sofa where it was, as a memory of this room filled with Reeves, and that finding Jamie hadn't cared to keep it might diminish it in her eyes. He also thought it was unlikely to fit neatly into the Dower House's parlor.

But he knew she wouldn't say so to Jamie, so he smiled. "She does. It was a bighearted notion."

Jamie shrugged, not looking at him. "I don't know what one man is supposed to do with such a large house. My rooms at Oxford would have fit into Wheatcroft's pantry."

Ash had remarked a certain lack of enthusiasm on Jamie's part towards any mention of his own future marriage or family. He wasn't sure if Jamie was molly, or if it was merely an unattached youth's dislike of being managed by relatives. He covered both possibilities by saying, "I imagine you could have splendid house parties for your friends. If you expected things to become rowdy, Mrs. Packham would always be welcome to stay at the Dower House."

Jamie winced. It occurred to Ash, too late, that maybe his friends at Oxford would also have fit into Wheatcroft's pantry. It had been a thoughtless remark after all.

Well, who could blame Ash for not being in top form? He was married and had yet to bed his extremely eager wife. It was enough to make anyone tactless.

"Or you could begin collecting things," he suggested, trying to salvage his mistake. "I'm sure that antique suits of armor could soon fill up some of the extra rooms."

Jamie's lips twitched. "All suits of armor are antique by definition," he pointed out with reluctant amusement.

It was precisely what Lydia would have said. Ash was filled with sudden affection. It was a useful emotion, but oddly unwelcome. Why?

You like everybody, he reminded himself. *It doesn't mean you're trying to make a little brother of him. It doesn't mean anything.* But he couldn't be sure. Maybe he really was so empty, so rudderless, that he would attach himself to the first people he washed up against.

"Are you all right?" Jamie asked.

"I just wish my brother might have been here." Ash's throat was dry as dust. "My au—" He choked on the lie. He couldn't remember the last time that had happened. "My aunt is too ill for him to leave her."

Jamie's face, for the first time, filled with sympathy. Then he remembered himself and looked sullen again.

"What did you wish to speak to me about?" Ash asked.

Jamie bit his lip. "Just that if you hurt my sister, I'll kill you," he said, rather apologetically. "I know I don't seem very menacing, but I'd wager I'm better with a pistol than you are, so take it seriously."

Ash thought it unlikely that Jamie had it in him to kill in cold blood. "I would never willingly hurt your sister," he said gently. "Her happiness is precious to me."

"Good. See that it stays that way."

Ash couldn't help smiling. "Do you think we might make another truce? This rift between the two of you is making your sister wretched."

Jamie lifted his eyebrows, reminding Ash again vividly of his sister. "She doesn't look wretched."

"I didn't say she was *all* wretched." He waited until Jamie met his eyes. "She doesn't wear her heart on her sleeve. But she feels very deeply."

"I know that," Jamie snapped. "I've known her a lot longer than you have, and if you hurt her, I'll kill you."

Ash nodded and held out his hand to shake on the deal. Jamie hesitated—but manners won out. Not shaking hands was a graver insult than he was willing to deliver.

"I know you've been making inquiries about me," Ash said. "And I know you haven't found anything, because there's nothing to find."

Jamie looked uncertain and stubborn. "I don't deny it—at least, I don't deny that my inquiries have been unsuccessful so far. My friend in Cornwall has turned up nothing against you. Your bank and the vicar of your home parish both vouch for you."

Ash kept his relief off his face.

"I can't shake the feeling that there is something odd about this whole affair, but I know it's no excuse for rudeness."

"It's to your credit that you want to protect your sister," Ash said. "I don't mind a little rudeness now and again. Politeness makes things go smoothly, but it's hardly a mark of good character."

"Exactly!" Jamie said with the relief of someone used to having to argue a point. He flushed. "We should be getting back to the breakfast." He held the door for Ash.

Lydia had promised herself she would stay exactly as long at Wheatcroft as she'd stayed in Lively St. Lemeston, so no one could feel slighted. She'd stayed in Lively St. Lemeston an hour and a half. Why? Why had she done it? If she'd stayed three-quarters of an hour, she could be taking Mr. Cahill's clothes off right now.

Don't think about taking his clothes off.

But she couldn't stop. She hadn't yet seen his naked body. She would take his cravat off first, she decided, and undo the first button of his shirt, and kiss the hollow of his throat.

There was something unbearably thrilling in the image—still in coat and waistcoat, with that one patch of bare golden skin, dark hair curling above his white shirt. Something that was always there, and that no one ever saw.

But perhaps we should wait until after dark, she thought. *What will the servants say?*

She'd always found the gossip and speculation about new brides extremely embarrassing. She had no doubt she would find it embarrassing when it was about herself. But even if they said Mr. Cahill was a fortune hunter who'd ensnared and enslaved her with lust, she…

Mr. Cahill tugged at the knot of his cravat. He saw her frown and made an inquiring noise.

"I forgot what I was thinking of." She glanced at the clock. Twenty minutes more.

The Wheatcroft carriage took them to the Dower House, knowing laughter at their haste still ringing in Lydia's ears. The carriage would stay with them until their own was finished later in the week. Jamie had said when he made the offer, "You know I prefer to ride," which hadn't much reassured Lydia, but the last thing she wanted was another argument with Jamie. She would visit the coachmaker and ask him to hurry, that was all.

Oh, but a bride wasn't supposed to go out visiting in the first weeks of her marriage. She would have to send a note.

Mr. Cahill slouched down among the cushions with a sigh. Lydia wasn't sure whether the movement naturally called attention to the fall of his pantaloons, or whether her own desire made it seem that way.

"I deserve a medal for this morning's work," he said. "I've burgled sturdy townhouses with less effort than it took to go through those breakfasts without an obvious cockstand."

She didn't know how to answer that; she was so unused to speaking plainly of such things. She supposed she should be more shocked by the mention of burgling than by the word 'cockstand'.

He leaned over and lifted her leg into his lap by her ankle, pushing her skirts up to show her stocking. "Maybe I could be awarded the Order of the Garter."

"We still have our own servants to greet," she said with an effort. So little—his hand on her calf—and already all her skin tingled and her breasts ached. She sent her attention to them, cupped and separated by her corset. The ache grew. Her nipples hardened, already humming with pleasure. How could they feel so good without even being touched?

The carriage jerked to a halt. He pushed her foot off his

thigh with a resigned sigh and stood. "Come along with you." Heaving her up into his arms as she descended from the carriage, he carried her up the walk, setting her on her feet with a flourish before the assembled staff in the entrance hall.

Wrenn and Gower had outdone themselves. The Dower House was cozy and warm, with Christmas greenery wound around the banisters, wreaths hung on the walls, and holly on the mantels. Everything in the house shone, gleamed, glowed, and otherwise reflected the light in a manner indicative of its extreme cleanliness and good condition.

"I cannot thank you all enough for your hard work this week," she began, once initial greetings and congratulations were exchanged. "Going to a new home can only be a wrench, and you have not merely done it yourselves with grace, but made it a joyful and easy occasion for us—"

"We're both very grateful," Mr. Cahill said with a grin. "But it's been a long morning, and though she'd never admit it, I think Mrs. Cahill needs to rest."

"Indeed, ma'am, you look worn out," Wrenn said dryly. Everyone else smirked.

Lydia couldn't bring herself to care. "Yes, indeed, I think I should benefit very much from a few quiet hours before dinner." The garden-and-stable boy, a lad of fourteen, fought for composure. "Thank you again, and thank you for your understanding. I look forward very much to our life together."

"Would you like me to attend you, madam?" Wrenn asked.

Lydia looked to Mr. Cahill, unsure.

"That won't be necessary, thank you, Wrenn," he said, offering Lydia his arm. She tried not to rush up the stairs to the two rooms that were to be theirs.

They were comfortable rooms—a little too dark-hued and

old-fashioned to be cheerful, but she liked that. Mr. Cahill led her through his, papered in silver and dark green, to her own in burgundy and gold. He put his hands in his pockets and turned a full circle, bouncing happily on the balls of his feet.

She realized, abashed, that while she had been thinking the rooms small and simple compared to Wheatcroft, to him two airy rooms for one couple must seem the height of decadence.

Feeling like a cat stalking a mouse, she watched him go across and lower the muslin window-blinds. She'd been patient, and soon she'd pounce. The room's light turned a white, clean shade, and she took a step towards him.

"May I take down your hair?" he asked.

She hesitated. She had wanted to luxuriate in their privacy, in being allowed to go as slowly as they wanted without fear of interruption. But now they were here—"I don't think I can wait."

He grinned at her and sat on the edge of the bed. "Let's take the edge off, shall we? Come here." He opened his arms, making space for her between his legs. When she sat between them, he wrapped his arms around her stomach and pulled her in close, pressing a kiss on the side of her neck. She gasped and squirmed.

"All right, all right, hold your horses," he said, laughter in his voice, and tugged her skirts up. He lifted her right leg and hooked it over his thigh, exposing her.

She held very still, half nervous and half not wanting to do anything that might discourage or distract him. Was she really ready for this? She had said she couldn't wait, though, and he took her at her word. When he put his hand there—

Abandon, this was abandon, but she couldn't even remember what she was abandoning. She whimpered impatiently as his fingers slid over her, desperate to reach the peak faster, now— "Do it yourself," he murmured in her ear, and slid his hands up her sides to cup her breasts.

Could she, with him watching?

A drop of sweat ran down her throat into the dark hollow made by the busk of her corset. He licked up the side of her neck, tasting her skin. Christ. Why on earth should that feel so good? She dipped her own finger into her wetness and circled her center of feeling.

"What do you think about when you do this alone?" he asked, carefully freeing one breast from her clothes and experimenting with her nipple in his fidgety way. Now he flicked it with his thumb and index finger, a hard, sharp sensation that felt the way champagne corks sounded. She spread her legs wider. He moaned, and she realized she had pushed her rear up against his manhood.

He put a hand on her hip to anchor her and rubbed against her. "Please," he said hoarsely. "Just one little imagining. The tamest one you have, if you like."

Her mind was blank. She didn't need any imaginings when the reality was so terribly arousing. "I—" She struggled to think. "When I was younger, I used to like to imagine coitus in one of the box pews at church."

His breathing quickened. "Really? Did you ever imagine that while *in* church?"

"All the time," she confessed guiltily. "I knew I shouldn't, and the more I knew I shouldn't, the more fun it was to know that no one suspected me."

It was fun to tell him about it, too. It felt wicked and free. There were so many thoughts she had never shared with anyone because she knew they would be shocked. She could say anything to him. She could ask him for anything.

"Did you imagine any particular person in the pew with you?"

She shook her head. "I don't like to imagine real people. It feels like a liberty."

"Have you ever imagined me?"

She nodded. "I didn't think you would mind."

He groaned and moved them, pushing her down on her back on the bed and climbing atop her. His hard cock pressed against her through his pantaloons, graceless and eager. "Tell me," he said.

She shifted until the wool scraped against her in just the right way, wrapping a leg around one of his for leverage. She loved the way her single bare breast felt, squashed wantonly against his silk waistcoat. Her head fell back.

"Tell me."

"I want you inside me. I want you to take what you need."

"You mean you want me to fuck you hard?" The words were crude; she had always imagined that would make them disrespectful, that a man said such things to a woman to master her. She had never objected to the idea—had even found it arousing. But Mr. Cahill was merely translating her round-aboutation into plain English, repeating it back to her because he liked the sound of it—and maybe teasing her a little.

All her life, honesty had been the most forbidden fruit of all. "Exactly."

He ground roughly against her, driving her into the bed. "I can do that."

Lydia spent, clinging to him as pleasure shook her out, ripped her apart at the seams, and pieced her back together with all her brightest, best parts facing out. She didn't even bother chasing the last tremors. There was more and better to come.

She lay back, sated and happy. Her own impatience gone, she relished the tension that was still in him, his arms braced to either side of her and his breath hot in her ear as he drove himself towards his peak.

"Sss—sorry," he said. "If—uncomfortable—"

Tenderness suffused her. "Take as long as you like," she said lazily, and tilted up her hips. "Dinner isn't until four."

He made a gurgling noise that might have started out as a laugh and pushed himself up on his forearms to look down at where he rutted in a froth of her skirts. The glazed, open-mouthed look on his face should have been comical or distasteful, but it wasn't. He dragged himself down her until she could feel the head of his cock bump over her pubic bone and push up against her naked slit.

"Soon," she said, and at the word some of the heat and impatience rushed back. "Oh, God, I've been waiting so long… do it. Unbutton your pantaloons and put your cock in me." She said it as crisply as she could, having noticed how gleeful it made him when she said coarse things in her educated voice.

He liked it now, very obviously. His jaw dropped, and he pushed convulsively up against her. "Do you mean it?"

Why not? She was as wet as she would ever be. That would help, surely. "Pull the counterpane from under me. We shouldn't get blood on it."

He had the quilt on the floor in under ten seconds. Her— she would have to ask him what to call it, all the words she knew were so precious—her female parts ached eagerly as he unbuttoned his pantaloons, fingers slipping on the buttons in his haste.

"Taking the care to do something correctly is faster than hurrying and fumbling," she teased primly.

He laughed and kissed her. "I think this will hurt about the same either way. It is what it is."

"I want it to hurt," she said, and meant it. She wanted to mark this connection between them with blood and pain, as Adam and Eve had marked it, tasting the apple in one another's mouth.

He took a harsh, ragged breath. "This is probably the least romantic thing in the world, but it will help." He spat in his hand and rubbed his expectorate over his member, his breath hissing through his teeth at the sensation.

Lydia tried not to make a face.

He laughed again, high and breathless and exhilarated. "We'll have a proper wedding night after dinner and strew the bed with rose petals if you like."

"Roses are out of seas—"

He pressed into her and her breath stalled in her lungs at the pain. He closed his eyes, breathing hard and shallow. "Shhh," he murmured, gentling her even though he was trembling.

He pushed in farther, which hurt more. But then he pulled out, and somehow when he came back inside it slid easier. He seesawed until he was all the way in, and then it wasn't bad at all. It felt good. Oh, it still hurt, a stretching, scraping hurt, but she liked it. It made things real. It made this something special, not something she would have wanted to do with just anybody.

"How are you?" he asked.

I love you. Lydia held the thought tightly inside her and smiled up at him instead. "Good. Oh! I forgot." She reached up to untie his cravat as he made slow, small thrusts inside her. She wondered if he needed to go harder or faster to spend. She should say something, give him permission, but she liked this. She didn't want it to end. They would never have another first time. She pulled his cravat off and undid the first shirt button.

"You forgot what?" She liked the sound of his voice, distracted and heavy and rough.

"I wanted to do this." She ducked her head and kissed along his skin at the edge of the linen. He tilted his head up obligingly. Somehow that pushed him more snugly inside her, and they both gasped. Her head was at an awkward angle and her shoulders were hunched, but she could see the pulse pounding in his throat, and his skin was smooth and salty and his hair was rough. She poked her tongue into the hollow of his collarbone.

"I'm sorry," he said. "I'm close, I promise—it won't be long now—"

Oh. That broke her heart. She was loving everything about this moment, and he thought she was wishing it was over, that he should have somehow made it better. "Don't apologize. Please. You don't have to—" *You don't have to try so hard.*

That would only make him feel ashamed. She would hate it if he said that to her, when she was doing her best. She was probably trying too hard right now, to find the correct thing to say.

"Nothing is perfect," she said finally. "I don't want it to be. I want th"—he struck some sensitive spot within her, and for a moment she couldn't breathe—"this. I like *this*."

He made a sound that was almost like a sob. "I think I li—" He pressed his face into the sheet beside her head and made three hard thrusts whose sharp, twisting pain almost made her spend again. He trembled violently, twitching inside her.

Oh. Oh, that was—strange and wonderful and unbearably intimate. He groaned and pushed into her a few more times, out of his own control.

They lay together silently until his cock began to soften and slip from her with a wet noise that was a little bit disgusting. He pulled out hastily and, heaving himself off the bed with an effort, wet a handkerchief in the basin. "Stand up carefully."

His seed dribbled out of her when she did. She made a face at him, tucking her breast back into her clothes, and cleaned up as best she could. It was difficult not to keep rubbing herself with the wet cloth. "What were you going to say?"

He thought back. "Oh," he said, grinning. "I think I lied when I said nothing was perfect. But maybe you're the exception that proves the rule."

It was a well-known fact that men in the heat of passion would say anything, but even so it gave Lydia the courage to say, "Would you—if you wouldn't mind—how you kissed my—in the greenhouse, how you—"

He blinked. "You mean you really did like what we just did? Well, of course I could tell you did, but enough that you—?"

"I don't think it will take long."

He collapsed back on the bed. "I don't think I can move," he said, eyes laughing. He tugged her by her skirts until she indecorously straddled his face, and yanked her down.

It didn't take long.

Lydia let Ash help her dress for dinner. "Can I take your hair down?" he asked.

She looked doubtful. "You won't be able to put it up again."

"Can't you?"

She considered. "Not well, but I suppose it's only dinner at home." Her mouth curved up as she said it.

Home. This was their home now. This was his house, at least for six months.

Suddenly he didn't know if he could spend six months in one house, using one name. He concentrated on taking out her hairpins, unrolling the rolls of hair. Untying the thread that held the end of her narrow braids, he unplaited them carefully. Her hair parted around the comb like water falling through his fingers.

Then he brushed it till it crackled and shone, coppery strands rising to meet the bristles. She shut her eyes and smiled. She always watched him. He liked that she trusted him enough not to, every so often.

She opened her eyes and caught him smiling. "Why do you like this so much?"

He thought. "I like the ordinary details of other people's lives. This is something you do every day, more than once. You don't even think about it. Yet no one but you and Wrenn has ever seen it."

She nodded and gathered her hair in her hands, rolling and pinning it quickly into a snail-shell at the crown of her head. Then he unbuttoned her dress and buttoned her into another, this one a deep turquoise blue.

It still filled him with delight that one person could have so many clothes, and that she now had another whole set he hadn't seen. How long would it take him to see everything, if he avoided snooping in her wardrobe? A fortnight, a month? How much longer to run through every hat and jacket and glove?

She fastened a string of fine large pearls around her neck and took up a rich cashmere shawl.

He didn't belong here. Not when he couldn't stop cataloging everything she owned. He knew to the penny how much that shawl could get him from a pawnbroker, and how much if he could find an outright buyer. She probably didn't remember what she'd paid for it.

You don't have to belong, he told himself. *You only have to blend in for six months, and then—if you can even talk her into it—visit now and again when you feel lonely.*

But he was realizing how much he did want a home. One place, forever. He couldn't understand it. He'd been in plenty of people's lovely homes before—maybe not quite as lovely as this, but better than anything he'd ever had. He'd never cared that they weren't his, or wanted to belong there. He'd always thought—

It hit him. He'd always thought, *Rafe and I will get ourselves a better one, one of these days.* Oh, there hadn't been any urgency to it. He'd loved his life the way it was. But he'd always planned to settle down, hadn't he? And he'd never noticed.

All at once he remembered how, as a little boy breaking into townhouses, he'd wasted precious seconds lying in a bed or looking at himself in a smooth new mirror and thought, *One day.*

What did it matter where he *belonged*? Did he want to be dirt poor again? Did he want to live among thieves and cutthroats and rivals and guard his back every moment from a knife or a constable's baton? Did he want to choke down sooty London air and breathe in the stagnant, filthy river all summer?

That was the only place he belonged that you could point

to on a map. He'd belonged with Rafe, but Rafe was gone and wishing wouldn't bring him back.

Ash didn't want to be a gentleman and really belong here, he only wanted to *have* it—and he did. He just had to hold on to it. By the end of six months, softhearted Lydia wouldn't want him to leave. He could probably even make her think that his staying was her idea.

Lydia might ask him to leave tonight if he couldn't pull himself together. But as centerpiece after platter after remove after entremets was brought out and lovingly arranged in a symmetrical pattern on the snowy-white tablecloth, Ash's stomach curdled further.

Duck, pheasant, roast chicken, apple compote without cinnamon, potato pudding, stewed red cabbage…every food he'd named as a favorite.

Why had he done this? It was exactly the kind of purpose-less lie he'd trained Rafe never to give. Yet somehow in that moment, he'd given her Rafe's favorite foods instead of his own.

Ash didn't look at the food. He ate it without letting himself taste it. Instead, he watched Lydia glowing at having done him a kindness—and a little at the enjoyment of playing devoted bride.

"Is the duck done to your liking?" she asked now, with a sweet, hopeful glance from under her lashes. "You must tell Mrs. Gower if there is anything you prefer differently."

Her turquoise-blue gown was bright in the clear, fragrant light of beeswax candles and a cherry-wood fire, and her hair gleamed like burnished bronze. The curve of her mouth gave him the same glad feeling as finding a penny in the street.

He smiled back and said, "Everything is to my liking," and ignored his stomach filling with Rafe's food. All those times he'd given Rafe his supper...he was being paid back in spades, now.

He managed it until dessert, when out from the kitchen came a glorious, towering tipsy cake, studded with slivers of almond. Ash imagined how Rafe's face would brighten to see it. His internal organs felt ticklish.

"It's beautiful!" he told the footman. "Tell Mrs. Gower she's an angel. A very talented angel."

These were going to be his servants. That cake had taken over an hour to make, and it had been made to please him. He couldn't insult the cook by not eating it. He couldn't even insult her by not taking a hearty portion and visibly enjoying every bite. So he chewed and swallowed and hummed with approval.

How often would he have to do this, now they thought tipsy cake one of his favorites?

He swallowed the last slippery mouthful and had a sudden vision of the dead moths in his chest awash in custard and soggy sponge cake, their wings disintegrating into the liquor. His throat rebelled, but he managed not to visibly gag.

"What is it?" Lydia said anyway. She watched him too closely. How was he supposed to fool her?

There was no way he could go back to her room and bed her and look like he was enjoying it. He was nauseated and his stomach roiled. But how could he tell her the truth? She would think he was mad.

Maybe he was. Why on earth would a person tell such a lie? There was nothing to be gained from it. It was a grotesque, unaccountable thing. He had already ruined their first tryst with his inexplicable melancholy. He couldn't spoil their wedding night too, not if he meant this marriage to be something she didn't want to let go of.

"I'm simply tired," he said. "I haven't slept properly in more than a fortnight, and the excitement of the day…"

Disappointment hovered around her mouth, and fled. She nodded at once, all sympathetic understanding. "Of course. We'll go directly to bed." By the time she was through the sentence her smile was genuine.

His heart ached. "Thank you," he said, and tried not to want to be caught in his lies.

As he undressed and pulled on his nightshirt, he could hear her moving around in the next room, she and Mrs. Wrenn speaking quietly—everyday domestic sounds. He fell backwards onto his new bed full of down and fresh straw and shut his eyes. His nausea receded. He was already half-asleep when she knocked shyly on the door and came in.

He somehow managed to align his limbs with the mattress and get under the covers. She followed, letting him pull her snugly against him. Jasmine and orange blossom and Lydia. She was warm and he could feel her breathing.

"Mrs. Cahill," he mumbled into her hair, and felt her cheek move as she smiled. Maybe he really was just tired. Why had he been so upset? He couldn't remember…

He slept.

Lydia had never shared a bed with another person in her life—well, except for Jamie once or twice when he was a very small boy and had nightmares, and that was a long time ago and didn't count. Mr. Cahill's body surrounded her, their skin separated by two layers of linen.

It should have been strange—it *was* strange, but the strangest thing about it was how much less strange it was than she had been led to believe.

Everyone behaved as though marital intimacy would be a terrible shock to a young woman's sensibilities, an alteration in her very mode of existence. But it all felt so natural, as if she had been made for it.

Bodies had been created to fit together, she realized, to share space and heat. How had she not known it before?

Chapter 21

Lydia didn't quite like waking in a strange bed with another person. It had been comfortable and pleasant the night before, but now her throat was dry and her mouth tasted odd and she couldn't move without disturbing Mr. Cahill, who hadn't slept well in two weeks.

She rolled over slowly. He had the blankets pulled up high and an arm wrapped round his head. All she could see of him was his close-cropped hair, his forehead, an ear and one eye.

There was nowhere she'd rather be, after all. She shut her eyes, moved a little closer, and commenced mentally planning the week between now and Gooding Day.

After a while, she got up, fetched the quilt from her own bed, and moved to his writing desk to jot down some thoughts and lists. Even with the quilt wrapped around her, the air was biting, and she had to hold the ink bottle in her hand to thaw it, but Mr. Cahill slept on.

At ten—Lydia had left instructions not to disturb them before then—Jeanie came in to light the fire. Mr. Cahill rolled over and did not wake. "If you would bring my morning correspondence and some breakfast on a tray," Lydia murmured to the maid, and moved the desk closer to the fire to read her letters while drinking chocolate and milky coffee and munching on buttered rolls.

It was two in the afternoon when Mr. Cahill finally stretched and said hoarsely, "What time is it?"

Lydia started a little guiltily, having taken a respite from her tasks to indulge in lustful daydreams. "Two o'clock."

He sat up. "Sorry I slept through our wedding night."

She shook her head. "Do you feel better?"

He blinked and considered. "Much. I don't think I even knew how tired I was."

"Would you like some breakfast?"

"In a moment. I'd better…" He went into her room to use the chamber pot. Lydia calculated how long it would be polite to wait before broaching the subject of intercourse.

Coming back in, he poured himself a cup of lukewarm chocolate, coffee, and milk. Lydia made a face, but he drank it with evident satisfaction, fingering her warm dressing gown. "You haven't dressed."

"No."

"How would you like to have that wedding night now?"

Lydia sighed in satisfaction. "Very much."

He put his hand under her elbow and pulled her out of her chair, untying her robe and sliding it off her shoulders, leaving only her thin nightgown.

Not sure what prompted her, Lydia crossed her arms over her breasts, shyly. "Wait…I've never…" The heat in her face had nothing to do with blushing confusion, but it could pass for it.

His eyes crinkled, immediately taking the cue. He gently uncrossed her arms and put them at her side. "Let me see you, angel." He shaped her with his hands through the linen. "My beautiful bride."

She shivered. "You'll be gentle, won't you?"

He kissed her brow, his unshaven cheek rough against her skin. "I promise not to hurt you more than I have to." He couldn't keep up the earnestness. *More than I have to* shifted into a teasing menace that made her want him to bruise her, bend her over the writing desk and take her hard…but there would be plenty of time for that later.

She pulled her nightgown over her head and held it to her chest for a moment, hesitating. His eyes were dark and hot. She let the linen fall to the floor, hands hovering as if she would have liked to cover herself. But she wanted him to see. She loved the way he looked at her, the frank lust in his gaze and the fond curl at the corner of his mouth.

"I'm going to worship every alabaster inch of you," he said huskily, and swept her up into his arms. Naked, it was a little awkward—her breast was mashed into his side, and she was extremely conscious of his gaze on the triangle of auburn—red, she corrected herself, the triangle of red hair between her thighs. But even though his mischievous glance told her his instinct was to toss her onto the sheets in a flurry of limbs and laughter, he set her down reverently on the bed, smoothing a stray bit of hair away from her face.

"Kiss me." She made it half a question, reaching up for him.

He pulled off his own nightdress, and finally, finally she saw him naked. It was even better than she had imagined. She wanted to rub her nose in the curly dark hair on his chest and press her open mouth to the smooth gap beneath the hair that came to a point at the base of his sternum and above the hair that marched in a dark line down to his navel. She wanted to put her mouth absolutely everywhere, feel the texture of every part of him.

But he lay beside her and kissed her, tender and sweet, and when he pulled away this wasn't a joke anymore. "Make me yours," she said with breathy overacting, but she meant it.

And he made her his, petting her until she opened her thighs, entering and taking her with slow, careful strokes. She wrapped her arms around him and uncurled herself like a closed fist, finger by finger.

He watched her face, intent and a little desperate, and she didn't know if this was real or if they were only pretending together, but she knew she'd never been so lost in anything in her whole life. The moment swept her up like a wave, and she let it, holding on to him and putting her heart in her eyes.

When the surge of pleasure came, she offered it to him, spreading her legs as wide as she could and pressing up against him and not holding anything back.

The week passed like a dream. They spent hours every day indulging in carnal pleasures, and hours more sprawled in bed talking. There was even a day or two when Lydia didn't bother to read her correspondence.

A few days after their marriage, visitors began to arrive in the mornings. Christmas was a season of visiting, and since a new bride stayed at home, the neighborhood came to her, bearing puddings and spiced brandy and most importantly, mince pies.

"It's important to eat twelve mince pies in the Christmas season, each made by a different baker," Lydia explained to Mr. Cahill as they sat in their snug parlor with Mrs. Cradduck, the brewer's wife.

"Aye, it brings luck for each month of the coming year," Mrs. Cradduck said.

Mr. Cahill lifted his small, cradle-shaped pie—and then put it down. "I—I think I've got more than my share of luck," he said, with a warm smile for Lydia. "There's a little girl in town who recently lost her family. Would you mind if I saved this pie for her, ma'am?"

Mrs. Cradduck agreed, of course.

Lydia couldn't breathe with how much she loved him, how kind he was. She had wondered if he even remembered his promise to take Mary to her sister on Christmas Day, and here... He carried on the conversation as if he'd done nothing out of the ordinary, and that night she saw the pie wrapped in brown paper, nestled in the corner of a basket on his dressing table.

He saw her looking and asked, "Do you think Mary will be pleased?"

Lydia nodded wordlessly and kissed him.

Over the next few days the collection grew. "Is your brother coming for dinner again?" he asked on Saturday morning. "Do you think you might ask him to bring a pie from the house? I still need five more by Christmas."

Jamie had been for dinner once already that week, an awkward affair where he watched the two of them for any sign of discord. She was not entirely looking forward to tonight.

Jamie arrived late, mince pies in hand. He was startled when Mr. Cahill set his carefully aside.

"You remember I told you of a girl from the workhouse, Mary Luff, the one with the sister?" Lydia said. "Mr. Cahill has promised to take her to visit Joanna for Christmas, and he's saving pies for her, to bring her luck in the new year."

Jamie looked uncomfortable at this evidence of Mr. Cahill's good character.

Dinner might have been worse. Mr. Cahill managed to engage Jamie in conversation about the Wheatcroft sheep. Lydia didn't understand why her own questions on the same subject fifteen minutes earlier had been met with monosyllables.

After dinner they went to the parlor. Mr. Cahill sat on the sofa and held out an arm. Lydia hesitated; she didn't want Jamie to feel shut out. But she took the seat, wanting Mr. Cahill's arm around her too. Wanting to feel wanted.

"You were happy to get the sofa, then?" Jamie asked.

In fact, Lydia's heart had sunk when she saw it in the parlor. Didn't Jamie treasure those memories of their childhood as much as she did? Had he spent so much time away that Wheatcroft things had lost the power to charm him? Did he consider the sofa one more sentimental fancy of hers?

Mr. Cahill's arm tightened. He knew how she felt, somehow, without her saying. She smiled at Jamie. "You know how much I love this sofa." She should be happy to have it. She and Mr. Cahill had coupled on it once already, the key in the keyhole to block the view of anyone in the hall.

Jamie patted the sofa on the arm, affectionately. "Do you remember when we used to pretend it was Gibraltar, and besiege each other?"

Lydia's heart leapt. "If you ever want the sofa back, Jamie, you have only to ask. You know that, don't you? It belongs to Wheatcroft, really." He might still want a family someday, and children. It upset her to think of the sofa one day meaning nothing to anyone.

Jamie scowled. "You mean it belongs to my children. I've told you I don't want any. You'll have children long before I do.

Why shouldn't they have the sofa?"

She knew she must look caught-out. To distract him from her silent meddling, she said, "Mr. Cahill and I aren't planning to have children."

Jamie's face changed. "Why not?"

The moment froze. Suddenly she heard Mr. Ralph's anxious voice: *Was it difficult? When you were so young too?*

What should she say? What *could* she say? *Raising you was the best thing that ever happened to me, and I wouldn't live it over again if you paid me half a million pounds* was the truth, but she didn't think Jamie would understand that. He'd think he'd been a burden somehow. Never mind that she'd seen it many times—women who'd brought up five or six children with aplomb dismayed at a pregnancy in middle age or at having to take in a grandchild.

"Chasing after babies is all very well for a young woman," she said, smiling. "I'm afraid I wouldn't have the energy for it now."

"You're only thirty." Jamie's voice was odd and tight. "Plenty of thirty-year-old women have children."

"*You* don't want children," she snapped. "So why should it bother you that *I* don't?"

Jamie's shoulders slumped. "I suppose we'll be the last of the Reeves."

There it was, the fear she hadn't wanted to say aloud. Everything their family had created, the love and the legacy, the political interest, the house, the laughter, the stories—it would pass away and there'd be no trace left of it upon the earth. It would all go to the family of their second cousin four times removed, whose name wasn't Reeve and whom they'd met once twenty years before. He'd been three years old and he'd shut baby Jamie's head in a door. Lydia had hated him ever after.

Their father had passed so much on to them, and a few months after his death, they'd already decided to let it die.

"It's only a name," Mr. Cahill said. "A man's life goes from dust to dust and ashes to ashes, but he lived it just the same whether or not anyone remembers it."

Lydia felt guilty that she couldn't feel the truth of his good advice, when Mr. Cahill's past might as well have been a picture drawn in the sand for all the traces that remained of it. But she met Jamie's eyes, and for a moment, they understood one another perfectly. They were Reeves, who had been brought up to leave their mark, whose roots were everywhere in the land and in the town. Plenty of people hereabouts spoke Lydia's great-grandfather's name as familiarly as their neighbors' children's.

"I'll sign over the money to you," Jamie said abruptly. "What are we saving it for, anyway?"

Lydia wished she felt happier.

Jamie had gone to see the family solicitor directly after leaving the house. Ash thought it a bit rude to bother the man after he'd left his office on a Saturday, but he supposed the Reeves had paid him enough over the years to compensate.

Sure enough, whatever Jamie said or whatever fee Jamie had offered convinced him to draw up the papers on Sunday so that they could all sign them Monday morning in his office. Ash would have his three thousand pounds before the Gooding Day auction started at three.

It was now Monday morning, and Lydia was dithering with Wrenn over what to wear. "We'll have to go straight to the auction." The door between their rooms was ajar, and her tense voice carried clearly. "Do you think such a bright color is suitable for a charity event?"

At that, Ash couldn't wait patiently in his own room anymore. "You've been to hundreds of charity events," he said quietly, pushing the door open and leaning against the jamb. "You know what's suitable."

She met his eyes in the mirror and nodded. The papillote curls framing her face trembled decisively. "It had better be the ice-blue wool. Festive but not too showy, and not too warm in the crush of the crowd."

He was going to have to buy more clothes. After today, he'd have the funds to do it. He could buy boots that had been made for his feet and break them in himself. If everything worked out as he hoped, he could keep them until he'd worn them out. He could own more than one set of evening clothes, maybe even something in the kind of flashy color that would draw attention to itself if worn twice in a row.

He was recalled from his daydream by Lydia's voice, twice as tense as before. "If you would give us a moment, Wrenn." The door shut quietly behind the maid.

She had something to say to him, then. Ash waited patiently, ignoring the fluttering in his stomach.

"You needn't answer me right away." She clenched her gloved hands together in her lap, putting taut wrinkles in the white kid. "We had a bargain, and of course I will keep it to the letter if that is what you prefer."

White gloves. He was married to a woman who didn't have to care if her clothes showed dirt. Had she realized he would always be unsuitable for every occasion? Was she going to ask him to leave early?

"I want you to stay," she said. "That is, I would like to invite you to stay, if the idea pleases you. On a permanent basis. I meant to wait, I meant to give you time to—to grow attached to me, I suppose. But I—I should like to know sooner than later. You must take all the time you need to consider, of course."

"Wh—" Ash's throat was too dry to finish the word. He swallowed. "Why?"

She met his eyes directly. "I find that I love you. I find that I'm happier with you than I have been before."

Well, there it was. What he'd hoped for. All he had to do was say yes. Why not? Why should he sacrifice this?

But he didn't believe in sacrifices, only swaps. He wouldn't be happy if she wasn't. That was selfishness too. "I can keep up this charade for six months. For a lifetime?"

She went, if possible, paler. "Do you mean you don't think you can, or that you would find it constraining?"

"I mean that I'm not a gentleman. And sooner or later, I'll make a mistake, or get to know someone well enough that they'd expect details of my life, and someone will guess. Or we'll come across one of my flats. I couldn't ever go to London with you—"

She shook her head. "I hate London. Once you've done it for six months, the rest will be easy. Don't—don't give me practical considerations. Tell me how you feel."

He tried to smile. "Since when have either of us put feelings above practical considerations?"

"I'm doing it now," she said. "Do it with me."

"I told you…" For once he didn't want to watch her face, but he couldn't take his eyes away, couldn't stop watching for a sign that something terrible was going to happen. He'd always been lucky, but this was too much. This was impossible. "I told you that you would start to question your own feelings. I promised I would know it was all a lie. I promised you, and you trusted me. I've never been trustworthy. Not once in my life. I'd like to be, with you."

He was in love with her too, but so what? He'd been in love dozens of times in his life. It had never meant a thing.

Because you didn't let it. The thought hung there. Maybe this time, it *could* mean something.

She looked uncertain. She wasn't sure either, then. Wasn't sure what she felt. "I don't…" She paused. "Wherever the feeling came from, it's here now," she said, her voice stronger. "If you know you don't want to stay, that's all right. Just tell me. But if you think you might…"

Oh, why not? She wanted it, he wanted it. Why think further ahead than that? "I want to stay. Of course I want to stay. Who wouldn't want to stay with you? You must know I adore you."

The words rolled easily off his tongue. Too easily, maybe. Surely something important should be difficult. But she bit her lip to keep from grinning and her eyes shone and she sat perfectly still, her hands still clenched in her lap.

He went down on his knees and kissed her. He didn't want to smear her rouge or her rose lip salve, so he covered her face with dozens of light kisses. "I love you."

After he said it once, it kept coming. He repeated it with every kiss, and she laughed and gripped his hands tight and said, "If you don't like the curtains we can change them, I thought—I thought you wouldn't have to look at them long," so he told her he loved the curtains too.

"I hope you can forgive my past rudeness," Jamie said, pulling Ash to the side. The papers had been signed and new instructions given to the family banker. Just as Ash had predicted, once Jamie had decided to give in he had done it all at once. "You've obviously made my sister very happy. Everyone has remarked upon it."

"There's nothing to forgive," Ash said. "I know you were only looking out for her. You had no reason to trust me."

"That's very good of you." Jamie smiled sheepishly, very clearly relieved not to have to be hostile any longer. "You've been nothing but kindness from the first. I am ashamed to think what my conduct has been."

"Let us forget it." Ash tried not to fidget. Somehow, joy was having the same effect on his nerves as a cup of strong coffee on an empty stomach.

Jamie nodded, and held out his hand to shake. "Welcome to the family."

Ash thought the auction was going well. He was keeping a running count as best he could, and by his tally, the Pink-and-Whites were far outstripping the Orange-and-Purples. He had spent almost twenty pounds already himself, on things he didn't want or need. He could afford it, so why not? Lydia hadn't stopped smiling all afternoon, and every time someone told her that married life agreed with her, she took Ash's arm and glowed.

This charity business was almost as good as swindling, really. He thought he could do it for the rest of his life.

When one of the ushers came to tell him that Lord Wheatcroft wished to see him outside for a moment, it didn't even occur to him to worry about anything except that Lydia's brother might have taken ill. He pushed open the door onto an empty street. Most of the shops had closed for the auction, and it was too cold to keep horses standing out of doors, so only one carriage lingered.

He walked out onto the steps and barely had the presence of mind to keep his face blank of recognition or surprise. Jamie stood in a corner of the portico with a dark young man of about his own age, but it was the third member of their party who transfixed Ash's attention.

"Wheatcroft?" Ash looked at the strangers with idle curiosity. "You wanted to see me?"

"Lord Prowse, this is Mr. Cahill. Mr. Cahill, do you recognize this man?"

This was the Cornish viscount, then.

Ash had built his life on the principle that a man couldn't be found once he disappeared into England—but that was with the resources his flats usually possessed, their circles of acquaintance limited, extending for the most part less than twenty miles in each direction. He had never realized how true it was that rich people all knew one another.

He shook his head, frowning slightly. "I'm sorry, my lord, have we met? Surely I would have remembered."

Jamie sighed impatiently. "Not Lord Prowse. *This* man." He pointed at the craggy old man to his lordship's other side.

Ash gave an embarrassed smile. "Oh, I'm sorry. Are we acquainted?"

"Mr. Maddaford, could you repeat to Mr. Cahill what you have told me?"

Fred Maddaford squinted uncertainly at Ash in the fading light. He'd always had bad eyesight. Ash could make something of that. "My name is Fred Maddaford. I live with my daughter and her husband near East Looe, in Cornwall."

Chapter 22

With his daughter? But Maddaford hated his daughter. He'd done nothing but complain that she was after him to live with her so she and her husband could have his money and his furniture, and from some of the things he'd told Ash, he was right.

Jamie's face was pale and set. His hands were in his pockets. Ash thought it was to keep them from trembling. "That is near your…home parish, is it not, Mr. Cahill?"

"Yes, but—I beg your pardon, Mr. Maddaford, for not remembering you."

Maddaford turned to Jamie. "I do believe it's him, my lord. Maybe he's swindled so many he can't remember them all." *There* was a flash of the cantankerous old sod Ash remembered. It was strange seeing the man so subdued. Maybe it was only the presence of two honest-to-goodness peers. "I'd recognize that voice anywhere. He went by Cas Carne then."

He turned back to Ash, and somehow those rheumy eyes seemed to see right into him. "Four years ago, you and your brother told me you'd discovered tin on my neighbor's land, and that if we could buy it from him…" Maddaford shifted uncomfortably at the looks of distaste on Jamie's and his friend's faces.

Ash would have liked to slap them. So the old man was

greedy—what of it? It was easy enough not to be greedy when you had plenty of everything.

"If we could buy it from him without him knowing why, we'd make a tidy profit. I gave the two of you a hundred pounds, and I never saw hide nor hair of you again. Well, I may be an old fool, Mr. Carne, but you are a thief, and that's worse."

"I am not," Ash said to Jamie, earnestly. "Bring out your daughter, sir. She must realize I'm not the man you knew." He tried to sound regretfully respectful of an old man whose memory might be unreliable.

"You never met my daughter, as you well know," Mr. Maddaford said scathingly. "I—" He faltered. "She always said I was an old fool," he muttered. "After I gave away a sum like that to a couple of strangers, I reckoned maybe she was right, and I'd no business living on my own, at my age."

Four years ago, Fred Maddaford had been nearly eighty. The amount of money had not been negligible to him, but it had left him with enough to easily live out the remainder of his life, however long. Ash had thought no more about it.

Now he remembered, again, Rafe's words: *You don't* know *what anyone can afford to lose. Maybe faith and self-respect were things they needed, things they couldn't live without.*

"I beg your pardon, Mr. Maddaford, for questioning you, but you cannot ruin a man on the evidence of a voice half-recognized from years back." The words were like sandpaper in his throat. Could he really look Fred Maddaford in the eye and tell Jamie that the man's senses must be going? Hadn't he taken enough dignity from him already?

Jamie looked wretched. "This is going to kill my sister," he told his friend Prowse. "You never met anyone so eager to help everybody. Such sordid cruelty—"

"This won't stand," Ash told him confidently. He could still carry this off, if he didn't look at Mr. Maddaford. "It's misidentification and slander, nothing more."

Jamie looked him in the eye. "You didn't go from robbing Mr. Maddaford to helping yourself to a slice of my sister's money with nothing in between. How many more such deeds will I find if I really go digging?"

If Jamie went digging, he might find Rafe. There was exactly one way to stop this now, and that was to summon Lydia and have her deal with her brother.

"Are you even a gentleman?" Jamie asked.

Ash found himself speechless before the question. What did that matter? If he were a gentleman who had talked an old man out of a quarter of his life's savings, would that somehow be better?

Lydia had been sure Jamie would never understand. She knew him better than anyone. And she'd said, *Of all the good opinions in the world, Jamie's is the one I cherish the most.*

"I blame myself," Jamie said to Lord Prowse, clenching his hands tightly together. Lydia had done that this morning, when she asked him to stay. "I knew something was wrong. If I had tried harder to stop her…"

"We'll send for her," Ash said. "See what she has to say."

Jamie turned on him. "If you imagine that I will allow you to continue living with my sister under *any* circumstances, you—" His voice failed him. "I won't. If you have any affection for her at all, you will leave now with Lord Prowse and go to your trial in Cornwall and allow her to live in ignorance of what she has married."

"You think she'll be happier having no idea at all why I left than—"

"Yes," Jamie said fiercely. "Yes, I do. As if she could bear the dishonor of—" He waved his hand in Mr. Maddaford's direction. When you got right down to it, Ash didn't want her to see the old man either. "Mr. Maddaford?"

"Yes, my lord?"

Jamie's eyes met Ash's. "Can you describe the gentleman's brother again? Blond, I believe you said, and very tall?"

So he could be ruthless too, like his sister.

Oh, Ash could fight this. He could risk Rafe, and tear Lydia and her brother apart. He had no doubt she'd refuse to abandon him. But why? For what? Did he really believe that he could make her so happy it would be worth the loss of her brother, maybe her friends and the life she'd planned and fought and schemed for? Did he really believe that his *own* happiness was more important than Rafe's safety? The idea was ludicrous.

"Leave my brother out of it," he said. "He hated this business with your sister. He tried to talk me out of it. Swear to me that you'll leave him out of it, keep him safe, and I'll go to Cornwall. Please, James."

Jamie rubbed at his temples and nodded. "Very well." That settled, he didn't seem to know what to do next. He looked at Lord Prowse, who looked back uncertainly. They were children, frightened by the magnitude of this disaster.

Ash took pity on them. "I'll write a note to your sister, telling her my aunt is on her deathbed and I've been called to go. I'm going to enclose a sealed note to my brother. I beg you will allow your sister to deliver it, should he ever come looking for it. I'll give you a draft on my account at the bank to repay Mr. Maddaford—"

Jamie shook his head jerkily. "My sister's money isn't going to pay for this. I'll pay Mr. Maddaford back, and I'll pay for your jailing and prosecution."

"Are you sure you wish to prosecute?" Prowse asked in an undertone.

Jamie pressed his lips together. "I said I'd kill him if he hurt her. I ought to do it." He shook his head. "I'm too much of a coward after all. But I'm not going to send him blithely off to defraud more innocent victims. It ends with my sister. I want him transported."

Ash could haggle. He could point out what had evidently not occurred to Jamie, that there were plenty of innocent victims in Australia. He could probably talk them into letting him walk away. It didn't seem worth the effort.

"I'll take care of everything," Lord Prowse said staunchly. He looked about twelve years old. "We'll charge him as a rogue and vagabond under the Vagrant Act. I'll keep your sister's name out of it. This is a rotten thing to happen."

"Don't ever come back here, C—" Jamie fumbled. "Whatever your name is. If once you've served your sentence you find yourself at loose ends—don't come back."

"I won't," Ash promised.

Jamie looked at him, a line between his brows, and Ash realized that in spite of everything, softhearted Jamie was worried about him.

"I've been in prison before," he said gently. "I'll be all right."

He mostly expected Jamie to take this as evidence he wasn't worth worrying about. To his surprise Jamie nodded, looking a little comforted.

Pencil and paper were produced, his letter to Lydia carefully supervised and his letter to Rafe honorably not looked at, and then Ash climbed into Lord Prowse's coach. He and Mr.

Maddaford sat in silence as Jamie and Lord Prowse said quiet, tense goodbyes outside.

He'd thought Jamie would be family.

"Mr. Maddaford," he said, "I won't tell them I only took fifty pounds off you if you promise me something."

Mr. Maddaford gave him the serene, noncommittal look of someone who knew he had the upper hand.

"If you ever meet with my brother, don't recognize him."

Mr. Maddaford shrugged. "He seemed like a nice boy. I've got nothing more to gain by denouncing him."

"Thank you."

The old man chuckled, not unkindly. "I always did think you worshipped the ground that lad walked on. Good to know I was right about something."

Ash's throat closed. "You were." He wondered if Rafe would ever come back for his letter.

Lord Prowse climbed into the carriage, and it rolled off down the street. There went the Market Cross, and the Drunk St. Leonard, and the Makepeaces' coffeehouse. Ash watched the town pass, streets and shops and houses. He'd thought he'd see them forever. He owed some of those shops money. He'd actually meant to pay them, for the first time in his life.

If you could open your heart a little farther, Rafe had said, and Ash had tried it. He'd thought that maybe, with Lydia beside him, he could take in a whole damn town. He'd pushed his luck, and now there was a big bloody mess.

They passed Miss Tice's. Mary Luff! He'd promised her he'd take her to her sister on Christmas Day. He hadn't wanted to break his promise—but maybe it was for the best. Maybe she ought to learn now that she had to take care of her and her sister herself, because no one else would do it for her, even if they'd honestly meant to.

Except that Lydia would. Lydia would remember. Lydia would take her to see Joanna for Christmas. He knew that.

Lydia had wanted to rely on him the way he was relying on her. At least he'd got her her money before he left.

He didn't know how much longer he could keep the real pain at bay, but for now, all he felt was a sad tightness in the muscles of his face and a heaviness in his chest. He didn't let himself think too much about Lydia.

He'd believed that eventually, she'd know everything about him. The things he hadn't told her—he'd believed there'd be a time and a place for all of them, even someday the ones she wouldn't understand, even the ones that would shock her.

He hadn't even seen all her dresses yet.

He could dwell on that later, when no one was watching his face.

It's just one more town, he told himself. *What difference does it make, anyway?* No doubt he'd manage to talk someone into loving him in Australia too. Or maybe he'd get lucky and die on the boat over.

Lydia had begun to think of going to look for Mr. Cahill when Jamie appeared beside her, pale and anxious. "Your husband gave me this." He thrust a packet of paper at her. *Lydia Cahill* was written neatly on the outside in pencil.

He had lovely handwriting, Mr. Cahill. He'd explained to her one morning that it was because he'd learned to write English when he already knew his way around a pen, and then hadn't written enough to develop any shortcuts or tics.

"Is he not feeling well?" she asked even as she unfolded the outer paper. Inside was another, folded smaller around something soft. It wasn't sealed, but it said in the same hasty, neat pencil, *If you are not Ralph Cahill, please don't open this.* "Please" was underlined heavily.

Lydia felt cold. But no, it couldn't mean what she thought it meant. It couldn't. Not today. Not in the middle of the Gooding Day auction. Not a scant few hours after getting his three thousand pounds. She unfolded the paper and read it.

Lydia, dearest,

I've had word that my aunt is on her deathbed and to my surprise, she's asking for me. I'll return as soon as I can. If by some mischance you see my brother before I do, give him this.

I love you more than life, sweetheart.

Yours, Ash Cahill

"He'll be back soon," Jamie said worriedly.

Lydia took a moment to compose her face. "Of course he will. I'm surprised, that's all. You know how I fuss."

There was nothing in the letter to mark it to any outside observer as the piece of cruelty that it was. To send her such a note, when she knew perfectly well he had no aunt, when he had promised to stay with her forever just that morning—

"Don't cry, Lydia." Jamie sounded desperate. "Why, what's the matter?"

But of course. He had had to send her a note she could show Jamie when he failed to return. Perhaps he had even considered to himself that he was acting in her best interests, when he wrote that.

No, Lydia thought. *This is wrong. He wouldn't. He wouldn't leave me.* Arguments against his leaving marshaled themselves neatly in her head, things he had said, things he had done, his hands in her hair, his hands—

He'd meant to stay that morning. She was sure of that. She supposed he must have changed his mind. Men were notoriously afraid of being tied down.

But he had seemed so happy.

Every argument led back to the one counterargument that couldn't be countered. He was a professional liar. She couldn't know what he had been thinking. She would never know what he had been thinking, about anything.

With a chill, she recalled that first time in the greenhouse, and his sadness afterwards. He'd been sad on their wedding night, too, hadn't he, and put it off? He'd never explained. She'd never asked him to.

He'd *seemed* happy this morning, but what did she know of his true feelings?

She had—God, she had *encouraged* him to lie to her. She had as good as given him permission to do this to her.

Maybe he would come back.

She hardened her heart. Was she supposed to wait patiently? Was she supposed to keep a light burning and watch the road for him? He was gone. *If* he came back, she'd decide how she felt about it then. For now—

He'd said he loved the curtains. Tears spilled over, and she couldn't stop them.

"Let me take you home," Jamie said.

"But the auction—"

"They'll manage without you," he said firmly, and Lydia let herself be shepherded out the door. She couldn't bear—oh, she couldn't bear to go to the Dower House and pretend to Wrenn that nothing was wrong. She knew already that if she did, she'd sleep in his bed and cry into his pillow and—

She was already grieving. It wasn't fair that she had to do it more, do it again. He'd *promised* to stay.

She leaned on Jamie. "Can I stay at Wheatcroft tonight? The Dower House will feel so empty—" Her voice broke.

"Of course. Lydia, is there something you're not telling me? Something in the letter…?"

She shook her head. "I don't know why I'm so upset. Perhaps a first separation from one's husband is always difficult."

He nodded and put his arm around her. She was terribly, terribly grateful to still have Jamie. "I love you," she told him.

His hand tightened on her shoulder. "I love you too."

This was her reward for putting feelings above practical considerations, she decided in the morning. She got up, dressed with the aid of one of the housemaids, and walked briskly back to the Dower House. She calmly informed Wrenn that Mr. Cahill had gone to visit his dying aunt. She answered her correspondence. She even saw a morning caller. Then she put a new mince pie carefully in Mr. Cahill's basket, lay down in his bed, pressed her face into a pillow that smelled like him, and cried.

She couldn't think about him. She couldn't stand to picture his face. He must have decided that whatever he felt for her didn't matter. He'd loved those girls he'd kept in London too. He'd told her that, and she'd foolishly thought it was sweet, pretending it didn't mean he could leave her as easily.

What had he called his victims? Flats? What a flat he must have thought her.

The worst of it was that she had no pride, no pride at all. She didn't care what he'd thought of her. She only wanted him back. She wanted him with a feeling like hunger or thirst, an elemental physical need that, unsatisfied, grew all-consuming.

She distracted herself with practicalities. How long should she wait before she became alarmed at the nonarrival of letters? How long before she pretended to write to his aunt, and how long before she could pretend to hear that he had never arrived, and become frantic with worry?

If she advertised for him in newspapers, would it put him in danger? But no, there were hundreds of thousands of dark-haired men of middling height in England. He'd be using a different name by now. He wouldn't be found.

She planned it over and over, and tried not to think about the rest of it.

She missed her father. Somehow all the sadness mixed up together, and it was as if she were back in those first few days without him.

Christmas visitors kept coming, that day and the next. The twenty-second was the last day Parliament sat before Christmas. Mr. Jessop and Mr. Dromgoole would be home soon, and she would have to tell them that Jamie would not be carrying on the Wheatcroft interest. It seemed surprisingly unimportant. She would be sorry to disappoint them, but that was all.

She didn't care, either, that the Pink-and-Whites had won the auction by almost a thousand pounds. The rivalry had only ever been intended to spur bidders on to raise more money for the widows and old women of the town. The total sum raised, though—that still gave her a dull satisfaction.

Maybe Caro was right, and she *had* been bored by politics all those years. Not her work, *politics*. She could do her work without the Wheatcroft interest. She could help people, and find apprenticeships, and organize charity auctions, and never have to manage an election again. That sounded terribly restful.

By noon on Wednesday, she only needed two more mince pies for Mary. When she had them, she could stop receiving callers.

Wrenn brought in a card, turning it over and over in her hands. "Mr. Sparks is here, madam. He brought his wife's card. Shall I show him in?"

Lydia was curiously glad to find Jack Sparks inspired the same hearty dislike as ever. She didn't want to insult Caro, though, so she nodded.

Mr. Sparks came in. He was a big man, imperfectly groomed and untidily dressed. His pale, fine hair stood up everywhere except where his hat had been a few moments before. He looked very out of place in her sitting room.

"Please sit down, Mr. Sparks. How do you do?"

He sat in a small, high-backed chair that looked like doll's furniture next to his size. She conjectured he had chosen it because he didn't wish to stay long. "I'm well, thank you. Mrs. Sparks wanted me to give you these as a wedding present." He held out a small box, of such a specific shape that Lydia knew even before opening it what it would contain.

She lifted the lid and pulled out a calling card. *Mrs. A. W. Cahill*, it read in sharp, clear, beautifully engraved letters.

A month ago, she would have been embarrassed to receive a gift from a friend made in her husband's own office, a clear reminder that Caro had married beneath her. A few days ago, they would have made her so happy. How she had thrilled, to be called *Mrs. Cahill*!

"Thank you," she said. "They're beautiful."

"Caro wanted to come," Sparks said abruptly. "I didn't think—I don't want to see her hurt. But you let me in. Would you receive her, if we came together?"

Lydia had always thought she and Caro would be two old maids together. She spoke with difficulty around the lump of bitter envy in her throat. "Yes. I would be happy to see her."

Sparks nodded and stood.

Caro had such beautiful manners when she wanted to— but Lydia knew her well enough to know she found Sparks's gracelessness charming. For the first time in two days, she felt an impulse to smile. "Ask her to come before Christmas and bring a mince pie. I'm collecting them for a little girl from the workhouse. And before you go, let me give you a draft on my bank for Christopher Tobill's bond."

Unexpectedly, he gave her a crooked smile. "I hoped I wouldn't have to dun you." He stood and waited while she wrote out the draft. Reading it over carefully, he folded it neatly and tucked it into his pocket. It was good to know he could be careful about some things, even if his personal appearance wasn't one of them.

"Did you like the column on your wedding?" he asked. "Caro rewrote it dunnamany times."

She and Mr. Cahill had read the column gleefully aloud to each other. She'd cut the paragraph out and saved it with her slipper.

Last night she'd burned the paper and put the slipper back in her wardrobe. It was only a slipper after all. Nothing special.

"It was lovely. Thank her for me." How could her voice sound so normal? "Happy Christmas."

When he was gone, she told Wrenn she was feeling unwell, and not to admit any more visitors. Lying in her bed, she stared at the ceiling and thought about walking to Wheatcroft just so she could sit in the window seat and stare at the Italian garden. It was so far, though. She lacked the energy even to sit up.

Wrenn knocked. "You have a visitor, madam."

"I'm not receiving," Lydia called, surprised Wrenn would ask.

Wrenn opened the door. Lydia sat up and tried to look as if she'd been reading. "I know, madam, but..." She handed Lydia a card. Lydia's heart pounded so loudly she could no longer hear Wrenn's voice.

Mr. Ralph Cahill.

Chapter 23

As soon as Wrenn was out of the room, Mr. Ralph turned on her. "Where is my brother?" he demanded.

Lydia's heart sank. "I was going to ask you the same thing."

He narrowed his eyes at her. "What is that supposed to mean?"

She glared back, not caring that he towered over her. "He left. He left in the middle of the Gooding Day auction and he didn't say goodbye."

"I'm sure that's what you told everyone. But I know it's a lie."

Lydia hated him. She'd already been over this so many times in her mind—*did he, didn't he, why?* She didn't want to go over it again. "It isn't! Why would I lie?"

"How should I know? But why would he call attention to himself by leaving in the middle of a public gala? Why would he leave without saying goodbye, unless he thought you would call the constables? I warned you—"

"Men leave women without saying goodbye all the time!"

Mr. Ralph paused, frowning at her as if she'd surprised him. But he shook his head. "No. He'd have waited until after Christmas. He promised that little girl he'd take her to see her sister."

Lydia had told herself that too. *Surely he wouldn't have*

left those mince pies, so lovingly nestled in their basket! She'd thought she was being naive, but if his brother agreed with her— At first she felt overwhelming relief, that she hadn't simply been lying to herself about everything.

Then she remembered the way Jamie wouldn't meet her eyes when he handed her Mr. Cahill's note. The first pricklings of fear began at the nape of her neck.

"He didn't take any of his money with him," she said. It hadn't occurred to her that that was strange. After all, he could come back for it whenever he liked.

"I know. I stopped at the bank." His mouth was a hard line.

She pulled the letter marked *If you are not Ralph Cahill, please do not read this* out of her pocket and thrust it at him. "Maybe—"

He tore the letter almost in half in his haste to unfold it. The soft thing inside was an old handkerchief. It didn't look like much, but Mr. Ralph went pale.

He went paler as he read. She would not sneak a look at private correspondence. She would not.

"What does it say?" she asked finally.

He turned terrible blue eyes on her. "Allow me to translate from the Yiddish. *Ralph— You mustn't tell Lydia the contents of this letter. Don't tell her for anything. Swear you won't. It's too late to do anything. I must be in Australia by now. I'm sorry for everything. You deserved the truth, since that's what you wanted. I'm sorry I never let you speak Yiddish after we left London. I'm sorry—well, you know everything I have to be sorry for. I'm proud of you for looking for something better.*"

Mr. Ralph pressed the back of his hand to his mouth for a moment before continuing. "*So here's the truth. Lydia's brother has dug up Fred Maddaford. I'm going to Cornwall to be tried for my crimes. Don't worry. There's three thousand pounds in the bank in town. I gave instructions that you can always draw on them. Take the lot, won't you? I love you, your brother, Asher Cohen.*"

Lydia couldn't move. She couldn't tell if the emotion paralyzing her was fear or rage or guilt. "He told you not to tell me," she said, as if his brother's small betrayal could make *her* less guilty.

"Yes, because unlike me, he gives a damn about how you feel," Mr. Ralph said. "Where's your brother?"

She had known Jamie was acting strange. She should have guessed why.

"At Wheatcroft. Wheatcroft—Wrenn!" she shouted. "Wrenn, we need the carriage! Pack an overnight bag and the biggest hamper you can. Mr. Cahill has taken sick on the road."

As she flew out the door a quarter of an hour later (the longest quarter-hour of her life), a thought halted her on the threshold. Mr. Ralph, following, cannoned into her and didn't apologize.

"Oh, and Wrenn," she said, craning her neck to see around him, "get two more mince pies, I don't care what you have to pay, and make sure someone takes Mary Luff to see her sister on Christmas Day."

They didn't speak on the way up to the house. There was nothing to say. Yet as they pulled into the circular drive, her head filled with words. "He said I should tell my brother the truth. He said—I never thought anything like this would happen. I thought at worst we'd have to leave town together, I thought—"

Mr. Ralph jumped down from the carriage without stopping to help her. "I'll forgive you when we've got him back.

Where's your damn brother?" He pulled the heavy front door open as if it weighed nothing. "Wheatcroft!" His shout echoed in the great hall. "Wheatcroft!"

Lydia called for Jamie too, but her voice was high and thready and didn't carry.

Her brother appeared at the top of the stairs at a run. "What is it? Is Lydia well—oh, Lydia, it's you." His gaze fell on Mr. Ralph, and he stopped running. His eyes grew wide.

She almost hadn't believed it until that moment. But she saw that Jamie knew who Mr. Ralph was, that he was afraid of what he would do. Jamie had sent Mr. Cahill to prison. He hadn't wanted to leave her after all, and here she'd been feeling sorry for herself when he was all alone, when he—

Coming down the stairs, Jamie showed them hastily into the study. Mr. Ralph lifted his hands as if contemplating violence, then lowered them. Then he raised them again and slammed Jamie hard against the wall.

"Where is my brother?" he growled.

"Let him go," Lydia said sharply, protectiveness cutting through the fog of self-recrimination. "Let him go now. He was only trying to protect me." She might never have found out. Jamie had done this terrible thing for her own good, and the secret would have stood between them, always. What had Mr. Cahill said? That secrets made a pane of glass between two people?

She couldn't bear to think of the long lonely life that might have been, the decades of missing her husband, and Jamie bearing the awful solitary burden of knowing he was the cause of it.

"Lydia," Jamie said. There was blood on his lip, where he must have bitten it. "I don't know what he's told you about Mr. Cahill, but—"

"I knew." The words dropped into the room like stones in a pond, so heavy they made almost no splash at all. "Jamie, I knew everything. I knew and I loved him—"

"You *love* him," Mr. Ralph corrected fiercely, dropping Jamie, and Lydia couldn't believe she'd used the past tense. "Where is he? We're getting him back."

"No, we aren't," Jamie said.

Lydia pushed herself between him and Mr. Ralph. "Yes, we are." Her thoughts flew ahead already. Of course they would get him back, and—and what? It didn't matter. It only mattered that he was in prison, he was alone and no doubt pretending not to be frightened, and she had put him in the way of it. "Where is he?"

Jamie looked incredulous. "Lydia, I spoke with an old man who says these men robbed him of a hundred pounds under false pretenses. They take people's trust and then they rob them. He…" Jamie looked so sorry, so sorry at having to tell her this, she almost laughed. She swallowed it. It wouldn't have been a nice sound. "He robbed you, Lydia. He wanted your money."

"We only took fifty pounds off Fred Maddaford, and he was a nasty old man who hated his own daughter," Mr. Ralph said loudly. "And if you don't help me, I'm going to the newspaper."

Lydia couldn't breathe. It was awful, it *was*, and yet she couldn't breathe for thinking that Mr. Cahill had probably liked that old man. He would probably defend him to his brother. That didn't make him a good man. But it made her love him.

Jamie had blanched at the dreaded word *newspaper*. She would have too, once. Even Caro couldn't save her if Jack Sparks got ahold of a story this good.

"I don't care," Lydia said through her teeth. "I don't care who he robbed, I don't care if the story of his life is printed in next week's *Intelligencer*, I don't care about any of it. Tell me where he is *right now*." She straightened and gave her brother a look that brooked no refusal.

She hated to browbeat him. She hated watching him crumple. But she hated it distantly. All that mattered was getting them in that carriage.

"Kellisgwynhogh," Jamie said. "Lord Prowse is taking him to the gaol there. They're using the name he gave Maddaford. Cas Carne."

Lydia's voice was steel. "Will you come with us and explain to your friend that you want him to drop the prosecution?"

"I'll put on my boots." Jamie looked at his feet. "Lydia…"

"It's my fault," she said flatly. "I should have told you. Only somehow, I didn't think you'd understand." That last part came out nastier than she'd meant it to.

"I *don't* understand!" he flared. "I don't understand. He told me he'd been in prison *before*, he—"

"I'm not listening to this," Mr. Ralph interrupted, and Lydia remembered Mr. Cahill saying, *It scared Ralph something awful.* "Get whatever you need to look rich and powerful and get in the carriage. We're leaving. And get someone to spell the coachman. We're driving through the night."

They drove for a day, a night, and a day in tense silence heavy with guilt and accusation. In answer to her questions, Mr. Ralph explained tersely that he had been working as a footman in Nuthurst and had been reading the *Intelligencer*—for news of his brother, Lydia thought, although he didn't say so. Mr. Cahill's abrupt departure had been reported in the article about the Gooding Day auction. She would have to thank Jack Sparks.

She couldn't meet Mr. Ralph's eyes and was too angry to meet Jamie's, but staring out the window, she could feel both their gazes on her. She knew what Mr. Ralph was thinking: that she had failed to look after his brother.

So did you, she wanted to protest. *You left him in pieces. At least I* tried.

But she knew Mr. Cahill wouldn't want her to say it, and besides—his brother had come to save him, when Lydia would have sulked till Doomsday and never *thought*. She should have known better. She should have had faith. She should have paid more attention to Jamie.

The worst of it was that she couldn't even believe Mr. Cahill would be angry. He expected nothing better.

She wanted him to be able to expect better of her.

She took out his letter, which she had thought so cruel. *I love you more than life, sweetheart. Yours, Ash Cahill.*

Why had he gone? He'd thought it was for her own good, she supposed. But she'd told him she didn't care about practical considerations. She'd *told* him. Did he think her an expensive China dish, that had lived in a glass case all her life and couldn't understand what she was risking?

Or maybe—no, it was unfair. The thought completed itself anyway: maybe he cared about practical considerations. Maybe he didn't love her *enough* to really want her, if he couldn't have everything that came with her.

She wanted to ask Jamie what Mr. Cahill had said before he left, what Jamie had said to make him go. But she was afraid the answers would provoke Mr. Ralph to violence.

She glanced at Ralph. Sensing it, he turned towards her, blue eyes hard and accusing. His easy charm was gone as if it had never been.

There was something besides anger, though—suspicion and puzzlement. He didn't understand where she fit in all this. He didn't believe she could really love his brother either.

Mr. Cahill would be so happy to see him. Overjoyed. Happier, maybe, than he'd be to see her. What if Ralph meant to leave again after?

She opened her mouth to ask, to convince him to stay, to defend Mr. Cahill—and, seeing him turn his glare out the window as if the landscape offended him by not being Cornwall yet, seeing the fearful hunch of his great shoulders, Lydia suddenly realized that it would be cruel.

For the first time, she allowed herself to think of the brothers' schism from Mr. Ralph's point of view. How must he have felt, to find out that his bulwark against the world had lied to him?

But she knew the answer to that. He'd been beside himself. *I would have forgiven him if he'd told me,* he'd said, eyes red with weeping. She'd seen it, and not much cared.

She turned towards Jamie. He sprawled sleeping beside her, long legs propped on the seat opposite, looking young and defenseless. How did he feel, knowing she had kept this from him?

Boys don't need to know everything about their big sisters, she'd told Mr. Cahill blithely. Yet she had known Jamie wouldn't expose her. She'd known she could talk him round. Once he'd signed over her money, there had been no practical reason to keep silent. She'd been afraid he wouldn't *respect* her anymore. That he couldn't love the truth of her, only a lie.

Jamie had believed the lie. He'd believed her so good, so respectable, so pure, that she could never love a man like Mr. Cahill. And her husband had paid the price for her fear and vanity.

How had she not noticed that Jamie was hiding something? How much had he hidden from her over the years, convinced she could only love perfection? There were so many panes of glass between them now that she'd lost the ability to distinguish between ordinary tension and a catastrophe.

Faster, she thought, listening to the hoofbeats and wheels on the road, leaning against the side of the carriage so she could feel its movement. *Faster.*

She slept fitfully, waking when they changed horses or when her dreams reached a particularly unpleasant pitch. By the second night their hamper had run out. Lydia insisted they stop for a few hours for supper, and for the coachman and groom to sleep.

Mr. Ralph's brows drew together forbiddingly. "They can pack us another hamper."

Even seated, his squared shoulders made the carriage seem tiny. For a moment she quailed; she didn't want to delay either, anyway. But that was the expression Mr. Cahill had said made him look like a little rabbi. Knowing that made it harder to be afraid of it.

"I need to talk to Jamie." She hired a private parlor, dragged her brother into it, and shut the door. "I've been thinking—"

"So have I." Jamie paced to the fire, taking off his gloves to warm his stiff fingers. "And I still think this is madness."

"I don't care what you think." She wished she could find a more tactful way to say that, but she was exhausted and her head had been aching for what felt like a week. She was cold too, but she wanted Mr. Cahill to warm her, not some impersonal fire. "Not about this."

His mouth set. "I was only trying to protect you. I *am* only trying to protect you."

As angry as she was, Lydia knew that feeling—trying so hard to make the right decision and being wrong.

Worry for Mr. Cahill and anger were a layer of down between her and her love for her brother. Carefully, she rolled them back. They would be there in an hour. Slowly, she saw Jamie again. Jamie, her darling, without her pain blurring his features.

"I know," she said. "I know. And—here's what I wanted to say. I'm sorry I tried to bully you into politics. I'm sorry I've tried to talk you into marrying. I'm sorry—I'm sorry I couldn't make Father listen to me about Eton. I tried, I did—and I'm sorry I never told you how hard I tried. I didn't want you to know that he wouldn't listen to me."

Jamie shifted uncomfortably, hair falling over his forehead. "Eton wasn't so bad."

"I wanted to protect you," Lydia said. "When Mama put you in my arms you were so small, and I wanted to protect you from everything. But I've been thinking, and—Father was trying to protect you too by sending you. From—from not having friends when you were older, from not being the kind of man he thought you should be."

Jamie hunched his shoulders. "Do we really have to dredge this up now?"

"I'm not defending him. What I'm trying to say is, I don't

think I ever really wanted to protect you. What I wanted was to be on your *side*, and I didn't know how to be. I want to do that from now on. I want you to know that no matter what you choose, even if I don't agree, I will always listen to you. I will always support you. Against anybody. It didn't matter that Father thought Eton was the right choice. What mattered was that you hated it, and we made you go anyway."

It had felt so wonderful to hear from Mr. Cahill that she could decide what she wanted and he would back her—even if in the end, he'd decided he knew what was best for her, like every other man in her life. She should have given that to Jamie.

"I got by. It was ages ago. I wish you'd let it go."

"*Jamie—*"

"God, listen to yourself," Jamie said furiously. "You really think I'm useless, don't you? I've blundered about like a bull in a China shop making a mess of your life, and *you* apologize to *me*? Because I'm just so pathetic you couldn't expect anything better!"

Lydia was aghast. "What? Of course I don't think you're useless. Why would you say that?"

"Because I sent you those letters!" he shouted. "I sent you those whinging, crawling letters begging to come home from school like a baby, and you've never forgotten it. You've never let me forget it. Why should you? What's changed? I'm still afraid of everything, and I still don't have any friends, and you know it!"

Lydia's mouth opened and closed. "But Jamie…you have lots of friends. I cried for days when you stopped coming home during the holidays because you always had invitations somewhere more exciting. Don't you remember? I tried to talk you into having a party for your friends at Wheatcroft and you didn't want to because home was so dull. You didn't even want to stay for Christmas this year."

"I didn't want to have a party because no one would have come," Jamie said. "Or they would have, and you would have seen how I was always on the edge of things."

Lydia rubbed her temples, trying to make sense of it. "I shouldn't feel so relieved by that, should I? I'm sorry, I'm appallingly tired. But I thought—I thought it was me. I thought you were embarrassed to have me as hostess. I thought you didn't want me to bore your friends with politics."

Jamie drew in a sharp breath, instantly remorseful. "Oh, no." He shook his head. "I've always been proud of you."

"And I'm proud of you," Lydia said. "No—Jamie, I am. You have been the brightest spot in my life for twenty-one years, and I think you're splendid. You're handsome, and brilliant, and funny, and so kindhearted, and talented—you'll find people who can see it, eventually."

Jamie put his head in his hands. "I don't know what I'm doing. I can't manage Wheatcroft. And everyone will be so disappointed about the borough."

"I'm sure not everyone will be disappointed," Lydia said, remembering with surprise that she had had a number of ideas on this subject, before Mr. Ralph's arrival had driven everything else from her mind. "There's room for enterprising men to move up, now. As for Wheatcroft, I've been turning it over, and I think all you need is a secretary you really like."

"But what about Father's secretary? I can't toss him out on his ear after twenty years."

"You'll have to talk to him about it, and see what he'd like to do instead, and help him do it."

Jamie made a face.

Lydia laughed. "I didn't say it would be easy. But nothing is. I've worked with him for most of those twenty years and I will be happy to provide excellent references."

"Everything's easy for you."

"I'm sorry I let you think that. It isn't at all true." She ruffled his hair. "You weren't supposed to have to manage Wheatcroft so soon. It's not your fault you aren't prepared. Father thought he'd be able to show you everything, now you were finished with school. Then after he—I meant to keep things going for a while, and smooth your path. I'm sorry I got married and left you to it."

Jamie gave her a suspicious look. "That was a lot of apologizing. Was all of this only to get me to help Mr. Cahill?"

"Not only." She tucked her arm through his and touched the malachite at her throat and didn't think of Mr. Cahill yet. "Never only. But tell me something. Do you think I could have said all that a month ago?"

Jamie shook his head.

"Mr. Cahill is good for me. I think—maybe I'm wrong, but I think you like him too."

"He's likable," Jamie said. It wasn't a compliment.

"What do you think about what I said? About being on each other's sides, instead of protecting each other?"

Jamie chewed on his lip. "You won't nag me about getting married anymore?"

Lydia took a deep breath and shook her head. She and Jamie would take care of Lively St. Lemeston and Wheatcroft while they could. That was enough; responsibility could not extend to eternity.

She'd been behaving as if the world would end if she wasn't

there to manage everyone, but the world had gone on before her, and it would go on after. Perhaps in several years, if Jamie still didn't want to marry, they could invite his heir the second cousin and his children for a visit.

Her father wouldn't like it, but she felt lighter already.

"And if I confess that I've fallen in love with the gardener, you won't stand in my way?"

Lydia blinked. "Which gardener? Not—not Andy Weller?"

Jamie made a retching noise. "Lydia, he's sixty if he's a day!"

She snickered. "He's still spry, though."

"I wish I could unhear that."

"You started it."

Jamie pinched the bridge of his nose. "I'm sorry about Mr. Cahill. I think—I think we can hush the whole thing up."

"So you'll accept him as your brother-in-law?"

Jamie's shoulders hunched again. "Lydia, how can you reconcile yourself to what he has been? I thought it would break your heart. We don't know how many innocent people he's stolen from."

No. She hoped with all her heart that she *would* know, someday, that he would tell her. She had never been as good or as kind as she'd tried to be. "You're right. But I know how many innocent people he's going to steal from in future. None. I know that. I'm not asking you to love him. I'm just asking you to receive him."

Ralph pounded on the door. "That's long enough!"

Jamie flinched. "Do I have to receive him too?"

"Not if you don't want to. He isn't always like this, though."

Jamie flung open the door. Ralph had one hand raised to knock again, the other arm effortlessly hefting an enormous hamper.

"What are you waiting for?" Jamie brushed past him. "Let's go and save your brother."

Ralph obviously didn't think that was very funny.

At the sight of him, Lydia's blanket of worry rolled back and smothered her. But she was the eldest, and she had to be practical. "The coachmen need to sleep," she said, entirely against her own inclination. "So do we. We need to be at our best when the time comes."

"One of them can sleep inside while the other drives." Ralph met her eyes unyieldingly. "Ash hates being locked up."

"They haven't slept in over twenty-four hours," Lydia protested, even though her heart failed her at his words. "It isn't safe."

"Then hire someone new!" Ralph roared. "You're rich, aren't you?"

"I can spell them," Jamie offered. "I've been sleeping."

"No."

Ralph looked at them. "Is he a bad driver?"

"Oh, he's an excellent driver. He just likes to go very, very fast."

Ralph grinned, looking at Jamie with something like approval for the first time. "Sounds good to me."

Chapter 24

There were four cells in the Kellisgwynhogh gaol. Ash didn't think they'd seen much use. Lord Prowse had had to go to the gaoler's house to fetch him out. As it was Christmas Eve, the man was both drunk and not best pleased. When Ash had asked politely for water, the gaoler had slammed shut the little hole that communicated between the cell and outside.

The straw pallet was moldy, so he sat on the floor and stared at the small square of cloudy sky he could see through the barred window. Outside, church bells began to peal. It must be midnight.

He had been looking forward to Christmas with Lydia.

The gaoler would surely not look in on him. It was safe, finally, to take Lydia's letter and her lock of hair from his breast pocket without fear of them being taken away.

He'd promised himself this throughout the days on the road, the last three nights when he couldn't sleep even though Fred Maddaford snored like a pipe-organ from where he lay stretched across the threshold to make sure Ash didn't escape. Lord Prowse had paid at each inn to have the shutters nailed shut and a guard posted outside the room, but Fred Maddaford trusted nobody but himself these days, even though sleeping on the floor must have hurt his old bones.

Ash had given him the quilt and pillows and lain awake in

the cold bed wishing he could take out Lydia's letter, that he'd saved for when he was really lonely. Oh, he could string it out, use the letter to keep himself going, tell himself this wasn't so bad—but why? Why keep going? Why be strong any longer? There was no one to be strong for, nothing to keep going for. And he wanted to read that letter.

Now, in his cell, he pulled it out and held it up to the window. Tilting the paper this way and that until it caught the greatest possible amount of moonlight, he at last made it out.

My darling Mr. C—

A letter ought to be for news, and here I can only manage to tell you what you already know: that I miss you when you're gone. I am missing you now. Time passes too quickly when we're together, and too slowly when we're apart. As you read this, the seconds are passing like minutes, and the minutes like hours, and the hours like years.

Come back soon.

Yours faithfully,

Lydia Reeve

That was the day they had playacted at love and laughed together. He'd said it was as good as the real thing.

He'd lied. The real thing was better, and worse.

He had the other note too, the one that started, *You were right. My hair is red.* He ran the braided lock of hair through his fingers. It still smelled faintly of jasmine.

He had all of her in those letters and that lock of hair—gleeful, sneaky, generous, thoughtful. Determined to mend things that were wrong. Beautiful inside and out. He had everything but *her*.

She was probably missing him right now, and he would never come back. He'd swindled her after all, taken her faith and her self-respect. Maybe she'd think he'd got itchy feet and taken to the highway. Maybe she'd think he'd never planned to stay at all, that he'd only ever wanted the money. All his life he'd lied and lied, and now here he was, perishing of sorrow that she'd never know the truth.

The Christmas bells stopped pealing, and Ash put his letters and his lock of hair carefully away in his pocket. He'd been married to her for a week. A week of perfection was more than most men got. He should feel lucky.

He'd always been lucky, hadn't he?

He couldn't even laugh. He curled up on the cold floor. The minutes didn't pass like hours. They passed exactly like what they were, one after another—second after second piling up, empty of any meaning or poetry at all.

It was Christmas morning when Jamie raced them into Kellisgwynhogh. Everyone was in church, even the local tavern shut for the morning. There was nowhere to change clothes or get hot water. Ralph cursed Christmas fluently.

"It's all right." Lydia was gripped by a curious calm that she suspected wasn't really calm at all. "Church will be over soon."

She pulled down her hair in the coach and repinned it carefully, tying the ribbons of her cap into a new bow and settling a fresh, uncrushed bonnet on top of it. Then she sat and thought sad thoughts. Terrible thoughts.

She thought about her father. She thought about last year's Christmas, how happy they had all been roasting chestnuts in the fireplace. She thought about Mr. Cahill and how much she missed him, and how he must think she'd abandoned him.

By the time the church doors opened and people streamed out, she was ready. She hummed her father's favorite ballad quietly to herself. Jamie threw her an unsettled glance just as her face crumpled and she began to cry.

Ralph grinned. "Good girl."

"I'm older than you," she sobbed. "Come on."

Jamie hesitated. "Maybe you should wait in the carriage," he said to Ralph.

Ralph's brows lowered.

Jamie squared his shoulders. "I promised him I'd keep you out of it."

Lydia winced, and Ralph's lips turned white. "I'm going to kill him." He swung himself down from the carriage.

Lord Prowse turned out to be a boy about Jamie's age, short and dark and rather square. His apprehension when he saw Lydia sobbing struck her distantly as amusing.

"I'm sure he's well." Ralph drew her gently away from Lord Prowse (who looked relieved) and let her sob against his shoulder. "Wheatcroft, can't we see him?"

The beautiful thing about tears was that once started, it required no effort at all to keep them going. She could barely speak by now.

Jamie pulled Lord Prowse into the empty doorway of a closed shop and spoke in an undertone. They'd agreed he would tell Prowse the truth, so the viscount would understand the need for absolute secrecy.

"Ma'am, we'll find somewhere to stable the horses and drink your health," called the coachman. Lydia trusted him and, seeing no alternative, had partially confided in him. But the groom she trusted with horses, not secrets. The coachman had promised to keep him occupied until Mr. Cahill could be produced, pronounced 'well enough to travel'.

The boys' conversation was lengthy. Lydia's tears dried, eventually, but she stayed huddled beneath Ralph's arm. It was stiff as iron against her. She was suddenly sorry she hadn't spoken to him more on the journey. He was her brother too, now, and she ought to look after him.

"Soon," she whispered. "We'll see him soon."

Ralph nodded. "I know. Because we walk the earth at the pleasure of folk like you."

There was nothing profitable to say to that, and it hardly indicated a great desire to speak to her. She waited in silence until Jamie and Lord Prowse approached.

"I apologize for any distress I may have caused you, Mrs. Cahill," Prowse said dubiously. "We believed ourselves to be acting in your best interests."

He was clearly still unconvinced, and annoyed besides. Lydia knew she ought to make a pretty speech and make him feel good about this. But she had no more patience left. She'd do it later. "Can we see him?"

"This way."

The gaol occupied one corner of the town Guildhall, a centuries-old granite building that appeared completely deserted. Lord Prowse let them in with a key, leading them up the stairs and through a timber-framed hall that looked as if it served half a dozen administrative functions.

Their footsteps echoed. Could Mr. Cahill hear them coming? Why did Lord Prowse walk so slowly?

The gaol was through the back of the hall, a small room with four barred doors whose heavy oak muffled any sound that might have come from within. A fire burned low in the fireplace, but there were no guards. For a terrible moment Lydia felt sure that he wouldn't be there, that he was gone and she would never get him back.

"What if the building catches fire?" Ralph said. "What if he takes sick?"

Lord Prowse looked uncomfortable. "It's Christmas morning. Someone will be back later, I'm sure."

Lydia clung tightly to Jamie's arm. She tried to call to her husband, to warn him that they were here. "Mr.—" She didn't even have the breath to get through his name.

Lord Prowse went to one of the heavy oak doors and unlocked it. It swung outwards, exposing a tiny room with a single barred window near the ceiling, narrower than a man's shoulders. A chamber pot and a pallet on the floor comprised its only furnishings. It smelled strongly of mildew and weakly of human waste. Mr. Cahill had only been there one night, thank God; Lord Prowse had traveled slower than they had.

He sat on the rough wooden floor, knees pulled up to his chest, looking at the sky. He didn't move when the door opened. The window did not admit enough light to see more than his four days' growth of beard, but she was sure that closer, she would find he hadn't slept.

"Cahill," Lord Prowse said. "You aren't going to be prosecuted."

Mr. Cahill frowned absently, looking up at Prowse as if he'd lost the ability to understand human speech.

"Ash," Ralph said, his deep voice cracking on the word.

Mr. Cahill stiffened. Slowly, he turned his head, taking in Jamie and Lydia and Lord Prowse. His eyes passed over his brother without recognition. "I'm sorry, I think there must be some mistake. Are you looking for someone you know?"

"I'm going to kill you," Ralph said, and threw himself at his brother, kneeling and burying his face in Mr. Cahill's shoulder. He was easily half a head taller than Mr. Cahill and possessed of half again as much muscle, but somehow there was nothing funny about it. "You son-of-a-bitch, I'll murder you while you sleep."

Mr. Cahill put his arms around his brother. Lifting his head, he looked directly at Jamie. "We had a deal."

Beside her, Jamie drew in a nervous breath. Mr. Cahill's voice was very cold, and there was a clear threat in it. Lydia had never heard that before.

But it was his voice, and it brought her own back. "Leave my brother alone." The words trembled, half playfully and half with tears. "Do you suppose Jamie could have stopped him? What did you feed him growing up, anyway, magic beans? Don't worry. We've come to get you out."

Mr. Cahill put a hand on his brother's hair and sighed as if recognizing the futility of further remonstrance. "Thank you. I didn't want you to—how did you even know?"

Oh, how Lydia wished she could say, *I guessed*, or even, *Jamie confessed when he saw how unhappy I was.*

"I had an eye on you," Ralph said. "Have you been eating? You never eat in prison."

Mr. Cahill laughed. "There's no one here needs bribing with my dinner. Of course I've been eating."

Lydia didn't believe him for a moment. "Well, come along. We'll get you Christmas dinner." But when she tried to take a step towards him, her knees gave way and Jamie had to catch her.

Mr. Cahill disentangled himself from his brother and rose,

gripping his shoulder hard as he did so. He came forward, making as if to reach out his arms to her—then put his hands in his pockets and rocked on his heels.

"On second thought, you'd better not touch me." His eyes shone as if this was a simple, happy moment, as if he hadn't put her through hell. As if she hadn't believed one of his lies above everything she knew of him. "I must smell awful."

He did, but she didn't care. She threw herself at him, her sobs entirely spontaneous this time.

He took her weight easily, his beard tickling her cheek, his chest more familiar and comforting than the heated wall of the greenhouse. For a moment it was hard to remember that *he* had been the one alone and in danger.

"You promised not to leave me. You *promised*."

"I'm sorry," he said, holding on to her tightly, but she didn't think he sounded sorry at all.

Lord Prowse soon took his leave. His mother was expecting him for dinner and he clearly had no intention of introducing Mr. Cahill to her. Lydia slipped out after him and found him waiting for his carriage on the granite sidewalk.

He looked a little apprehensive when he saw her, though whether because he thought she might be angry with him or because he thought she might cry again, Lydia couldn't say.

"I hope you'll allow me to apologize again for all the trouble we've put you to. You've been a good friend to my brother."

"Thank you," he said warily.

"I… My husband got in among bad people very, very young," she said at last. "He never knew another way, or thought to look for one, until recently. But he has a good heart, and I love him, and I hope—I hope you'll find it reconciles with your principles to keep his secret. I've always been taught that God treasures the lamb who was lost better than all his well-behaved flock."

Lord Prowse didn't reply right away. She didn't know him and couldn't read him. His face would one day be weighty and full of character, but on such a young, quiet man the heavy Cornish brow and long nose gave him the look of an unfinished carving, unformed and uninformative.

She didn't try to smile at him, or look pretty, or do anything except let him see how much his answer meant to her.

"These explanations would have saved Wheatcroft and me a good bit of time, money, and embarrassment a week ago," he said.

She flushed at being scolded like a schoolgirl—and with justice—by someone a decade younger than her. "I know."

"And I've always thought that was pretty hard on the well-behaved flock. But I gave Reeve—Wheatcroft, I mean— my word that I would keep silent, and my word is my bond." He looked at her, sober as a judge.

Of course, he *was* a judge. A justice of the peace at twenty-one! She wondered how she would feel when she was eighty, and everyone conducting all the business of the world was her junior.

"You ought to know that your husband has conducted himself well through this whole affair. He could have made it very unpleasant for Wheatcroft and myself, and he didn't. Nor did he attempt to slip away on the journey here, when I don't think he would have found it too difficult. I believe he wished to honor his promise to Wheatcroft that he would not. His crime was black, of course…but I watched him with Maddaford, and I think he felt the weight of that."

He twisted his signet ring on his finger. "They say love is blind, but I've rarely found that affection made me less aware of the faults of others, only led me to forgive them. Do *you* really believe he has reformed?"

"I do," she said without hesitation. "I will admit, when I found he had left me with no explanation, I doubted—but now I know he had a reason, and I would give surety for him as I would for myself."

Lord Prowse nodded. "Then I wish you joy." He broke into an awkward but genuine smile. "And my best hopes that your children will resemble you and not your husband."

Lydia thought that was an impolite and unwitty jest, but she laughed obligingly and thanked him, offering him her hand.

"Shhhh, don't say that!" Ash said, catching sight of Lydia returning from her bath in a fresh dress. He had bathed too, and shaved. If the inn aired its sheets and she was forgiving, they'd have a clean, sweet-smelling night of it.

He didn't think about what would happen if she was unforgiving.

She frowned in good-humored suspicion. "Don't say what?"

Rafe turned a blank face on her. "Pardon?"

It was too much. He was free, and his brother and his wife were in one place, being themselves. Ash was lucky, but not *this* lucky.

"Mr. Ralph said his favorite food in the world was tipsy

cake," Jamie said, "and if he was going to sit through Christmas dinner, he wanted one."

Lydia looked at Ash. "What are your other favorite foods, Mr. Ralph?"

Rafe looked at Ash too.

He threw his hands up. "You might as well."

"Roast duck," Rafe said slowly. "Roast fowl of any kind, really. Potatoes, cabbage, cooked fruit. Without cinnamon."

Ash shrugged sheepishly at Lydia. "I'm sorry. I don't know what came over me."

"And what are your brother's favorite foods, Mr. Ralph?" she asked.

"Pasties, mostly. All kinds of pasties."

"Pasties are the perfect food. Delicious, filling and portable." It was perfectly true, but Ash didn't feel much of the insouciance he put in his voice. He didn't feel any of it.

"This is a very embarrassing conversation I'm going to have to have with the servants," she said severely. She was smiling, but Ash couldn't help but think he'd embarrassed her a great deal with everyone she knew. There were shadows under her eyes, and he'd put them there.

Had she met Fred Maddaford?

"Are you sure—" He took a deep breath. "Are you sure you want me to come home with you? I—you've fetched me out of gaol and risked your reputation, and you don't owe me anything beyond…"

Lydia sighed, her brows drawing together a little in concern. God, he loved her face. "I had hoped we could delay this conversation until after we'd all eaten," she said, "but perhaps we'd better have it now. Jamie, Mr. Ralph, if you would give us the room for a few minutes."

Chapter 25

A sh did not quite like to let Rafe out of his sight. He felt the sound of the door shutting in his bones.

"You don't owe me anything either." Lydia sounded nervous, of all things. Her hands curled tightly around each other in that way she had, as if she couldn't hide her anxiety but refused to fidget. "I ought to have guessed the truth. It should not have required your brother to make me see what was before my eyes."

Ash tried to decide if her nerves were more likely to be because she'd somehow managed to twist this into her fault and thought he blamed her too, or because she'd decided it would be better if he stayed away and dreaded hurting him. "How could you have guessed? I told you I had a wandering soul the first time we met. I wouldn't have guessed myself."

Her crooked smile was sad. "I thought you might say that. But I'm sorry, nonetheless. And you don't owe me a thing." She took a deep breath. "Now that we've agreed that we do not owe each other anything, can we talk about what we *want*?"

"What do you want?" Ash asked obligingly. Surely now his luck would run out. Now she would say, *I've been thinking, and...*

"You ought to know that by now," Lydia said. "But I'd like you to go first. *You* left *me*."

It was an easy answer, and yet the words felt like great weights torn clumsily from his throat. "I want you."

"Me, or our life in Lively St. Lemeston, and our nice house, and our money?" she asked inexorably.

He might cost her all that if any of this came out. All but the money. He'd got her that, anyway. But she'd asked what he wanted.

"You," he said unhesitatingly. "I've thought of nothing but you these last days, and the way your hair smells."

He came forward, almost surprised when she let him take her in his arms. She wore a cap, but he pressed his face into the lace anyway, smelling jasmine through the starch. "Please, Lydia. You were the only appetite I had left."

She didn't relax against him. "If we have to leave home, I might change my soap."

"I hope that if I disliked the new smell, you would consider altering it," he teased, watching her for any hint of a smile.

She pulled back. "I mean it. I'm sorry I wouldn't speak of practical considerations, before. Apparently it led you to believe I hadn't weighed them. I had. I decided I would barter everything to be with you. I'd rather not, of course. I don't think I'll have to. I'm a political hostess for the government's party. I've seen worse scandals hushed up. In five years, who will even remember your face well enough to accuse you? But I would do it. Without a second thought."

She still wanted him. He should feel more relieved. Why couldn't he ever let things be simple with her? Instead, he kept trying to be honest, and he was newborn-foal clumsy at it. "I know you'd do it. I knew it when they arrested me. You would no more turn your back on someone you loved than you would steal from the poor box—a thing I once did regularly, by the by."

She grimaced, but she didn't pull away. Why not?

"Then *why*?" she demanded, and it shocked him that she really couldn't understand, that she was angry. That she thought it was as simple as that. "You promised me you'd back me. You promised me, and you knew I wanted you to stay, and you— If you knew how unhappy I've been—"

That was a blow. He had promised that, hadn't he? "I said I want you, and I do," he told her. "But I want you to be happy more than that. I would hate to make you unhappy." His brain caught up with his ears, then. She'd just said that very word. He'd made her unhappy already by leaving.

He'd known she'd miss him, that he was failing her. He'd been sorry for it. But why hadn't that felt as real as making her unhappy by staying? Because he wouldn't have to watch it, he supposed. Well, he'd never said he wasn't selfish.

And he'd been so sure that no grief at his loss could be as bad as the damage he might do if he stayed.

She watched him, sardonic and expectant even with tears swimming in those great brown eyes. A body wasn't meant to contain this much love, was it? He felt as if it would split him in two.

"More than being alone, I would *hate* that," he said. "I make people unhappy professionally, Lydia. I never saw it, but—did Jamie introduce you to the old man I…" He couldn't finish the sentence.

She shook her head. "Was he very unhappy?"

Ash couldn't even look at her. He couldn't watch for her reaction. "He was the proudest, stubbornest man I ever met, and I knocked all the fight out of him."

Out of the corner of his eye, he saw her nod. "Then I

expect you want a new profession. I'm offering you one."

That was it? "But—"

She sighed. "Loyalty isn't—you *know* this. You might as well have chosen a brother at blind man's bluff, and you stuck by him all the rest of your life. Was it because you would have felt guilty if you didn't? Did it make you unhappy, to give things up for him?"

Ash shook his head. "I thought they were good swaps for what I got." He gave her a lopsided smile. "But you know, I got Rafe, who is, by my estimation, the most wonderful person in the world. You'd only get me, and I turn melancholy at odd times and lie about strange things for no reason."

"So do I," said Lydia. "Rafe hurt that old man too."

There was nothing to say to that. If he said it was all his fault, she wouldn't agree. But he knew it was true.

"You can't change the past," she said. "I never told anyone this…"

In spite of everything, his ears pricked up.

"The night my father died, I told him not to ride home. I told him he'd had too much champagne. But he said, 'Don't fuss, Lydia, I know that road by heart and so does this horse', and I was happy and busy and didn't want an out-and-out argument, so I shrugged and let him go. Now he's dead, and Jamie is an orphan."

Oh. Oh, his poor Lydia. As if that were the same, at all. "I'm sorry."

"So am I. I'll never forgive myself. For days after, all I could think about was going back and doing it differently. But we can't ever go back. We all do things we can't forgive our-selves for, and we can't change them. Some of them are worse than others, maybe. I'm not telling you not to be sorry. But what good will it do anyone to send me away? Will it change what happened? Will it take away one drop of Mr. Maddaford's unhappiness?"

In spite of himself, he smiled. "I think seeing me miserable comforted him plenty."

Her eyebrows lifted wryly. "Oh, well in that case."

"You're right. I can't change it. But I can try to be better in the future. That's what I'm doing: trying to be better. I'm trying not to hurt you any more than I already have."

"Then stay with me," she said. "Because I know that if it comes to that, I'd be happier living under another name with you in some port town than I would be living without you at the Dower House. Change your name back to Cohen and grow a beard, and who could find us?" She tapped her mouth with her forefinger, consideringly. "In fact, it might be nice to take a few months' holiday now and then and do that anyway."

That *would* be nice. He couldn't quite breathe with how nice it would be. He couldn't breathe with how complete this reprieve seemed. "What would you do in some port town?"

She smiled a little pityingly, as if the answer should have been obvious. "People need help everywhere. I'd do what I do at home."

"What about your brother?" *Don't push your luck,* he thought instinctively. But he always did push his luck, didn't he? And as much as he loved walking the cliff-edge, she made him believe for the first time in his life that ground could be solid under his feet, if he had the courage to push far enough.

He remembered thinking that if he showed her his secret drawers, she'd put things back where she found them. But it was more than that. Maybe— It felt dangerous even to hope for it. He poked at the thought carefully, looking for the sharp edge he knew must be there.

Maybe she'd like what she found in those drawers. Maybe there wasn't anything he could show her that would make her want to leave him.

She gave him a brilliant smile. "I'll always have my brother. No matter what."

He blinked, realizing what that meant. "You sorted things out with him, then."

"I had to. I needed him on my side."

She was magnificent. She'd untangled her own heart, to help Ash.

"I know you've loved women before, and left them." The deep coffee brown of her dress made her eyes, fixed on his, seem darker and her hair stand out like jewels on dark velvet. "I know you've liked people and taken their money. But you've also been a brother. Love isn't just a feeling, is it? It's a choice. I've chosen you. You have to choose too. Now." She hesitated. "Well, I suppose if you need time to think it over..."

"I do." He hated to see her uncertain. But he had to do this honestly, instead of pleasing her now and balancing the accounts in his head later. "I need—I need a moment, to think about everything you've said."

She sat down in a chair and waited patiently.

There was no doubt Ash loved her. But he'd loved all his mistresses when he was a boy. He'd chosen girls because they were kind to Rafe, and he'd fallen for them anyway.

He'd always known, though, that he'd throw them to the wolves in a second if he had to, to protect himself and Rafe. Because he'd known it, he'd never let love matter.

Could he have been happy for life with one of them? Maybe, maybe not. It was hard to imagine he could ever fit with anyone else the way he fit with Lydia, neater than a dove-tail joint. But he'd never given himself the chance to find out.

Lydia wanted to let love matter.

He felt a surge of pride at the idea, the kind of pride that came from seeing someone else achieve something that you aspired to someday. Ash had never realized he wanted that.

He'd thought it would hurt to open his heart, but suddenly he understood: it was keeping it closed that had been hurting all along. He had connections with twenty people a day, and he'd turned away from all of them. He'd ripped them out and pretended it didn't sting. He'd thought there was so little to him that caring about one person at a time was all he could manage.

He'd been wrong to leave her. He'd torn out half his heart to do it, and hadn't seen any reason not to. But he'd been wrong.

I'm not nothing, he told himself. *I was never nothing. My feelings aren't nothing. And there's plenty of me to go around.*

It felt wonderful, better than stepping out of a prison cell, better than a bath when you were covered in a week's dirt.

People torture themselves, you know, he'd said to her once. *They put themselves through a regular Spanish Inquisition, and nobody asked them to do it. Nobody enjoys it but themselves.* True, he'd always been far too easy on himself, but he was right about that—nobody ever enjoyed self-flagellation but the person doing it.

He could throw all this away and pretend it was justice, pretend he'd atoned, or he could make a new profession out of making people happy. Starting with Lydia.

Ash chose.

"I want you. I'll never leave you. I promise."

"I told you that you could lie to me," she said, "and you

can. You can lie to me about your favorite food, you can tell me you love the curtains when you don't. You can lie about everything but this. Me, and only me, forever."

"You and only you, forever," Ash repeated. He smiled. "And I adore the curtains."

She nodded, all the tension leaving her body. As she slumped back into her wing chair, he saw all at once how tired she was, how much he'd frightened her. "Then I promise you the same thing. Convenient, isn't it, that we're already married?"

They'd be sharing that clean bed tonight after all. "I want you," he said. "I've wanted you for days." He went down on his knees to kiss her, desperately. It was oddly like that last morning in the Dower House, and nothing like it. He felt lightheaded, lighthearted. He understood now that this was more than luck. It was a miracle. A miracle they'd created themselves, together.

She kissed him back, and then she said, "Dinner first. Our brothers are waiting, and so are the servants, and anyway I don't want you to faint halfway through."

But they stayed there a little longer, talking and kissing, before she got up to open the door.

Lydia felt as if she'd used up all her words. She was floating on a blissful, exhausted cloud, and there wasn't a single syllable in her head. She didn't know how they were going to get through dinner.

But to her surprise, dinner was easy. Now that he wasn't worried about his brother, Mr. Ralph proved entirely capable of charming Jamie, plying him with warm, bright smiles and apologetic good humor and questions that said Jamie was the most interesting person he'd met in months. Lydia was sure Jamie saw through it, but that didn't mean he was immune. Probably Ralph's good looks didn't hurt, either.

Soon Jamie was talking of gardening and horses and exactly what a day at Oxford was like with less self-consciousness than Lydia had ever seen him display with strangers. Then he and Ralph spent some time agreeing that physical work with a tangible result was more satisfying than work that was all talking with people.

By the time dessert was brought, Jamie was flirting a little. Subtly, nothing undeniable, but definitely flirting. He even allowed that he preferred spring holidays to Christmas, which Lydia happened to know was a bald-faced lie. Greenhouse gardeners loved winter.

Ralph had succeeded where Mr. Cahill had failed, in less than two hours and after terrorizing Jamie for several days beforehand. Lydia gave her husband a bemused look.

Mr. Cahill glowed at her. He'd been glowing all evening. Leaning in, he whispered in her ear, "I told you my brother is talented."

"I thought you were being partial."

Ralph caught Mr. Cahill's eye about something and grinned. Mr. Cahill's beam increased until he was nearly incandescent. Her heart swelled.

It occurred to Lydia that since his arrest had brought about Ralph's return, Mr. Cahill would be more ready to forgive Jamie. It was a calculating thought, the kind she'd always pretended she didn't have. But Mr. Cahill liked that she was calculating.

She leaned her head on his shoulder. "I've never seen you

so quietly content before. I've seen you happy, but—I thought that was how you were, that your joy had an edge of wildness. Like the delight Jamie takes in going much too fast and almost breaking his neck."

He grinned at her. "I always felt like I was in a lightning storm before, with you. Surrounded by light and glory, but sure to be struck down at any moment." He ran a finger down the back of her neck. "The sun's out now."

Lydia understood that. She'd also been drawn to Mr. Cahill by the contrast between how he made her feel and her misery over her father, and the knowledge that it couldn't last with him had made it headier, more urgent. It had been glorious, but she was looking forward to something a little less desperate.

She grinned back. "We probably won't be quite this happy *all* the time."

He leaned in and winked, and there it was again, that exhilarating rush like falling from a great height. "Care to put money on that?"

"You look tired," said Ralph from across the table, smirking. "We should let you get to bed."

Jamie looked embarrassed, but he stood.

"Just try to keep the noise down, will you? I'm in the room next door."

Jamie made a face, obviously grateful that he was in the room on the far side of Ralph's. He had flatly refused to share, much to Ralph's good-humored scorn of people with too much money.

"Don't congratulate yourself too soon, Jamie," Mr. Cahill said. "He snores louder than anything we're likely to do."

"Ash!"

"He'd have found out soon enough. These walls are thin."

Ralph turned to go, and Mr. Cahill said, "Wait. Ralph—I—I know we're all tired and I meant to let you rest before—I don't think I can sleep until I talk to you."

The easy good humor fled Ralph's face, leaving it closed and apprehensive. But he nodded.

Ash sat on the edge of Rafe's bed, watching his brother clean his boots. There was nothing to distinguish it from hundreds of other evenings in their lives. But everything was different.

"Thanks," Ash said finally, when Rafe didn't speak. "Thanks for telling her who we really were."

Rafe shrugged. "I never would have believed she'd marry you anyway, not with that butter-wouldn't-melt-in-her mouth air."

Ash grinned. "You know how deceiving appearances can be." He hesitated. "I hoped you'd marry her," he confessed. "Really marry her. I thought it would be a good life for you."

Rafe looked incredulous. "You're joking."

Ash shook his head. "I had a feeling about her."

Rafe laughed. "What on earth gave you the idea I wanted to bury myself in the same small town from now till Judgment Day?"

"You wanted a respectable life," he protested, startled.

"I said I wanted an honest life. It isn't the same thing, Ash."

Ash knew that. He just hadn't realized Rafe did. He'd thought Rafe meant, *I wish I'd grown up somewhere else, with someone else.* He'd thought Rafe was saying something about *him*, when Rafe had been trying to talk about himself.

"I'm sorry," he said. "I never knew it scared you that I lost weight in prison. I reckoned a few pounds would bother you less than a black eye or a broken nose, so when someone asked for my food, I gave it to him."

Rafe sat on the bed. "You can stop apologizing. You should have told me."

"I know."

"Then that's all you can do." Rafe sighed. "I'm sorry too. I'm sorry I lost my temper. I didn't mean for us to part like that."

"You had a right to be angry." Ash hesitated. "Do you—do you wish I'd left you in the workhouse?"

Rafe shook his head vehemently. "Of course not. I'm glad to be your brother. I'm proud to be your brother. But we were both finished with that life. You know we were. You simply didn't want to admit it, any more than you'd ever admit when something was wrong."

He remembered Rafe dropping his muffler around Ash's neck, muttering, *You never dress warmly enough.* Ash had always thought he was protecting his brother by pretending everything was all right, and instead he'd only taught Rafe that he needed careful watching, that Ash couldn't be trusted to know when something was wrong. Rafe had kept watching him even after he left, and he'd been right to. He'd saved Ash.

It was a humbling realization, that his little brother had been looking after him all this time. "I'm sorry."

"Thank you for being sorry." Rafe smiled crookedly. "Ash, I'm angry. I'll be angry for a long time. But you always say that anyone who tells you he isn't angry with his parents is either lying to the world or lying to himself. I've been doing both for a long time. It's nice to just be angry instead. It makes me like you more."

Tears stung Ash's eyes. "I love you," he said, because he didn't know what to say. "I wish there were words for how much."

"I know. I've always known that." He hesitated. "I'm not going to Canada, and I'm not joining the army."

Ash tried to contain his relief. "Do you know what you'd like to do instead?"

Rafe shrugged. "There's no hurry. I can do whatever I like in the meantime."

Ash smiled. He might not have given Rafe a trade, but he'd given him the ability to talk his way into a job without references. "Write to me, will you? Every fortnight or so? Just to tell me you're safe. And if you ever need anything—"

Rafe rolled his eyes. "I'll apply to your bankers."

Ash laughed.

"Do—do you want me to write in English?"

English was safer. Rafe had been a child when they left London, and Ash had kept him safe as best he knew how. Now Rafe was old enough to choose for himself. "Write in whatever language you like," Ash said in Yiddish. His native language felt unfamiliar on his tongue, his mouth shaping the words awkwardly.

Rafe looked stunned. "I want to ask you something," he said in the same language.

Ash hadn't expected the sound of it to affect him so strongly, but it did. The Dower House was home now, but this would always be where he was from. "Anything."

Rafe pulled Leah's handkerchief from his pocket and turned it over in his hands. "Can I keep this?"

Ash nodded. "Carry it in good health." He'd said those

words so many times, they rolled off his tongue without effort. He hadn't lost this at all. It would come back, if he let it.

Rafe stroked the faded L with his thumb. "What name did she give you? Your mother?"

Ash made a face. "Rafe—oy, I—if you really want to know, I'll tell you. Just because you want it. But that name—I wouldn't think to turn around if someone called it after me on the street, and there's nobody living who'd know it to call. I'm Asher Cohen. It isn't less my name because some man with a beard didn't write it down according to the law."

Rafe looked a little forlorn. "Does that mean you'll be Ashford Cahill in twenty years?"

"Of course not. I plan to live a respectable life, not an honest one. I'll die Asher Cohen. I promise." He shook his head in bemusement. "Lydia told me tonight she wants to raise money for Jewish charities. She's more reckless than I am, I swear."

"You should do it."

"And so are you!"

Rafe laughed. "Consider it, anyway."

"I'll consider it," Ash promised. Why not? Lydia had actually spoken of working with Lady Tassell—who apparently was already acquainted with a number of leading Jewish philanthropists in London—and if she was willing to consider *that*, who was he to be stubborn?

"What about you? Are you going to change your name? It's more fun than you'd think." He hoped his apprehension wasn't written on his face as plainly as Rafe's had been.

"No," Rafe said gently enough to make Ash think it had been. "I'd rather have the name you gave me. Are you sure you'll be happy, pretending?"

"I'll be happy with Lydia at the Dower House," Ash said.

"If I told everyone I was Jewish, it would be the same life, with the same people, except that everything would be more difficult, and I'd have to hear them do and say things that would make it hard to like them. Why should I? Do I owe it to *them*? Lydia knows who I am. That's enough for me. That was always enough for me. Did you think I was longing to tell the world the truth, all the years we spent together? I don't wish I was honest, Rafe. I only wish I'd been honest with you."

Rafe frowned. "You're finished with swindling, though, aren't you?"

Ash spread his hands wide. "I'm finished with stealing. But raising money for a hospital or a school exercises all the same muscles. I won't be bored." He bit his lip. "The difference is that now when I'm done, the flat and I both leave happy. I'll have built something. You understood that that mattered before I did."

Rafe bumped shoulders with him. "I grew up in a kinder world than you."

Ash looked away. He wouldn't embarrass his brother by crying. "Do you think you'll visit? If you don't want to pretend to be Ralph Cahill anymore, I'll understand. We could meet in Brighton."

Out of the corner of his eye, he saw Rafe grin. "Jamie's already invited me for the lambing in the spring."

Ash raised his eyes beseechingly to Heaven. "It took me weeks to get that boy to *look* at me without glowering."

"You put too much pressure on people," Rafe said. "He's shy. He doesn't want to make a deep connection with you. He just wants to talk to someone who's entertaining and interested in what he has to say."

Ash stuck out his tongue. "The eggs are teaching the hens

now!" *Di eyer lernen di hiner* had been one of Ash's favorite sayings when they were boys. Later, he'd substituted *Don't teach your grandmother to suck eggs*. It had never felt quite right, but it had made Rafe glare the same glare, which was the main thing.

This time, Rafe beamed at him. "I haven't heard you say that in a while."

Ash must have done something right, because he'd brought up the best kid in the world. "Come again in the fall," he said. "For Rosh Hashanah. We'll throw bread in the water, feed our sins to the fish and start new."

"I'd like that." He sprawled back on the bed, gazing pensively at the ceiling. "Ash...tell me about the day you found me. Would you?"

Ash nodded. "I was eight years old, and I was working for Izzy Jacobs, the resurrection man…"

It was a long time before Mr. Cahill finally knocked lightly on the door of their room and came in. He pulled off his boots and laid his coat over a chair. Then he came silently to the bed and gathered Lydia in close, the two rows of buttons on his waistcoat nestled on either side of her spine.

She could feel his happiness in his body. "How did it go?"

"Shhh," he whispered, nipping her ear. "The walls are thin."

He did his level best to make her moan, and she retaliated, but they both had plenty of practice at silence, she who'd always slept with a maid within call and he who'd spent his youth in one-room lodgings with a younger brother. He thrust into her slowly, delicately, to keep the ancient bed from creaking—then tickled her when she was pinned to the mattress. She clenched her teeth together, her helpless writhing rubbing her sensitive places against him. When she pinched him, he jerked inside her.

Their pleasure drew out and out like a violin string vibrating just on the edge of hearing, until that became a game too, how long they could put it off.

The distinct sound of snoring came from the room next door. Their eyes met. They pressed their lips together and stayed absolutely still for probably ten seconds before they were shaking with laughter and making awful wheezing noises trying to stay silent.

Those few moments of lost control were all it took. Lydia went off like a firework, in bursts and sparks and sudden flares. It wasn't until Mr. Cahill bit her shoulder that she was even aware he was spending too.

They fell back against the pillows, drawing in ragged, giggling breaths and arguing in whispers over who had spent first, and whose fault it was that Lydia had hit her head against the headboard at the last with a small but distinct thud.

There was a brief lull in the whispers, and Mr. Cahill fell swiftly and thoroughly asleep. Lydia nestled against him, reveling in the particular pleasure of a warm bed when one was utterly worn out.

She didn't think she had ever before looked forward to a morning with such certainty of its living up to expectations.

Author's Note

T hank you for reading *True Pretenses*! I hope you enjoyed Ash and Lydia's story.

Would you like to know when my next book is available? Sign up for updates at RoseLerner.com or follow me on Twitter at @RoseLerner. You can also support me on Patreon, and receive weekly sneak peeks at what I'm working on!

Reviews help other readers find books. I appreciate all reviews, positive and negative.

This is book 2 in my series about the little market town of Lively St. Lemeston. Book 1, *Sweet Disorder,* is the story of Nick and Phoebe Dymond, whom you met in this story, and Book 3, *Listen to the Moon*, is about Nick's very proper valet and Phoebe's snarky maid-of-all-work, who marry to get a plum job. And by popular demand, Book 4, "A Taste of Honey," is a sexy novella set in the Honey Moon bakery!

Visit my website for free short stories (including one about Ash and Rafe running a con on Aaron Burr), plus *True Pretenses* extras like deleted scenes (in the first draft, Lydia let Ash sneak through her window at night before they were married), an Ash/Lydia music playlist, Pinterest boards, and historical research. You can learn about Regency con artists, greenhouses, Christmas puddings, criminal slang—and lots more.

Turn the page to learn more about my other Regency romances.

MORE BOOKS BY
Rose Lerner

LIVELY ST. LEMESTON
Sweet Disorder
Listen to the Moon
A Taste of Honey (novella)

To find out when new Lively St. Lemeston books release,
sign up at RoseLerner.com!

RYE BAY
(f/f Gothics set in the world of Lively St. Lemeston)
The Wife in the Attic (an Audible Original, coming February 2021)
The Wife in the Attic (print and e-book, coming late 2021)

To find out when new Rye Bay books release,
sign up at RoseLerner.com!

NOT IN ANY SERIES
In for a Penny
A Lily Among Thorns
All or Nothing
(novella, first published in the *Gambled Away* anthology)
Promised Land
(novella, first published in the *Hamilton's Battalion* anthology)

TURN THE PAGE for an excerpt from
Listen to the Moon, in which a very proper valet and a
snarky maid-of-all-work marry to get a plum job.

Listen to the Moon

Always the bride's maid, never the bride...

John Toogood always prided himself on being the perfect gentleman's gentleman, skilled, discreet, and professional. But now he finds himself laid off and blacklisted, stuck in tiny Lively St. Lemeston until he can find a new job. Any job.

His instant attraction to his happy-go-lucky maid Sukey Grimes couldn't come at a worse time. Her manners are provincial, her respect for authority nonexistent, and her outdated cleaning methods...well, the less said about them, the better.

Sukey can tell that John's impeccably impassive facade hides a lonely man with a gift for laughter—and kissing. But she also knows he'll leave her sleepy little town behind the moment he gets the chance, and she has no intention of giving him her heart to take with him.

John learns that the town vicar needs a butler—but the job is only for a respectable married man. Against both their better judgments, John and Sukey tie the knot. The ring isn't on her finger long before Sukey realizes she underestimated just how vexing being married to the boss can be...

Chapter 1

S ukey Grimes, maid-of-all-work, gave the chipped mantel a last pass with her duster. Empty of furniture, the two attic rooms looked nearly a decent size. But on a rainy day like this, nothing could hide the leak in the roof. The boards in the ceiling swelled and rotted, and water dripped into a cast-iron pot with a constant *plip plip plip*.

Someone knocked.

"Mrs. Dymond, is that you?" Sukey called. "I've been over these rooms, and if your sister happens to be missing a hairpin with a lovely rosette on it, I simply can't *imagine* where it could have got to." She pulled the pin from her hair and held it out as she opened the door.

It wasn't Phoebe Dymond, former lodger in these rooms, or her new husband Nicholas Dymond either. It was a very tall, very well dressed, very—"handsome" wasn't in it. Oh, he was handsome; there weren't any bones to be made about that. But handsome was ten for a penny. This man had *character*. His jaw might have been hewn from oak, and his nose jutted forward, too large on someone else's face but perfect on his. His warm, light-brown eyes stared right into her, or would have if he'd seemed the slightest bit interested in her.

He glanced down at the hairpin, lips thinning. His eyebrows drew together, one bumping slightly up at the side. The tiny, disapproving shift brought the deep lines of his face into sharp relief.

Oof. He as good as knocked the breath out of her, didn't he? "I'm that sorry, sir, I thought you were somebody else." She tucked the pin back into her hair with relief. Mrs. Dymond's little sister had made the rosette from a scrap of red ribbon that showed to advantage in Sukey's brown hair. "Are you here about the rooms for let? They come with a bed," she said encouragingly, quite as if the mattress had been restuffed in the last half a decade.

The eyebrows went up together this time. "I am Mr. Toogood. Mr. Dymond's valet." The calm, quiet growl of his voice knocked the breath out of her too. Deep and powerful, it was made for loudness, even if he kept it leashed. Tamed, he probably thought, but Sukey didn't think you *could* tame a voice like that, only starve it into temporary submission.

She wondered what Mr. Toogood would sound like tangled with a woman in that lumpy bed. Were bitten-off growls all he'd allow himself there as well? She'd never find out—she had never tangled herself up with any man yet, and never planned to—but it was nice to think about nevertheless.

Tardily, her brain caught up with her ears. "Not anymore, are you? Or you'd know not to look for him here." She didn't expect Mr. Dymond could afford a valet now he'd married beneath him.

Mr. Toogood didn't flinch. If anything, he looked more calmly superior than before. "No, not anymore, that's correct. Can you tell me where I might find the Dymonds?" That voice rubbed up and down her spine.

She made a show of considering. "I don't know as I'd ought to tell you. How am I to be sure you are who you say you are?"

To her surprise, his lips twitched. He pulled a card out of his pocket. *John Toogood,* it read. *Gentleman's Gentleman.* His own card! Upper servants were another species, right enough.

She pocketed the card to show the maid next door. "Oh, that don't prove a thing. Anybody can have cards printed."

His lips curved, the lines between his nose and the corners of his mouth deepening in a very pleasant way. "And anybody can sweep a floor thoroughly, but I don't accuse *you* of doing it."

She laughed, startled. "You'd better not. I don't like having false rumors spread about me." So she'd missed some spots in the corners. Who cared? Mrs. Dymond wasn't paying her to clean this attic anymore. She'd done it out of the goodness of her heart, and to help lure a new tenant. Old Mrs. Pengilly, who owned the house, didn't seem in any rush about that, but Sukey needed the money.

She eyed Mr. Toogood. "*You* must need a place to stay now you're out of work."

He looked about the room. "I don't plan to be out of work for long."

"Nobody does." He was too tall for the place. He'd hit his head on the eaves dunnamany times a day. Sukey didn't say so.

"I don't need anything so large."

She smothered a laugh. "It's cheap. On account of the leaky roof. And Mrs. Pengilly might give you credit for furnishings, if you engaged to leave them here when you go."

"And what is your interest in the matter?"

She grinned at him. "It'll cost you threepence a week to have me clean and cook for a bit Friday and Saturday afternoons."

"I see. Are you a good cook?"

"I'm not *bad*."

He sighed. "If you give me the Dymonds' direction, I'll

stop by again this afternoon to speak with…Mrs. Pengilly, I believe you said?"

Mr. Dymond surveyed his Cuenca carpet as if it could tell him what to say. This gave John Toogood, gentleman's gentleman, ample opportunity to observe that his former master's hair was growing far too long, that he had been consistently failing to shave a spot under his left ear, and that his cuffs were ink-stained. He did not dare look about the room.

"My mother's refused to find you another position, hasn't she?"

John kept his hands folded behind his back. "I wouldn't say 'refused', sir. She has not replied to my letter. Naturally the weeks after an election are a very busy time for her ladyship."

They both knew that Mr. Dymond's mother, the influential Countess of Tassell, never neglected any correspondence unless she meant to.

"I'm so sorry, Toogood," Mr. Dymond said. "I never expected this. I was sorry to have to let you go, but it never occurred to me that Mother would put you on the black list. You're bound to find another place, even so. You're an exceptional valet."

"Thank you, sir. Please do not apologize. I would not have troubled you in the first weeks of your marriage, had I not hoped for a letter of reference."

"Of course." Mr. Dymond went at once to a writing table and exchanged his cane for a pen. It became clear as he wrote that the pen needed mending.

John clasped his hands tighter together so as not to reach

for the pen-knife. He wasn't looking forward to going about town, hat in hand, asking for work. He'd never done it before, having worked for the Dymonds all his life.

He hadn't even been Mr. Dymond's valet anymore. For the past four years, John had worked for his elder brother Stephen, Lord Lenfield, who sat for Sussex in the House of Commons.

But when Mr. Dymond sold his commission after a serious injury, the Tassells had judged a stranger's care too much for their son's nerves. The countess had asked John to serve him through his convalescence as a particular favor. She'd promised both John and Lord Lenfield that they'd be reunited in a matter of months.

Few politicians, asked what smoothed a man's way in government, would mention a close shave, clean linen and polished boots. Yet those things took subtle root in the minds of others, hinting softly, *This is a fellow worthy of respect, who knows how things ought to be done.* Lord Lenfield would be a great man someday, and John had thought to help him in his rise to greatness.

That was before Mr. Dymond married a poor widow and broke all ties with his mother.

Now the most glowing letter of reference wouldn't help John if the angry countess had really put him on a black list among her acquaintances. He had few connections outside that circle, and no man in it would alienate powerful people like the Earl and Countess of Tassell merely for an improvement—however marked—in his comfort, appearance and mode of dress.

And by the time Society trickled back to London for the opening of the new Parliament in a few weeks, news of Mr. Dymond's fall from grace would be through the entire *ton* like wildfire. Everyone would know John had been dismissed from the family's employ.

Unless he was minded to work for a Tory, which he wasn't, he'd have to seek a position among strangers who cared nothing for politics.

No, John wasn't pleased about the current turn of events. But unlike Mr. Dymond, it had occurred to him that the countess might punish him for failing to warn her of her son's inappropriate attachment. He'd done it anyway, and he regretted nothing. He would just have to venture into new spheres of greatness.

It came to him with a sinking feeling that many distinguished professions were famed for inattention to dress. Might neat attire even hamper the career of a scholar or man of science, raising suspicions that he couldn't be so brilliant as all that?

Mr. Dymond sanded his letter. "Stephen will stop in Lively St. Lemeston on his way to London. Mother wants him to make me forgive her. Maybe if you talked to him…"

John had written to Lord Lenfield already and received no answer to that letter either. His lordship would never rehire his valet against his mother's wishes, but a personal appeal might persuade him to help John find a position elsewhere. "Thank you, sir. If you might tell me when you expect him?"

"If you give me your direction, I'll ask him to come and see you."

Heat crept up the back of John's neck. He wasn't sure why this should be embarrassing, but he was embarrassed nonetheless as he said blandly, "I was thinking of letting your wife's old rooms, as it happens."

Mr. Dymond blinked. "Can you afford them?"

John (when employed) likely earned twice what the new Mrs. Dymond did with her pen. But Mr. Dymond saw only that he was a servant and she was a respectable lawyer's daughter. "I have a little money put by. And I am told the rooms are cheap, on account of the leaky roof."

Told by that puckish maidservant, who didn't clean worth a damn and had a retroussé nose and pale blue eyes tip-tilted like a cat's.

That wasn't why he was taking the rooms. She was too young for him, and besides, the last thing he wanted was more scandal. Which there'd be if he was kicked out of lodgings for making advances to the maid. Or debauching her.

An image of her—naked, tossing back her unbound hair as she straddled him with a sly half-smile—appeared with startling speed and had an equally startling effect on him, though fortunately not to a degree visible to Mr. Dymond.

On reflection, John supposed it was only natural. While no Lothario, he enjoyed the company of women, both in and out of bed. He'd been accustomed to a healthy dose of it, living in London or traveling with Lord Lenfield to house parties that were nearly as convivial for the servants as their masters. Now for months he'd slept within call of a convalescent who barely left his rooms. There'd been few chances even to take himself in hand.

Lively St. Lemeston was full of women. He'd find someone older and more discreet.

Mr. Dymond nodded. "Be careful of the eaves. I've cracked my head on them more than once."

John grimaced. He was at least three inches taller than his former master. "Thank you for the warning, sir. Pardon me—" Unable to resist any longer, he reached out to tighten the uneven knot of Mr. Dymond's cravat. Their eyes met for a moment before John dropped his respectfully.

"I'll write to some of my school friends and see if any of them are looking for a valet," Mr. Dymond blurted out. "I really am sorry. If you ever need anything, you must come to me."

I'm richer than you are now, John thought. "Thank you, sir. You're very kind."

Read the rest of Chapter One and buy the book at smarturl.it/ListenDotCom

Made in the USA
Middletown, DE
01 September 2021

47427912R00227